Also From Cohesion Press

🌐 🌐 🌐

<u>Horror:</u>

SNAFU: An Anthology of Military Horror
– eds Geoff Brown & Amanda J Spedding

SNAFU: Wolves at the Door
– eds Geoff Brown & Amanda J Spedding

SNAFU: Survival of the Fittest
– eds Geoff Brown & Amanda J Spedding

SNAFU: Hunters
– eds Amanda J Spedding & Geoff Brown

SNAFU: Future Warfare
– eds Amanda J Spedding & Geoff Brown

SNAFU: Unnatural Selection
– eds Amanda J Spedding & Geoff Brown

SNAFU: Black Ops
– eds Amanda J Spedding & Geoff Brown

SNAFU
RESURRECTION

Edited by Amanda J Spedding & Matthew Summers
Senior Editor – Geoff Brown

Cohesion Press
Mayday Hills Lunatic Asylum
Beechworth , Australia
2019

SNAFU: RESURRECTION

Amanda J Spedding & Matthew Summers (eds)
Senior Editor: Geoff Brown

Anthology © Cohesion Press 2018
Stories © Individual Authors 2018
Cover Art © Dean Samed 2018

Print Version 2019

Set in Palatino Linotype

As seen on Netflix

COHESION PRESS
THE BATTLE HAS JUST BEGUN

Cohesion Press
Mayday Hills Lunatic Asylum
Beechworth, Australia
www.cohesionpress.com

CONTENTS

The Shadows of Teutoburg

Evan Dicken

Back in line, you miserable—" A javelin caught the third cohort's centurion in the mouth, erupting from the back of his neck in a spray of blood. Quintus Pontius Varro struggled to lift his waterlogged shield, eyeing the mob of barbarians pounding down the hill toward him. Desperately, he cast about for the optio and found the man lying face-down in the trampled muck, pierced through with German darts.

With its leadership down, the cohort descended into chaos. Spread out along the muddy road soldiers shouted and screamed, their calls lost amidst the high, unnatural barks of their ambushers. The barbarians were too close for pila, not that Quintus could've managed a decent throw in all this rain. Shouting desperately for his contubernium to form up, he shrugged out of his heavy pack and drew his gladius.

The barbarians were close enough now for him to see their teeth and eyes, wild flecks of white swirling amidst the mud-daubed savagery. Otho stepped to Quintus's side, the big man's shield a welcome presence. The other six soldiers of Quintus's unit struggled into formation, their kit in various forms of disarray.

"Shields," he shouted as the barbarians came crashing in.

The blade of one of their long lances scraped across Quintus's shield, and he jerked his head out of the way just in time to avoid losing an eye. Lunging forward, he hammered the lower edge of his shield into the barbarian's knee. As the man stumbled, Quintus stabbed him in the neck, a quick, punishing strike that left the German twitching on the ground.

There was barely time for Quintus to step back in line, let alone catch his breath. A barbarian in Roman chainmail stepped

1

over the body of his tribesman, broad-bladed axe slashing down like a bolt from Jupiter. Although Quintus caught the blow on the curve of his shield, there was enough force behind the strike to numb his already exhausted arm. Driving his shoulder forward, he knocked the sword aside to give Otho a clear strike, and the big man obliged by punching his gladius into the barbarian's side.

The man's mail would've turned almost any slash, but it was little proof against the tip of a fine Roman blade.

A slash is a wasted strike. Stab deep, my boys, and kill.

The admonitions of Quintus's old weapons trainer rang through his muddled thoughts like the peal of a festival horn. He twisted to the left to cut the hamstring of a barbarian hacking at Rufinus. The German toppled forward and Rufinus finished him with a quick chop to the back of the neck.

Quintus grinned through the sheeting rain. *Slashes have their place, old man.* His grin disappeared as a wave of howling barbarians crashed over them. Quintus cut and thrust at the shouting throng, blade licking out around the edges of his shield to cut exposed tendons and sink into flesh. Like his comrades, he used his shield to frustrate his attacker, but when Quintus struck, it was not at the man in front of him, but the one to either side. It was one of the many tricks that gave the Roman legionaries the ability to face the barbarians head on.

Fight together or die alone.

Not all his old trainer's advice was misplaced.

Rufinus fell, pierced through with a long-bladed lance. To Quintus's left, Lamiskos quickly moved to dress ranks, but the line was already broken. A barbarian shouldered into the breach, a sword in each hand. Snarling curses, he hammered at Quintus and Lamiskos's shields like a blacksmith pounding iron. Such was the man's fury that it was all Quintus could do to keep his shield up, each blow jolting his shoulder and sending a painful tremor down his arm. Lamiskos cried out as the German's blade carved a red slash down his thigh. The Tarantine infantryman stumbled but did not fall.

Breath hissing through clenched teeth, Quintus swore to raise an altar to Jupiter Maximus if the god would see him clear of this battle.

As if in answer to his plea a javelin sprouted from the huge German's shoulder, his swing faltering. Ceorix, one of the Gallic auxilia assigned to Quintus's contubernium, stepped into view, another javelin poised to throw. With a nod to the Gaul, Quintus pushed in, pinning the man's wounded arm to his chest even as he stabbed his gladius down. Bright blood welled around the blade as it pierced the barbarian's neck.

The German fell back, spitting blood and teeth, and Quintus spun to take a spear thrust on his shield, warding Lamiskos. The Tarantine offered a grateful nod but could manage little else before the barbarians were on them again.

This was more than just a raid. There seemed no end to their opponents. More breaches opened along the ragged Roman line, the edges beginning to curl back like a bent bow. Soon the two wings would meet, and they would be well and truly surrounded.

A glance up the road showed fighting as far as the eye could see, waves and waves of screaming Germans washing over the Roman units. It seemed impossible that three full legions could be overwhelmed so quickly. Just an hour ago they had been marching to quell a minor uprising. It had been such a trivial action that General Varus hadn't even bothered with scouts, trusting Arminius and his German allies to guide them.

As the line contracted and their casualties grew, discipline began to falter. Quintus and his men were no strangers to fighting barbarians, but the sudden ambush had put them on the back foot. If the hordes didn't relent soon, they would die together here in the mud.

The battle eddied as the battered legions formed up, beating back assault after assault. At Quintus's call, his contubernium took shelter in the dubious safety of an overturned wagon. Of the eight soldiers under Quintus's charge, only Otho and Lamiskos still stood, although the latter leaned heavily on Ceorix.

"Decanus," the Gaul met Quintus's gaze. "We should withdraw."

Quintus took a shaky breath. "I won't abandon the Seventeenth—"

"Those are Sicambri." Ceorix thrust his chin at a knot of tall, mustached barbarians that were ransacking a provisions cart, then he nodded at a line of warriors on the hill, their bare chests painted with swirls of dark colors. "And those are Marsi. I've also seen Bructeri, and Chauci, and Chatti as well – many, many tribes. Also, there is something in the air Decanus. Something that makes my skin cold."

"Yes, *rain*," Otho rumbled, shaking his helmed head to spatter the rest of the squad with drops. "I don't know about you, Decanus, but I've never run from a little water."

A cold fist clenched in Quintus's breast as he surveyed the slaughter. Three legions, *three*, and they were being worn away like a dam on the Tiber. He'd seen tribal alliances before, but never like this. Could this be another Carrhae? Another Caudine Forks?

"Sir." Otho pointed his gladius at the crest of the distant hill.

Quintus turned to see a formation of Romans descending towards them. No, their armor and helmets were similar, but they were *not* Romans.

"Arminius," Quintus said.

A ragged cheer rose from the beleaguered legionaries at the sight of the German auxilia. But any shred of hope Quintus might have conjured that they were here to rescue Varus's legions was dashed as the auxilia drew up and launched a hail of pila into their former comrades.

"That bastard led us into an ambush." Otho spat the words.

"We need to withdraw." Ceorix glanced at the sky, his face paler than usual. "Before it's too late."

Quintus rubbed one eye with the heel of his hand. Suddenly the close coordination of the German ambush made sense. Arminius had been raised in Rome, trained and trusted by the Senate. A close friend of General Varus, he had even been awarded the rank of equestrian – a privilege bestowed on very few barbarians. He knew their tactics and their fighting style.

He knew how to beat them.

"Decanus?" Otho asked.

Quintus looked around, desperate for order. The cohort, the *entire* Seventeenth legion was being cut to pieces. There was nothing he could do, nothing *any* of them could do. And yet the idea of running stuck like a bone in his throat.

He stepped from behind the wagon, sword in hand. "C'mon lads, let's make these traitors regret—"

Ceorix grabbed the straps of Quintus's armor, dragging him back. "Stay down." The Gaul's lips drew back from his teeth like the snarl of a cornered wolf. "They come."

And Quintus suddenly felt it – the damp heaviness in air just before a storm rolled in off the sea.

From the tree line atop the hill came a line of hunched shadows. Twice the height of a man, the things were long-armed with legs that bent backwards like a dog. They loped down the hill, crocodilian mouths open wide in snarls, eyes like flecks of obsidian in their triangular heads. There was a shambling grace to their movements, every step like the hungry lunge of a cat snatching prey. They hit the Roman lines like an avalanche. Armor crumpled like linen before the slash of their gnarled claws, their jaws crushing helm and skull alike. Quintus watched in horror as one of the things was pinioned by a scorpion bolt, but continued to charge, twisting the heads from the artillerists who injured it before finally collapsing to the bloody earth.

"Ceorix, what are those things?" Quintus had to force the words through lips gone numb and wooden from the shock of what he'd just witnessed.

"Ancient." The Gaul flinched from the carnage, his eyes wide in the gathering gloom. "And powerful."

"How do we fight them?" Otho's anxious question was almost lost amidst the screams of dying men.

"We don't," Ceorix's gaze flicked to the tree line, his muscles tense as if the Gaul was ready to bolt.

They looked to Quintus. The decision sat like ashes in his mouth. As the squad's Decanus, Quintus's duty was to his men. He couldn't ask them to face such abominations. Varus's legions were doomed, but there were more legions across the Rhine, more men Arminius and his monsters could catch unawares. Someone needed to carry word of this betrayal across the Rhine so more Romans didn't fall to the German chieftain's sorcery.

With a scowl that felt bone-deep, Quintus tossed his heavy, waterlogged shield aside. "We run."

Quintus couldn't decide which was worse, the Germans or the boggy, shit-filled forest they called home. The mud sucked at his sandals, dragging at every step like the clutching hands of the dead.

"Emperor's balls," Ceorix cursed as a sling stone rattled off a nearby tree. The wiry Gaul knelt to snatch up a rock of his own and hurl it at the Germans, but the throw fell woefully short.

Quintus squinted at their pursuers through the sheeting rain – eight shadows ranged among the distant trees, whooping and laughing as they lobbed shots at the Romans.

Still, at least those who pursued them were human.

None of the contubernium had inquired as to what had slaughtered the legions, as if even voicing the question would bring the crook-legged creatures shambling from the swamp. Quintus caught their anxiety in sideways glances, mumbled prayers to Apollo, and the white-knuckled grip they kept on their weapons. The memory plucked at Quintus's thoughts like the strum of a poorly-tuned lyre, a dissonance echoing again and again.

He shook his head. "Ceorix, what were those things?"

The Gaul made a strange sign with his hands, fingers crooked as if to ward off a curse. "The Germans call them *thurisaz*, although I've heard the name has its roots farther north, where they are known as *trolls*."

"Where do they come from?" Otho asked.

"Once, long ago, they were everywhere, but were pushed back." Ceorix shrugged. "Now, the creatures dwell amidst shadowed cliffs, pits and caverns, places where the sun has never touched."

"You said they were pushed back," Quintus said. "They can be killed?"

The Gaul gave an irritated wave of his hand. "By heroes, *gods*."

"How did the heroes do it?" Quintus asked.

The Gaul frowned. "Fire, enchanted blades, dropping a mountain on them…"

"We don't have any mountains or magic." Otho flicked a spray of rainwater from his fingers. "And we can't set any fires in all this damp."

"There must have been a *dozen* tribes back there. It seems impossible, but Arminius has forged the Germans into a coalition, and I think these trolls have something to do with it." Quintus ran his tongue across his teeth, gathering his thoughts. "If we can reach the Garrison at Aliso before Arminius, we can warn the prefect."

"What good will that do?" Ceorix asked. "Even if they do hold out, most of the legions are in Illyria with Tiberius."

"The first and fifth legion are south of the Rhine." Otho slapped the hilt of his gladius. "I'd wager those trolls wouldn't fare so well in a stand-up fight."

"I aim to find out," Quintus said. "Although our first concern is staying alive."

As if to punctuate Quintus's point, there came the whir of a sling from behind. He hunched his shoulders, but the rock just hissed by, accompanied by a chorus of derisive hoots from their pursuers.

"Why don't they just advance and be done with it?" Otho rumbled, shifting to get a better grip on Lamiskos. The young Tarantine was badly injured, but was struggling along without complaint, jaw clenched, lips pressed into a thin, bloodless line.

"Why risk battle when you can let the land do your killing?" Ceorix spat into the mud.

"Barbarians are all cowards," Otho said, then blanched, glancing at the long-haired auxilia. "I didn't mean—"

Ceorix waved the insult away. "I *am* running away, aren't I? If this rain would just let up, I'd show them their mistake." He gave the string of his bow an irritated flick. The Gaul was the squad's best hunter. Quintus had no doubt he could see off their attackers with some well-placed shots, but the constant rain had left the sinew string of Ceorix's bow slack and useless.

Conversation lapsed as the Romans continued to struggle through the knee-deep mire. Quintus knew it was futile to run; they'd discarded most of their equipment and still the damned Germans hounded them like wolves.

"By Jupiter, I'd give Ceorix's left arm for a hot meal," Otho said.

The Gaul snorted. "Wager your own limbs, ox."

The laughter that followed was weak, forced. Quintus felt the hopelessness of their situation settle on his shoulders like a sodden cloak. The squad looked to him for leadership – he was their Decanus, a veteran evocatus with more than two decades of legionary service, and yet none of his experience had prepared him for the unnatural horrors that had slaughtered his legion.

The shame of it nested in his breast, as bitter and twisted as the scrubby trees that grew in this cursed marsh.

Another sling-stone rattled through the brush just off to their left.

"They're toying with us," Otho said.

"Leave me." They were the first words Lamiskos had spoken since before the battle. The resignation in the Tarantine's voice broke something in Quintus – a barricade that held back the whole of his helpless fury.

"We fight together or not at all." He nodded to where the gnarled trees thickened a few dozen paces ahead. "Right there."

"Sir?" Otho asked.

Quintus smiled for the first time in what felt like days. "*There* is where these bastards learn their mistake."

🜨 🜨 🜨

Lamiskos moaned again, a pitiful sound that raised the hairs on Quintus's arms. They'd propped the wounded legionnaire against one of the trees, sword in hand, their single remaining shield laid over him like a blanket. Quintus hoped the Germans would prefer to finish off the Tarantine by hand, but he left the shield to ward any remaining sling stones. The rest of the squad lay amidst the sodden shadows, half-buried in slushy mess the rain had made of the forest floor – faces, armor, and clothes smeared with muck. A fat-bodied spider tickled across the back of Quintus' hand, but he did not move, even when the thing paused to deliver a stinging bite to the webbing of his thumb.

If he and his comrades were spotted, the Germans would send them to Hades.

The barbarians entered the tree line slowly, weapons out, eyes wide in their mud-spattered faces. They fanned out to scan the forest, advancing more confidently when it became clear the Romans had abandoned their wounded comrade. One of them barked something in their hard-edged tongue and the others laughed.

Quintus waited in the cold mud as his prey crept closer. The muck was in his hair and clothes, the chill seeming to sink into his very bones. He clenched his jaw to stop his teeth chattering.

A tall German with a longsword crept warily toward Lamiskos. He prodded the Tarantine with his blade, and Lamiskos swept it aside, cursing the barbarian for a coward.

The German snorted, then called something back to his comrades. More laughter rang throughout the forest. A few more barbarians entered the trees, weapons raised, but when no one descended on them, they straightened, relaxing.

The tall man, the leader apparently, said something to his companions, then gestured with his sword. Two of the barbarians moved further into the wood, looking for signs of the Romans. Quintus hoped Ceorix had been able to leave a clear enough trail for them to follow.

The leader poked at Lamiskos again, then turned to discuss something with his five remaining comrades.

When the man glanced away, Quintus finally struck.

Rising from the mud like an avenging revenant, Quintus lunged with his gladius, slashing for the vein on the barbarian chieftain's inner thigh. The blade bit deep, the spray of blood speckling Quintus as the man fell shrieking to the mud. Turning, he leveled a hard kick at the groin of the barbarian closest to the writhing chieftain, then drove his blade into the man's throat as he hunched forward.

Otho burst from the muck on the other side of the startled barbarians, deftly gutting one of the Germans with his gladius then turned to bury blade of his entrenching pick into the neck of another. Even Lamiskos did his part, hurling his gladius overhand at one of the barbarians. It was a bad throw, the handle of the blade striking the man's shoulder, but the impact distracted him enough for Quintus to slip the blade of his dagger between the barbarian's ribs.

One of the two remaining Germans tackled him. White sparks danced across Quintus's vision as his head rebounded from a tree root. By the time his sight cleared the barbarian was on top of him, pushing his face into the mud. Quintus's sword arm was pinned below him, his dagger scraping uselessly across the barbarian's chain shirt. He bucked and twisted, but the man might have been a boulder for all Quintus could do to move him.

Mud filled Quintus's eyes, nose, and mouth, smothering him. He struggled to raise his head, to breathe, but the barbarian bore down with almost inhuman strength. The world became nothing more than a cold damp pit as the swamp closed over Quintus. His struggles slowed, his thoughts slipping away.

Dimly, Quintus felt the man on top of him jerk, then suddenly the pressure lifted. Strong hands grabbed his shoulders, dragging him up into the air. Quintus took a greedy breath, then gagged as mud filled his throat. Gasping, he clawed it away, coughing as he fell back against the tree.

"Thought he almost had you, sir." Otho's grinning face bobbed into view. He brandished his bloody pick.

Quintus stifled a laugh. He could feel it – the mixture of joy and relief that always came after a fight. Against all odds, he had survived again. He tamped the feeling down. "Everyone up, there are at two more barbarians ahead of—"

"I wouldn't worry about them." Ceorix stalked from the trees at the far side of the clearing. With a thin-lipped frown he made a show of wiping the blade of his long dagger on the leaves of a nearby tree. "Looks like you cleaned this lot up nicely."

Otho slapped his chest with the flat of his gladius. "Lucky for you lot, I'm the best fighter in the legion."

"Debatable." Ceorix knelt to slit the throat of a writhing barbarian.

The big man chuckled. "Care to wager on that, cupid?"

Yesterday, the joke would've brought a round of laughter from the squad. Now, they simply looked to the ground, silent and uncomfortable.

"Do you think there are more Germans?" Lamiskos' question came as a pained whisper, his breathing sharp and quick.

"Always." Ceorix sheathed his knife.

"I want to put more distance between us and the battle." Quintus pushed to his feet, nodding to Ceorix. "Which way to Aliso?"

The Gallic hunter squinted up at the flat, grey sky. After a long moment, he spat, then thrust his chin at a sharp angle to the direction they had been heading. "That way, near as I can tell." Ceorix scratched the back of his neck, heavy brows knitted above his shadowed eyes. "They will have put out pickets to catch any survivors making for the river. It's what I'd do."

"Leave me." Sweat stood out on the Tarantine infantryman's brow, his lips pressed together in a pained scowl, jaw clenched with the effort of pulling himself upright.

Quintus waved a hand to silence the man. "We fight together or not at all. Is that clear?"

"Never any question, sir," Otho said.

"I'll make sure to burn offerings to your good fortune when we get back to Rome," Lamiskos said through pain-gritted teeth.

Grinning, Otho bent to help Lamiskos to his feet. "Better yet, pay for dinner and drinks."

"My friend," Lamiskos gave a weak laugh. "If we get out of this, I'll buy you a damn tavern."

"Sir," Ceorix hissed from where the trees thinned further ahead. "You're going to want to see this."

Not wanting to risk a camp, they'd been walking for the better part of evening, stopping only to share a hurried dinner of dried meat and to bind Lamiskos's wound. The darkness left them poking the swampy ground with a stick to keep from stumbling into a mire, but gradually scrubby trees gave way to pine and larch even as the earth became more firm.

Around midnight, the gods had finally answered Quintus's whispered prayers – the rain had ceased, clouds shifting to reveal a gibbous moon, its wan light enough to pick out trees and rocks. For a moment Quintus almost believed they might survive.

He should've known better.

"In Jupiter's name, what is it?" Lamiskos's voice broke like a man on the edge of panic.

Quintus stepped into the clearing to gaze up at the massive wooden structure. The scaffold was as tall as the Arch of Augustus and nearly twice as broad. Roughly man-shaped, it was a thing of salt-bleached wood hung with bones and ragged bits of cloth. No… not cloth, Quintus realized with horror – tanned skins. The odd structure hunched forward like a man on the verge of collapse, its limbs at odd angles, arms and legs twisted by too many joints. Strips of braided sinew bound the scaffold together, the pale wood appearing like bones in the moonlight. Skulls lined the top, a jumble of animal and human remains that lent the structure a low, brooding aspect, as if it were a titan prepared to snatch them up.

Runes were carved into every exposed surface. The strange, curling sigils looked nothing like the Germanic script he had seen etched into stones and trees. They seemed to crawl across the wood like insects as the squad crept towards the thing, shifting in a way that made Quintus feel as if he were trying to focus on a heat mirage.

"Is it a shrine?" Lamiskos asked, glancing at Ceorix.

The Gaul sucked his teeth for a moment, then winced. "Not sure."

"You're a barbarian." Otho mimed stroking a beard. "Surely you must recognize *something*."

"What do you know of Egyptian tombs?" Ceorix grunted. "I'm a Gaul, idiot. My people are no more German than yours."

The big legionnaire scowled but held his tongue.

Quintus squinted up into the vast, open interior of the scaffold. It was hung with what looked to be twists of grass and sticks, but on closer inspection proved to be the desiccated bodies of thousands upon thousands of insects. He took a surprised step back, grasping the structure for support, then yelped and snatched his hand back.

It was warm to the touch. Not the stolid sameness of wood or cloth, but genuinely *warm*, like the body of a living man.

Bile rose in the back of Quintus's throat as he prodded the structure with his sword. He almost expected it to bleed as he tentatively carved into the strut, but the strip just curled away like normal.

The breeze picked up suddenly, causing the dead insects to rasp and rustle as they brushed against one another. Wind blew through the hollowed skulls atop the scaffold, the sound like a storm shrieking around the edges of a door. For a moment, Quintus thought the scaffold might come to life, tearing free of the moss and vines to stand like some colossus of legend, but the wind died as suddenly as it started, and with it, the high, skirling moan.

"Can you read any of this?" Quintus glanced back at Ceorix, then thrust his chin at the runes.

The Gaul padded forward to examine the rough sigils then drew back with a low hiss as if the writing was an adder about to strike.

"It's not Gallic," he said, his wary gaze fixed upon the runes. "Or German."

"That makes no sense." Lamiskos glanced around. "Isn't this Cherusci territory?"

"It is." Ceorix's voice trembled. "But this is no human tongue."

"Sir," Otho hissed. "Someone is coming."

Quintus glanced back, cursing as he saw the dim glow filtering through the trees. He cocked his head, trying to judge the distance, but the pines muffled the footfalls of the approaching party. From the light, he guessed it to be a large group.

Quintus and the others padded back to the tree line, bodies low to cast smaller shadows in the moonlight. Unfortunately, the ground around the scaffold was flat and open, the spreading pines having left almost no cover apart from a few bushes choked by a smothering carpet of pine needles.

The torches had drawn much nearer, enough that Quintus could see individual shadows through the trees. Close enough they would notice if Quintus and his comrades fled.

A breeze whispered through the pines, thick limbs swaying with a soft hiss. The sound tugged at Quintus. He glanced up, the beginnings of an idea tickling at the back of his mind.

"The trees," he whispered to the others. "We climb."

"What about Lamiskos?" Otho asked.

"I'm wounded, not invalid." The Tarantine infantryman pushed free of the big man's grip, then stumbled over to a nearby tree. With a pained groan, he hauled himself into the lower branches, his bandaged leg dragging stiffly behind.

"You heard the man." Quintus nodded at the pines. "Up. And be quick about it."

Quintus leapt to catch a branch, grunting softly as he pulled himself up. Thankfully, the limbs were closely spaced. With a bit of effort, he managed to shinny up to where the branches were thickest. Although he couldn't see his comrades, the occasional grumbled curse from below told him they were making good progress.

After a few shaky moments, Ceorix clambered into the branches across from Quintus, Otho helping Lamiskos to brace himself against the trunk below.

They waited, silent and still, as the procession approached the scaffold.

Torchlight cast the clearing in shadowed relief. The first barbarian to step into view was armed and dressed as a Roman officer, the high crest of his helm gone lank and wet.

Even without the uniform, Quintus would've recognized Arminius.

The traitor general was followed by a score of men and women swathed in hide cloaks, gold and silver bracelets clattering on their well-muscled arms. From their weapons and armor it was clear they were chieftains. Quintus recognized some of their attire from the battle and, from the way they eyed one another and kept their hands close to their weapons, it was clear they hailed from rival tribes.

Behind them came Arminius's guards – turncoat auxilia. Bearing torches, they led coffles of bedraggled prisoners. The captured Romans shuffled forward, heads down and shoulders rounded. They had been stripped down to their mud-spattered tunics, so Quintus couldn't tell if there were any of rank.

Beside him, Ceorix drew his bow as the prisoners were forced to their knees before the scaffold, but Quintus laid a hand on his arm. There was nothing they could do against so many.

Arminius raised his arms, holding forth in the halting, hard-edged tongue of his folk. He spoke at length, gesturing both to the scaffold and the assembled chieftains.

"What's that bastard saying?" Otho whispered to Ceorix.

"He's blowing air," the Gaul replied, voice low. "Promises of land, victory, and wealth to those who help him crush the Romans."

For their part, the German chieftains seemed just as skeptical as Ceorix. One of them, a short woman in white furs, even went so far to spit at the traitor's feet.

With an irritated scowl, Arminius turned to mutter something to the man next to him in a centurion's helm. At the officer's call, the auxilia behind the line drew their gladii.

It happened so quickly Quintus barely had time to register the motion as the auxilia stepped forward and slit the throats of the kneeling prisoners. The captured Romans fell forward, feet drumming on the soft earth as their blood spread below the scaffold.

Fingers of dark red touched the edges of the great creaking structure that seemed to almost vibrate with energy. Threads of shadow crept from the cracks and joints of the scaffold to spread through the pool. Like ink in water, the fingers of darkness spread back to the Roman bodies, which began to twitch and convulse.

Quintus gave a low moan as the corpses split open, bursting like overripe fruit to reveal a seething mass of chitinous bodies. Mandibles clacked and chittered as papery wings unfurled to bear the churning horde aloft. As large as scarab beetles, with clutching legs and long centipede-like bodies, the swarm circled the clearing once, before diving deep into the scaffold.

Something stirred inside. Not the papery rustle of insects, but pale, snuffling things. The trolls did not step so much as tumble from the darkness, their flesh slick with inky effluvium, their limbs wrapped tight around their ungainly bodies. Quintus was closer to the things than at the battle, but he still couldn't focus on the creatures, his gaze sliding off every time he tried to look at them directly. The clearing filled with the smell of rotten leaves, of earth and old, decaying things.

With a thin-lipped smile, Arminius shifted his gaze at the woman in white furs. She barely had time to draw her blade before the trolls descended on her like crows on a fresh kill. They pulled he chieftain apart, bones cracking in jagged mouths as they rooted around inside her, squabbling over craps of bloodied viscera. The other German chieftains watched the slaughter in sullen silence.

Arminius spoke to them again, his tone short and clipped.

"They're to gather more prisoners, bring them here. He

plans to push for the Rhine," Ceorix translated. "Any who resist will be given to the trolls."

At Arminius's gesture, the chieftains fled, casting anxious glances back at the scaffold and the trolls. Even Arminius's guards seemed unsettled by the unnatural things. With a snarled command, the traitor general waved them back into the forest, the trolls loping after.

"Now we know how that bastard brought the other tribes to heel," Lamiskos murmured. "But what do we do about it?"

Quintus let out a shaky breath, chewing on his lip. "We can't hide forever."

The squad managed to descend with only a modicum of rustling. Thankfully, the thick blanket of pine needles muffled their footfalls as they crept away.

"Sir," Ceorix hissed suddenly, his voice low and urgent. "I think I heard something over there."

Quintus squinted into the dim, predawn light. Pines made jagged shadows in the murk, the ungainly form of the scaffold looming behind like the shrine of some ancient and terrible god. For a moment, he thought he saw movement among the trees – a flash of pale skin, a twist of spidery limbs.

Quintus cursed inwardly, his stomach clenching with dread. Bad fortune clung to them like flies on rotten meat. They were in no shape to face one of Arminius's trolls. They could die facing the beast or flee and hope to lose it in the forest. Quintus chewed his lip once more, considering. With a start, he realized everyone was looking at him.

"Decanus?" Lamiskos asked.

"Aliso. We must reach Aliso," Quintus said. "The prefect will know what to do."

At his nod, the legionnaires headed out, moving as fast as they were able. No one glanced back at the bulky shadow that slipped through the trees behind him, as if by ignoring the thing they could somehow deny it form and substance. There was no need to track its progress; the creature made no effort to hide. It simply stalked through the underbrush, snapping branches in its claws, the low rasp of its breath seeming to swallow up all other sounds.

Quintus moved to the rear of the group, bared blade in hand. He had done all he could. Their fates were in the gods' hands now.

🜨 🜨 🜨

"Execute these deserters." Prefect Lucius Cedicius scowled down at Quintus. Lit by the braziers outside the garrison gate, the man bore little resemblance to his uncle, Varus – long-faced, with high eyebrows and a thin blade of a nose.

Quintus struggled to stand, but the two legionnaires holding him only tightened their grip on his shoulders. "Sir, you must get inside, one of those things—"

"Do not tell me what I *must* do, pleb." The prefect shifted on his horse, causing the animal to sidestep. "You and these other fugitives come shambling out of the forest with tales of barbarian hordes and boogeymen and expect me to welcome you like conquering generals?"

"It's true, prefect." Otho's voice came low and raspy, muffled by the mud. Like the rest of the squad he'd been shoved facedown on the field outside the garrison walls, the point of a spear resting just between his shoulder blades.

When they'd encountered the mounted Roman patrol, it had seemed like Fortuna's wheel had finally turned but Quintus should've known better. The patrol's commander assumed they were deserters and took them into custody. To be honest, based on Quintus and his companions' ragged appearance, he couldn't blame them.

"I know this sounds like madness, sir," he tried again. "But Arminius—"

"Is a friend to the Empire." The prefect scoffed. "And to me."

"Kill me if you must," Quintus said. "But please, call the men to arms."

Cedicius's scowl relaxed barely a fraction. "They *are* at arms.

18

Three legions under my Uncle Varus, who is due back any day now."

"They're gone, sir," Otho said. "All of them."

"Maxentius," the prefect glanced to one of the spear-wielding cavalrymen. "If that man opens his mouth again, I want you to take his tongue." He turned back to Quintus. "This isn't the first time I've heard deserters spin lunacy to save their—" The prefect cocked his head, glancing toward mist-shrouded trees at the other end of the killing field outside the garrison. "What was that?"

"You have to get back inside." Quintus winced. Already he could feel the damp, clinging chill that followed the creatures like a miasma. "One of those things has been stalking—"

The troll burst from the trees in a spray of scattered leaves, crossing the killing field with preternatural speed. Quintus barely had time to flinch before it was amongst the panicked cavalry. Men were torn from horses in a maelstrom of blood and shrieking steel. A cavalryman's scream ended in snapping bones as the thing snatched the man up and bit down on his head, the troll's jagged fangs crushing steel, skull, and flesh with equal ease.

To his credit, the prefect reacted quickly, wheeling his horse to charge the thing. "To arms, damn you! Romans are dying!"

He slashed at the troll, drawing a thin dark line across the creature's shoulder. It spun to slap the prefect from his horse as easily as a man brushing away a fly. Cedicius hit the ground hard, rolling through the mud to lay still.

The soldiers holding Quintus released their grip to fumble at their blades. He stumbled to his feet, snatched up two swords from where the guards had piled the squad's weapons beside the braziers, then turned to toss one to Otho.

The big man caught his blade with a savage grin, bending to retrieve his entrenching pick. "Another minute and we'd have been crow fodder."

Ceorix scrambled over to snatch up his bow and quiver. "Is it wrong that I'm happy to see that thing?"

"Help Lamiskos." Quintus nodded to the Gaul.

"I can take care of myself." The Tarantine waved off Ceorix's ministrations with an irritated scowl. "Just help me to my damned feet."

"You," Quintus shouted to the man Prefect Cedicius had called Maxentius. "Back to the garrison, bring help."

The man's gaze flicked to the downed prefect, lips pursed as if he were about to argue, then he gave a quick nod and wheeled his horse, galloping back to the garrison walls.

Quintus turned to the rest of their former captors. "Advance with us. And spread out, we want to surround it – formations are useless against this thing."

As they stalked forward, weapons at the ready, the troll drove a clawed hand into the stomach of the last cavalryman. Tearing out a handful of slithering guts, it paused to regard the steaming innards like a child with a new toy.

The prefect's guards were well-trained. They fanned out to surround the beast, which continued to maul the dying man, seemingly unconcerned.

Quintus nodded the advance, hand tight on the grip of his sword. It wasn't an enchanted blade by any means, but he hoped good Roman steel would be enough.

He stabbed for the inside of the beast's thigh, hoping there was an artery there to cut. The point of his gladius scraped across the troll's flesh leaving barely a mark. It was as if he were back at the training field hammering at a post with a blunted blade.

The troll swung a hooked claw and Quintus had to throw himself to the ground to avoid the slash of the beast's talons.

"Like a tree from the halls of Dis," Otho shouted as his blade hacked a hunk of hard flesh from the thing's hip. "Let's fell this oak, lads!"

The others came charging in, hewing at the troll's legs. Chips of hard flesh flew through the air like wood from a lumberman's axe, and the creature stumbled. Huffing like a pregnant sow, the troll roared and tore the head from a nearby guard, then casually backhanded another a dozen paces. It caught another man, hooked claws perforating the guard's mail as if it were wet papyrus, then it simply folded him in half, the crack of the man's spine unaccountably loud amidst the shouts and clatter of arms.

Quintus scrambled to his feet, backpedaling to avoid a kick from one of the troll's heavy feet. His blade licked out, scoring a thin slash along its calf. It charged after him, gnarled talons flexing, ready to crush and rend. Quintus tried to dodge, but the thing was simply too fast.

Ceorix's arrow thudded into one of the troll's wide, dark eyes. The shot seemed to enrage the thing, and it reeled back, shaking its head violently.

Quintus heard the beat of hooves behind him a moment before he was dragged off his feet and up onto a horse.

"That was close, " Lamiskos shouted to be heard over the melee. He deftly maneuvered the horse away from the snarling troll, which was now slashing at the remaining guards.

"I didn't know you could ride," Quintus said.

"Better than I can walk." Lamiskos gave a wild smile. "I'm from Tarantas, sir. We're born to the saddle."

The troll looked like a taproom table covered with scrapes and gouges, but barely a half-dozen Romans remained standing. Quintus was heartened to see his comrades among them. Otho and the remaining guards were bringing the thing down, but far too slowly. Even as Quintus watched, the beast tore the arm from a screaming guard, then hurled the limb into the face of another.

Shouts rose from inside the garrison, the clatter of armor and hobnailed sandals, but no soldiers had yet emerged from the gates. Quintus cast around the field for something, anything that could be of help.

His desperate gaze fell upon the crackling braziers outside the garrison gates. With a shout, he directed Lamiskos toward the fire. Leaping from the horse, Quintus tugged off the tattered remnants of his cloak. He wrapped the sodden fabric around his hands, then grasped the handles of the great bronze bowl, lifting it from its cradle.

The heat from the burning coals scorched Quintus's exposed flesh, the air suddenly thick with the reek of burnt hair, but he ignored the pain. Stumbling toward the troll, Quintus hurled the bowl of coals at the beast.

Flames burst on its bark-like flesh. Skin blackened and burned, layer upon layer peeling back like the pages of a book. Still it fought on, dragging another man into the burning maelstrom and biting his head off.

With a shout, Otho skipped forward to bury his pick in the troll's knee.

At last, the creature toppled, the few surviving guards backing away as the troll thrashed and screeched, flames rising like a bonfire at Vulcanalia.

Quintus watched horrified as the thing collapsed in on itself, its flesh like thick hide stretched over an armature of wooden bones. For a long moment, no one spoke, the field silent but for the hiss and crackle of the troll's corpse.

"In Jupiter's name."

Quintus turned to see Prefect Cedicius sitting up, eyes like silver coins as he watched the creature burn. Groggily, he pushed to his feet, regarding Quintus with newfound respect. "Are there more of those things?"

"Dozens," Quintus said.

"And the Germans?"

"Many, many more."

"Is my uncle is truly dead?" the prefect asked.

"We didn't see him fall," Quintus replied. "But the legions are almost certainly gone."

Cedicius stepped forward to prod the ashes with his spear. "Where did it come from?"

Quintus frowned. "Arminius has worked some manner of dark sorcery in the wood. He summons the beasts with sacrifices, somehow controlling them through offerings of blood."

With a shout, Maxentius burst from the gate at the head of a phalanx of Roman soldiers. At the sight of the burning troll, they clattered to a halt.

"Stand down." The prefect waved a tired hand. "Spread the word: the barbarians are coming."

With a tight-lipped nod, Maxentius turned to the assembled troops, already shouting orders.

"We barely survived one of those beasts," Quintus whispered. "With the Germans they'll be almost invincible."

The prefect swallowed. "I'll have the onagers rigged with fire pots – we might get lucky."

Quintus turned and regarded the smoldering corpse of the troll, then took a deep breath as an idea came to him. "We might not have to face them."

The prefect raised an eyebrow.

"The sorcery, I think I know how to stop it," Quintus said.

"I can't spare many men." The prefect gestured at the garrison. "But anything else you need…"

Instead of answering, Quintus turned to regard his squad, forcing humor into his voice. "Fancy another jaunt into the woods, lads?"

Otho snorted. "Just point me at them, sir."

"If I can keep the horse," Lamiskos said, patting the beast on the neck. "My leg's a little sore."

After a long moment, the Ceorix shrugged. "Can't have you idiots stumbling into a bog now, can I?"

Quintus turned back to the prefect. "We'll need a few hours rest, not to mention new weapons, equipment, oil, kindling, mounts—"

Otho cleared his throat loudly.

Quintus grinned. "And a hot meal."

"So what gave you the idea, sir?" Ceorix asked, bow held low, an arrow nocked and ready.

"It was your tale, actually." Quintus nodded. They'd managed to get some sleep while the garrison was mustering, and while not quite recovered, he wasn't on the verge of collapse. "Our blades weren't doing the trick, and we certainly didn't have a mountain to drop on the thing. I figured fire might be worth a try."

"It *was* satisfying to see that thing burn." Otho grunted, patting his stomach. "Although not as satisfying as a bowl of stew and good hard bread."

"You think the scaffold will burn, too?" Lamiskos asked. The young Tarantine seemed to have taken on new life on horseback, guiding his mount with a thoughtless ease Quintus couldn't help but envy.

Quintus massaged the back of his neck, working out a kink. "When I stabbed the troll, my blade didn't pierce, but it carved a piece off – just like at the scaffold."

"You think they're made of wood?" Maxentius asked. The prefect, still visibly shaken, had dispatched the cavalryman and a score of soldiers to assist Quintus and the others. A small group, traveling quickly and quietly, or so they hoped.

Otho gave a bitter laugh. "Wouldn't be the strangest thing we've seen in the last few days."

The conversation lapsed, each man looking away, lost in their own thoughts. Quintus couldn't blame them, memories of the slaughter loomed at the edges of his mind as well, lurking like a troll ready to leap from the brush and snatch his sanity away. They rode in silence for some time, the forest quiet but for the muffled thud of hooves on pine needles.

Ceorix's hiss snapped Quintus from his painful rumination.

"We're almost there." The Gaul slipped from his horse, tying the beast to a nearby tree. "Best to continue on foot."

At Quintus's nod, the others dismounted and began to unpack their equipment. He laid a hand on Lamiskos's shoulder. "I need you to stay back."

The Tarantine's glare could've etched copper. "Sir, I—"

"You're our best rider." Quintus held up a hand. "We may need your help later. If this goes *very* poorly, you're to ride for Aliso and tell the prefect we've failed."

Lamiskos gave a quick nod, not meeting Quintus's gaze.

"Good." He clapped the young man on the shoulder, then turned away. "The rest of you, load up on firepots. No armor, no helms, blades blackened – nothing to catch the eye."

"And if they catch us?" Ceorix slung two of the cord-wrapped clay vessels over his shoulder.

Quintus returned a tight-lipped smile. "Then we burn them out."

They stalked through the darkened pines, slipping from tree to tree. Quintus heard the scaffold before he saw it – the low droning of thousands of wings filled the forest like the buzz of some monstrous cicada. Figures stood silhouetted in the torchlight, the tall unnatural shadows of trolls as well as those of men. *Many* men.

Quintus let out a soft curse, pressing himself against a wide-boled pine. Arminius had returned, and he'd brought a small army with him.

Scores of German auxilia ringed the clearing, shields resting on the ground, their hands on the hilts of their blades. Perhaps a dozen trolls squatted like guard dogs near a crowd of German chieftains and their warriors, regarding the sullen barbarians with hungry eyes.

Arminius stood a few paces from the scaffold, arms raised, exhorting the thing. His chant seemed to blister the air, snaring Quintus's thoughts with images of deep, dark places; of eyes and blood and shadow. Of things long buried.

"Sir," Otho whispered, nodding at the far side of the scaffold.

Quintus shook his head to clear it, then followed the big man's gaze.

Row upon row of captured Roman soldiers knelt before the structure, their hands tied behind their backs, sacks over their heads. More of Arminius's guards stood among them, blades bared.

"There must be a few hundred, maybe more," Maxentius whispered, his voice caught between awe and horror. "Poor bastards."

Ceorix grunted. "Think of what's going to come crawling out of that thing when Arminius finishes his little chant."

25

The hair on Quintus's arms prickled at the thought – a few dozen trolls had been enough to slaughter three legions. What would a hundred do to those Romans who remained?

He chewed his lip, eyeing the gathered horde. "Maxentius, give me your firepots. You and your men are going to slip around the other side and try to free as many captives as possible."

"More blades in Roman hands could be helpful." The cavalryman nodded. "What are the rest of you going to do?"

Quintus gave a thin smile. "We'll be causing a scene."

They waited as Maxentius and the others slipped into the darkness, giving them a slow hundred count to edge around the clearing. Fortunately, everyone was focused on the ritual.

When the count had wound down, Quintus glanced at Otho and Ceorix. "I feel like I should say something profound."

The big man grinned. "When we tell this story later, we'll say you did."

With a deep breath, Quintus pushed from the tree and padded towards the torch-lit clearing. A dozen paces from the edge he paused to light the fuses of the first firepots. The clay jars were meant to be hurled from an onager, but Quintus had fitted them with dangling cords, allowing them to swing the pots like hammer throwers. He was too far to hit the scaffold, but after a quick turn the pots tumbled through the air, arcing down to explode among the trolls.

The beasts ignited as if they had been soaked in oil. Flames spread, the trolls shrieking as they thrashed around the clearing. The German chieftains drew back in confusion, then, as the beasts began to topple, drew their weapons. Some fled back into the forest while others advanced on the startled guards.

Traitor auxilia snatched up their shields, slipping into a close formation to ward off more missiles, but pots were already in the air, and the tightly-packed mass proved an excellent target.

Men screamed as the pots exploded, spraying them with burning pitch and saltpeter. Arminius's chant faltered. The traitor's lips twisted into a vicious snarl as he gestured to the guards holding the prisoners, then he turned and continued his terrible invocation. The high, keening buzz rose above the shouts and screams, the shadowy innards of the scaffold twisting like a heat mirage.

Arminius's guards hacked down at the bound and blinded Roman prisoners, bodies falling like cordwood. Quintus saw a barbarian raise his blade, then drop as one of Maxentius's men stabbed him in the side. Beyond the spreading flames, freed Romans now surged to their feet to struggle with their captors.

A burning barbarian stumbled toward the scaffold, arms flailing, only to have Arminius run him through without breaking his chant. Although the flames licked around the edges of the structure, they did not catch as they had with the trolls.

"We need a solid hit." Quintus hefted one of the last pots, judging the distance. "Keep lobbing these and I'll try to—"

"No time." Otho drew his blade and pick, nodding to the blood that was creeping toward the scaffold. He stepped from the shadows, face grim. "Stay behind me, sir."

Quintus opened his mouth to order Otho back, but the big man was already moving.

Muttering a curse on all bull-headed infantrymen, Quintus snatched up another pot and ducked after Otho, a lit taper clenched in his sweaty fist as he called to Ceorix to cover them.

The clearing was a tumult of shouting, struggling men. A few of the Germans tried to form a shield wall, but a burning troll scattered them like leaves, shrieking and snorting as it gutted a man then fell to roll in the spilled entrails like a dog in carrion.

Arminius's auxilia had kept their Roman arms and equipment down to the tunics and caligae, so they were slow to respond to two similarly dressed men charging into their midst.

Otho buried his pick in the helmet of the first barbarian to bar their movement. Twisting to punch his sword into the stomach of the next auxilia, he kicked the man sprawling into his companions, then dropped a shoulder into another barbarian. A man to Quintus's left fell, pawing at the arrow in his throat, and suddenly the way was clear.

"Go!" The big man bellowed as the Germans closed in around him. "In Mercury's name, go!"

Quintus knew better than to look back. He bulled toward the scaffold, sandals churning the soft loam as he closed on the thing. Close up again it seemed less a structure and more a living thing. The hide-covered bones of its chest rose and fell with unnatural breath, its twisted shoulders hunched forward, hands outstretched as if to beckon the carnage closer. The first runnel of blood touched its base, and Quintus groaned as black tendrils crept back up the stream of red. He heard the buzz of membranous wings, the high whine as the first of the Roman bodies burst open. In a heartbeat, the air was full of swirling insects.

Shifting the pots, he touched his taper to the wick of the first. It hissed and popped as Quintus steadied himself for a throw right into the center of the cursed structure.

He saw the descending blade a moment before it tried to take his hand. Arminius's sword caught the firelight, and Quintus twisted away just in time.

Roaring like an injured lion, Otho surged from the fire-lit shadows, bulling Arminius to the ground. Although of a similar size and build, the traitor general seemed imbued with a terrible vigor, ending up on top. Teeth bared, he hammered the heavy pommel of his blade into the big man's skull, and Otho went limp.

Arminius stood as the first of the trolls tumbled from the scaffold, slick with shadowstuff. The traitor nodded at Quintus, ordering the beast forward.

On reflex alone, Quintus swung the fire pot like a ball-and-chain. It struck the creature in the torso, flames spreading across its boney chest. The troll batted at the flames, which only served to spread them to its hands and chest. Burning like Vulcan's forge, it stumbled into the traitor auxilia that were coming to save their chieftain.

Unfortunately, Arminius didn't need saving.

Quintus dropped the taper to draw his own blade, bringing it up just in time to parry another blow from the traitor general.

"You think the world is yours, Roman." Arminius followed

up his swing with a kick that sent Quintus stumbling back. "We are not your dogs to be leashed and broken."

Quintus snarled and lunged only to have his gladius slapped aside, Arminius's backswing almost opening his throat. The barbarian wielded the heavy blade like a willow switch, the blows quick and powerful. It was all Quintus could do to keep the bigger man from cutting him in two. Breath rasped through his clenched teeth as he parried strike after ringing strike, his sword arm numb. Arminius's sword slashed across him with ease. His tunic was soon soaked in blood, his limbs loose and weak.

Darkness roiled within the scaffold. The thing seemed to balloon outward, swelling like a sea-bloated corpse as it prepared to unleash its rot upon the world.

Quintus lunged for the scaffold, but Arminius blocked his path. The traitor general was Roman trained and had fought with the legions – he knew every trick, every ploy. Quintus was overmatched, every moment only weakened him. He fought alone, no brothers at his side.

"You come to our home! Claim *our* land, *our* children!" Arminius shouted down at him. "We are *not* yours!"

With a despairing cry, Quintus threw himself at barbarian general, who calmly sidestepped and brought his blade slashing down.

There was no pain, only a terrifying coldness that spread through his arm. He fell to the ground, gasping, barely able to keep a grip on his sword, let alone the firepot.

The insects swarmed to the scaffold, crawling inside to disappear in bursts of greasy black smoke. Quintus fumbled in the bloody earth, struggling to reach the fire pot even as Arminius raised his blade.

An arrow pierced the darkness, and Arminius stumbled as it ricocheted off his helmet. Ceorix stalked from the swirling smoke like a wolf scenting prey, another arrow already nocked and ready.

Quintus seized on the distraction to crawl backward toward the firepot, the bloody earth seeming to churn beneath him.

More arrows came as fast as Ceorix could fire them, but Arminius seemed a colossus, a titan imbued with terrible might, blade glittering in the firelight as he parried the bolts with almost contemptuous ease. Darkness slipped from the cracks in the scaffold to wreath the barbarian like smoke. An arrow thudded into the traitor general's shoulder but he seemed hardly to notice.

At last, Quintus's trembling fingers closed around the firepot. Feeling almost drunk, he turned toward the scaffold, fumbling at his side for flint and steel.

Arminius closed the distance to Ceorix in three quick strides. Knocking the Gaul's bow aside, he hammered him to the ground with a clenched fist.

His fingers gone wooden from blood loss, Quintus awkwardly struck the flint. Sparks showered over the firepot, but the wick did not catch. The flint and steel slipped from Quintus's numb hands. He cursed, pawing at the blood-soaked earth.

"It's over." Arminius's voice echoed unnaturally, seeming to come from all around Quintus. "You have fought hard, but you have failed."

Through the haze of pain, Quintus heard a distant clamor draw closer, the thud of hooves on soft soil. His questing fingers closed again on the fire striker. Hunching protectively over the fire pot, he hammered flint to steel, almost crying out as the wick finally caught.

"I do not hate you, only what you represent." The tip of Arminius's blade pricked the back of Quintus's neck. "Give in. Your legion is shattered. Your comrades have fallen."

"Not all." Quintus gave a bloody smile as Lamiskos charged from the smoke. The Tarantine's horse seemed at the point of panic, its muzzle flecked with foam, its eyes rolling white, but Lamiskos somehow kept control.

With a shout, Lamiskos bowled into Arminius, sending him tumbling back into his men. Swinging a firepot over his head, the Tarantine wheeled his horse to put it between Quintus and the traitor auxilia.

Quintus pushed to his feet, barely keeping his footing as

he staggered toward the scaffold. It was like a fever dream. The darkness inside the scaffold had deepened, becoming an inky tunnel – no, not a tunnel, a *well*. Quintus saw them then, rank upon rank of trolls. Hundreds. *Legions*. They boiled up from the murk, pale bodies writhing as they clawed up from whatever underworld they called home.

Dimly, he heard Arminius shouting, anger and panic warring in the general's voice. Quintus dismissed it with a grin. Arminius didn't matter, all that remained was Quintus's duty – not to his Empire or his people, but to his comrades.

Straightening his shoulders, he tossed the fire pot into the scaffold, letting the arcane gravity of the place drag it down. He saw the trolls turn to watch it fall, their eyes like stars on a moonless night.

Quintus muttered a quick prayer to Jupiter as he staggered away from the scaffold. There was a moment of silence, quick as an indrawn breath, then the chest-rattling boom of the scaffold catching flame. The explosion knocked him face-first into the muck, and Quintus covered his head, expecting the end.

Slowly, the shouting began again. A hand plucked at his arm, and Quintus turned, fist clenched.

Otho's bruised and bloodied face grinned back at him. The big infantryman nodded at the mighty bonfire behind them. "Fucking profound enough for you?"

"It will have to do." Quintus let the big man help him to his feet.

Arminius's shouts drifted over the roar of the flames and the howls of maddened trolls. Freed of whatever dark hold the scaffold held over them, the beasts attacked any who came within reach, stumbling through the firelit shadows, every slash of their jagged claws echoed by a scream and a spray of blood.

Arminius beat at a passing troll with the flat of his blade, exhorting the creature to strike down the Romans, to drive the invaders back across the Rhine. It turned on him with a wide-mouthed snarl, its answering swipe gouging deep furrows in the barbarian's shoulder. Grimly, Quintus hoped the beast would finish the job, but it turned away to bury its gore-streaked maw in the throat of a staggering barbarian, dragging the man off into the forest.

Tears cut silver lines down the Arminius' cheeks, his lips twisted in an expression partway between fury and sorrow. He pressed towards the burning scaffold, but was dragged away by his warriors, raving like a man possessed.

"Care for a ride, sir." Lamiskos cantered up. The Tarantine had earned another cut for his trouble, his arm held close to his chest, but his smile seemed genuine enough.

"I think he needs it more." Otho nodded at Ceorix, lying face-up in the bloody muck.

The Gaul opened one blood-crusted eye, regarding them with barely concealed irritation. "Jupiter's balls, for a moment I thought I was finally free of you lot."

"Stubborn as we are?" Quintus snorted. "We'd find you in the underworld."

Most of the trolls had disappeared into the woods or lay in burning heaps upon the blackened earth. Those few barbarians who continued to fight seemed primarily concerned with escaping the clearing. When Quintus turned to look for Arminius, he found the traitor general fled. It was too much to hope they could cut the head from the snake, but they had dealt the German coalition a staggering blow this day.

The heat of the fire like a burning hand at their back, they loaded the Gaul onto the snorting horse then shambled toward Maxentius and the others. Quintus felt his wild elation echoed by the grins of his companions. One day, he wouldn't make it out alive, but that hardly mattered.

Although Quintus might die, he would never fight alone.

The Deicide Machine

Justin Coates

The Chicago front was in the process of collapsing when the *Andrada Ascendent* arrived. The *Montgomery*-class super tank rolled over a field of corpses, crushing them to dust beneath her gargantuan frame. The ragged survivors of III Army Corps, barely half of the 250,000 that had marched to war a month ago, cheered for the magnificent war machine. She was 10,000 tonnes of steel and murderous intent, her 85-meter tall frame instantly attracting the bulk of enemy small arms fire. The alien weapons glanced harmlessly off her scorched armor as she crossed over the trenches and into the ruins of the city.

Her captain, PSICOM officer Mercy Ubuntu, watched tactical data flow across her comscreen from the handful of surveillance drones still airborne. The situation was worse than her superiors knew. III Army Corps had held the enemy back, but at an unspeakably high cost. Chicago was reduced to a smoldering ruin, cloaked in a vast cloud of ash and dust.

The city was lost, but III Corps might be able to withdraw if the *Ascendent* could cover their retreat.

It's up to us, Ubuntu thought, before addressing her gunnery officer. "Commander Nguyen. Ensure the Voidborn know we are here."

"My pleasure, ma'am. *All conventional platforms, fire for effect.*"

The *Ascendent* woke, and the earth shook. 120mm mortar platforms along her spine hurled white phosphorus rounds at enemy positions. Sponson-mounted 25mm Bushmaster cannons filled the air with depleted uranium rounds. Nearby battalions fell back to safety, dragging their dead and wounded by the furious light of her howitzer and missile batteries.

Her artillery batteries ruptured gibbering N'nogug bio-tanks as they slithered among the ruins, reducing them to stinking black smears on the war-struck earth. Unprepared for the sheer violence and rapidity of the armored assault, two entire companies of squid-like Voidborn clones were caught in the open and fell in their hundreds to the *Ascendent's* scything broadsides. Her rockets punched through hive-bunkers and armored reefs, incinerating dug-in enemy artillery in titanic eruptions of smoke and fire. Her main guns, two massive 50-inch Void Eater cannons, each hurled 7-ton psychoreactive shells that vaporized enemy bio-armor reinforcements nearly twenty kilometers away.

"Enemy advance is stalling," Commander Burley said. The navigation officer turned to look back at her captain. "We've blunted the assault across five kilometers."

"My regards to the weapon crews," Ubuntu replied.

It was difficult to stay professional with the *Ascendent* grumbling violence in her mind. The product of a union between strange science and even stranger sorceries, the *Ascendent* was described as 'semi-sentient' in PSICOM training manuals.

Ubuntu knew better. There was nothing 'semi' about it, and the *Ascendent* found no satisfaction in killing mortals (alien as they were). It hungered for worthier prey.

"Incoming plasma barrages detected," Burley said. "Deploying countermeasures."

Multiple jets of superheated gas struck the prow of the land cruiser. Electromagnetic pulse defenses dispersed the worst of it, but Ubuntu could physically feel an outer layer of armor strip away through her connection to the tank.

The *Ascendent* rocked sideways, but her hundreds of crew members were well trained. Loading teams kept up with her voracious demand for ammunition. Command and signal units, located on her uppermost decks, swiftly abandoned damaged stations for redundant platforms deeper inside the vessel, even as security teams escorted welders and mechanics to repair internal damage. Burley's superlative helmsman skills kept the assault moving forward, and that mattered most of all.

"I want those plasma cannons gone, Commander Nguyen," Ubuntu said, effortlessly overseeing both the battlefield and the *Ascendent's* interior operations.

"Working on it," Nguyen replied, her fingers dancing across her comscreen.

"Commander Burley, inform Phantom 6 to continue a fighting withdrawal from the city limits. We will cover their retreat."

"Yes, ma'am," Burley said, hastily firing off the messages via comscreen. "Be advised: I'm picking up dispersion rates above .6 in multiple locations."

"How many are stable enough for a breach?"

"Over a dozen."

"Plot coordinates for those closest to us. We will strike them as they deploy from the noosphere."

The *Ascendent's* atomic heart rumbled with barely-restrained impatience as Burley charged the nearest dispersion point. Ubuntu took a breath to center herself, then opened her invisible third eye to the swirling hell of the Otherworld. She could see the thin spots between realms as pulsing lights on the battlefield. Some were brighter than others, and from these she knew the dreadful deities of the Voidborn might emerge. These alien gods were titans in their own right, hideous constructs of flesh, machine, and insatiable hunger.

There was already a god on the battlefield, however. The *Ascendent* lurked just behind her, speaking in furious, bloody whispers that Ubuntu knew better than to heed.

Those deific whispers caught the attention of beings lurking on the other side of reality. Entities made of fanged nightmares turned their baleful gaze toward her. One of them, older and hungrier than its kindred, snarled in a language that made Ubuntu nauseous.

The *Ascendent* howled in response. Ubuntu closed her third eye, shivering from the awful rage bound up in the war machine's heart.

"Dispersion spikes in three locations," Burley said. "We're at .75 and climbing."

"That got their attention," Nguyen said. "Permission to prep tactical sleds."

"Granted, but hold for my signal," Ubuntu said. "I don't want to destroy any more of this city than we have to."

They rumbled through the barren New City district. Voidborn small arms fire all but ceased, though the *Ascendent* herself continued to punish any enemy ground forces with the temerity to occupy her battlespace. The tank's restless spirit made its impatience known through groaning treads and spiking reactor heat output. A whisper, one Ubuntu knew only she could hear, hissed across the net.

Is it time?

Burley called out a warning. "Dispersion rate of 1 detected! Breach initiating!"

A portal between dimensions opened six hundred meters to their west and stayed open just long enough to spit out a spindly-limbed void hound. The alien demon gibbered through a hundred fanged proboscises. Particle cannons, crudely sutured to its rigid exoskeleton, flashed a vivid blue through the dust clouds.

"Concentrate howitzer fire on the target," Ubuntu ordered. "Commander Burley, bring us close enough for the tridents."

Plasma bombardments hammered down around them. The comscreens stuttered in and out. Messages between maintenance crews flew back and forth across the net with a renewed sense of urgency.

"I want that enemy artillery dealt with, Nguyen!"

The void hound trumpeted and charged. Its cannon struck their armored prow. Ubuntu grit her teeth. Despite no visible wounds, she felt as though a hot iron was scalding her flesh. An auto-generated report revealed damage to the tank's superstructure on her uppermost levels.

"Fire the first trident," the captain ordered.

"Trident away," Nguyen replied.

The massive harpoon soared through the air, launched from a rocket-assist platform along the *Ascendent*'s spine. It slammed into the hound just below its right shoulder. The meter-thick cable tightened, pulling the extradimensional horror off balance.

"A fine shot, Nguyen," Ubuntu said. "Reel it in, Commander Burley."

The *Ascendent* dragged the hound through the steeple of a church. The super tank swerved, dragging the beast through burning ruins. It shrieked, its cannon discharging wildly into the air, the ground.

"All howitzer batteries, fire for effect," Nguyen ordered.

Twenty-one 105mm cannon shells and a dozen 8-inch high-explosive penetrator rounds struck the creature around its face and forelegs. It turned, snarling, only for a double volley from the *Ascendent's* massive pair of 50-inch 'Void-Eater' guns to strike it midsection. Its torso vaporized in a spray of acidic blood. The trident snapped off, the cable whipping through the air in the vessel's wake.

Prow-mounted horns on the *Ascendent* blared a victory anthem. Her crew members cheered and stamped their feet. Back at the front, the survivors of III Army paused in their consolidation efforts to join the battle cry.

Burley shouted, "God kill confirmed!" Then, louder, her voice rising in pitch: "Breach imminent! Brace for—"

Something hard and heavy slammed onto their right flank.

Ubuntu cursed. Connected as she was, Ubuntu could feel talons made of otherworldly material raking across her ribs. Vile fluids poured through her rent armor, damaging internal systems.

"Void Crawler," Nguyen stated, her voice calm. "Bastard is trying to gut us."

"Get it off, Commander Burley," Ubuntu ordered.

The *Ascendent* roared through an overpass. Concrete and asphalt shattered on the war machine. The cackling demon on her flank paid the debris no heed. Its mandibles dug deep into the vessel, ripping chunks away and vomiting venom into the tank's interior.

"Fires on Decks 3 and 4," Burley said. "Fire suppression systems are damaged. We're open to the air in nine locations."

"Send security teams to defend possible entry points and compartmentalize damaged sections." Ubuntu breathed through the pain, eying a series of office buildings ahead. Most were ruined skeletons, but a few – taller than the *Ascendent* – looked to be mostly intact.

"Commander Burley, all ahead full through those buildings."

"We risk tremendous damage to the structural integrity of our prow," Burley said, even as she ceded more power to the engines.

"Then you'd best double-check your restraints," Ubuntu said, ensuring hers were tight across her chest. "Let's see the bastard hold on through this."

They were going nearly 120 kilometers an hour when they hit the first building. The structure turned to a moving wall of debris, crashing into the next just moments ahead of the *Ascendent*. Ubuntu clutched at her arm rests, fighting through the pain of her chest being struck with sledgehammers. She spit onto the floor of the bridge, wiping away a trickle of blood from her nose.

Surviving external cameras showed the crawler digging its thousand claws into the vessel's flanks. The *Ascendent* roared, not in pain, but outrage at such audacity. Perhaps showing some latent psychic connection to the warmachine's spirit, Burley accelerated further, coaxing even more energy from the strained reactor, grinding the alien demi-god through thousands of tons of debris.

"It's off!" Burley said, sparks flying from her console as the world shook apart. The *Ascendent* emerged from a titanic dust cloud, smashing abandoned homes beneath her treads. "Enemy is clear!"

"Direct all Hellfires to fire for effect," Ubuntu said. "Fire for effect. ***Fire. Burn these motherfuckers and eat the ashes.***"

The voice that came through her lips was inhuman: the sound of the wounded and dying in the midst of ceaseless artillery bombardment, if such noise could be turned to speech. Nguyen turned to her, hesitating, fear reflected in her eyes.

Get back, you bitch, Ubuntu snarled, shoving the *Ascendent*'s psychic will away from her mind. *Your hour isn't here yet.*

Ubuntu met Nguyen's gaze. "It's me, Leesh. Launch the Hellfires."

Nguyen nodded, relieved. "Hellfires away."

A flight of missiles burst from sixty vertical launch platforms near the *Ascendent*'s stern. They arched briefly through the air before screaming toward the shrieking void crawler. The thermobaric weapons blistered its alien form. The abomination caught fire. Strips of smoking flesh peeled from its body. It shuddered, curling up on itself like a dying insect, and lay still.

"God kill confirmed!" Burley declared.

Nguyen thumped her small fist into her tactical console, shouting, "burn, you bastard!"

The *Ascendent* howled her victory anthem again, but Burley's voice cut quickly through the noise. "Captain, we've got three squid swarms heading this way. Estimate 1,200 enemy infantry in the open."

"What's our armor integrity?" Ubuntu asked.

"Compromised. If they get past the Bushmaster cannons, we *will* be boarded."

"That's a big if," Nguyen said, updating firing plans for the sponson guns. She pointed to a pulsing icon on her display, growing closer to them by the second. "Last target is inbound. We'll need to use the sleds."

"That is absolutely out of the question," Burley said. "We'll kill our own crew and cause additional and unnecessary damage to the *Ascendent*."

"Irrelevant," Nguyen replied, her voice sharp. "Our mission is to cover III Corps' retreat."

"III Corps is made of men," Burley insisted. "But the *Ascendent*..."

"Is made *by* men, *for* men. Our mission is paramount. Should she be lost, others can be built to replace her."

"There is only one *Ascendent*," Burley said stiffly. "And the loss of this vessel is too high a price."

"I'm the judge of that, Commander," Ubuntu said, the slightest raise of her voice signal to her subordinates that she would brook no argument. "As it stands, I've no intention of surrendering the *Ascendent* or the battlefield to the enemy."

A warning klaxxon sounded on their comscreens. The tides of the Otherworld rippled out of a yet-invisible dispersion point.

Burley's shouted warning was entirely unnecessary. The hair on the back of Ubuntu's neck stood up. Weird, alien whispers filled the net. Impossible glyphs flashed across the comscreen, then disappeared.

Ubuntu switched her radio channel to address every human unit that could hear her. Her throat was dry; she swallowed, trying to still the twisting knot of terror and anticipation in her gut.

"All elements, this is the *Andrada Ascendent*. A MIDNIGHT-Level event is occurring. Break." She hesitated, then added, "Use of atomics on the battlefield is imminent. Break. All units are advised to withdraw. Godspeed, and *Contre Noctem*"

"*Contre Noctem*," the two commanders muttered. Nguyen genuflected.

The shrieking klaxxon grew louder. The *Ascendent's* psychic growling grew with it. Two of the dispersion points collided. The breach appeared as a brilliant sphere of light on the battlefield. Ruins near it began levitating strangely, the tides of gravity warped by such aberrant, otherworldly power.

The breach swelled in an obscene parody of birth, and a true Voidborn god tore its way out of the madness of the Otherworld. Even at a distance Ubuntu could see how it towered over the *Ascendent*, supported on bulging tentacles and vaguely simian legs. Psychic assimilation devices of bone and sinew, their method a mystery to even the most brilliant minds of PSICOM, spun wildly as they soaked up the energy from the breach.

The name of the god was written with glittering alien runes on each of its titanium scales. The squid infantry advancing on the *Ascendent* took up that name as a battle cry, even as the deity itself roared the name into the mind of every living being within twenty square kilometers.

UZHAIOGACH!

Nguyen whistled. "That's a big fish."

"Captain Nguyen, hold sled fire for my signal," Ubuntu said. "All other systems are yours."

"Yes ma'am. All howitzers batteries, fire for effect!"

Four kilometers of ruins lay between the *Ascendent* and Uzhaiogach. Every one of her guns covered that distance in a heartbeat.

"Rocket pods 1-20, fire for effect!"

200 Hydra 70 rockets screamed from their launch pods. The demon roared, recoiling from the heat and pressure of the multiple blast waves.

"Mortar batteries, bracketing fire from the following coordinates! Exhaust all ammunition!"

The 120mm mortars fired at high angle, raining down burning white phosphorus as close as 200 meters away. The flames spread quickly, punishing the advancing enemy infantry and creating a field of fire that Uzhaiogach would have to cross.

The demon regarded them for a moment. Ubuntu could taste its thoughts: brackish and alien, possessed of unfathomable purpose. Its mere presence drove the *Ascendent* into blind fury. The ghost in the machine struck at Ubuntu as though she were an enemy. For a terrifying moment Ubuntu thought she would be lost, her mind soaked into the vessel's pulsing reactor heart, but her own stubborn refusal to cede control to a damn vehicle kept her conscious.

"Not yet," she hissed through clenched teeth, heedless of the concerned looks both Nguyen and Burley gave her. "Not bloody yet."

The demon god boomed with laughter. Its slime-covered tentacles pushed it faster toward the *Ascendent*.

"Noospheric spike detected!" Burley shouted. "Brace for impact!"

The demon's psychic attack hit the tank hard enough to push it sideways on its tracks. Sparks flew from the bridge's command screens.

The *Ascendent* screamed, and Ubuntu screamed with her. An invisible spear pierced through her ribs, its cold touch profaning her organs. She could *feel* cancerous tumors sprouting inside her lungs and liver, sprouting in stigmatic sympathy with the tank's injuries.

"Major hull breaches on the second, third, and fourth decks," Burley said. Blood oozed from a wound on her forehead. Nguyen was silent, her head lolling on her chest. "Enemy dismounts are boarding on the fourth. We've lost all sponson guns on our starboard side. Locomotion failing. Reactor close to critical."

"Prepping remaining Trident missiles," Ubuntu said, taking over Nguyen's responsibilities. "Once they've fired, the bridge is yours." Then, though the words were her own, the voice was once again that of the *Ascendent*. ***"Don't let that bastard get away from us."***

Burley gave a crisp salute. Her eyes shone with near-cultic fervor. "*Contre Noctem*. It has been my honor, and privilege, to serve You."

Ubuntu opened her third eye and turned to behold the *Ascendent*. It was a column of atomic fire, a towering psychic whirlwind that was at once familiar and more alien than even the Voidborn.

Is it time? The god demanded.

Ubuntu nodded. "Yes. It is time."

There was no hesitation. The *Ascendent* took Ubuntu, bringing her into the heart of the tempest until She and her were one.

Burley's voice seemed to come from a thousand miles away.

"*Tridents away. Happy hunting, Captain.*"

The metal goddess drove her talons into the demon. Three of them failed to penetrate, but a fourth stuck in a gap between its armored scales. Burley accelerated at a tight angle, yanking it toward them.

Squid clones crawled over and inside her. Security teams with shotguns and riot shields battled next to ammunition chambers and fuel supplies, making the enemy bleed for each step.

Integral systems failed. Coolant lines evaporated. Locomotion systems shuddered and threatened to go dark forever.

Together, Ubuntu and the *Ascendent* held on. The strain was tearing her apart, but she forced her atomic heart to stay online, to continue working with what limited power it had.

The part of her that was still Ubuntu shouted: *Come on! We aren't finished yet!*

They turned. Uzhaiogach came on. They collided like mobile mountain ranges, two gods of war desperate to consume the other. The buildings between them were reduced to dust and ashen embers.

Its mantis limbs hacked deep into her spine. She pummeled it with her howitzers and remaining 25mm Bushmaster cannons. Her Void-Eater cannons blasted meters-thick chunks of armored plating from its eldritch form. It seized the yawning barrels in its jaws, chewing through the explosion of the gun's magazine.

Uzhaiogach swung her around. She dug in, her treads roaring, then pushed back. The demon slithered backward, prevented from disengaging by the trident embedded in its torso. The phosphorus firestorm scorched alien and human god alike.

I will devour you, the *Ascendent* seethed. *And shit you out my exhaust pipes.*

They roared from the flames and into the frigid waters of Lake Michigan. The sky overhead broke with forks of green lightning. Downed alien craft drifted in the cursed waves battering the shore.

The trident snapped free. Uzhaiogach broke away, lumbering down the rocky beach. It sucked in energy from the noosphere, preparing itself for another brutal psychic attack.

Bleeding from one hundred thousand wounds, the *Ascendent* pivoted, feeling the fusion reactor in her heart beginning to flicker.

She charged the enemy, hurling her remaining rockets and howitzer rounds. She slammed into its crustacean torso as its main weapon fired. It scoured her back, peeling off her mortar platforms and drone landing pads, but did not pierce her heart.

She did not notice the pain. Her momentum was unrelenting. She rammed Uzhaiogach, piercing it on her armored prow. The god machine forced the demon back into the ruins, through the flames, through a kilometer of pitched battlefield.

She was screaming by the time she shoved Uzhaiogach into the rusted remains of a toppled skyscraper. Dozens of massive structural beams burst through its chest. The *Ascendent* hurled herself into reverse, her treads shredding on razor-sharp debris. For a moment she was stuck, battered by the howling demon's claws and teeth, her cannons and missile systems reduced to sparking wrecks.

Burley came through in the end.

They limped away, fires spreading on multiple decks, smoke pouring from the wounds in her armor.

I am the memory of the great Andrada.

Squid infantry poured through her hallways and corridors. Security teams fought to give loading crews and engineers time to complete their tasks before being overrun by alien horrors. Uzhaiogach pulled itself free, emerging from the rubble of the collapsing skyscraper with hellfire in its crushing claws.

I am a child of the all mighty Behemoth.

She activated her recoilless sleds at last. The devices hurled twin M-422 bombs at Uzhaiogach. The projectiles opened seconds before impact, revealing dozens of fin-steered devices that aimed right for the alien's heart.

The ensuing detonation formed a nuclear fireball nearly 60 meters wide. A newborn sun kissed the earth, sucking in fountains of irradiated ash and spewing it into the air. The blast-wave formed a toxic cyclone that pummeled the *Ascendent* and her foe.

Uzhaiogach burned.

The elemental fury of sundered atoms torched its otherworldly frame. Its accumulated psychic energy ran out of control, mutating and warping its flesh in great heaving loops. Its compound eyes burst. It screamed, and collapsed under the weight of its own mutation, rapidly dissolving into stinking, purple flames.

Ubuntu and the *Ascendent* were one, and then they were two again. Ubuntu gasped, her fingers curled from the agony of her wounds. A thousand warning sirens sounded from multiple systems throughout the *Ascendent*.

Burley held an emergency oxygen mask to Ubuntu's face. Nguyen was still in her chair, barely conscious, clutching a pistol and staring at the door leading out of the bridge.

"God kill confirmed," Burley said. "Ironside 6 is reporting a full withdrawal. III Corps lives to fight another day."

Ubuntu's cracked lips opened.

"Boarders?"

Screams, shotgun blasts, and the gibbering of Voidborn clones on the other side of the bridge's blast doors answered her question. Ubuntu got to her feet, waving away Burley's protest. She reached out her hand; after a moment of hesitation, Burley armed her with a stout pump-action shotgun. Ubuntu racked the chamber.

"Get us off this battlefield, Commander."

Wincing, Ubuntu leaned against Nguyen's chair for support. The *Ascendent* whispered through the rumble of the engines and the ceaseless work of the surviving crew members. A voice that was once bellicose and challenging now seemed almost grateful, ready to lend its strength for the battle to come.

The door to the bridge shook. Burley shouted orders across the net. Slowly, torturously, the god of steel and fire turned away from the irradiated remains of its foe.

Ubuntu aimed her shotgun at the door and whispered, "The honor is mine, my friend."

STAINS

Daniel Finley

He hated it. The black tar. It coated everything. Burrowed into the nooks and crannies of his gun, rooted underneath his fingernails. Even contoured the creases in his skin. Except it wasn't tar; it was something else.

Mattock scrubbed the Fostech Origin SBV until near perfection and moved on to the machete. Black sticky liquid spattered the blade. A solvent was the only thing that could remove it, and yet, it never did. Years of tar matted the outdoor wooden table he sat at. In fact, the entire way station carried the stain of the black woods. Small and squat, the structure stood half a mile away, but the forest left its mark in the form of a tar trail trampled into the green grass. This black path led mercenaries to fame, fortune, or the end of their lives. This way station stood as the last reprieve before they left the rational world behind.

As Mattock sharpened the blade, Griff and Padoo lumbered out of the building. He'd ventured into the black woods with the two tar mercs once before on a shit show of a mission. They'd gone in with twelve tar mercs. Only four came out.

Griff and Padoo were leaving, lugging their weapons in stained duffle bags that were once camo green. Padoo recognized Mattock, gave Griff a tap on the shoulder, and changed direction.

Griff eyed Mattock's setup. "Jesus, man. Is that a machete or sword?"

Mattock grinned and stroked the edge with a whetstone. "I let the thing on the receiving end decide that." A chuckle bounced between them.

"You ain't going back in there today, are you?" Griff asked.

Mattock just frowned and shrugged. "Why not?"

"You crazy, man? The sun is gonna set," Padoo said. "You win a bid we don't know about?"

"Nah, just a couple-a tourists. We go a hundred yards in. See the sights. Shoot a leech-bat for them so they can talk about it at their next soiree."

"Holy shit," Griff said. "First time I ever heard someone work that angle. Damn, I gotta give you credit, bro."

"You know me. GTGP, baby."

Griff smiled, threw out a hand, and did a bro hug by touching shoulders, speaking in sync, "Got to get paid!"

"We got tourists now?" Padoo scowled. "Fuck that. Last thing I want to see is a souvenir from in there. People got enough nightmares."

Mattock shrugged. "They don't. But they about to."

Griff laughed while heaving his tar-stained equipment to the other shoulder "Hey, do me a favor, Mattock…"

"Yeah?" Mattock looked up from his work, half expecting Griff to wish him well and be safe.

"Now that you rollin' in it, wire me that money you owe before you go in. Because I don't want to go in after you to get it."

They all chuckled and Mattock nodded. "I was hopin' to borrow a little more."

"Fat chance of that," Padoo said. "He about to lose it all on a stripper named Jasmine. Come hit us up after, man."

"Will do." Mattock threw them a nod as they turned to hike the dirt road. On the horizon, Mattock eyed a Bentley kicking up dust and cruising his way. He packed the seventy pounds of gear, threw it on his back, and shuffled inside.

It was a spacious room. One wall was covered in maps of the black woods and several lost IDs. The largest map displayed North America, a large black scar running from the tip of Canada down through the Midwest, tapering at the Gulf of Mexico: the corrupted land. The other side of the room held the kitchenette area and two vending machines. One with snacks, the other filled with various ammunition. Black tar splotches covered the floor, reminding Mattock of a city sidewalk covered in old gum.

The couple sat at a plastic folding table filling out paperwork. Henry looked young for his fifty years, silver hair combed back and framing an arrogant smile. The woman next to him, Cassie, looked like his daughter but Mattock could tell she wasn't by the way they joked with each other.

He couldn't take his eyes off them. They were so clean. Their matching khaki outfits were spotless. Their skin, ivory white. They even smelled good. Mattock looked at his reflection in the lone mirror hanging in the kitchenette. He looked like he had smeared black grease paint all over his face. The whites of his eyes stood out in stark contrast. It reminded him of old photos of coal miners covered in soot.

"I think we're ready." Henry offered the paperwork and their picture IDs to Mattock.

"Oooh, this is so exciting," Cassie squealed. "Aren't you excited, baby?"

Henry nodded like he had already answered a hundred times on the trip here.

"Great," Mattock said, "Let's go over some ground rules. First rule, I lead. Stay behind me at all times. If something moves, shout, point, and get out of the way. Second rule, no weapons. Only I'm—"

"Wait, wait, wait." Henry raised his voice and puffed his chest. "No weapons? What's the point of being on a safari if we can't shoot anything?"

"You didn't pay for a safari, you paid for a short tour."

"If it's more money you need—"

"No. It's not about money. I only let people carry guns when I know they can shoot." Henry was about to speak but Mattock held up a hand, knowing what he was about to say. "And I'm sure you've trained at a shooting range, but what we find in there makes people squirrelly and I ain't aimin' to get shot today, ok?

You wanna shoot? We can go through some basic training until I'm confident you ain't gonna shoot me in the ass, but we don't have enough time to do that today."

Henry threw Cassie a smarmy look. "So he can make more money."

Mattock clenched his teeth shook his head, telling himself to be calm. "There ain't no law preventing you from going in on your own, guns blazing. But I ain't gonna be with you. I'll refund your money right now. We'll go our separate ways."

Mattock watched Henry lift his chin, working up courage. "Fine, I'll call your bluff. We'll go in alone." Henry pulled a stainless-steel Smith and Wesson Model 66 revolver from his duffle bag. He held it at his side, palm open, flaunting it.

"Baby!" Cassie pulled on Henry's arm, urging him to put it away.

"Pretty," Mattock nodded. "I hope you're going in there though with more than a wheel gun. If you're not, then best of luck." Mattock grabbed his stuff. Midway through the door, Cassie called after him to wait.

She threw her doe eyes at Henry. "Baby, can't we just check it out today? We can always come back. I've heard stories. I don't think we should run around in there on our own." They both glanced out the window to gauge the truth. The woods sat black and barren and Mattock could have sworn he saw them both shiver at the sight of it.

Mattock watched Henry wrestle with the decision, then Cassie put the nail in. "For me, baby? Please?" Henry caved and put the gun back in his duffle bag.

"Good," Mattock said. "Now fill your water bottles. 'Cuz there ain't none in the black woods."

Mattock led them down the inky path. Before they reached the edge of the thicket, he heard the complaints.

"Eww, it smells like death and asphalt." Cassie waved a hand in front of her face then held her nose. "Do you have masks or something? That smell is probably toxic."

Mattock grumbled to himself and soldiered on, enjoying how much worse it would get for them. He imagined how black those pressed khakis were about to become and the earful Henry would endure on the plane ride home. It would take them weeks of scrubbing before she got all the tar stain off her.

They strolled up to where the green stopped and the corrupt woods began. It was as if someone had coated the forest with black enamel paint. Trees twisted and bent before them, stretching out for light and begging for life. It was a fruitless gesture. A thick and permanent cloud hung over the blackened land like a sheet draped over a rotting corpse.

Cassie stopped in her tracks, eyeing the strange landscape. "I don't know, baby. Something's not right."

"Oh, c'mon, Cass. I thought you wanted some adventure in your life."

"I do, but this… this doesn't feel right."

Mattock understood where Cassie was coming from. Everything in there was wrong. It felt rotten to the deepest part of his soul, and every time he approached it, he wanted to throw up. If he was lucky, these two might change their mind. That was fine by him – there were no refunds. Mattock smiled to himself. It might be a short day after all.

"We've come this far. Let's go a little further." Henry waved her over to follow. Cassie teetered closer, still not convinced. A wind whistled through the dead branches and her eyes darted across the thicket, searching for reassurances.

Slick, sticky, wet ground sloshed under Mattock's feet, each step trying to hold him down. He heard their footsteps following.

The light refracted in odd ways inside the black wood. Shadows no longer represented their source, and murky shafts of light seemed to stretch and bounce through the branches. The air itself felt claustrophobic and stale.

They advanced through a landscape that evolved from black mud to black marsh. Cassie squealed as her new boots sank deep into the muck. Mattock had taken them so far in that the green behind them had disappeared. He stopped and peered around. Henry and Cassie paused with him.

"What are we waiting for?" Henry snapped.

"For a souvenir. Something should come through soon."

They waited. Henry scanned the dark sky for a prize. Time stretched on and the man grew impatient. "I thought we'd be on a boar chase or something. Have you ever hunted elephant in Africa? That's an experience. This? A fucking snoozefest. Everything is dead."

"It's so quiet," Cassie whispered, hugging herself tight as she shivered. "Where are the birds? Not even the sound of leaves rustling."

"There's nothing happening here." Henry kicked at the mud in disappointment. "Let's go further in."

Mattock was only willing to take them this far. This was considered a safe distance in his experience, but his muscles still tensed, eyes laser focused on any movement. Any farther and this wouldn't be a babysitting gig. No, they'd wait until some mutated creature flew by or crawled up out of the muck, shoot it, and then be on their way back.

Henry trod a circle in the sludge. "This would be much easier if I knew what we were hunting for. There's nothing here!"

Mattock didn't answer. He took a swig from his water bottle and kept his eyes on the horizon.

"My buddy got one of those worm things mounted on his wall, I don't remember what it's called. It looks like a giant black maggot as big as my thigh. Big green fangs as long as my fingers. Have you ever seen one? Where do we find those?"

Mattock had seen one once. He was with a group of tar mercs on a rescue mission. A mile and a half in and they were fighting for their lives. One of those maggot things jumped up out of the silt and bit a merc on the hand. Didn't think much of it at the time. Tried to treat it in the field. By the time they got back to the way station the skin around the wound became ashen and spread up to the guy's elbow. The forearm was veiny with red welts bubbling up and chunky puss oozing out. At the hospital, the doctors couldn't figure out what was wrong. Had to cut that arm off. Apparently, a science lab has it now. The severed limb still moves. Claws at the air like it's still alive.

The black maggot that bit the guy was as big as Mattock's thumb. "Nope, never seen one. And I don't know where they are." The memory still made him nauseous and beads of sweat collected at his temples.

"Well, this is bullshit," Henry said. "I shoulda hired my buddy's guide. I knew it."

"Why didn't you?"

Henry's lack of reply told Mattock what he suspected. That guide was dead. Mattock eyed the horizon, waiting, hoping something would fly by.

"Fuck this," Henry said as he marched past Mattock.

"Hey! Hey! Where you think you're going?"

"I didn't come all this way and spend all this money to stare at trees. I came to hunt, and that's what I'll do." Henry yanked the pistol from his pocket and pushed further into the woodland.

"Baby! Wait! What are you doing?!" Cassie chased after Henry.

Mattock closed his eyes and cursed their stupidity and his own luck. If he walked away right now, he was certain he would never hear from them again. But then he'd have to deal with the questions from the police, and after that word would get around that he was getting innocent tourists killed. That would put a big dent in his extra income. Or he could go after them and save two idiots who didn't know what they were getting into, putting his own life at risk.

For Mattock the answer was easy. He turned and stormed back toward the way station to bunk down for the night and catch up on some sleep, imagining how comfortable that cot would be.

Mattock eyed and cherished the green on the horizon when Cassie's shrill scream pierced the vacuum of the black woods behind him. It cut into Mattock's brain so hard that it froze him in his tracks. His body tensed, hand gripping his Fostech. He cursed, spun on his heel, and ran in their direction.

Mattock hustled through the woods. Three gunshots and another shrill scream echoed through the oppressive air. *What did they run into? Fuck. Fuck. Fuck.*

He crested a black hill that rose out of the marsh and discovered Cassie, covered in black tar, aiming the gun at Henry. No, not Henry, the thing holding Henry. It had a milky white tentacle wrapped around Henry's chest, lifting him three feet off the ground. The creature, whatever it was, remained under the marsh, but a second tentacle lashed out at Cassie. She fired two more shots. Both missed their mark.

"Cassie! Back here!" Mattock shouted.

"Help! Help!" she screamed as she crawled through the black liquid.

Fuck, I need a bigger gun.

Mattock knew he'd need some serious firepower and pulled out a disc that held eighty rounds of triple-aught buck. He latched it onto the Fostech, which now looked like some kind of Tommy gun on steroids. He quickly aimed and blasted five rounds into the second arm, sending it flailing. The tentacle clutching Henry thrashed. His screams of agony silenced as he was yanked under the tainted water.

Mattock rushed to the frothing black liquid only to discover a lake of black tar sprawled before him. He toed the edge, only daring to go in ankle deep, gun muscled into his shoulder.

"Shit. Shit. Shit," Mattock said to himself. "I shoulda' kept on to the way station."

"Where did he go?! Save him!" Cassie screamed.

"I'm tryin'! Shaddup!" Mattock swatted at her to be silent. He peered into the lake, realizing the top layer was a translucent blackish-green. Heavier black tar floated a foot below that and made it impossible to view further.

He waded in up to mid-calf. The wet ground shifted under his feet. The water rippled and refracted the barren trees that now looked like deathly claws reaching toward him. A low rumble reverberated through the depths of the water and a terror stabbed into his heart.

Air bubbles belched through the surface and Mattock snapped his aim to it, but nothing else came after it. Was that Henry's last scream?

A full minute had passed, or had it been ten? Cassie's rhythmic sobs filled the silence. He inched forward one more step—

The water exploded, knocking him off his feet. Four white tentacles surged from the water, whipping around searching for him. He aimed the gun and fired. *Click.* He glanced at the gun; the firing mechanism was caked in thick black tar. *Fuck me.* A tentacle thrashed toward him, and Mattock whipped his machete out and severed the thing as it went for his face. The white squirmy arm separated from its host and splashed back into the lake. The rest of the creature reacted with violent convulsions. This time Henry emerged with a huge gasp. The white tentacle still wrapped his chest, but was now spiraling around his neck, the nubby end sliding up the side of his face. Henry's eyes were wide, his pupils pinpricks in comparison. Mattock caught sight of blue and green veins through the tentacle's milky, translucent skin as Henry screamed.

Mattock lunged into the fray of whipping tendrils, swinging the blade like a madman. He ducked, weaved, and slashed, fighting his way to Henry. Mattock cut at the tentacle enveloping Henry with a sickly *ca-chunk*. Another swing and the tentacle gave way. Henry dropped back into the tar water. Mattock felt the liquid suck and surge as the creature leapt into the air and revealed itself. At that moment, through webs of black splashing tar, Mattock got a brief glimpse at the thing, but couldn't comprehend it.

Two eyes stared back at him. Human eyes. Looking at him in either shock or awe. A gaping mouth lay underneath. Mattock's view widened, and he realized he wasn't looking at the beast's face. He was looking at its stomach. Three more heads were next to the first. Eyes closed and puffy, chunks of their flesh bobbing around in the viscous fluid. For a millisecond, Mattock could have sworn one of them blinked.

The creature splashed down into the tar water and swam off. Mattock dragged Henry out, the severed tentacle still clinging to him.

Cassie appeared and helped drag Henry onto the hill as he moaned in pain. He clutched the tentacle wrapped around him and stifled a scream. His coiffed hair was now matted, his whole body coated in black as if dipped in a vat of black crude.

Cassie tried to pry the tendril free but Henry recoiled in more pain.

"Wait!" Mattock pulled a flare out of his pack, struck the end and sparked it to phosphorescent red. He pressed the burning tip into the tentacle and it squealed, though it had no mouth to squeal from. The pale appendage writhed and released Henry, curling up and rolling to the side, dead.

Henry shuddered. The tentacle had left a pattern of holes that were now oozing blood.

"Oh my God, baby! Are you ok? Henry? Are you ok?!" Cassie hovered over him, trying to comfort him but not wanting to touch him.

Mattock looked from Henry to the curled tentacle. He kicked it to make sure it was dead, then burned it with the flare again. Nothing. He picked up the white wormy arm and examined the suction cups on the underside. With some mild pressure he exposed a three-pronged barb, that looked like three fish hooks bound at the spine. He pulled a black garbage bag from his pack and threw the tentacle in. He might make extra cash off this sample if the scientists didn't have this specimen already. *Today wasn't a complete loss.*

"We need to get him to a hospital. Now!"

Mattock looked Cassie in the eyes. He knew there was nothing a hospital could do. For thirty years the best of humanity had studied this place, and the only thing they'd discovered was nothing followed the laws of science in here. If there was an injury it always led to an infection, and there was no cure. When you came to the black woods you either survived, or you didn't.

Mattock touched Henry's wounds to identify if they were superficial. Each of the holes oozed white liquid against his tarred black skin. Henry wasn't talking, just looking up at them, shivering.

"We can't do anything for him. I'm sorry."

"Wha… What do you mean? We're taking him to a hospital!"

Mattock studied the determination in her face. She lifted Henry's revolver, dripping with black gunk, and aimed it at Mattock. "We're taking him to a hospital."

Mattock doubted the gun could still fire but decided to play it safe. "Okay. Okay." He spoke in a soothing tone, trying to put her at ease. "You're not strong enough to drag him out of here on your own, so why don't you put the gun down." She didn't move. "Do you even know which way is out?"

It took a moment to sink in, but she lowered it in small increments as common sense filtered back into her brain. She dropped the gun and wept, salty tears streaking down the black mud that had spattered her face.

Henry suddenly moaned and coughed up white, creamy fluid. He turned to his side, eyes rolling into the back of his head as his body convulsed.

"Shit."

"Do something!"

Henry's body ran rigid like an electric current shot through him, back arching, fingers hooked. Then his body relaxed. Dead.

Cassie hyperventilated, forcing out panicked squeals between breaths.

Mattock eyed the body, not quite believing what he had seen. Every time he'd witnessed someone die in the black woods it was different, but he had never seen someone succumb to their wounds so fast. Then he noticed movement in the holes left by the creature. It was almost imperceptible at first but as he watched, little white strings emerged. They grew at a rapid pace, in a staccato motion, gaining length with pulsating bursts of energy. The threads crept out, wagging their ends as if discovering their new surroundings. When the tiny strings found one another, they tied together. They kept growing and attaching until there was a webbing of crystal threads surrounding the body.

Mattock and Cassie exchanged a worried look, and as soon as they looked back, pods were growing at random places on the strings. They were swelling quickly, pregnant.

Mattock's eyes widened in horror. He'd seen this before. "Fuck! Back! Back! We gotta go! Now!" Mattock retreated, but Cassie stared at him in confusion. He grabbed her arm and yanked her away from the body as the bulbs popped and released fine white spores.

Mattock dragged her against her will. "Cover your mouth and nose. Do not inhale those things!"

The cloud of spores coasted on a breeze, fanning out through the space. Mattock angled back towards the way station when a curtain of spores spiraled in, cutting them off.

They dashed left and ran as hard as they could, putting some distance between them and the threat. Mattock's pulse thumped in his temples as he eyed the landscape, catching twinkles of light where spores still floated.

He retrieved a bandana from his pack and handed it to Cassie.

"What's this?"

"If you inhale those things, they'll incubate inside you and you'll end up like Henry. You need to cover your nose and mouth." He opened his shirt and used a Ka-Bar knife to cut up his undershirt, pouring the last of his water over the swatch and wrapping it around his face.

Mattock then broke off a black tree branch, wrapped the rest of his undershirt around the end and ignited it. "Keep your face covered and stay behind me." The torchlight betrayed Cassie's tear-glazed eyes. Her breathing shuddered as she managed a shaky nod in confirmation.

The sun was setting, and what little light pierced the dark… the day was fading fast. Mattock guessed they had thirty more minutes before the forest would go completely dark. They didn't want to be in here after sunset. Not without a full squad of tar mercs to stand guard all night.

They raced through the forest until a curtain of spores drifted in front of them. The minuscule particulates hung in the air, twisting on an invisible axis. "Hold your breath. Okay? Don't talk or breathe unless you absolutely have to."

Cassie nodded. They took a deep breath and pushed into the veil. Mattock waved the torch in front of him. When the flames touched the particles, they emitted tiny squeals of pain.

Mattock eyed the organisms and realized they were the same shape as the tentacle's barbs.

Cassie froze, eyes locked on something in the distance. "Did you see th—" She stopped mid-sentence.

Mattock yanked her arm, forcing her forward. She resisted, and he pulled harder until they had made it through the cloud. When they'd cleared it by thirty feet, they removed their masks.

"Did you see him?" Cassie asked with a dazed expression. She looked like a shell-shocked child, confused, lost and searching for a familiar face.

"See who?"

Cassie's eyes locked on the woodland behind them, almost like she wanted to go back.

"What's wrong with you?" Mattock asked, shaking her by the arm. "We need to get to the way station! We've got about fifteen minutes before it's pitch black in here and a thirty-minute hike if we move fast."

Cassie shook her head then shook off his arm and focused on Mattock. "Yeah. Yeah. All right."

They cleared the black forest, collapsing onto the grass. The fresh, clean smell hit his nose and told him he was safe. They stared up to the sky, breathing hard, trying to collect themselves. The sun's final luminescence painted the heavens in navy blue, with a deep fade to black.

Cassie sat up and peered into the woods. She squinted, focusing on something deep inside. "Do you see that?"

Mattock turned and scanned the darkness of the wood. "See what?" It was impossible to discern anything beyond twenty feet in. He didn't understand what she was talking about. "There's nothing there. C'mon, we need to get back and notify the authorities." Mattock helped her up, and they shuffled back to the way station. Every few yards, Cassie would look over her shoulder like she caught sight of something. This unnerved Mattock most of all.

Inside, Mattock flipped the power generator on and the wooden building lit up. No one else was here on the weekends. They were all most likely out drinking or gambling away their money. Nobody wanted to be here longer than they had to.

Mattock retrieved a bottle of Brennivin from his rented locker. Cassie had already found a stained seat among scattered tables and chairs. He grabbed a coffee mug from the kitchenette and parked in front her, pouring her a finger of the clear liquid. She didn't acknowledge it, holding herself as she stared through the table.

Mattock took a slug from the bottle and let the licorice spirit burn down his throat. He took a deep breath, grateful for having survived. Again. "I called the authorities. They'll be here in the morning."

Cassie snapped out of her daze. "In the morning? They need to get here right now! We need to get his body."

Mattock shook his head. "They won't set foot in there during broad daylight. There's no way they're going in at night. As far as the police are concerned, their jurisdiction ends at the forest's black line. You get lost in the black woods, then that's the end of you. There ain't no rescue. They just write it up. Told us to stay put until morning."

She was looking over her shoulder again, out through the window. Mattock wished she would stop. "Thirty years, and nothing's ever come out of those woods," Mattock said. "We're safe." She turned back to the table and nodded, grabbing the coffee mug and drinking the liquor without so much as a blink.

🌑 🌑 🌑

That night Mattock showered up, cleaned his guns, and lay down on a cot in the next room. He wanted to sleep but every time he closed his eyes, he saw that face floating around in that intestinal sack, staring back at him. Except it was no longer in the beast, but part of it. All three faces melted together as a part of the monster's outer skin. Each face stared at him.

He sat up and took a deep pull of the liquid mash, noticing Cassie wasn't on her cot. Stumbling into the kitchen, Mattock found her standing at the window, staring out at the black woods again. "You gonna be okay?" he asked.

"Are you sure he's dead?"

The question hit Mattock so hard, he flinched. "What do you mean, am I sure? I'm about as sure as sure as I can get," he said, an image of those white threads growing out of Henry's blackened face rising like a fever dream.

"Because I… I see him. He's there. At the edge of the woods. Right now."

Mattock hustled up to the window. She pointed into the darkness. The forest was a half mile away. There was no way she could distinguish anything from this distance. The perimeter lights were throwing anything beyond it into a black abyss.

She pointed again. "See that little dot of light? I saw him as we were running out. He was watching us. And then when we got out, he was right at the edge of the forest, staring at me. It was him, but it wasn't him, you know?" There was a lilt of hope in her voice, but she looked confused, like she wasn't sure if she could trust her own senses.

Mattock shook his head; he didn't know. "You've been

through a lot. Get some rest. We got a long day of paperwork in the morning. You should call his family."

She nodded and pried herself away from the window. "He didn't have any family left. I was it."

That night, neither of them could sleep and they ended up talking about Henry. Mattock had gotten it all wrong. When he first met them, he thought Henry was the rich guy with some arm candy. Turned out Cassie was the heiress, and Henry the broke musician she met and rescued from poverty. The trip was a gift to him. He'd been talking about proving himself for so long she'd got fed up with it. That, and his constant competing against her friends. She bought this trip to shut him up. She didn't realize she'd get her wish.

It had to be three in the morning when Mattock woke with a start. That damn face was staring at him in his dreams, but this time it was his own floating within the sickly white beast.

He took in the room, relieved to be out of that nightmare, and used the space to ground him back to reality. The perimeter lights cast soft oblong shadows inside. It took a moment for him to realize Cassie wasn't in her cot. *Probably staring out that damn window again.* Still, it was better to talk to someone than fall back asleep. Mattock got up and shuffled into the main area. The door leading outside sat open. The screen door out of its hitch. Mattock looked around for her. "Cassie?"

Maybe she was on the front deck. He moved outside and found her running down the tar path, back to the black wood.

"Cassie!" he shouted, but she never looked back. "God damn it." Mattock bolted back inside, threw on his boots, a headlamp, and grabbed his gun.

He gave chase, but she had a good amount of distance on him. Mattock kept shouting, but she ran as if she couldn't hear. Or didn't want to.

As he followed her back to the black woods, he spotted a glow of light at the edge of the forest. Faint. Cassie ran right for it. "Cassie, don't!" But it was no use. He was still a hundred yards away when she stopped at the light.

As Mattock closed the gap, the glow became more defined. He froze. *Henry.* But at the same time, it wasn't. What Mattock saw was an image of Henry that shimmered as if looking at someone's reflection in a pool of water. This ghostly visage looked dead straight at Mattock and his body went cold. Mattock swallowed the dry air trying to push away the heavy, sinking feeling in his chest.

The Henry-illusion held out his hand to Cassie. With her left hand she took his, and with her right, she raised the revolver to her temple.

The shot echoed across the land and her body dropped like a marionette cut from its strings. The shimmering image of Henry still held Cassie's dead hand. He took one last look at Mattock, smiled, letting out an extended breath of air, like someone trying to fog up a window. A slow, drawn out, ghastly laugh erupted from the thing. Then it dragged her corpse into the darkness.

🌎 🌎 🌎

The police arrived when the sun rose. Mattock told them everything in his statement and they nodded like they had heard it before. The police never even bothered to look at the scene where Cassie shot herself. They wrote it up as a missing person and impounded the Bentley.

After the police left, Mattock went back to the edge of the woods. Silver glinted in the black grass. Mattock snatched up the silver Smith and Wesson Henry had flaunted. Blood stained the ivory handle, mixing with the black tar that consumed the gun. It was a nice piece. Maybe he could fix it up. He cinched the gun in his waistband and double-timed it back to the way station.

Mattock packed up his things then took Henry and Cassie's IDs from the folder and pinned them to the corkboard along with the fifty others. Each of the faces stared out at him, their pictures a testament to how unforgiving the black woods were.

Then there was one that stood out. The face that was in his dreams. The face that was in the belly of the beast.

Mattock swore to himself that he would never come back again. But those who did this kind of work were just as lost as those in the black wood. And no matter how hard they tried to get away, the money always brought them back to be a face on the wall.

RAGNAROK

Mark Renshaw

Lost in unsavoury memories of a grisly breech in Syria, Sargent Falkner failed to respond to his unit's coms check.

"Sarge, ready to rock and roll and boogie till we puke, on your order!" This came from Brody, a brazen behemoth of a man. Ex-Special Air Service and one of five equally imposing soldiers under his command.

Falkner nodded. "Go, go, go!"

They entered the old Burley estate via the servant quarters at the south-east entrance. Brody took point with Jones, Johnson, Douberman and Hans zipping in behind him. Falkner brought up the rear. He clocked a police enforcer battering ram among the splintered remains of the door as he stepped over the threshold. This was the only sign that a counter-terrorist unit had already entered the ancient building. Inside, his men had formed a perimeter. Beams of light from their torch attachments splayed across the mouldy walls.

"No good," said Hans as he removed his night vision goggles. "Everything is lit up like a Christmas tree, just like the thermals. I can't get clear visuals. Did they put lead or something in the walls back in the good old days?"

"Maybe they were worried Superman would spy on them," said Brody.

"Zip it," ordered Falkner. "Let's do this old school using our eyes, ears and balls, just like God intended. Move out."

They headed down a corridor that connected the servant's quarters to the main building, spot checking each room they encountered. Falkner recalled the schematics he had memorised. Built in 1902, the blueprints hadn't mentioned what building materials had been utilised, but he couldn't imagine what substance could fool thermal imaging or cause drones to malfunction. Yet that was exactly what happened when Command had tried to throw modern technology at the mystery his men were now investigating.

The search continued, and at nearly 90,000 square feet with 130 rooms covering three floors, the abandoned mansion was an imposing area to cover. Despite this, his 'immediate action' squad certainly lived up to their name and completed the first-floor sweep in less than an hour. As communications with the outside world were almost non-existent, Falkner flashed Command a pre-arranged message in Morse code from a first-floor window: 'Nothing found so far. Moving to the second floor.'

As his squad ascended, he noticed symbols scrawled on the wall. Most were faded but the odd one here and there appeared fresh. Falkner recognised some. Inverted pentagrams and similar cultish tokens. Most of it appeared to be gibberish. In his briefing, the building's owner, self-made millionaire Joseph Burley, had tastes rumoured to be exotic, his appetites – legendary. He was a known associate of occultist Aleister Crowley, as well a member of the Hermetic Order of the Golden Dawn, whoever they were. Maybe some nutter cultists had abducted the others rather than Command's assessment it had to be terrorists. Everything was bloody terrorists' fault these days. If in doubt, get the terrorists out. His musings were interrupted by Johnson.

"Got something here, Sarge." He indicated an area of the wall revealing a single word. 'RAGNAROK'. The colour and consistency of the liquid suggested it was blood. It had been applied recently as well. Streaks of the crimson fluid were still dripping down the wall.

"What the fuck is a Rag-nar-ok?" asked Brody.

"It sounds like this online role-playing game me little brother plays all the bloody time," offered Douberman. "It drives me mum mental."

"Are these terrorists or virgins playing Dungeons and Dragons?" said Hans. His Austrian accent made it difficult to tell if he was being sarcastic or serious.

"It's a Norse legend," pointed out Johnson, his voice hushed. He remembered being absorbed in Thor comics as a child. "It's an account of the fall of the gods and the end of the world; an ancient extinction level event."

The men's nervous glances to each other spoke volumes in the deep silence.

"Well that's cheered me right up," said Brody, breaking through the gloomy atmosphere. "Let's have an end of the world party!"

Falkner did not like the implications of such a word, or how it spooked his men. He needed them focused and disciplined. "Enough of the sightseeing, ladies," he barked. "Move out!"

Falkner took point, leading them down the murky corridor. Thoughts of disastrous military interventions into cult compounds danced along the periphery of his mind as they continued their sweep. Something didn't add up though. This didn't feel like a hostage scenario, be that terrorist or cultists. Zero communication from the so-called abductors for one. All they knew was several police officers and a counter-terrorist unit had entered this building, none had returned.

The second floor cleared, he again signalled the outside world. In silence, they ascended to the final floor.

Falkner couldn't shake the sense of foreboding. The whole house had an atmosphere that went beyond a spooky old building. Even the smell was odd. At first, he assumed it was just dust and decay. Then he swore he could smell rusted iron. Now on the third floor, it had taken on a sickly, sweet fragrance. There was no denying it any longer, the stench of blood permeated the air. His men knew it as well. When Jones reported yet another room clear, there was a questioning look in his eyes. "What's with the stink, Sarge?"

"Just mould. Keep moving."

"Mould? Are you joking? This is worse than the East Hama offensive without the bodies!"

The squad froze.

"I said keep moving. And cut the chatter." Falkner barged

ahead, breaching one door after another door. Each time, he swept his weapon from one corner of the room to the other. Each time he hoped they would find some enemy his men could attack, something normal to explain this unfolding nightmare. All they found was rotting wood, emptiness and more symbols scrawled across the walls.

The final bedroom lay at the end of a tight corridor. They, whoever 'they' were, had to be in there. Falkner held up a fist. The squad halted. He crouched, motioned ahead with two fingers. Douberman crept forward. He primed a flashbang, opened the door, chucked it inside. The light from the detonation splayed through the cracks in the walls. Weapon raised, Douberman charged inside. The squad followed. Falkner took up the rear, praying for the sound of gunfire. Yet when he entered, he found his men stood in another room that hadn't seen a single soul in decades.

Brody was the first to break the silence. "What the fuck?"

"Stay focused. They may have snuck around us," warned Falkner.

"Bullshit. The house is empty, Sarge!" Brody protested.

"I'm not going to repeat myself, soldier!" Falkner's voice took on a dangerous tone.

Their torches failed, plunging them into darkness. Falkner slapped the side of his weapon. The light flickered a few times, then died. "Spread out, check the exit and stay sharp!"

The squad obeyed, eyes adjusting to the point where they could distinguish the shapes of their comrades. Falkner felt along the ridge of his Streamlight rifle attachment until he found the tab. He flipped it up. "Change batteries," he ordered. It seemed unlikely all their batteries would drain at the same time, but it was the obvious solution.

They fumbled to comply. Seconds later, their lights fluttered back into life.

That was when *It* entered the room.

The thing was so big it had to crouch through the doorway before lifting itself to full height. Even then its head was about an inch off the ceiling. Under the glare of torchlight, it was completely naked. Its skin was grey and dotted with red blotches that throbbed and pulsed with an eerie light. Its arms and legs were elongated, as if they had been stretched out on a rack.

It flexed its hands, revealing claws several inches long. A sticky substance oozed from each tip and dripped onto the floor. Falkner moved his torch up to its face. No eyes, ears or nose but its lower jaw bristled with several rows of teeth. Each row moved from side to side, at different angles from the rest. Spikes covered the rest of its head.

Falkner pulled the trigger. His men joined in. The fire spewing from six SA-80 assault rifles lit up the room like strobe lights. The bullets had no visible effect. They didn't tear flesh or push the creature back. There were no visible signs of impact as if it absorbed each slug.

"Changing!" yelled Jones. He ducked down. Douberman and Hans providing cover as he popped in a fresh clip.

The creature cocked its head to one side and despite the lack of eyes, it seemed to home in on Jones. It strode forward. Fear of crossfire made the rest of the team cease theirs. Jones fumbled with his rifle as he backed away. He stopped short, his back against the wall. The monster casually swiped its vicious claw, removing half of Jones's face. Falkner roared and opened fire again, aiming at the creature's legs. Jones let out a gurgled scream as the monster picked him up and tossed him into the corner of the room. His body hit the wall with a sickening crunch and he collapsed into a heap.

It snapped its head to Brody and trapped him as easily as it had Jones. Brody continued firing at point-blank range as the monster gripped him by the shoulders then slowly inserted its claws into Brody's chest. It cleaved through Kevlar and bone and plucked out Brody's heart. Somehow, Brody was still alive. He was still alive as he watched the creature bite into his heart, tearing off a large chunk and gulping it down. And he was still alive as it carried him over to the corner and dropped him where Jones moaned in agony. Like a medieval king at a feast, it casually snapped off Jones's arm, pulled out a bone and chewed away at the marrow inside.

Falkner had used four magazines to no effect. Lowering his weapon, he stared dumbstruck at the carnage before him. The thing was ignoring them! It was far more interested in its feast. From the corner, he heard the unmistakable voice of Brody calling out for help while the creature consumed more body parts. He must have been in excruciating agony, but it was impossible – he'd seen the monster remove the man's heart! Jones was also becoming more vocal, the shock giving way to terror and pain. Both men had suffered fatal injuries yet were still, somehow, being eaten alive in front of him.

Falkner found himself moving on auto-pilot out of the room and sprinting towards the main staircase. He glanced around, relieved to see what remained of his squad had followed. His mind struggled to accept what he's witnessed was real, he fell back on training and standard operating procedure. "Johnson, move down to the second floor and take position. Hans, you're in the middle. Douberman, you're with me at the rear. Let's move!"

The group descended the stairway, their guns sweeping to cover every angle. They regrouped on the second-floor landing. Falkner was about to order them down to the first floor when he heard a noise from a door to his right. "Quiet," he whispered. "Everybody listen and be on alert."

Approaching the door, the sound became clearer. It was a woman calling out 'help' over and over.

"What are we hanging around for?" pointed out Hans.

"Yeah, I say we carry on. Let's get the shit out of here," said Johnson.

Falkner turned his torch on Johnson, "I'm giving the orders soldier. We may have an injured civilian here. Hans, keep an eye on the stairway."

"This is bullshit," Hans said, as he moved into a flanking position.

"Johnson, open the door then move back. You two, cover him."

Side by side with their weapons raised, Douberman and Falkner stood ready. Johnson placed his back to the wall. Reaching over, he pushed the door open. Clear. They strode in. Their lights shone all over the room as they surveyed it with practised efficiency. Yet the room, which once had been some kind of study, looked exactly the same as when they first swept this floor; empty.

"This is fucked up with a capital F!" said Doberman.

"I agree, let's go people!" ordered Falkner.

Falkner and Douberman headed out first. Johnson backed out slowly, his gun rifle sweeping the room as if he didn't quite trust the emptiness. As he reached the doorway, he heard a large popping sound like a burst balloon. A huge disembodied hand materialised out of thin air right in front of him. "What the…"

Falkner looked over his shoulder and couldn't quite comprehend the surreal scene before him. A hand. A hand almost as wide as the doorway held Johnson in a bone crushing grip! He raised his weapon, but before he could squeeze the trigger, Johnson was dragged back into the room and the door slammed shut. Falkner slammed into it with all he could muster. It didn't budge. Hans and Douberman joined in, adding their weight. Despite the rotting wood, it held fast. A wet tearing noise joined Johnson's screams. Bones cracked and crunched. A vivid image of Jones and Brody being eaten alive invaded Falkner's mind.

His knees felt weak. His world was collapsing. All his training, all his experience with the so-called evils of the world paled in comparison to… to… *this*. Escape. It was all he could think to do. His men were frozen to the spot. He grabbed them by the shoulders, propelling them forward. "Let's go. Now! Move it! NOW, NOW, NOW!"

All professionalism left them as they took the stairs two at a time, feet pounding, hearts racing, running on pure instinct. Douberman tripped on the final step. He went down hard, sprawling across the marble floor of an enormous ballroom. Beyond rational thinking, Falkner fled past his fallen comrade until he found himself in the centre. He halted a moment to gather his bearings and finally noticed a voice screaming in his head, telling him that something was out of place. Hans approached, supporting a limping Douberman, blood gushing from the man's smashed nose. "Which way, sir?"

Falkner shushed him as he trained his torch around, trying to figure out what was amiss. Then it came to him. When they'd swept through earlier, there were two sets of support columns at each end of the room. Now there was an extra set. He trained his torch at the base of one of the extra columns. He tried to convince himself that what he was looking at had the consistency of stone. Then, like a deer caught in headlights, he stood staring as steel grey claws extended from what was a massive paw. Hands shaking, sweat pouring down his face, he raised the torch towards the ceiling. But that was no ceiling. It was a mass of familiar-looking grey skin with throbbing red blotches. He trained his torch ahead, towards the exit. In the distant gloom, he could just about make out an enormous bulk hovering above the doorway. The head of the beast, waiting to eat them alive if they passed that way.

A section of his mind observed it almost casually while the rest of it began preparing for a short, sharp descent into madness. The rational part noticed that Douberman was jabbering. "That can't be real. It can't. I want me mum. Sir, tell her to come pick me up. She won't mind. Please, sir!"

His rational mind took hold, and he slapped Douberman far harder than he intended. "Get a grip solider, we are leaving... now! Fire in the hole, gentlemen, light that bastard up!" He pointed with two fingers towards the exit, then with one towards the wall on their far right.

Their training kicked in, experience and thought of escape keeping them focused. Each tossed stun grenades towards the main exit then slid regular grenades towards the wall. The trio curled up on the floor, closed their eyes and covered their ears. The flashbangs erupted, and the beast roared. Moments later the concussive force of the grenades added to the sensory overload.

Falkner was disorientated. Visions of retaking Kunduz against the Taliban overlapped the reality of the moment. Part of him wanted to hide in those memories. Back then it was horror, but at least it was a horror he understood, an enemy he could fight.

He forced himself kicking and screaming into the present. Yanking his men from the floor, he shoved them forward. "GO, GO, GO!"

With a roar, he opened fire. Hans and Douberman followed suit, emptying an entire mag at the wall as they charged. The combined fire was enough to punch several small holes through. Their torches revealed what appeared to be a kitchen on the other side.

"Douberman, provide cover!" Falkner ordered as he and Hans pulled at the bricks and mortar and hacked away with the butts of their rifles. Hans reloaded, then sprayed and prayed.

A few agonizing moments later, they had a soldier-sized hole cleared. Hans wasted no time scrambling through.

Falkner turned to Douberman and froze. The man was held inches off the floor, a monstrous tentacle wrapped around his waist. *Why hadn't he called...* Falkner's gut lurched. At the tip of the tentacle, a grotesque mouth filled with razor-sharp teeth was chewing through the Douberman's throat.

The soldier's mouth flopped open in a desperate attempt to scream. All he could manage was a blood-filled gurgle. Bile burned up Falkner's throat, and without a second thought, he raised his weapon and shot him. It was clean, right through his forehead. But he didn't die. He continued twisting in agony as the monster bit deeper into his neck. Despite the insanity of the situation, Falkner found himself assessing the threat as he would normally. It was just like Jones and Brody. Once the thing had you in its grip, some aspect, be it biological or supernatural, kept you alive while it feasted. *Pain, torment, and suffering must flavour the meat like sugar and spice and all things nice.* That thought made him giggle as he scampered through the hole. Every second he expected the grasp of a slithery tentacle to drag him back. This made him laugh harder. By the time he made it through, he was hysterical. He spotted Hans throwing up in the sink. Falkner collapsed in a heap, tears streaming down his face, laughing so violently his stomach cramped.

Hans grabbed him by the shoulders. "Get a grip, sir! We're almost out." Falkner could smell the vomit on his breath, and somehow this brought him back from the brink.

He wiped his eyes, nodding. "Let's fucking *do* this."

Both men switched to pockets torches, discarded their useless rifles in favour of increased speed and mobility – their fight or flight response indulging the latter with increased urgency.

They sprinted, reaching the main hallway without any sign of the creature. Escape was but a few scant seconds away. *If we could get out, we can report back to Command.* Command would know what to do. They could explain it all away. They had explanations and contingency plans for everything.

A dark swarm of shadows formed before the main entrance.

"What the *fuck*?" said Hans, as they halted.

The swarm merged into a humanoid shape but with the signature long arms and legs of the creature. Falkner tried to come up with options. His mind drew a blank. He had nothing left. The shape blurred as it surged forward at incredible speed. Falkner tensed.

Shit—

Hot liquid splattered his face. He glanced around. "Hans?"

Falkner stood alone in the gloom.

It took a few seconds for his brain to catch-up. Like viewing a video recorder, Falkner rewound the event then played it back in slow motion. The creature had moved at such high velocity, Falkner barely registered it. It had run straight through Hans, who exploded with the force of the impact. What was left of the last man under his command, now decorated the walls of the mansion

He let out a slow moan that soon built up into a war cry, a roar filled with pain, rage and terror. His eyes bulged, the veins on his neck threatening to burst. Falkner catapulted himself forward, convinced he was going to die. All sense of reason lost, the only shred of humanity left was a grim determination to go out like a solider; fighting until his last breath.

Somehow, he reached the entrance and almost wrenched the door off its hinges. A spotlight of blinding light trained on his position. He shaded his eyes and stepped outside but was brought up short. His heart pounded in his chest. Something held him fast from behind.

This is it. This is where eternal pain begins.

Claws sliced through the armour at his back with ease, tearing into his flesh. He screamed. The sensation was greater than pain. It was fire, ice, eternal darkness and damnation. It felt like the culmination of every wrong deed, every injustice he had ever inflicted onto others had returned tenfold. As it reached a crescendo where the suffering threatened to become all-consuming, it ceased. Something shoved him forward. Using this momentum, he managed to get a few feet clear of the building before collapsing.

Moments later he felt arms around him as officers picked him up and carried him away. Questions assaulted his ears, a babble of voices that made no sense. He mumbled something unintelligible. He wished they'd shut up. All he desired was a hospital bed, drugs and the comfort of blessed oblivion. A sudden flurry of activity sparked his interest and rekindled a faint flicker of fear. He opened his eyes and sat up. He'd been dumped unceremoniously just short of the main command tent they had setup on the front lawn. Soldiers were shouting and pointing at the house.

Huge spotlights, trained on the entrance where a huge, grey hand was visible just inside the doorway. A spiked tongue curled around one of its talons, licking away Falkner's blood.

The hand withdrew. Then a face appeared. *Hans.* but... it wasn't. It was impossible, and impossibly large – almost as large as the doorway. It spouted an evil grin, displaying rows of sharp teeth drooling with blood.

Several soldiers opened fire. No order was given but the commanders also drew their side arms. Within moments, it was a free-for-all.

"It's no good! It's no good!" Falkner shouted, but no one could hear him over the gunfire.

The bombardment decimated the main entrance and side windows. Enough hit their mark though. Slugs from various calibre weapons bounced off the face, others were absorbed into its skin. One soldier lobbed a grenade, it was a perfect shot. But after the explosion cleared, the creature's taunting face remained. Finally, the shooting ceased, although the trigger-click of empty weapons filled the silence.

With a smirk, the thing pulled itself back into the shadows.

Falkner's superior ran over, grabbing him by the shoulder. "Falkner! What the hell happened in there? What is that thing?"

He tried to explain. Words failed him. All that came out was fractured comments. "Evil... no... survivors. All dead, but still alive. Forever alive, forever dead!"

His commanding officer cursed and barked out orders as he strode towards the communications tent. It didn't take long for three camouflaged soldiers to make their way to the house where they placed small devices around the sides of the estate. Several more were thrown through the windows. Their task completed, they withdrew. Falkner knew they had planted laser markers. Despite the horror he had been through, Falkner smiled at the thought of the trouble this would cause the government. An authorised air strike on British soil! Oh, there would be hell to pay, even though the estate was miles from the nearest populated area. Unless, of course, they could cover it up. They were very good at cover-ups.

All units were pulled back to minimum safe distance. It would only take a few minutes before the planes arrived. Falkner felt disconnected. It all seemed a bit surreal like it had happened to someone else. The creature or whatever it was, possessed abilities beyond human understanding. It wasn't afraid of their guns and Falkner was sure it could have taken them all out at any time. Yet it chose to play with them as if it was showing off. Why had it stayed inside the mansion? Why hadn't it come out of the house to finish the job? He gazed at the sun sneaking up over the horizon. Tears tracked down his cheeks, as one of his favourite Bram Stoker quotes came to mind. *'No man knows till he has suffered from the night how sweet and dear to his heart and eye the morning can be.'*

Had the creature sensed the oncoming dawn? Was it afraid of the sun just like Bram Stoker's creation? He could hear the roar of planes approaching, and Falkner's smile widened. If the creature was averse to daylight, it was about to get more than it bargained for. Then a stray thought pierced his mind. Why *did* it stay in that house? A being of that magnitude shouldn't be contained by mere bricks and mortar.

As the aircraft unleashed its deadly cargo, Falkner recalled the pentagrams and other strange symbols on the walls. His smiled faltered. What if Burley and those other cultists had summoned the monster by accident while playing around with the supernatural. He remembered in his briefing, Burley had abandoned the estate back in the 1950s but refused to sell it. Had instructions left in his will to ensure the property remained intact but untouched. Folks at the time assumed it was his ego, a desperate attempt at enshrining his legacy. What if it was some-thing else entirely?

Each bomb hit their mark. All detonated with devastating effect. The mansion imploded, over a hundred years of brick and mortar reduced to rubble in an instant.

When the dust soon cleared. Troops returned cautiously to the remains of the house. There was no sign of the creature. Falkner breathed a sigh of relief. *Let it rot.*

The ground shook. He thought he'd imagined it but a nearby soldier was staring at the ground. "Earthquake?" he said to no-one in particular.

The ruins of the house suddenly exploded outwards, sending soldiers scrambling for cover. Several men caught in the upheaval disappeared under a pile of rubble. Falkner looked on with a growing sense of dread as an enormous hand emerged from the wreckage. A warped version of the creature shook itself free of the wreckage. Its anatomy shifted at incredible speed. A transmogrification of thousands of different beings every single second.

The creature swelled to twice its original size and showed no sign of stopping. Some soldiers fired weapons, others ran. Falkner heard sobbing. It took a few confused moments before he realised it was him. Wiping his tears, he saw his fingers covered in blood.

Beyond the perimeter, a journalist was broadcasting her latest report. She tried to maintain a professional demeanour, but her quivering voice betrayed her fear. Turning to point to the creature, she made the fatal mistake of looking directly at it. She screamed, then proceeded to gouge her eyes out live on national television. The camera stayed transfixed on the scene. It captured the chaos. Some soldiers mutilated themselves, others turned on their comrades. Most stayed transfixed on the being, their eyes bleeding, their hands clenched so tightly they snapped the bones in their fingers.

Falkner's sanity teetered on the edge of madness. He didn't want to die but he didn't want to be trapped in an undead state. The very thought of being eaten alive and becoming part of that thing was too much to bear. He didn't know how the creature kept its victims living but he hoped it required physical contact to do so. This seemed to be the case with his men anyway. He prayed he was right.

The ancient being stepped forward, causing a tremor that surely rattled the breadth of England. Falkner felt some sort of connection to the being. Images from other times and other places flooded his mind. He also felt subtle links to billions of other terrified beings. Together, the human race bore witness as the being strode across the world consuming the dinosaurs. A blink of time later, it devoured the Mayan civilisation, followed by the Cahokia, the Göbekli, and a myriad more civilisations Falkner had never even heard of. He felt the vast, all-consuming desire to feed. He witnessed the culling of entire species across different timelines, different dimensions and different planets.

Finally, it brought him back into the near past and the people it had consumed within the house, *his men*, to absorb all it needed about modern man. They had forgotten the old ways, the true ways, and posed no threat. Now that it was free from its makeshift prison, nothing would stop it.

Now it would feed again.

With a silent prayer that this would be his last thought, a thought that was his alone, Falkner drew his pistol, put it in his mouth and pulled the trigger.

How Zeke Got Religion at 20,000 Feet

John McNichol

Poppa used to say: when a man says he's scared, he usually ain't lying. He could lie about how many gals he done the hokey-pokey with, how many guys he beat down in a bar, how much money he's got, or anything else. But when a man says he's scared and he says it to other men, well, he ain't lying.

So I'll say it: I was scared. And so was Tex, Wrenchie, Sharkey, Booger, Preacher and the others. You'd be scared too, if you was in a giant metal tube flyin' in the dark waitin' to get shot at while the engines hummed, the wind whined through the chinks in the Belle, and all you can think about is how far from home you are. It don't matter how many times you get in a bird or make it back. Every time you go off to drop some on Fritz, you're hoping you don't roll snake eyes.

Heck, Preacher already knew what was waiting for us on the other side, and still kept them beads around his neck, his Saint Christopher medal pinned under his web belt and said a Hail Mary each time a Mister came out of the clouds. But there was one of us who waren't scared, and that was Zeke.

If he was scared, he hid it good. Zeke was from New York City, which maybe explained a lot. He was good at talking, and he and Preacher would go at it for hours 'til the rest of us was tired and went to bed and put the pillows over our heads so we wouldn't hafta hear Zeke say why there warn't no God and Preacher say there was.

Zeke said he didn't believe there was nothing but what we could see, that there wasn't no Heaven to hope for and no Hell to be afraid of. So why worry? If you're gonna die, it ain't gonna hurt or help.

Well, I saw that as plumb foolish. I didn't know if the Devil wore red pajamas like he did in the Sunday School pictures, or flew around on black bat wings like those in Preacher's book about Paradise being lost. I'd known enough bad folks that was gonna get theirs, here now or there later. It's something you just know inside. But for some reason, Zeke never got those inside-eyes.

We knew something was up when they gave us, and only us, a bunch of coffee and candy bars and a movie. When anyone out here is that nice, and you ain't no officer? Means they're gonna drop you in something, and it might as well be a big bucket of the ole' warm-and-brown.

Sure enough, a half hour after the movie was done, the call goes out over the speakers. Usually that's enough to make your insides turn to water, but we was hyped up from John Wayne and good coffee and everything else. So we jumped to it and was formed up on the square in under five minutes.

Then some Major came by with two guys in suits and glasses.

"Let's go, ladies," yelled the Major once he got to the doorway of one of the meeting tents.

Another officer waited in the room. "Gentlemen," he said. His voice sounded rich like velvet but cold like ice. I got prickles on my neck just knowing he was talking to me. He also talked like a Brit, and that was different. We got to sit, and that was different, too.

"I won't mince words," the Brit said. "You don't have the expertise we need to make sure this mission is a success, but right now you're all we've got. Tonight, you'll be going into Germany. Normally, Americans don't do night missions, and almost never as a single bomber. But this is different."

He looked at each of us in turn. "You're going to bomb a church," he said, and his voice dropped almost to a whisper when he said it. Made my skin go all prickly again, and my mouth went dry. "Jerry's got something inside it important enough that Command wants us to drop a bucket load of Black Betty and her fat ugly sisters on it, tonight. You'll have fighter support part of the way, but then you're on your own. Any man who has a problem with either of these two points can withdraw now."

None of us backed out.

They'd been getting the Belle ready the whole time we'd been watching the movie. We double-timed it back to the bunks, dropped our fatigues, got our flight-suits on and double-timed it again out to the tarmac.

"You ready?" Preacher asked me as we got in line. I looked at the nose of our bird, how beautiful the blonde gal looked on it, smiling at me in a WAC uniform shirt that was just a little too tight and shorts a bit too short as she leaned against the cracked bell waving at me. The 'Liberty Belle'. She was a good seventy-four feet o' pure, B-17 Bomber death with wings, and I got scared to death each time I walked in her, and happy as a horse in a field o' green grass every time I stepped out after we was done.

"Yeah," I said to Preacher. "I'm ready. You?"

"Always," he lied. Same as me. "I can't wait to drop a bomb anywhere in Fritz's backyard. Even if it is on a church."

"You got any idea why they got us doing this one?"

"Tap," he says to me, 'cause Tap was my nickname. "You got me on that one. My best guess is that Fritz hopes we won't drop one there 'cause it is a church. They know we won't run night missions. Maybe they've got something there really, really good. Something worth turning a church into a shield over. Last Limey I talked to saw something pretty weird behind enemy lines. Said Fritz took a cathedral and done some real bad things inside it. Painted stars on the walls and floor, blood, other things. Something weird, you know?"

No, I didn't know. But I nodded just the same.

The inside of the Belle was lit up, and Cap and Eggs headed to the pilot an' copilot seats and started their talk about numbers, oil pressure, oxygen levels an' all that. Tex went in the belly gun and did all his checks, telling Wrenchie everything was A-Ok while he rotated the ball and made sure he had his ammo. Sharkey went up top, Booger in the nose, Preacher in the tail and Zeke an' me went to the waist, all of us checking out .50 cals an' making best sure they didn't jam. Zeke an' me, we made sure the ammo belts were straight and laid out zig-zag over the top of each other in the hopper and then loaded up for bear. Almost nothin' feels quite so good as clamping down the lid on the feeder of a .50 cal Browning, you know? Makes you feel ten feet tall and ready to kick the Fuhrer in the balls. Now what warn't so good was putting on the jackets, the gloves and the masks. See, when you're a waist-gunner, you got more room to move but you've gotta wear jackets and gloves so thick you felt like you was wearing a live grizzly, and then you've gotta put on your mask, or you faint from how thin the air was up there. Try pushing the buttons on a .50 grip with thumbs that feel like bricks wrapped in cotton batten and you get the idea.

"Wrenchie? They still didn't fix the right grip. I gotta push it twice as hard as the left. Can you take a look?"

"Love to, Tap, but I gotta check a dozen other things first. And I don't think I can take it apart until I get back."

Crap. It's not life-or-death, but it is a pain in the ass.

A half hour later, the engines started. The Belle lurched forward, and my stomach made a little flip-flop like it always does, then we hit sky. Man alive, it was cold once you got all the way up. Colder than a snowman with an icicle up his ass, even with our heater vests plugged into the Belle.

But the cold ain't your worst enemy; Fritz is. And even though we had a few jugs flyin' alongside, you never get more'n half way before the fighters gotta turn back.

I took a bit while we still had the fighters at our back to look at the stars. We'd taken off in the dark, and there warn't much to see this time. Usually it was light out when we flew, and while we was flyin' Preacher'd be sayin' his prayers, an' Wrenchie'd be fillin' out forms for the Engineering school he wanted to go to, or Zeke'd be looking at pinups of some movie-star gal he thought he'd get to step out with if'n he got enough Confirmed Kills on his record.

But since it was dark, most of us couldn't do the things we did to pass the time. I heard Preacher prayin' a bit, and Tex took out his harmonica and started playin' it soft and slow in the belly. Somehow it made me feel a little sad and better at the same time- Tex could do that when he played, you know?

Then after a bit I heard the Mustangs' engines turn as they did their 180 to leave us and head back home. The moonlight was bright – real bright. I could see the tail of the last Mustang disappear behind the clouds. And right after that, Booger yelled from his place in the nose gunner's seat:

"Misters! We got Misters! Two and ten o'clock!"

"Shit!"

"Shitfire!"

You yelled. You hadda yell or your balls shriveled up an' died.

"Two o'clock, Tap!"

"I see 'im! Shit!" He was a speck on the moonlight, then a little flash.

Then the bullets started whizzing, whining and slamming on the Belle. Heavy thunks where they hit metal, sparks where they hit wire.

"Fucker! On 'im!"

I opened up, trying to put that flashing speck in my crosshairs. Then it stopped flashing.

"'Ja get 'im, Tap?"

"Dunno! They still shoot—"

More flashes, moving back. More hits! Fuck! I felt hot beestings on the back of my head.

"Dammit, Zeke! Hit those fuckers! I'm taking shrapnel."

"You hit 'em! Like getting flies with a fucking sledgehammer!"

"Sharkey! He's goin' up!"

"Shut the fuck up, Booger, I see 'im!"

A mister's engine roared over us. Fuck!

"What the hell? Cap, you got the radar – he trying to ram us?"

"Just kill 'em, Sharkey! Ask me later!"

Sharkey'd already done that, his .30 cals punching a Mister into a bunch of screaming, flaming metal pieces.

"Leave some for me next time, Shark!"

"Get your own Gawldarn CKs, Tex. Mebbe grow a foot or two an' you'll get outta th' belly!"

"Where's the rest?"

"Can't see the—"

More flashes. The Belle rattled and cried. My hands were sore, my left thumb ached were I hadda push the trigger harder and my arms had started to shake.

No, fuck no! Can't get the shakes now! Not 'til we're done!

"Tap! You see 'im?"

"No!"

"Shit! Where'd he—"

The flashes came, so close we heard the '.30 mil pills drill into the wing.

"There you are!"

"Fuckfuckfuckfuck—"

I held the grip tight as I could though my hands screamed at me near as loud as Sharkey was screamin' in the dorsal.

"Tap! You clipped him! There's pieces of his ass on fire!"

Tex had the best eyes. I couldn't hardly see – my goggles were starting to fog up.

All I needed was a flash and—

"Engine fire!"

When I heard Zeke yell that one, I tried to keep my eyes on the Misters. But you still hear the chatter and the yelling from the Captain to the rear to the Engineer and everyone else in the whole blamed plane.

"Number?"

"Two, Cap!"

"Wrenchie!"

"On it, Cap! Pulling the plugs!"

"Engine Fire, number one!" yelled Zeke.

"Wrenchie!"

"Already out, Cap! One's out! Two's out! Just oil leaking. We're oka—"

Bullets slammed in the hull. Wrenchie stopped talking.

You know what that means nine times out of ten, but you keep pouring it on, waiting to hear from the other gunners.

"Tap!" Tex yelled from the belly. "Coming your way from below!"

"Shit," I yelled. "On it!"

The Mister came up from under at six o'clock. It was the last mistake he was ever gonna make. When Tex yelled from the ball below I started pumping lead straight down before I saw anything. When Fritz flew out from underneath, I swear I heard his canopy crack even before my bullets started tearing the rest of his plane a new set of ragged metal armpits and assholes. I'd wanted to tear into a Kraut ever since we came back from the trip where Whitey bought it.

"Got 'im, Whitey," I mumbled, watching the sky while I heard little pieces of the Mister shred and spin off into the night. I even thought I could hear Fritz screaming.

"That's for Whitey, you fucker!" I yelled, seeing poor Whitey's face gettin' whiter, then yellow after he died slow in the ward.

We all waited a minute, and when we couldn't hear any more fighters nor feel any more hits, the guys cheered. I'd unzipped Fritz and his Mister, and the cheer meant we could relax. And if they were relaxed, it meant there weren't no more Misters either.

We breathed easy. I let the shakes come. While I'd been busy tapping away and blasting Fritz into whatever special hell God made for Nazis, the other guys'd been having their fun, too. Tex in the ball, Zeke at my back, Booger in the nose, Sharkey up top and Preacher over in the tailgun had ripped the other Misters apart. But that's the way of it. You look so much at the Misters you're trying to kill, you don't hear nothing else. Zeke took a few seconds to grab a blanket out've the emergency kit and cover up Wrenchie, as much to soak up the blood so we wouldn't slip in it as out of respect for the dead.

It was maybe five minutes after the Misters got sent packing before we started hearing the ack-ack. Someone really didn't want this church to get it. None of it was touching us, though. Not right away. It sounded in the air like thunder, far off and away from us. The brass had finally made a right call by sending us in at night.

I started breathing faster. My chest got all tight inside. Through the radio I could hear Preacher whispering his prayers on his beads and Sharkey started to babble again.

Then flak got closer, louder.

The Belle shook, then another thunderclap, this one sounding like it was right outside the door. The Belle rattled and screamed as more flak blew up in the air and peeled the skin off the bird.

Then the flak hit everywhere. A hundred booms, bangs, and big black bombs, all up and over. Flak ain't some Jerry pointing his .30-cal at you and pulling the trigger. In daylight you can see a hundred, maybe a thousand pockets of black air booming around you, and any one of 'em kills you if it's close enough.

I looked back; Zeke was calm, like he near always was. The others?

"Fuck the flak, fuck the flak, fuck the flak, fuck the—"

"Se do bhetha, a Mhuire—"

"Goddamn that's close! Crazy fucks!"

An explosion rent the air, and the Belle lurched like it had been punched.

"Cap, I heard something tear off the . . ."

"FUCKFLACK!"

"Stay on target!"

"Ata lan de ghrasta…"

"Can't we shoot 'em? Can't we . . ."

"Steady, boys! Eggs?"

"Close, Cap. Less than twenty!"

The next burst shook the whole damn bird.

"FUCK!"

"Closing in, boys," said Cap. "Sharkey, shut up. Eggs, get down there and start talkin' to Norden."

Eggs had already jumped from his co-pilot seat to move down beside Booger in the nose. Eggs was a cool, quiet guy. Had no trouble aiming then dropping as we got close. Me, I liked gunning way, way better than egg-dropping.

He sat and looked in the Norden bombsight, spinning the dials like a science guy playing with a microscope.

"C'mon, honey," he said, his eyes hidden by the viewer. "C'mon, where're ya hiding? Where you at? Inputting altitude . . . heading . . . estimated windspeed . . ."

I was already at the spot where Wrenchie would've usually been, getting ready to pull the levers and drop the payload.

"Aaaaaaaaand... NOW!" Eggs shouted, and you could hear just a little of the New York in his voice he'd tried so hard to get rid of ever since he'd gotten here. I pulled, the bombs slid down with that scream of metal-on-metal you never get used to.

"Turning around," said Cap over the horn as soon as the bombs dropped out of sight. Eggs was already heading back to the cockpit. We saw the flashes, but we almost didn't hear the bombs go off over the sound of the engines and the yelling of Cap and Eggs.

You didn't usually hear the bombs much, 'specially when the wind was up and the engines were all in your ears. Maybe a muffled piece or two.

But we all knew when our bombs hit. Not just from the noise, but from the color the sky and the ground turned. It made this sick-lookin' green cloud that got bigger an' bigger until it looked like it hit the sky. Then the sky turned red, the kind've red blood looks like when it hits dirt and dries up a ways. My guts did a flip-flop, and I could tell by Zeke moanin' into his radio that he felt it too. The whole damned world seemed to rise, fall, stretch and come back t'gether again, like a belch you just couldn't quite make come up and out.

Then it was all done. We were back to seeing the black and hearing the engine and the whistling of the wind outside through all the holes in the Belle.

"Cap?" Booger whispered. "Cap? Whut... wuzzat?"

"Shut up and keep your eyes open, Booger. You see anything, anything moves, you kill it."

"Even civvies?"

"I don't give a fart in a hurricane if it's your baby sister on her baptism day! It moves, you kill it! Copy?"

"Copy that, Cap."

"Okay, listen up, ladies. I want battle damage and casualty reports, on the double."

"Bombardier, OK."

"Nose gunner, OK."

'Left gunner, OK."

"Right gunner, OK."

"Tail gunner, OK."

"Belly gunner, OK."

We waited a few seconds. "Radio op-engineer? Guys, how's Wrenchie?"

I turned. In the dim moonlight I could see a dark stain where the blanket covered the hole in his chest the size of a fist. The flak jacket was great against small arms and shrapnel, but not when a shell from a Mister punches through your plane.

"Wrenchie didn't make it, Cap," I said.

Everyone was quiet. And we kept for home. My gut calmed, but we were all feelin' pretty antsy. Even with no more Misters in the air, no more typewriter-sounds of ack-ack from below, we still all felt like there was an itch we couldn't scratch.

Preacher came outta the tailgun and walked along the plank down the center of the fuselage, holding onto the cord for balance. He knelt best as he could, pulled out a little blue book and started mumbling prayers. He wasn't supposed to leave his post, us being over enemy territory an' all. But Zeke an' me let it go, and Cap pretended not to notice. It made it better somehow, him doing that, and he went back pretty quick.

For maybe a half hour it was quiet, 'cept for the rattling of the Belle, the roar of the engines, and the shriek of wind through her belly.

That's when things got real bad.

"Bandits, up top!" Sharkey yelled from the dorsal gunner nest.

"FUCK!"

"Sonovabitch…"

"Se do bhetha…"

"Shut the fuck up. We got more Misters?" Cap said.

Then I saw 'em.

"Shadows," I yelled. "Shadows! On the goddam moon. See 'em?"

Sharkey piped in, "They's too small for Misters, but too big for pigeons. I... I dunno what in Hell they are, but they's in the air, an' they's gainin' on us!"

"Cap? What's out there?" I hoped he couldn't hear how scared I was.

"Shut up, Tap. Preacher? Wait 'til they're in range, then fill 'em fulla holes," Cap said.

So we waited. I could hear Sharkey breathin' heavy. Tex was countin' backwards. My heel kept tappin' and tappin' like it did when I got the shakes. Preacher in the tail started whispering in his radio, and I just knowed he was saying some more of those prayers he's always saying with the beads. He said it helped him to not be afraid.

But this time, it didn't help him pull the trigger fast enough.

The sound of flapping wings beat faster, closer, and the bandits dove right, just before Preacher opened up on 'em with his .50 cal.

"Tap!" Preacher screamed as I saw them flush over to my side of the aircraft. A hundred rounds of hot, shiny lead leapt from my gun, and two of 'em come apart

"That's two, Tap!" I heard Zeke yell from behind, and then I heard his own guns start chatterin' with our new friends. He cheered – that meant he saw another one go down, maybe two.

Then Preacher started screaming.

"A dhia sabhail sinn!"

Everybody got real quiet. Preacher only started yelling Irish when he was real scared 'bout something. Everybody shut up. Even with the engines and the wind, it felt like things just changed and we were playing a whole different game. The walls seemed closer and I wanted to take off my mask, no matter how little oxygen there was up here.

"Preacher?" I yelled. "You all right?"

He yelled something down the tube I couldn't get.

"Par boiled?" I said. "Iissat more Irish?"

"No! That's what they are," he said.

I dunno. Hard boiled? Was it a Catholic thing? It made more sense later, but right then, in that moment, no.

Zeke's browning suddenly started belching bullets and he cheered. "Got two," he yelled. "Got two! I saw 'em fall apart! Just like shooting clay pigeons back home!"

"Where?" Sharkey yelled. "I got nothin' up here. They's—"

We all heard the smash and shriek of metal as Sharkey's canopy got ripped open, and the air started blowing all through the Belle. Then we heard Sharkey screaming, screaming like something was tearing him up.

Then he stopped screaming, and all we could hear was the wind.

Cap climbed down the steps, then ran four more big, leaping steps to the dorsal gunner's stepladder. His face was white, and his eyes were red as a Christmas fire.

"What the fuck?" he shouted. He got to the ladder, stepped on the first rung, and wiped something out of his eye.

He blinked, and wiped again. I turned and got a closer look. There was a long, red string, like a long piece of spit, dangling down and splatting in Cap's face.

And sitting on the floor where Sharkey's boots shoulda been was a little white blob with a dark spot on it.

Sharkey was gone, and he'd left his eyeball behind.

Cap didn't panic. He pulled his piece and pointed it straight up as he climbed the ladder.

He poked his head up there a minute, maybe more. His legs stood still and straight then he stepped back down slow, bloody prints from his shoes leaving rust-colored streaks on the ladder rungs.

"Sharkey's gone," he said, his voice raised just enough so we could hear him over the wind blowing through the destroyed canopy.

He shut the door above him. A small line of red moved around the rim of the hatch.

Cap's eyes just got real wide, like he'd just figured out something that scared the willies outta him. "We gotta get back," he said, and ran for the cockpit.

"Eggs!" he yelled, jumping up the ladder. "Hit it full throttle! Get us outta here, now!"

"Cap, all due respect—"

"Eggs!"

"Cap, at full throttle, we'll let every ack-ack, fighter—"

"EGGS!"

"and EVERY GODDAMN FARMER in the FATHERLAND, CAP, is gonna HEAR US AND START SHOOTIN'! Remember the Cat's Eye? The Lucky Seven? They went full throttle and they got—"

Cap pulled his pistol and pointed it at Eggs. "Direct order, Eggs," he said all quiet.

Eggs paused just one second, looking at Cap's eyes that'd gone all narrow. We could all see him from the tube – they been so loud we'd heard the whole thing, and we could read his last words on his lips.

"Goddam death sentence!" Eggs said as he pulled the throttle.

"We already got one a' those, Eggs, if we don't shake these things! Now move it!"

Now the engines started roaring even louder, and the Belle started rumbling hard enough I thought it was gonna shake itself to. . .

Oh shit... I saw it through the cockpit window, right in front of Cap.

Two bright red eyes looking in at him.

And a smile. Big and white like a crescent moon.

"CAP! In front!"

Cap looked forward and roared, pointed his pistol and started panic firing out the window. Stars and spiderweb cracks bloomed like sick white flowers on the window in front of Cap and Eggs. Eggs screamed, and the face dropped outta sight.

"Cap! What the fu—"

Now Booger started screaming below them in the nose gun. Then we heard another crash and more wind, and Booger stopped screaming.

"Gunners!" Cap yelled. "Gunners! Into the fuselage!"

Preacher'd just gotten through the hatch from the tail, and Tex was coming up through the ball-turret when we heard more glass breaking near the back of the bird. Preacher's face was ghost white, his eyes wide as dinner plates. He was scrambling on his hands and knees, one hand held his beads in a dead-man's grip, the other hand was grabbing and clawing the walls, the steady cord, the floor, anything to pull himself forward and away from what was behind him while he gibbered and blubbered, hollering louder than even the engines and the wind. "It's coming!" he yelled. "It's coming! IT'S COMING!"

And then I saw it.

Whatever it was scrambled after Preacher into the fuselage. And it wasn't like nothing you ever saw before. I thought at first it was like a giant bug, what with those big black eyes with red glowing behind 'em. But then there was the teeth, they unfolded out of its mouth like a mix of knives, spikes and long, sharp needles. And even though its mouth was open, we couldn't hear no sound. It looked like it'd roar at us if it could, but it couldn't.

And the horns, they warn't like the little curve jobs they got on Halloween costumes. Nossir, these were big jobs, the kind you'd see on a Memphis bull about to gore you through the gut for just lookin' at him wrong.

Preacher scrambled past me, still yellin'. I stuck myself in a little door space where Wrenchie kept his stuff, and watched the thing crawl past me, squirmin' and writhin' like a sidewinder. I warn't being a coward but thinking I could attack from the rear when I had the chance.

I wish now I'd been thinkin' straighter, but I wasn't. None of us were. I grabbed the biggest wrench I could find, but when I poked my head out, Preacher had slipped and fallen. He turned over quick but the thing was on him, ripping at his chest and making blood splash on the walls, the floor, the ceiling. Preacher was screaming in a high, shrill shriek while his chest and guts all got stripped away like cheap wallpaper off a barn door.

No.

Not Preacher.

Not after Shark, Booger and Wrenchie.

I started throwing every tool I could at the thing while Preacher's blood sprayed around me. Everything bounced off the thing. Nothing worked. The walls of the Belle were getting tighter and tighter. I couldn't breathe. Then I could and I wished I couldn't, because I could smell Preacher's blood and shit as his guts got opened up.

It all happened in maybe five seconds, but then I saw Preacher look at the beads in his right hand just long enough to stop screaming. He looked back at the thing and started slapping it in the head with his right hand, doing the worst, weakest punches you ever saw. But… but the thing winced, and backed off just a little, then shook its snout like a dog that'd been slapped upside the head.

Preacher didn't scream now. He roared. Roared with what was left of his throat and kept hitting the thing. I saw little pieces fly off it like sand where he hit, and that took all of another two seconds.

The thing looked down at Preacher, and its eyes got so red, so help me God, it lit up the inside of the Belle like a lantern. Its teeth unfolded and was about to chomp down on Preacher's face.

Then Cap screamed. It warn't a scared scream, but a mad one. I'd seen Cap mad before, and I knew what made him madder'n anything was someone acting wrong on his plane. He pointed his gun and emptied the clip into the thing's face. Behind him, Eggs had grabbed the fire extinguisher and started blasting at its eyes.

Nothing happened.

Not on the monster, anyways. The Belle was goin' crazy; the engines were making me deaf, and I thought I could see the treeline through all the holes in her side. The wind wasn't frost-bite-cold this close to the ground, but it was still cold enough to feel against my face and through my gloves and jacket. The Belle started to rock back an' forth, making it tough to stand straight. Eggs must've hit the autopilot, but it sure didn't feel that way.

The thing's face jerked a little with each hit, and then it got all covered in the white stuff. But before it got all hidden I saw little bits of its face get chipped away like a claw hammer hitting granite.

It didn't stop the thing a bit. It couldn't move forward, on account of Preacher's body and Eggs and Cap blockin' its way. Now that it was out of the tail gunner pit, we could see why it'd been able to keep up with us. Its wings grew out of its back like an angel's, but they were huge and grey with black ribbing. Like a giant bat.

It had claws on haunches for legs, but it couldn't stand inside the plane. It crawled, trying hard to move faster while looking for someone else to rip up.

And then I remembered what it made me think of. Last time I'd been in a big city –New Orleans – there was a huge church down there. The kind of church Preacher said he'd gone to, all made up of stone, colored windows, and giant wooden doors.

And it had these funny looking monsters carved on top. They showed what you'd be like outside of Heaven, if you didn't get your sorry hide into church and stayed good.

Well, this thing was one of those things. We'd bombed a church, one that Fritz'd been messing with big time. Whatever evil Fritz'd been doing down there made this thing get madder 'n a hornet in a kicked-up hive.

Though its head was all covered up, I could still see its body. Saw the thing flinch when Preacher swung and hit it again, pulling back just a little when Preacher hit it for the last time. He'd run outta gas, or maybe had just enough for one last shot. I heard him say somethin' in the Irish – don't rightly know what – but I bet now it was something to Jesus, or Jesus' momma.

Eggs was still blindin' the thing best he could, and the blast shot something right over the thing's head and straight at me.

The monster'd taken one last good slash at Preacher and taken his hand with the beads clean off, and Eggs had blasted it right at me while Cap loaded another clip into his piece.

Preacher's hand turned end-over-end. It was like slow motion – a long necklace of beads with a cross at the end.

I grabbed 'em, had to pry Preacher's fingers to get at 'em, then let the hand fall. The beads was hard brass threaded on knotted paratrooper cord and tough enough to choke a pig. I figured I was gonna die, but I wanted to die like Preacher, fightin' this sick and ugly bastard hard as I could until the Belle hit the ground. And I had the one thing I'd seen work on it in a fight.

Preacher's getting killed pulled something loose in all of us. Cap was the only one with a pistol, and he kept shootin'. The other guys took whatever else they could. Tex was under it in the ball, tryin' to stab it upwards with his kneecapper. Zeke had a torn-off piece of metal and was wavin' it, tryin' to get the thing to look at him while Cap shot and Eggs blasted. Everyone was screaming, louder than the wind and the Belle doing it's roaring and rattling. The thing slashed at Zeke and slammed his shield, smacking him so hard against the wall he went down and I couldn't see him in all the ruckus. We couldn't see much 'cept when Cap's gun fired and flashed. There wasn't much room and I don't think anyone thought we'd survive much longer inside a plane with that ripping up the bird's insides the way it was doing.

So I jumped on its back. Well, climbed on, maybe. I don't right remember now exactly. And I don't recall just how I got Preacher's beads around its neck neither. All I knew was that my hands were crossed, the cord with its beads was around its neck and all I had to do was pull hard.

So, I pulled. And I kept on pullin'. And the thing realized I was there when Eggs' fire extinguisher ran outta white stuff, and it started to get ornery. It bucked like a bronco, but I kept on pulling. And my head hit the ceiling more n' once, but I kept on pulling. And laws, did my noggin hurt like the dickins and make everything go all blurry. But I kept on pulling.

Then I saw blood.

It started comin' out where the beads were wrapped around the thing's neck, oozing from under the monster's stone skin and running down the string and the beads. My hands started to feel slippery and hot, like I'd dunked 'em into a vat of cookin' oil.

But I kept on pulling, and slowly the beads started sinking into the thing's neck. It felt like rock to sit on or hit, but where the beads were, it was soft as cheese 'gainst a wire, cutting through slow but never stopping, so long as I was pulling.

It still kept rearing up. But soon the monster jumped less. And it screamed quieter each time too.

Then all a sudden like, I wasn't riding it no more. It just came apart and I was sitting in a pile of black sand. My hands were all bloody, and it was drying up and flaking off. Someone was still screaming. Cap come up and shook and smacked me a few 'til I figured it were me screaming. Then he got in my face up close and told me to stop, so I did.

He looked me over, then got back into the pilot seat where Eggs'd been flyin' the Belle. Don't even remember Eggs leaving the fight with the monster, but he took back his seat, and I shuffled back to my position near the door. Tex stayed in the ball and didn't move nor speak. I heard he was like that for a long time after we got back, but that's another story for another day.

Zeke took another blanket and covered Preacher's front where his guts were trying to hang out. I pretended not to notice, but Zeke looked at Preacher's body a long time. Then he reached for one of Preacher's chest pockets, and found that little blue book he always read from when one of us bought it. He opened up to a page and started reading. I couldn't quite hear him over the noise of the wind whining through the holes in the Belle, but I'd heard the quiet sounds over the radio enough to know he was saying the same words Preacher'd said so many a time: "Eternal rest unto him, O Lord, and may your perpetual light upon him, may he rest in peace . . ."

We got the Belle back, 'most in one piece. We'd lost Sharkey, Wrenchie, Booger and Preacher, and we was sad, sure. But not as much as you'd think. Crews came back worse, or didn't come back at all, so I can be glad of that. Whitey was the last one I got real sad about. After that, you learn.

The sun had just started comin' up when we touched down, cold wind blowing in our faces. The landing strip looked the same, but it was different. Sometimes when we'd get back, the ground crew'd cheer us. Now, no one cheered for us 'cause no one was there. We landed and we stopped, and guys we didn't know ran out and hooked the plane safe and put the stoppers under the wheels.

When we got off the Belle, no one we knew was there. Even the new guys had run back to the buildings, didn't say nothin' to us. The base was empty. Only the two men we'd seen over at the briefing room were there, watching us with their glasses, their arms crossed about a hundred feet away on the tarmac.

A couple of soldiers drove up in a truck and told us to get in the back. They helped Tex out, and I was right impressed they didn't have to hold their noses with him, covered in shit as he was. where he messed himself

We drove away, and I was still tired, more tired'n I ever was. I couldn't even think of a time that was close. Then I heard something from Zeke next to me. Cap was still wide up and Eggs was lying on the floor of the truck. Tex was staring with eyes that looked hollow and dark, his mouth half open and spit going down one side.

"It's real," Zeke said, his eyes wide and bloodshot.

"What's real?"

"All of it. All of it. All I ever said to Preacher, it's only because it was all I saw. And now that I've seen something else, I know there's something else."

Well, I coulda asked for more. Coulda asked him what he meant. But I knew something was going on inside Zeke. And I couldn't help it go faster or get bigger, but I knew I'd jinx it pretty bad if'n I talked any more.

So while the sun came up behind us, I just kept my mouth shut and let Zeke keep getting religion.

DANNY

Dirk Patton

Danny Britton awoke in a panic, sweat immediately popping out on his forehead as he lurched to a sitting position and looked around the hotel room. A dim slice of light from the bathroom revealed hastily scattered clothes, a half empty bottle of tequila with two glasses on a table and several discarded condoms on the floor. Taking a deep, calming breath, he raised his hands and rubbed his face in relief. Whatever he'd heard hadn't been his wife bursting through the door to catch him red handed with another woman.

A brief, gurgling snore from the other side of the bed drew his attention and he looked down at a pile of blonde hair spilling across a pillow. Janice. Or at least that's the name she'd used on the Internet hookup site where he'd first contacted her. He hadn't cared if her name was Adolf. She was stunning and the most enthusiastic and unrestrained lover he'd ever had. It had been a good night.

But it was morning now, or soon would be he noted after checking the bedside clock. Time to shower her smell off, dress and head home. If he hurried, he could make it before his wife, Theresa, got out of bed and woke the kids for school. She wouldn't be happy that he hadn't made it home last night, but was accustomed to him spending at least one late night a week in the office.

Moving carefully so he didn't disturb Janice, Danny stepped out of the bed and padded silently to the bathroom, closing the door softly before cranking the shower on to hot. Waiting for the water to begin steaming, he cursed when the light went out, plunging the room into impenetrable darkness. Fumbling a hand across the wall, he found the switch and flipped it several times to no avail. Water still running, he opened the door and peered out into the room. Tried to spot the glowing digits on the clock next to the bed, but they weren't there.

"Fuck," Danny mumbled under his breath when he confirmed the power was out.

For a long moment, he stood naked in the open bathroom door, the shower hissing behind him, and hoping the electricity would come back on so he could clean up. Last night's sex had been vigorous and had lasted a long time. He could smell the scent of the woman as well as the musk of their mingled sweat coming off his bare chest. There was no way Theresa wouldn't notice, nor would she be understanding of any excuse. He needed to bathe.

Resigned to showering in the dark, he was turning away from the room when Janice wheezed a deep gurgle that ended in a guttural sound that was eerily like the snarl of a wild animal. The blood in Danny's veins ran cold as he looked at the bed in fear. He wasn't concerned for the woman, he was terrified at the thought of something happening to her in a hotel room rented in his name.

It's just from last night, he told himself.

The sex hadn't only been vigorous, it had been rough. The woman liked to be slapped and pinched. And choked. Danny had been only too happy to accommodate her, losing himself in the moment of squeezing her neck until the blood flow to her brain was restricted as she writhed beneath him.

That's got to be it! Bitch has a sore throat.

Before he could turn away, Janice growled again. This time there was no dismissing the possibility that something was wrong. Danny stood rooted to the spot, staring at the covers as the woman began moving, occasionally emitting more of the sounds. Had he damaged her throat? Was she choking? Unable to breathe? Concern over being caught and the resulting consequences spurred him to action and he rushed forward.

"Hey, Jani…"

Danny froze in place, hand extended to pull back the sheet when she sat bolt upright and looked around at the sound of his voice. Then she screamed. But it wasn't the sound of a frightened or injured woman. It was a voice of unbridled rage as she leapt off the bed, reaching for him.

Stumbling away in surprise and fear, Danny's feet tangled in her dress and he fell backward onto a small, round table placed between two chairs. Never designed to hold the weight of a full-grown man, it collapsed, dumping him and its contents onto the floor.

Stunned and flailing about, the breath in his lungs whooshed out of his body when Janice slammed down on top of him. Instantly, she was ripping at his chest and neck with her nails, another scream loud in his ears as she tried to bite into his face. With one hand, he fought to fend off her attack as he felt his flesh tear open under the assault.

Fear-induced adrenaline surged through him and he hit her as she screamed inches from his face, then used all his strength to push her away. She tumbled across the floor, limbs flailing, then came to a stop against the side of the bed. Sitting up, Danny watched in horror as she immediately sprang into a crouch and let out with the loudest scream yet.

Scrambling away to open some room between them, his hand landed on the smooth glass surface of the liquor bottle as Janice leapt with a snarl that made his balls shrivel and the hair on his arms stand on end. Reacting to the attack, he grasped the bottle by the neck and swung it up to protect himself.

Glass exploded when it impacted the side of Janice's head, but the blow didn't stop the momentum of her leap. Slamming into Danny's chest, their arms intertwined as he struggled desperately against her. Knocked back half a dozen feet, it took several long seconds for him to realize he was the only one participating in the battle. She was completely limp. For a heartbeat, Danny held her upper arms in a tight grip, then panic set in.

Shoving her aside, he scrambled away and climbed to his

feet. His breath was coming in short pants of fear as he stood over Janice's limp form.

"Oh, God... no," he breathed, shaking uncontrollably and unable to force himself to bend down and check her injuries.

Rank sweat ran down his nude body, mixing with the blood from his injuries and stinging the open wounds. He ignored the discomfort, standing there for what felt like hours as his mind whirled, playing out the consequences of the situation.

He was in a hotel room with a woman who wasn't his wife. His DNA was both in and on her body as well as the bed. His skin and blood were under her nails. What if he'd killed her? Who would believe he'd only been defending himself? That she'd gone crazy after a night of drunken sex and tried to bite his face? He wasn't even sure he believed it himself. Slowly, he knelt next to her, ready to leap away at the slightest hint of movement.

Janice was face down and there was a small amount of light leaking around the heavy curtains that covered the window. Enough for him to see the dark blood that stained her thick, blonde hair. Tentatively, he reached out and touched her shoulder, jerking his hand away as if he'd received an electric shock. When she didn't respond, he carefully placed two fingers on the side of her neck. Held them there for a moment, then probed around toward the front. Seeking her carotid artery.

"Fuck me," he said when he couldn't find it.

He thought about turning her over. Checking to see if she was breathing. But that idea was dismissed as soon as he had it. He was already in enough trouble without adding in disturbing the scene. Any half decent prosecutor would use that to justify seeking a more serious charge.

Standing, Danny looked around the room with an investigator's eye. He'd once been one of the prosecutors he was now worried about, but that had been a long time ago. Now, he was a junior partner in a White-shoe law firm who never handled anything other than contracts. He hadn't even set foot in a courtroom in more than a decade. But his firm employed an entire floor of top-tier defense attorneys that were available to their corporate clients. Lawyers that could and did get CEOs and board members off the hook for everything from DUI to sexual assault, and even a charge of involuntary manslaughter.

Ignoring the woman, Danny leapt across the room to where his suit had been tossed carelessly. Ripping pockets, he fumbled out his phone and opened the contact list. He knew several of the attorneys that specialized in criminal defense. Played golf with them on Saturdays when he couldn't stand to be around Janice and the kids. They'd help with the call to the police and make sure the right narrative was spun from the outset of the investigation.

Finding the name he was searching for, he pressed the dial button but the call failed immediately. Frustration surging, he tried twice more before noticing the no service indicator at the top of the screen. Resisting the urge to fling the handset against the wall, he reached for the hotel phone, freezing in place when he heard what sounded like muted gun fire. Looking at the window, he listened closely, but there weren't any more shots. If that's what it had been.

After several seconds of staring at the curtains, waiting, he frowned. Something was odd about the quality of the light leaking into the room around their edges. Walking to the window, he parted the drapes with his finger and peered out, expecting to see a stormy sky was the culprit. His mouth fell open in shock when he saw the horizon consumed in towering flames that were sending dense clouds of black smoke billowing high into the air, filtering the morning sun and turning its light a smoky, bloody red. Atlanta was burning.

Danny stood immobile, curtains thrown wide as he stared at the inferno consuming Atlanta. After several long minutes, he stiffened and looked over his shoulder at the unmoving woman. The sun was fully up and bathing the room in light and he could see the damage done to her head by the tequila bottle, including a wicked shard of glass protruding from her eye. But fear of the police and prosecution had evaporated. He didn't know what had happened, but with Atlanta on fire there wouldn't be time for anyone to worry about some blonde slut that had died in a hotel room. A smile of relief crossed his face and he turned back to watch the smoke and flames.

Movement in the parking lot three floors below caught his attention. Several bodies were on the ground and a man with a gun and a woman were walking quickly toward a row of parked vehicles. He leaned closer to the glass when he realized the woman was nude, then stepped back quickly when the man suddenly stopped, slapped his pant pockets and looked up at the hotel. Danny didn't know why, but something told him he didn't want to be seen.

After a few seconds, the man turned away, slowly scanning across the parking lot and surrounding roads. No traffic was moving and from Danny's elevation he could see several groups of pedestrians, all apparently converging on the man and woman. They saw them too, breaking into a run away from the hotel.

Fascinated, Danny watched as they approached a small cluster of vehicles that had been abandoned at a nearby inter-section. A group of people, probably the drivers, milled around amongst them and turned to meet the new arrivals. The breath caught in his throat when a woman suddenly leapt onto the hood of a car and launched herself at the man like a missile. He saw the gun come up and buck once in the man's hand, the attacking woman falling to the ground and tumbling to a stop at his feet. A second later, the sound of the shot reached him faintly through the heavy glass.

"What the hell?" Danny whispered, a thrill of fear passing through him.

Turning, he looked down at Janice. She'd behaved the same as the woman he'd just seen shot in the head. Attacked for no reason.

"WHAT THE HELL IS GOING ON?" Danny cried loudly, turning back to the window at the sound of more gunfire.

The man stood over several bodies, searching them for some-thing as the nude woman looked around nervously at multiple groups of pedestrians converging on their location. Seemingly finding what he was looking for, the man made a gesture and the pair raced to a big Ford truck and leapt into the cab an instant before grasping hands began slapping on the sheet metal. Within moments, the truck was completely surrounded by dozens of people and two women leapt onto the hood to pound on the windshield.

Checking his phone, Danny cursed to find there was still no service available. Rushing across the room, he yelped when he stepped on a shard of the shattered bottle. Ignoring the pain and blood that began to soak into the carpet, he snatched up the TV remote with a trembling hand and pressed the power button. In his state of mind, he'd forgotten the power was out. With a curse of frustration, he flung the remote across the room where it bounced off the dark TV screen.

Sidestepping the broken glass, he returned to the window. Something seriously bad was going on and he needed to get out of here. Maybe he could draw the attention of the man with the gun and catch a ride with him. Danny didn't like guns. Didn't believe anyone needed one or should be allowed to have one, but right now seemed like a good time to be standing behind a well-armed man.

He sighed in dismay when he saw the Ford hadn't moved. In the brief time he'd been away from the window, the size of the mob surrounding it had doubled. It didn't look like those people were going to be able to help him. Terrified, but more freaked out by the thought of remaining in the room with the dead woman, Danny grabbed his clothes off the floor.

He was ready to dress quickly and go but hesitated when he saw the gash on his foot was still bleeding freely. The thought of ruining the eight-hundred-dollar pair of shoes he was about to put on sent him to the bathroom where he washed the injury while sitting on the edge of the tub. The amount of blood was surprising, the hot water causing the wound to flow freely.

Satisfied he'd administered all of the basic first aid of which he was capable, Danny wrapped a white washcloth around his foot, hissing in pain as he pulled it tight across the cut. He needed stitches, but this would have to do until he could get home. Theresa, once an emergency room nurse, would know what to do. Theresa!

Thoughts of his wife electrified him. Atlanta might be burning, but if he walked in smelling of another woman, he'd have bigger problems. He had no doubt his wife was capable of ruining him in a divorce. Half of all his assets, plus their palatial new house in Buckhead. A more than generous monthly alimony to keep her flabby ass living in the style to which she'd become accustomed. Then child support for their two daughters, privileged little monsters both. He'd be ruined.

Ripping the cloth from his foot, he stepped into the still running shower. Leaning to the side to take pressure off his injury, he vigorously scrubbed his body with the small bar of soap provided by the hotel and shampooed his stylishly cut hair. With a growing sense of urgency, Danny toweled off quickly, rewrapped his foot with a fresh cloth and hurried out of the bathroom.

He paused for a moment, hoping this had all been a nightmare. Atlanta still burned and there was still a dead woman on his hotel room's floor. Ignoring everything, Danny dressed in a rush, grimacing in pain when he forced his injured foot into a shoe. Standing, he quickly checked himself over, satisfied when he felt his keys and wallet in their normal pockets. Without even a glance at the corpse of the woman he'd spent the night with, he limped across the room, scooped his phone up and opened the door.

The hallway had no exterior windows. Battery powered emergency lights were located every hundred feet and cast small, isolated pools of illumination. Between them were large swaths of darkness and Danny hesitated. Goosebumps raced along his arms and back as he stared in the direction of the elevator bank. Two lights broke up the long stretch of gloom to the alcove where the cars were located. Gloom that was impenetrable. Anyone, or anything, could be waiting for him and he wouldn't see them.

Swallowing hard, he looked in the opposite direction. A long, unlit stretch to the end of the corridor with a softly glowing exit sign. Stairs! Of course! And not only were they closer, but with the power off the elevators wouldn't be working.

Taking a deep breath for courage, Danny finally stepped fully out of the room and released the door. It closed with a soft hiss of hydraulics, then whether by design or a faulty mechanism, sped up for the final foot and slammed hard enough to rattle in its steel frame. Immediately, from the darkness in the direction of the elevator, several hisses and growls sounded.

Whirling, Danny stared hard, trying to penetrate the gloom. He couldn't see anything, but the sounds were coming closer and he was certain there was more than one of whatever was making them. Memories of Janice attacking him caused his breath to catch and he turned to flee in the direction of the stairs.

Two limping steps and he pulled to a stop despite the still approaching sounds. A fifty-foot stretch of darkness separated him from escape into the stairwell. What if something was waiting for him in there?

Sweat beading his forehead and trickling down his back, Danny glanced over his shoulder. The sounds were still approaching. Looking back to the front, he hesitated. Tried to work up the courage to move forward. To…

It's quiet, he thought, almost saying it out loud.

Squaring his shoulders and taking a shuddering breath, he hurried forward into the dark. Halfway to the exit sign, he risked a glance behind. Three men were visible in the pool of light outside his room. They moved slowly. Uncoordinated. Clumsy as they shuffled after him. And they were making the sounds, hisses ending with guttural snarls.

Danny frowned, unsure what to make of them. For that matter, what the hell had been wrong with Janice? Why had she attacked him like that? Like a wild animal. For a few seconds he stood immobile, watching the men come closer. It was only when they passed out of the light and disappeared into the unlit area of the hall that he turned and fled.

Fled didn't exactly describe the limping, shuffling run to the end of the corridor, but he was moving faster than they were.

Reaching the steel fire-door that opened into the stairwell, he paused with his hand on the crash bar. The men were invisible in the darkness, but he could hear them coming. Cautiously, he pushed the door open, brilliant light from large banks of emergency lighting flooding through the opening.

Stepping through onto the poured concrete landing, he controlled the speed at which the door moved, letting it close with only the soft click of the latch re-engaging. Exhaling a shuddering breath, Danny looked around at the raw, gray steps and walls. Iron railings protected from a drop to the first floor. He stayed there, closing his eyes and willing his heart to stop racing as he leaned against the door.

Danny shouted in fear when the door was violently shoved. Stumbling forward, he nearly fell down the first flight of steps as it slammed inward against the concrete wall with a resounding boom. Whirling, he saw two of the men momentarily wedge themselves into the opening, their hisses and snarls loud and echoing off the hard surfaces in the stairwell.

Frozen in place, he watched in horror as the larger of the pair gained the upper hand and squeezed through. The man was big, easily outweighing Danny's trim frame by fifty pounds. And his two companions were right behind him.

The brightly lit area gave Danny his first good look at them. All three had red orbs for eyes and black blood dripped from their ears and nostrils. Transfixed, he stared at them as they shuffled forward, then he turned and began hobbling down the stairs. From behind, there was the sound of flesh striking concrete as the lead male stepped blindly off the landing and pitched forward. He never stopped snarling as he tumbled down the steps, seemingly impervious to the damage being done by the iron caps on the edge of each.

The body slammed into Danny, taking out his legs and sending both of them bouncing to the landing below. Ending up in a tangled pile, Danny cried out in pain when the male, unfazed by the fall, grasped his leg in a viselike grip. Kicking with his free foot and trying to pull away, Danny panicked as he was steadily pulled toward the man's snapping teeth. He watched in terror, unable to free himself. His kicks were useless, and the man was frighteningly strong.

"HELP!" Danny screamed as the male lowered its open mouth toward his foot.

Grabbing the railing in a last, desperate attempt to escape being eaten alive, Danny pulled for all he was worth. Adrenaline fueled his efforts and for a moment he achieved a stalemate with the man. Then, slowly, he was drawn back toward the hungry mouth.

"NO, NO, NO, NOOOOoooo," Danny began to wail.

His mind was already prepared for what was coming. The dull, tearing sensation of teeth piercing his flesh. The searing pain of a chunk being torn free. And… the blood. It would spurt and spray and flow, coating everything as it was pumped out of his body by his wildly beating heart. The teeth came closer, hovering over him. Ready to rend and tear.

Then the second male arrived. Its body tumbling and bouncing down the steps to slam into the first one an instant before Danny would have become the main course.

The impact broke the man's grip and Danny jerked his lower body away, pulling on the railing with all his frightened might. In his panic, he slithered beneath the bottom rail before he realized there was only open space beneath him. Now he clung to the railing, dangling over a long drop to the first-floor landing.

The two males were still struggling to extricate themselves when the third bounced down the steps and crashed into them. Hisses and gurgling snarls seemed deafening to Danny as he dangled by his hands, watching his attackers. He cast several terrified looks down at the ten-foot drop to the concrete landing. To his frightened mind it might as well have been a hundred. There was no way he could force himself to release the railing and fall.

But gravity and too many hours in a comfortable office chair had different ideas. Quickly, Danny's hands began to ache and his arms shook with the effort of maintaining his grip. The three males were still trying to sort themselves out and he ignored them, struggling to pull himself up enough to hook an arm around a vertical post.

He might have made it if he were younger or had spent any time in the gym. In fact, he was almost there, twisting his body and digging at the sheer wall with his feet. Only inches from thrusting his arm past the post and hooking it so the stress was off his rapidly failing hands. Perhaps he would have if one of the males, in its efforts to disentangle from the pile, hadn't kicked out and crushed Danny's hand between the railing and the sole of its shoe. Danny lost his grip and fell with a cry.

The impact with the landing came much faster than he expected. But that didn't make it any less brutal. Legs buckling immediately, he fell to the side, absorbing more punishment with his left shoulder before rolling and coming to a stop against the wall.

Danny was unable to move. About all he knew was that he was conscious. For several very long seconds he remained perfectly still, waiting for his body to report in with a damage assessment. The glass cut on his foot was the first thing to hurt, sending a bolt of white-hot pain up his leg. Then everything else began to make its presence known. Ankles. Knees. Hip and left shoulder.

The males a floor above were still hissing and snarling and even though he had no idea if he was seriously injured or not, Danny decided he had to move. Had to get out of the stairwell before they fell down the final flight and trapped him. Feasted on him.

Forcing his bruised and battered body to roll over, he groaned and had to stop twice as more areas announced they had been abused. Making it to a sitting position, he gulped air and glanced up the stairs, afraid the males were already on their way down. He could see them, but they were still apparently hopelessly entangled, or perhaps injured by the roll down the stairs to the point they couldn't keep pursuing him. Dismissing them for the moment, he began taking stock of his condition.

"Fuck," he mumbled, seeing both knees of his suit pants had been shredded by the rough concrete, the skin beneath raw and bleeding. "Five-thousand-dollar suit. Trashed."

A change in sound from the males snapped his head up. At least one of them was free and clambering to his feet. Fear made Danny forget about his ruined bespoke suit. Stiffly, he got to his feet, cringing when he was barely able to put weight on an ankle. The one opposite the foot he'd sliced open. He might be standing, but he wasn't going anywhere fast.

The ground-floor door swung into the stairwell and Danny jerked it open as the male who'd managed to regain his footing began tumbling down the final flight of steps. Ignoring the pain as much as possible, he hobbled through as the male's body slammed against it, closing it with enough force to rattle the walls.

Without even a glance to see if the door was remaining shut, Danny shuffled around a corner and through a small kitchen where breakfast for the hotel's guests was prepared each morning. Stepping into the lobby area, he stopped in surprise when he saw a young woman looking at him from behind the front desk. She was dressed in slacks and a button-down white shirt that no one would willingly purchase and wear, marking herself as a hotel staff member. Most likely the lone night-shift employee. She'd been crying, broad black streaks of mascara trailing down her cheeks and she looked appropriately freaked out.

"Stay back!" she shouted, clutching a large butcher knife tightly to her breasts.

"What the hell happened? What's going on?" Danny shouted back, shooting a glance over his shoulder to make sure the males weren't through the door yet.

"You... you're not sick?" the girl asked, doubt clear in her voice.

"Is that what's going on? A virus?"

"I don't know. Maybe. New York was attacked with nuclear bombs, then everything went off. All I know is there's something wrong with people."

Tears were streaming down her face as she said the last. A moment later she looked briefly to the side before turning back to watch Danny. He followed her gaze, feeling a chill wash over him when he saw a pair of feet sticking out into the lobby from the far side of the desk. For several moments the woman watched him staring at what had to be a body on the floor.

"What happened?" he finally asked.

Slowly, he shuffled forward, angling to the side for a better view and to keep plenty of room open between himself and the big knife. She watched him the way a cat watches a mouse hole but didn't answer his question.

Reaching the center of the lobby, he could see a woman dressed in exercise clothing lying face down on the shiny marble floor. A large pool of blood had formed beneath her, congealing into a thick morass. He didn't need to approach any closer to confirm she was dead.

"She attacked you, didn't she?"

He looked at the woman, meeting her eyes and waiting for an answer. She finally nodded, sniffing back tears.

"I was in the kitchen," she said, nodding at the area Danny had just walked through. "I'm supposed to be an auditor, but part of my job is to do some food prep. I was cutting fruit when the front desk phone rang and I ran to answer. She... she just leapt at me out of nowhere. Screaming. The knife was in my hand and I guess I held it up to protect myself, because... I wasn't trying to hurt her."

As she'd spoken, the woman had turned to stare at the corpse on the floor. Her head snapped around and she extended the knife protectively when a pounding sounded from the direction of the stairwell.

"What's that?" she shouted, voice cracking with fear.

"More like her," Danny said, edging toward the exit into the parking lot. "They're in the stairwell. I barely got away."

The woman's breath caught in her throat at his words and she stood there, eyes riveted in the direction of the pounding. It took her several seconds to realize Danny was still moving.

"Where are you going?" she asked frantically, taking a step out from behind the desk.

"Out of here," Danny said, shooting a nervous look toward the stairwell.

The males were still pounding, which he realized was a good thing. It meant they hadn't gotten through. Yet.

The woman took another step away from the desk, dividing her attention between the racket the men were making and Danny. He was nearly to the automatic sliding door that opened to the outside.

"Take me with you!" she suddenly cried, moving several steps closer.

"You should wait here for the police. You killed someone. They're going to want to talk to you."

"There are no police!" she cried. "No phones. No 9-1-1. No Internet. Nothing! Whatever's going on, there's no one coming!"

"Bullshit," Danny said without conviction.

Whether he was ready to admit it or not, part of him knew from the moment he saw the raging inferno that had once been Atlanta that the world had permanently and drastically changed. Acknowledging this to himself renewed his sense of urgency to get to his house. Moving to the door, he stopped when it didn't automatically open and glanced up at the sensor.

"Power's out," the woman said.

Turning so he could grab the door and still keep an eye on her, Danny tugged hard, but it didn't slide on its track.

"And I locked it," she said.

"Unlock the door," he said, eyes locking onto her.

"Only if you take me with you," she said, determination clear in her voice.

Facing her, he considered trying to take the key from her. But she still tightly clutched the bloody butcher knife and he had no doubt she was frightened enough to use it without hesitation if he tried. He wasn't a fighter and even though she was far smaller than him, he had no confidence in his ability to take it or anything else she didn't want him to have.

"You don't even know where I'm going," he said in a last-ditch effort to dissuade her from insisting on coming along.

"I don't care, as long as it's away from here."

Danny hesitated. He didn't want company. All he wanted was to get home where his new Jeep was parked in the garage with a full tank of gas. More than enough to make it to his lake house where he could hunker down in luxury until whatever this was had blown over. Isolated on the north shore of a sprawling lake, the closest neighbor was miles away. It was powered by its own generator and the perfect place to ride out the storm.

Glancing through the glass door, he could just make out the Ford truck with the man and woman he'd seen earlier. It was mobbed with people, well over a hundred. His eyes drifted back to the parking lot, coming to rest on his shiny red Tesla. For the moment, there was no one anywhere near it. He had an opportunity to reach the car and be on his way, but not if he kept wasting time with this bitch.

"Okay. Fine," he said, looking back at the woman. "Let's go while we can."

She hesitated a beat, then shifted the knife to her left hand and rushed forward. Digging a set of keys out of her pocket, she quickly unlocked the deadbolt and stepped aside. With a sigh, Danny worked his fingers into the seam and pulled it open. Warm, humid air, rank with the smell of the fire that was consuming Atlanta flooded into the lobby, but they both ignored it and rushed outside.

"Where are we…" the woman began to ask as they rounded a thick hedge that separated the walkway from the parking lot.

A blood chilling scream caused them to whirl about. From the opposite direction, coming from behind a different hedge was a female charging in at full speed. The woman emitted a squeal of fright, reflexively raising the knife and stepping back, closer to Danny. He acted without thought, reaching out and shoving her in the back with all his strength.

Not expecting the push, she stumbled forward, arms flailing in an effort to maintain her feet. Before she regained her balance, the female slammed into her and they tumbled across the walkway into a planting bed full of flowers.

Danny had gone into motion the instant he'd pushed the

woman. Shuffling sideways and now hobbling toward his car as fast as his injured foot and leg could carry him. Behind, the woman's screams mixed with those of the female for a few moments, then there was only the sound of clothing and flesh being torn.

A fresh scream snapped his head around. Two more females had come around the hedge and were sprinting directly at him. Pushing his injured body as hard as he could, he flopped against the side of his car and fumbled with the recessed handle. It finally released and he yanked the door open, sparing a glance at the swiftly approaching women as he threw himself behind the wheel. Pulling hard, it slammed into place as they arrived.

Fists immediately began pounding on the side window, then one of them leapt onto the hood and pressed her face to the glass. Danny's breath quickened as he stared into her eyes. The whites had turned a deep, blood red and no sign of humanity remained. Only unbridled rage and predatory hunger.

Time stretched out as his eyes remained locked on the female's. Neither moved, both ignoring the frenetic attempts of the other woman to gain entry into the car. Finally, with a shake of his head, Danny looked away. The female instantly began screaming and attacking the windshield.

Pressing the button to activate the car, Danny held the brake as he shifted into reverse. Instead of just going, he once again caught the female's eyes. She calmed, staring back. Blood stained her face and he could see bits of flesh trapped in her teeth as her lips peeled back into a silent snarl. Emboldened by the protection the Tesla provided, he leaned closer to the glass, a sneer on his mouth. She pressed her face against the windshield, creating a grotesquely distorted death mask.

"Fuck you, bitch," Danny whispered, then hit the throttle.

With a spinning of tires, the car shot backward out of the parking spot, the female losing her grip and sliding off the hood. She tumbled across the asphalt but was back on her feet in a flash. The second woman had been sent flying when he cut the wheel, the Tesla's fender knocking her well clear. She, too, was up in a heartbeat, both pursuing as he shifted to forward and screamed away across the lot.

🌐 🌐 🌐

"Where have you been?" Theresa screamed, rushing forward to throw her arms around him as Danny stepped into the house from the garage.

Surprisingly, he'd made it from the hotel to his home without encountering any problems. He'd seen plenty of the insane men and women, even witnessed multiple murders as they ran down unaffected people. He'd been chased by the frighteningly swift females, and had even hit a few with his car, but they hadn't been able to stop him.

The roads heading away from the city were hopelessly clogged, but he'd been driving against traffic. Several times he'd questioned the wisdom of going closer to what he believed was the epicenter of the chaos, but that was where his house was. The Tesla was down to less than a third of a charge and there was no way he could make the drive to the lake house. He needed the Jeep. But when he whipped into his driveway, the garage door was up, and it was missing.

"Where the hell's the Jeep?" he asked, roughly grabbing his wife, pushing her back and holding her at arm's length.

"Jerry took it," she said defensively.

"WHY THE HELL DID YOU LET HIM DO THAT?"

For a beat, Theresa stared at him with a look of shock on her face. Then, she lowered her gaze as tears began flowing down her cheeks.

"He had a gun," she said just above a mumble.

"What?" Danny asked incredulously.

Jerry and his wife Anita had lived next door when they'd bought this house a little less than a year ago. They'd been good neighbors, always friendly and quick to invite them over for cocktails and cookouts. There were even a couple of times when they'd watched the girls so Theresa could attend corporate functions with him.

"He came over looking for you before the sun even came up. When he found out you weren't here, he asked for the Jeep. I thought he was joking. After I said no, he went away, but came back a few minutes later with a gun! What was I supposed to do?"

She was nearly blubbering as she spoke. Danny stared at her in amazement, his anger over the missing vehicle tempered by the story. As his grip on Theresa's arms slackened, she moved in and wrapped her arms around his waist, seeking the comfort of physical contact.

"Did you fall down, Daddy?"

They both looked around to see their youngest, Hailey, standing in the middle of the kitchen with a frightened expression on her face. Theresa started to step over to comfort her daughter but paused when she glanced at Danny. It was the first time she'd actually looked at him since he'd walked into the house.

"Oh, my God! What happened? Are you all right?"

She stared in horror at his torn and bloody suit and the bruises on his face from fighting with the males in the stairwell and falling to the ground floor.

"I'm okay," he said. "But we need to get out of here. You still have a first aid kit?"

Theresa nodded, her eyes cataloging her husband's injuries.

"My foot is gashed open. Can you get the kit while I change?"

"Change? Where are we going? What's going on?"

"Just do as I say, Theresa! We're going to the lake house. We'll be safe there until the authorities get this all straightened out."

"How will we get there without the Jeep? That's why you bought it."

A note of a whine crept into her voice. One of many things Danny found himself less and less able to tolerate.

"Damn it, Theresa, just get the fucking kit, will you? I'll worry about how we're going to get there without a Jeep."

Without another word or a backward glance, Danny turned

and hobbled away. He didn't see the momentary flicker of anger that passed across Theresa's face as she watched his back. But as suddenly as it had appeared, it was gone and she turned to face her daughter.

"Hailey, honey. Go find your sister. I need each of you to get your backpacks ready to go. Okay, sweetie?"

"Why's Daddy mad?" Hailey asked. "Did I do something bad?"

"No, baby," Theresa said softly, wrapping the girl into her arms. "He's not mad, he's just had a bad morning and he's worried about us. Okay? Now, go get your sister and be sure each of you puts a change of clothes and clean underwear in your backpacks. Got it?"

"And our iPads?" Hailey asked, already moving on from the scene between her parents she'd just witnessed.

"Yes, baby. That's fine. As long as you have clothes and clean panties. That's what's important. Now scoot! Mommy has to help Daddy."

She planted a kiss squarely on Hailey's forehead then the girl ran off shouting her sister's name. With a deep breath, Theresa straightened, took a first aid kit off the top shelf of a cabinet and headed for the master bedroom.

When she walked in, Danny was in the bathroom, wearing nothing but a pair of boxers. Sitting on the edge of the tub, he was trying to loosen the knot in a blood-soaked rag that was wrapped around his foot. Her eyes traveled over his unclothed body, professionally cataloging all the bruises and scrapes, then paused at the deep slash marks on his torso where Janice's nails had torn open his flesh.

"What happened to you?"

Danny didn't bother to look at her.

"I was at the office and was attacked by this crazy woman." As he spoke, Theresa casually picked up his discarded clothing and moved to a laundry hamper. "She broke the big plate-glass window in the conference room, you know the one, and that's what cut my foot."

"Your shoes were off."

Her tone was matter of fact. Danny looked up, evaluating her expression and deciding how best to respond.

"Yes, Theresa. They were. It was a long night and I was tired of wearing them."

The knot finally released, and he gently unwrapped the bloody cloth with a hiss as it pulled on the edges of the cut.

"Why was your shirt off?"

"What?" he asked, not looking up from his injured foot.

"Your shirt."

She held it up with two hands by the shoulder points. Other than blood stained, it was undamaged.

"What?" he asked again, looking at the piece of clothing and frowning.

"Don't understand how you can get your chest torn up like that without a mark on your shirt. Unless you weren't wearing it at the time. Why was your shirt off, Danny?"

An awkward silence settled over the room. They stared at each other, neither saying anything. Finally, Theresa shook her head, sighed and stepped forward. Sinking to her knees in front of him, she roughly grabbed his ankle and lifted so she could examine his wound.

"Look, I really don't—"

"Just stop, Danny!" Theresa barked, cutting him off. "I'm scared. The world seems like it's falling apart and I just don't have the energy for your bullshit. You think I don't know you're fucking around on me? I'm not stupid!"

"You're wrong! I swear to you, I've not touched... OUCH!"

He jerked his foot away when she probed the edge of the wound. Looking up, she met his eyes.

"God help you if you've brought any diseases home," she said before turning away and busying herself with opening and preparing the first aid kit.

"Honey..."

"Don't honey me," Theresa snapped. "There's things a woman can put up with if it means her children will have a good, stable home. I've put up with your cheating, your condescension and all the rest of your bullshit. The least you can do is not lie to me and expect me to believe you. I'm not stupid. Just tell me the truth!"

After a moment of glaring into his eyes, she looked away, pulled on a pair of latex gloves and tore open a small packet of betadine. Lifting his foot, she squeezed the brown liquid directly into the wound, flushing from the top. Satisfied, she none too gently wiped the area dry with a large square of gauze. Danny grimaced in discomfort as she worked.

"You want the truth?" he asked when she set the gauze aside and picked up a small bottle of super glue.

"That would be refreshing," she said as she pinched the edges of the wound together and began sealing them with the glue.

"Ewwww, that's gross!"

"Hailey, did you do what I asked?" Theresa asked without turning away from her work.

"Yes, ma'am. I'm all packed."

"What about Lisa? Did you tell her?"

Lisa was the older sister by three years.

"She just told me to get out of her room. I don't think she's doing it."

"Go tell your sister she's in big trouble if she doesn't get ready to go," Danny interceded, earning a sigh from Theresa.

"Where are we going, Daddy? Are we going to find Uncle Jerry?"

"We're going to the lake house, sweetie," Theresa said, adding another spot of glue. "Won't that be fun? We can swim and make s'mores over the firepit at night. And no school for a couple of days."

"Really?" Hailey asked, the prospect of going to the lake house instead of school for a few days brightening her mood.

"Really, baby. Now, go tell your sister I expect her to be packed and standing in the kitchen in ten minutes. Can you do that?"

"Yes, ma'am!" Hailey cried, turning and running off, shouting the news about no school to her sister at the top of her lungs.

"She won't be ready," Danny said, pointedly not looking at what Theresa was doing to his foot.

"Probably not, but I'll deal with it. Just like I always do."

She worked in silence, finishing sealing the cut and giving it a once over to make sure it wasn't seeping any blood.

"What about infection?" Danny asked, lifting his foot to peer at the results of his wife's work.

"Here."

She tossed a single-use packet of antibiotic ointment at him and he fumbled it out of the air. Quickly gathering up the kit, she stuffed the trash into a waste basket beneath one of the sinks. Danny remained seated on the tub edge, watching her studiously avoid him.

"So, what do you want to do?" he asked to stop her when she headed for the door.

"About what?"

Theresa turned and glared down at him, hands on her hips.

"Well, us. You seem unhappy."

"Do I? Nice of you to finally notice. I've been unhappy for so long, I don't remember what it's like to be anything else."

"That's not an answer."

"I don't have an answer, Danny," she said in exasperation. "Right now, it's more important that we get our children away from the city and somewhere safe. Once things calm down, we can worry about us."

Without another word, Theresa turned and left. She was calling Lisa's name before she was out of the master bedroom. After several seconds, Danny sighed and got up, hobbling into his closet. An old elastic bandage from the back of a drawer wrapped his injured ankle, relieving some of the pain of standing on it. He smeared antibiotic ointment on his freshly treated wound before pulling on a thick pair of socks, then dressed quickly in jeans and a polo shirt with his law firm's logo emblazoned on the left breast.

Grabbing a duffel off the top shelf, he stuffed in several pairs of clean underwear and socks, added another pair of jeans and a couple of shirts. He didn't expect they'd need to be gone for long, but even if they were, all of them had extra clothing at the lake house. They just needed to get there.

Stepping back out into the bathroom, he paused when Theresa walked in. Ignoring him, she breezed into her closet, returning less than a minute later with a small bag. He moved to step in front of her and she stopped with a sigh, refusing to meet his eyes.

"We have a couple of minutes," he said gently, reaching for her free hand. She pulled it away, tucking it behind her back. "Can we please talk about this?"

"Kids. Safety first. We're not important, Danny," she said, looking up and meeting his gaze.

"Theresa, please…"

Both of their heads snapped around at the sound of gunfire from outside. Before either had even had an opportunity to process what they were hearing, Hailey and Lisa both began crying for them.

Theresa shot forward like a race horse out of the gate, elbowing Danny out of her way. Casting a frightened glance at a window that overlooked the direction the gunfire had sounded, he followed at a slower pace.

Hobbling into the living room, he found Theresa huddled on the floor at the end of the sofa, Hailey and Lisa under each arm. The girls were crying, their mother speaking softly as she tried to comfort them.

"What happened?" Danny asked, then dropped to the floor when more shots sounded from right outside.

Scrambling across the carpet to his family, he tried not to flinch as still more gunfire erupted, punctuated by the screams of several females. Chills running up his spine, it took him a moment to summon the courage to raise his head high enough to see out the window. When he did, the breath caught in his throat.

Four bodies lay on his perfectly manicured front lawn. As he stared at them, trying to tell if he knew any of the people, a man ran past with a gun in his hands. Danny had no idea what kind it was, but it looked like what he'd seen soldiers carrying on the news. The man came back into view, angling across the driveway, then a pair of females flashed past.

Several fast shots that were loud even inside the house and both of them fell to the ground. Apparently, one was only injured as she immediately began dragging herself forward, still in pursuit of her prey. The man cautiously came forward, stopping ten yards from the slow-moving female.

In horror, Danny watched as he raised the rifle, aimed carefully and pulled the trigger. The female's head ruptured, and she lay still. Fighting the impulse to throw up after witnessing the brutal murder of another person, he panicked when he saw the man look around and take off at a trot.

"Oh, shit!" he said, hurrying toward the kitchen as fast as his injuries would allow.

"What's wrong? Danny! What?" Theresa called after him.

"Man with a gun heading for the garage!" he shouted back, hearing his wife and daughters cry out in fear at the news.

He was moving slow despite the medical treatment he'd received and pulled to a dead stop when he stepped into the kitchen. A large, black man, the one who'd just shot the woman on his lawn, stood inside the door from the garage with the evil looking rifle in his hands.

"What the fuck?" Danny blurted, nearly pissing himself at the sight.

"You alone?" the stranger asked intently.

The weapon wasn't pointed at Danny, but it still drew all of his attention and turned his bowels to water. When he didn't answer, the man glanced around, then reached behind his back and threw home the deadbolt on the door with a loud click. The implications of what the stranger had done helped Danny find his voice.

"Get out," he croaked.

"Not gonna hurt you, man. Just can't be out there. It's getting worse!"

"Get out of my house!" Danny repeated, his voice stronger.

The stranger squinted and shook his head slowly.

"Sorry to bust in on you uninvited like this but didn't have much choice. Saw four more of 'em skulking around on your neighbor's lawn and I'm runnin' low on ammo."

"Four more of what?" Theresa asked from behind Danny.

The stranger leaned to the side, apparently not having seen her and the girls approach.

"Females, ma'am," he said.

"Excuse me?"

"Nerve gas. Sending people into a rage. You folks didn't know?"

"TV and Internet are out," Theresa said, moving a step closer but still keeping Hailey and Lisa sheltered behind Danny.

"Radio, ma'am. AM band. Not much news, but there's a couple of guys broadcasting and that's what they're saying. Makes sense too, what I've seen."

"Nerve gas?" Danny asked incredulously. "Where?"

"Sounds like everywhere. Heard some guy calls himself Max. Says most of the big cities in the country got hit."

"Oh, my God," Theresa said. "What do we do?"

"Get out," the stranger said. "Away from the city. Least that's what I was trying to do but didn't make it very far."

"Why do you have a gun?" Hailey asked, leaning out to peer around her father's leg.

"Hello, little miss," the stranger said, giving her a smile. "Well, the gun is for protection. Make sure I can defend myself if anyone tries to hurt me."

"Look," Danny interrupted impatiently. "We can't help you and we don't want you here. You need to leave. If you need a car, that Tesla outside is mine. Take it!"

The man looked at him for a long stretch, eyes boring into Danny's as if he were trying to read his soul. After an uncomfortable silence he nodded to himself.

"You take care of your family," he said softly to Danny, then leaned to the side to see Theresa. "Ma'am, sorry to have frightened you and your young ladies."

Turning, he released the deadbolt and grasped the knob to open the door into the garage.

"Wait!" Theresa said, pushing the girls behind her and stepping forward to stand next to Danny.

"What are you doing?" he snapped, looking sideways at her.

The stranger paused and looked over his shoulder.

"Please wait," she said to the man.

When he nodded, she grabbed Danny's arm and ushered her family into the living room.

"What the fuck are you doing?" Danny hissed once they were around the corner.

"Daddy said a bad word!" Hailey said, sounding happy about it.

"Hailey," Theresa said in warning, silencing the little girl. "Danny, you just saw what happened in our front yard. You were attacked, you said. And Jerry took our Jeep because he had a gun. And things are probably going to get worse before they get better. Maybe we should ask him to come with us."

"Are you crazy?" Danny's eyes were wide in shock. "We don't know anything about him! Nerve gas? Sound like bull... BS, to me. If it's nerve gas, how come everyone isn't affected?"

"I don't know, but I do know we need to get out of the city and we need to go now. But if we run into someone with a gun who wants to take what we have, we won't have a choice. Maybe if he's with us, they'll think twice and leave us alone."

"And he's black," Hailey piped up. "Didn't you say that a black man with a gun was the scariest thing you ever saw, Daddy?"

"Hailey..." Theresa said sternly, delivering another warning.

"That's the most ridiculous thing I've ever heard!" Danny said, ignoring his daughter's comment. "He won't protect us, he'll just get us caught in the middle of a gunfight! Look, you want to let him stay here and us leave, that's fine, but he's not coming with us!"

"Excuse me, folks."

They turned to see the stranger standing in the doorway. Apparently, he'd been listening to their conversation.

"Perhaps this will ease your mind."

The rifle was held pointed at the floor in his right hand, his left deftly flipping open a badge case.

"Special Agent Tony Busey, FBI."

They all stared at him in surprise, unsure what to say.

"Is that real?" Hailey asked suspiciously, starting to step forward for a better look at the ID.

"Hailey!" Theresa snapped, grabbing her shoulder and pulling her back.

"Yes, little miss. It's the genuine article!" Busey smiled.

Danny tentatively stepped forward, reaching out. Busey hesitated for a beat before handing over the case.

"What's that? Genuine article?" Hailey asked as her father examined the credentials.

"Means it's legit, dummy," Lisa said derisively, earning a dirty look from her little sister.

"This says you're retired," Danny said, returning the case. Busey took it and slipped it into a back pocket.

"True. I am. Two weeks ago."

"Where's your family?" Theresa asked. "They didn't come with you?"

"FBI life is hard on a marriage," he said, shrugging and offering no further explanation. "Now, this is all nice, but if you folks were serious about leaving and you don't mind some company, it would probably be best if we got on the road. As I said, it's getting worse out there by the minute."

"Yes," Theresa said without bothering to consult Danny. "We'd be happy to have you come with us. We've already had one car stolen by a neighbor with a gun."

"Yes, ma'am. People tend to go off the rails a bit when bad things happen."

"Theresa," she said, stepping forward and extending her hand.

Busey shook it then nodded and smiled at each of the girls as she introduced them.

"What about you?" he asked, turning to Danny. "You okay with me coming along?"

Danny held his eye for a beat before letting his drift to look at the floor.

"Sure. Why not? You were FBI, after all."

"Then we best get going," Busey said. "We're not going to try and squeeze into that Tesla, are we?"

"No, we're taking Theresa's Mercedes," Danny said, picking up his bag. "S Class. Plenty of room."

The girls were quickly herded to the garage door, Theresa keeping a protective arm around each of them. Danny started to lead the way, pausing when Busey held up a big hand.

"Okay, we're going straight to the car," he said, all business. "Ladies in the back, Danny driving and I'm riding shotgun. Seatbelts on the instant your butt hits the seat. Got it?"

He looked at Hailey and Lisa and softened the instructions with a wiggle of his eyebrows. Hailey giggled and nodded, but the older Lisa only rolled her eyes dramatically. He glanced up at Theresa and she nodded acknowledgement of his instructions.

"And you," he said, moving to directly face Danny. "You stop for nothing unless I tell you."

"I made it home less than an hour ago," Danny said petulantly. "I think I can handle this."

"That's good. Very good. But there may be some people who are trying to take advantage of the circumstances. Your family is in the back seat. Movement is safety. Do you understand what I'm saying?"

His eyes bored into Danny's who, after a beat, swallowed hard and nodded.

"Then let's go!"

Busey unlocked the door and pushed it open, the rifle already to his shoulder and scanning for danger as he moved into the large garage. Danny, keys in hand, hobbled across the floor to the driver's door as Theresa rushed the girls into the back seat. While they loaded into the car, Busey remained near the rear bumper, weapon ready to engage anyone or thing that threatened them.

Behind the wheel, Danny pressed the starter and the powerful twelve-cylinder engine rumbled to life with a sound of subdued power. Hearing the seatbelts behind him click, he pressed a button on his door that clunked the locks into place.

"What are you doing?" Theresa called in alarm.

She was starting to lean over the seat to grab his arm when he shifted into reverse and hit the throttle. The heavy car rocketed backwards out of the garage, missing Busey only because he leapt to the side when the engine note changed.

Steering around the Tesla, Danny ignored him as well as the shouts of protest from the back seat. Whipping through the circle driveway, he aimed for the street and took an instant to glance in the mirror. Theresa and the girls were all turned, looking through the rear glass. Busey stood at the entrance to their open garage, watching them leave without him.

Before they lost sight of him, he opened fire on a group of females that had been attracted by the sound of the Mercedes driving away. After two shots, the rifle ran dry and he dropped it, turning and running for the door into the house. The females rounded the corner at speed, their screams audible even in the superbly insulated luxury car. There was a small cry from Hailey, then Danny turned onto the street and they lost sight of Busey and the attacking females.

"He didn't make it," she said in a very quiet voice, turning and burying her face into her mother.

Danny glanced in the mirror again as he accelerated away. Theresa met his eyes, disappointment and anger shining brightly in hers.

The drive out of the Atlanta area was perilous, but they made it without any serious consequences. The freeways that led away from the city were hopelessly clogged. The people in the stranded vehicles were either unfortunate enough to become one of the infected from contact with residue from the dispersal of the agent, or they fell victim to those who had already turned.

Using the Mercedes' satellite navigation, Danny stuck to smaller roads. Crossed major arteries carefully and only at minor intersections. Several times he tried to engage Theresa or his daughters, but none of them would respond to his overtures. He understood their anger, but they had to understand that he was only trying to protect them. Bringing along Busey and his gun, FBI agent or not, was only asking for more trouble.

Finally leaving the Atlanta suburbs behind, the countryside opened up and turned to gently rolling hills. It was a beautiful day, the sun shining brightly as he accelerated smoothly past a blue sign marking a large marina. His house was on the same lake, but still many miles ahead, then back through the forest for more than a mile. Isolated as isolated could be.

It had cost a small fortune to construct, but now more than ever he was grateful he'd spent the money. He and his family would be safe. The road in wasn't marked and other than boaters on the lake who would have noticed the massive, two-story structure with its boat dock, no one knew it was there. In fact, the trail through the forest was so well hidden by the overgrown shoulder that he drove past and had to turn around.

Nosing into the thick grass, he brought the big sedan to a stop. Ahead was a narrow tunnel through primeval forest that wound its way to the lake. He'd never driven it in anything other than a Jeep that belonged to the realtor or one of the construction crew's trucks and wasn't at all sure Theresa's heavy, low slung car could make it. But, even if they couldn't, it wasn't that far of a walk. He'd just have to listen to his daughters complain the entire way.

"Can't make it in this."

The first words Theresa had spoken to him since he'd abandoned Busey.

"Going to try," he replied, no longer in the mood to hear anything she had to say.

She mumbled something he didn't catch as he gently accelerated onto the rough track. Within a hundred yards, they had bottomed out twice and scraped the passenger side on the bark of a massive oak. The overhead foliage was dense enough to activate the automatic headlights and wildly growing blackberry bushes made a screeing sound as they dragged along the sheet metal.

"I don't feel good."

Lisa's voice from the back seat.

"She's gonna hurl," Hailey chimed in, drawing a sharp look from her mother.

Danny glanced in the mirror, unconcerned. One of the kids always had something wrong. More often than not it was simply to get attention or to get out of doing something. Besides, he knew Theresa would deal with it. He could see her turned to their oldest daughter, feeling her forehead and speaking to her in low tones.

"She's got a fever," she said a minute later, worry clear in her voice.

"There's Tylenol at the house," Danny said dismissively.

"My head hurts," Lisa said, commanding Theresa's full attention again.

"We need to turn around," she said firmly after another mother's examination of the girl.

"And go where?" Danny asked, irritation clear in his voice.

Theresa didn't have an answer for that, glaring at him in the mirror before turning back to press her hand against Lisa's flushed face.

"I feel bad, too," Hailey said a minute later.

Danny sighed loud enough to be clearly heard in the backseat. He knew his youngest well enough to recognize a ploy to pull attention from her sister when he heard it.

"Hailey," he said, warningly.

"She's hot, too," Theresa said a moment later after feeling the smaller girl's face. "Danny, we've got to do something!"

"Everyone relax," he said as he carefully steered the heavy Mercedes around a massive tree stump. "We'll be to the house in a few minutes and there's medicine, then you can lay down and rest."

The girls fell silent, which was unusual. When either was sick, they complained incessantly. This reinforced for him that they were just reacting to the stress of the circumstances. Not that he blamed them. There'd been several times in the past few hours that he wanted to throw up then crawl into a corner and curl into a ball.

"Why didn't you have this path cleared into a real road?" Theresa asked.

She knew the answer. They'd spent so much on the construction of the house and dock that there hadn't been enough money left over to build a more than mile-long driveway. Danny's solution had been to buy the Jeep which would have handled the terrain with no difficulties. Unlike the Mercedes, which bounced over a gnarled tree root, bottomed out then came to a stop. The engine revved as he pushed on the accelerator, but the only result was the high-pitched sound of a spinning tire. They were stuck.

"Just great," Theresa mumbled.

Danny shot her a look in the mirror but didn't respond. Popping the driver's door open, he leaned out and looked back. Shifted into reverse and pressed on the gas while he watched the rear tire. More whining, but the car didn't budge.

"How much farther?" Theresa asked as he continued trying to get the heavy vehicle to move.

"Maybe a quarter of a mile," he said, slamming the steering wheel with the palm of his hand.

Releasing his seatbelt, he shut off the engine and pushed the door fully open.

"What are you doing?"

"We're stuck, Theresa. I have to find some rocks or branches to put under the tire," he said, his voice dripping with condescension.

Stepping out, he slammed the door and moved to the back of the car for a closer inspection. Both rear tires had dug ruts into the loose soil around the edge of a rotting tree branch that was thicker than his leg. That was the bad news. The good news was that it looked like he could drive it out if they could only gain a little traction. Hobbling as he moved, he began looking for anything he could use to help free the vehicle. He turned when the back door opened and Theresa stepped out.

"I got this," he said, thinking she was coming to help.

"I'm not waiting," she said, turning back to the interior and helping Hailey climb out. "They're getting hotter. I'm taking them to the house."

"I'll have us unstuck in a few minutes," he said, upset that she was taking action without discussing it with him.

"Then you can pick us up," she said firmly, helping Lisa out and wrapping her arms around both girls. "But we're going. Now."

Danny opened his mouth to argue with her, but the words died unspoken when he got his first good look at his daughters. Both were ghostly pale, clammy sweat beading their faces. Lisa looked like the only thing keeping her on her feet was her mother's embrace.

"Okay," he said, concern for them finally overriding his irritation with his wife.

"Hurry," Theresa said, fear for her children clearly written on her face.

Danny nodded and watched for a moment as they moved slowly down the path to the lake house. When they disappeared around a bend, he looked down at the car and cursed, then began gathering fallen branches.

Jamming them under the front of each rear tire, he briefly surveyed his handiwork. Satisfied, he jumped behind the wheel and started the engine. Putting the car in gear, he gently pressed on the accelerator. Nothing happened, which encouraged him. If the tires weren't spinning, that meant he had traction to get free.

Pressing harder on the throttle, his heart leapt when the car moved an inch forward. A little more gas. Another inch, then another. The rear started to come up as the Mercedes climbed out of the ruts. A little more pressure. There was a sudden racket from the back then the whine of spinning tires as the vehicle rolled back into the ruts.

"Goddamn it!" Danny screamed at the windshield.

He sat there for a few moments, panting in frustration. When he regained his composure, he stepped out and looked at the tires. They had grabbed the branches, spitting them out when he applied too much power.

"Goddamn it," he muttered, bending to collect a softball sized rock.

Twenty minutes later, he had built an impromptu rock path that ran for several feet in front of each rear tire. Digging out some of the soil from in front of each, he jammed fallen tree branches and smaller rocks into the void, giving the front of the tires something to grab so they could climb up onto the paths he'd made.

It was oppressively hot and humid in the forest and Danny's clothes were soaked in sweat, clinging to his body. Slipping into the Mercedes, he started the engine and took a moment to relish the cold air coming from the air conditioning.

"C'mon, bitch," he said under his breath as he shifted into gear.

Pressing on the accelerator as if there were an egg beneath his foot, he held his breath and willed the car to move. Slowly, an inch. Almost imperceptible, but it was there. Then a couple more, the back end rising slowly as it climbed out of the ruts again. A few more inches. A little more gas and with a whoop of victory from Danny it bounced free.

The excitement of successfully freeing the car momentarily brightened his mood, but it didn't last long. The weight of his circumstances crashed back down and he stepped on the brakes. For a long time, he just sat in the idling Mercedes, staring through the windshield.

They'd been closer to the house than he'd realized. Close enough that when the breeze moved some tree branches in the right direction, he could catch a glimpse of blue water. His house was just around the next turn. An impressive two story painted a gleaming white with a dock that could accommodate the largest of cabin cruisers. Somewhere he'd planned on entertaining the senior partners from his law firm when he was ready to make his pitch to join them on the fifth floor. Once there, he was set for life. An astronomical salary and more perks than even he could imagine. But that dream was gone.

Danny was realistic enough to understand that only one of two things was going to happen. Either the world as he knew it had ceased to exist, or this was all going to blow over in a couple of days and things would slowly get back to normal. Neither scenario favored him, though. He'd already seen the brutality resulting from whatever had happened and knew he wasn't someone who could survive in that type of environment.

But what if things went back the way they were? Just as bad. A dead woman in a hotel room rented in his name. DNA. Fingerprints. A digital trail of their online communications. A first-year prosecutor wouldn't have to break a sweat to secure a conviction or force him to plea to a lesser charge. Either scenario would almost assuredly result in some amount of prison time, and he was no better equipped to survive in that environment than he was in the world unfolding around him. At least in this one, he wasn't disgraced and behind bars.

Taking a deep breath of resignation, Danny caught a glimpse of the house as a particularly strong gust of wind bent a leafy branch aside. Theresa and the girls. He cared about them but had never felt the husbandly and paternal love he heard his friends and co-workers profess.

Life was better with them because he was expected to present a specific appearance as a member of his law firm. Solid. Dependable. A family man with his head on straight. That's what was expected. Not someone who trolled Internet sites and chat rooms, looking for anything with a pair of tits that was willing to hop into bed with him. No, he never would have gotten even a first interview with the firm were it not for Theresa and his daughters, let alone have made junior partner in less than ten years.

She had been the perfect wife. Always knew the right things to say in social settings. Made sure the family was active in volunteer work and was properly deferential to the spouses of the senior partners. In a word, they all loved her, and she had furthered his career immeasurably. But now… in a world collapsing in on itself, why did he need her? What did he need with the girls? In one day, they'd gone from asset to burden.

Still unmoving, Danny made a mental checklist of the pros and cons of having a family in the apocalypse. None of them could help with protection. That would all fall on him, whether he wanted it to or not. Food? Shelter? The basic necessities? Again, he wouldn't only have to provide those things for himself, he would be expected to for them as well.

His list was short, but it only consisted of cons. Try as he might, he couldn't come up with one single reason to continue being burdened with a wife and kids. Besides, there would be plenty of women out there willing to do whatever he asked if he could provide any of those things. Women a hell of a lot sexier and more interesting than Theresa.

Danny had his answer and he didn't feel even a twinge of guilt. Perhaps a tad bit of loss as life with Theresa had once been exciting. But that had been a long time ago and hadn't lasted past the first year of their marriage. After that, it had been nothing but bills and kids. This was his golden opportunity.

Decision made, he looked at the forest that was tight against the narrow trail. There was no way to reverse course. He would have to drive on to the house where there was a concrete driveway he could use to turn around. And if Theresa saw him, he'd simply ignore her and keep going. No need for an emotional parting. It would be easier on everyone if he just drove off and never came back.

Easing forward, he navigated slightly more than a hundred yards of forest before emerging into brilliant sunshine and bouncing onto a broad driveway. He breathed a sigh of relief when he didn't see Theresa or the girls. Not that he'd expected to as he was sure she had them tucked into bed, cold compresses on both their heads.

Keeping his speed low to not alert them to his presence, he steered into the circular drive, following the curve as it turned back to the forest. A flash of movement from the corner of the house snapped his head around, then Theresa appeared at a dead run. Bright blood stained her blouse and she was screaming as she angled for the driveway.

Danny nearly accelerated before she could reach the car, but years of conditioning took over and he stepped on the brakes as his frantic wife ran in front of the Mercedes. She was screaming unintelligibly, shooting terrified glances at the side of the house as she worked her way around to the driver's door. As she drew closer, Danny could see numerous gashes and what appeared to be bite marks on her exposed skin.

Pounding on the glass with bloody hands, she continued to scream something about the girls. Danny was momentarily frozen. Afraid he knew what was going on and unable to step out of the car and face it.

Chilling screams brought his head around to see his youngest daughter approaching at a full sprint. Blood stained her face and she ran like a gazelle despite having never been athletic in the least. Theresa screamed his name, grasping the door handle and tugging frantically. Danny looked down at the controls, spotting the unlock icon, but made no attempt to press it.

Theresa screamed for his help a final time before turning and running for the forest. Secure in the Mercedes, Danny watched in fascination as Hailey, then Lisa streaked past the grill in hot pursuit. Seconds later, before she'd gone twenty yards, they caught up with their mother.

Hailey launched herself into the air like a missile. Striking Theresa in the middle of the back, they tumbled to the concrete driveway, Lisa falling onto the pile an instant later. More screams pierced the air as they savaged their mother, then blood spurted, brilliant in the Georgia sunshine and silence fell as they began to feast.

Danny was absorbed in watching the carnage and jumped in surprise when several gunshots suddenly rang out. Hailey and Lisa flipped off their mother's body and lay still, gaping wounds in their heads. Terrified, Danny gasped as two men stepped out of the forest onto the driveway. Immediately, like prehistoric beasts, several battered and muddy four-wheel-drive trucks emerged from the path and neatly boxed him in.

More men stepped out and formed a loose group around his

wife's and daughters' corpses. They looked like what Danny had always privately thought of as hillbillies and each was armed. Cold fear flushed through him as the apparent leader strode to the car and tapped on the window with a chrome plated pistol.

He didn't know what to do. Terror had him frozen, unable to respond. Until the man took a step back and aimed the revolver at his head. He'd never realized the hole in the end of a barrel was so big until that moment when he looked down one.

"Gonna count ta three, boy," the man shouted in a thick, southern accent. "One!"

Hand shaking, Danny fumbled for the handle and pulled, popping the door a few inches. The man jerked it fully open before reaching in and grabbing a fistful of his shirt. With frightening strength, he pulled Danny from the car and shoved him against the fender.

"Watched ya let her die," he said, sour beer breath washing across Danny's face. "Ain't no call for that shit. We needs women!"

"What?" was the only thing Danny could say.

"You slow, boy?" the man asked, earning a chuckle from the others.

He peered at Danny from beneath the brim of a greasy baseball cap. A grin spread across his face as he pushed his face close.

"Don't always need women, though. Ol' Tommy over there done a long stretch in the state pen. Says one hole's perty much same as another when your dick's hard."

It took a moment for realization to dawn on Danny. A groan of fear escaped him as he looked around for any way to escape. He was completely surrounded with nowhere to go.

"Oh, God. No!" he breathed.

"God ain't got nuthin' ta do wit' it, boy. Best put on ya best smile."

CONVICTION

N.X. Sharps

On the 152nd day of our posting at Fort Conviction, Private Olyver Bagwell shit himself to death. His passing marked the third that week and the forty-third in total since the Stonewall Sharpshooters arrival.

Death had claimed a third of our unit, and another third had elected to gamble their lives fleeing into the swamp rather than man Fort Conviction another day.

Doc Dunbarr did the best he could with the tools at his disposal, but we infantry are a superstitious lot. Had Bagwell not been of my own company I would not have stepped foot into that temple of death we had for an infirmary. But when the summons came, I grabbed a couple lads for funeral duty, and headed on down. When Doc saw us, he began to pry the sheets from Bagwell's rigid death grip.

We were dangerously depleted of all supplies, linen included, and were unable to bury our dead out in the muck so we had taken to cremating them instead. It was preferable to being left to the wetland scavengers or, worse, the mirefolk and their profane ceremonies.

"Has Father Fehervari been by to anoint the body?" I asked.

"Aye, left shortly 'fore you arrived. Commissar caught another one. Piotr couldn't wait for you slugabones to show on account o' needin' to hear the lad's confession 'fore 'e's hanged."

"Who?" I asked with trepidation.

Doc stopped cleaning, his eyes darting between Corporal Cobb and Private Soward. I gave a curt nod.

"Corporal Bahr," said Doc.

"Feck," I cursed.

Ever since Private Antony Lovatt abandoned his watch and

walked into the night all those months ago, desertion had been an ongoing issue of no small severity. Commissar Normann stalked the renegades into the surrounding wetlands with his faithful hound. Whether he executed them, or they escaped his clutches the final result did naught to improve our dwindling number. It genuinely surprised me someone had yet to stick a knife in the bastard's belly while he slept. Still, I did not expect the political officer to survive the coup we were concocting. Unless Corporal Bahr blew the bloody lid off the operation.

"Don' fret," said Doc, "Piotr's goin' to 'ave a word with the dumb bastard about 'is eternal soul, an' you know how persuasive he can be."

I spat. "We need to act."

"Have we got the numbers? Aren't some o' the boys still on patrol?" he asked, applying a fresh layer of scented jelly above his lip to disguise the reek of the infirmary.

"Just be ready to move when you receive the signal," I snapped. "Cobb, Soward, haul Bagwell here off to the pyre. Once you finish, grab your rifles and all the dry powder you can secure and inform the others to be ready. I'm off to speak with Father Fehervari."

The deteriorating conditions at Fort Conviction and Major Tybalt's pigheaded refusal to address it propelled me to act.

Our expected resupply was months past due and our orders were dreadfully outdated. The nearest village with which we could trade was days away and the inbred buggers were none too friendly. The reserve of tolerably clean water was perilously low and rats the size of round shot plagued what dwindling rations we still had. And the threat of the rebels and mirefolk loomed large over the Fort.

I bumped into Father Fehervari as he exited the brig. "Father," I greeted him, bowing my head and making the sign of the Dual Pillars of Crown and Church over my heart.

"I assume you have heard of Corporal Bahr's capture," Father Fehervari said.

"I have, Father," I whispered.

"He asserts that his lips are sealed, and he will not betray our confidence."

I released a sigh of relief.

"The scum-sucking bastard is lying," Father Fehervari said.

"What?" I asked, heart seizing.

"The conspiracy is safe for now, else you and I would be dancing a jig with ropes around our necks, but I could see it in his beady eyes. The blighter is going to sell us out in return for a pardon, may rats nibble on his rotten bollocks in the Abyss," the priest sneered.

Private Weese, passing by on the way to his shift posting, reacted to the cursing as if physically struck, mouth gaping and eyes growing wide.

"Blessing be upon you my son," said Father Fehervari with a smile and we continued at our leisurely pace.

"I can kill him," said Father Fehervari, returning to his muted tone.

"Private Weese? That seems unnecessary, Father, I do not believe he heard anything that should concern us," I said.

"Not Weese, you pillock. Bahr. I can go back there and slip him a splash of 'holy water' if you catch my drift. Next thing you know he's slipping into a sweet, peaceful rest and the Commissar is none the wiser."

"Peaceful? Truly?"

"Oh my, no, it is a horrible death. Headache, dizziness, vomiting, seizures – a most unpleasant way to meet the Lord."

I frowned and shook my head. "Bahr is a complication. We need to address the root of the issue and we cannot stall another moment. We need to remove Tybalt from command now."

"You don't have to sell it to me, Lieutenant. If my addled mind can recall correctly it was a certain man of the cloth who has been proposing immediate action for weeks—"

"Father, I take it the deserter has confessed his sins?" came the boisterous voice of most hated man residing in Fort Conviction.

Commissar Normann strode toward us, that slobbering mutt close on his heels. I saluted as he approached, and he waved it off.

"Corporal Bahr has made his peace with the Lord," said Father Fehervari.

"Good, good. Now he must make peace with me," Commissar Normann sneered. "Would you care to sit in on my interrogation, Lieutenant? Not much else qualifies as entertainment around here."

"Thank you, sir, but no. I have duties I must attend."

"Do you see this dedication, Father? Lieutenant Skynner has no time for leisure, not when there are obligations to fulfill. With work ethic like that, I suspect Lorne here will make Major sooner than anyone expects," Commissar Normann said with a wink.

"Indolent hands are the Archfiend's manufactory," recited Father Fehervari.

"With your leave, sir?" I asked the Commissar.

"Dismissed Lieutenant," he said.

I saluted again and skirted the panting hound, heart hammering and cold sweat breaking out across my palms. I hated leaving Father Fehervari behind with the Commissar but if anyone could go toe-to-toe with the political officer it was the company priest. Besides, time was running out if we were to affect a coup with minimal loss of life.

An hour later and with the weight of our crimes hanging over our necks like a guillotine, I performed a final circuit of the Fort, noting all my men in their intended positions then headed for the Officer's Quarters with five reliable soldiers in tow, my pistol and saber at the ready.

I prayed Major Tybalt would relinquish command peacefully, and neither weapon would be required. My prayers went unheeded as we turned the corner of the storehouse and saw Commissar Normann and a selection of riflemen arrayed around the Officer's Quarters, muskets unslung.

"Feck," I muttered under my breath.

My fingers tightened around the grip of my pistol and I wondered if I could get a shot off before Normann's lackeys blew me apart. With the sun sinking lower over the horizon we stared each other down across the avenue, daring the other to blink. My body ached for release, muscles compressed like coiled springs.

The sentry bell rang out loud and clear across the Fort, shattering the tension and nearly triggering a shootout. Incomprehensible shouting accompanied the clamoring bell, and, in my periphery, I could see the Commissar's men glance about, straining to hear. Still his gaze remained locked on me, and mine on him.

"What are they saying?" asked one of the riflemen across the street.

"Artillery," Sergeant Coates screamed from his position behind me. "Artillery fecking incoming!"

"Is this your doing? A diversion perhaps?" Commissar Normann hissed.

"No. Is it yours?" I retorted.

A series of deep crumps shook the ground and resolved the question for us.

"Take cover," I bellowed.

I made three steps before the projectiles rained upon us, whistling all the way down. Lobbed on high arcs over timber walls, the shells began detonating indiscriminately within the midst of Fort Conviction. Fragments scythed through the air and men came apart in welters of gore. A shell punched through the roof of the stables before detonating, and the blood-curdling screams of the few remaining horses that had not yet graced our supper bowls, rent the air. The surviving equines bucked madly to flee the stables as the wooden structure ignited. I kissed the mud and prayed.

The bombardment lasted less than a minute, but it felt the length of an entire campaign. I did not immediately register the cessation of fire until I was kicked onto my back. I thrust my pistol into the face of Commissar Normann, and he batted the barrel away with the back of his hand and hauled me close. With his nose inches from my own he spoke with sedate emphasis. I blinked and shook my head.

"We are not finished, you and I," he said, and I heard it clear as day.

"No, we are not," I spat, but Commissar Normann had already stormed off.

I picked myself off the ground and looked around to get my bearings. A smattering of men littered the avenue, some motionless, the majority merely shocked by the shelling. I about stumbled over the jellied remains of a soldier, swallowing my revulsion and snatching up a rifle and cartridge box. I waved the rifle over my head and shouted for the men's attention.

"You four," I singled out the boys who appeared most distressed by the bombardment. "Fetch buckets. Let the fire spread no further beyond the stables. The rest of you follow me."

To their credit the shell-shocked lads leaped to their given tasks. I bolted for the palisades with the remaining troopers on my heels. We climbed the ramparts and took cover behind the protruding lip. Corporal Fadley, arguably the finest marksman in a company famed for its marksmen, had already claimed a spot and begun firing. Rebel irregulars approached through the brush, their unkempt beards, mud-daubed faces, and impromptu uniforms had the bastards look half-mad. They advanced without a perceivable degree of unit cohesion like the peasants they were. I aimed down my barrel and fired at a bear of a man with a leather coat and twigs in his hair. I cursed as my shot flew wide but Corporal Fadley fired a heartbeat later and his aim proved true. I dropped back behind the rampart and began reloading.

Fadley rose again and I joined him, scouring the greenery for a target. Most of the enemies' shots impacted against the palisade, chipping off splinters and doing little other harm, but one musket ball zipped past with alarming proximity. My eyes darted from bush to tree to rotten stump and then back to the tree. Movement caught my eye. A rebel crept through the greenery, reloading his rifle as he edged closer, near enough for me to see the necklace of severed and desiccated ears strung around his neck. I fired reflexively and when the smoke cleared, I had missed again. Cursing, I reloaded quickly and fired just before he lined me up in his sights. The bullet struck him in the torso and he collapsed to agonized screams. The pounding boots of Sharpshooters arriving and taking up position along the ramparts had the advancing force withering under the additional fire, and the rebels retreated. The boys let out a ragged cheer at the sight, but a fresh series of crumps and flashes in the gloom cut their celebration short.

"Take cover," I ordered.

This time the cannons directed their fury at our gatehouse to the north, hurling solid iron shot into the timber at high speed. A cannon ball hit several lengths down the rampart, easily penetrating a rotted section of the palisade and pulverizing the rifleman kneeling behind it. I left Corporal Fadley and a meager crew behind to man the walls and raced headlong into Fort Conviction with the rest of the soldiers.

We reached the ruins of the gatehouse with no time to spare. The blood-slicked arms and legs of defenders protruded from the debris at unnatural angles as rebels swarmed the breach. They nearly doubled our number, but we hit them hard. I fired my rifle from the hip as I ran, discarding it as I drew my saber. A rebel charged, brandishing his rifle like a spear toward my face. I swatted the barrel away with the flat of my sword and the bayonet thrust into the midsection of an unsuspecting Sergeant Coates. The rebel heaved on the stock to free his rifle, but the Sergeant latched on, refusing to relinquish it. He lurched forward as Coates yanked on the barrel in a final act of defiance and I delivered a swift chop to the attacker's neck. Both men tumbled to the ground; one dying, the other dead.

Sergeant Coates mewled like a babe as blood pumped from his ruptured organs, the roars and shrieks of battle a rising din as my men met the enemy blow for blow – killing with rifles wielded as clubs, bayonets dripping red, knives and bare hands; punching, biting, tearing as they brawled. Movement the other side of the breach, and a rebel had his rifle trained squarely on me. I grabbed for my holstered pistol knowing I would never reach it in time. I watched him squeeze the trigger, bracing myself for the sensation of a round shredding through my chest, but the gunpowder fizzled rather than ignited. Before I could line up the shot, his right eye exploded, and a welter of gore ejected from the rear of his head.

"Cast them from the light! Consign them to the Abyss!"
came a welcome voice.

Father Fehervari, rifle in hand, led a contingent of soldiers to
relieve us. The reinforcements swung the battle in our favor and
the surviving rebels withdrew, leaving behind those too injured
to flee. I approached the priest, sheathing my sword and returning my pistol to its holster.

"Well met, Father."

"Well met Father? Is that all you have to say to me? That son
of a bitch was a ball hair's breadth from severing your mortal
thread and I put a bullet through his eye at twenty goddamn
meters," said Father Fehervari.

"That was your doing?"

"Don't be so impressed, I was aiming for his left eye," he
said with a grin.

Without another word he clapped me on the shoulder, slung
his rifle, and began to tend to the wounded, ours and the enemy.
To the former he spoke words of comfort, bolstering the spirits
of those who would endure a while longer and blessing those
who would not. To the latter he granted his own form of mercy
via a hooked dagger across the throat. I instructed the men to
construct a makeshift barricade from the detritus of the gatehouse. Next, I dispatched couriers to assess the situation around
the Fort and to locate Commisar Normann. We had unfinished
business to attend to.

Before the couriers could return a burst of rifle shots erupted
from the swamp. I rushed into cover, expecting another wave of
rebels. Instead, naked men and women, armed with flint-tipped
spears and knobby war clubs, hurtled toward us out of the
darkening swamp. They made no sound as they ran, no war cry
save the slap of their feet on the yielding soil. A pasty white substance clung to every inch of their skin from the crest of their
heads to the tips of their toes. They practically glowed in the
moonlight.

It made them ideal targets.

"MIREFOLK! MAKE READY!"

Our first volley, rash and lacking discipline, felled only a handful of the charging beasts. The ashen-skinned barbarians died in silence as they closed the distance rapidly. I bellowed out each step of the reloading procedure to my men, and they sped through in record time. Our rifles spoke with one voice, musket balls punching great craters into the ranks of the mirefolk, fouling ghostly paint with geysers of crimson. Those struck by our fusillade dropped away as the unaffected strove on. Still, they produced no sound. Before we could muster a third volley, they fell upon us.

We met their charge with a line of bayonets and swords, and the battle became a blur of blood and violence – flesh parting bone, the stink of ruptured guts. Father Fehervari rallied the men with a hymn, interspersing the traditional anthem with vulgarities as he tangled with the heathens. He slew the mirefolk with a tempo that belied his age, and that same fervor animated the men on his flanks. Howling with rage, I hacked through the aggressors, carving rents into their unprotected tissue. Two mirefolk advanced on me and I shot the farthest through the heart to even the odds before almost splitting his comrade in half on my keen blade. Paste-smeared bodies covered the ground and draped across the splintered timbers of our bulwark. It wasn't enough.

For each one we killed two more poured into the Fort, overwhelming us by sheer weight of numbers. I bawled desperately for my soldiers to close ranks, but they surrounded and isolated us before any could heed my command. I clutched tightly to my saber as several of the bastards encircled me, spears poised. So engrossed in the spears, I never saw the swing of the club that bludgeoned me into oblivion.

My faculties did not return in earnest until I found myself wading waist deep in putrid water with a cloud of famished insects harrying my every step. I whipped my head back and forth, unable to swat at the pests with my bound hands. The motion failed to deter the bugs and jostled my already throbbing head. A string of men slogged through the muck ahead of me and more prisoners, I suspected, followed behind. It was difficult to identify men by the backs of their heads, but I thought I spotted Father Fehervari as well as Commissar Normann in the gloom.

Mirefolk ranged ahead in pairs, gliding through the night like ghosts. Rebels flanked the procession with rifles and lanterns. The privileged among them poled along in rafts laden with the same cannons that had cracked open Fort Conviction like a nut. The less fortunate grunted and cursed along beside us as they trudged through the wetlands. One of the irregulars serving guard detail looked oddly familiar.

"Antony? Antony, is that you?" I whispered.

He only glanced my way for a moment, face half obscured by shadow, but that was all I required to confirm my suspicion. Private Antony Lovatt, the first member of the Sharpshooters to abandon post and flee into the swamp was not simply a deserter – he was a bloody turncoat to boot.

"Antony, where are you taking us?" I hissed.

The rebel stared ahead, ignoring my question.

"Look at me you bastard. Where are you taking us?"

A mireman appeared at my side and rammed his war club into my gut. I doubled over and vomited. After several heaves the white-painted man hooked his club under my jaw and tilted my head up. He did not speak but pressed a finger to his lips and held it there. Message received, I nodded vigorously, bouncing my aching brain around to the point I nearly vomited again.

We marched through the fetid slime for what felt like hours. Whenever a prisoner lagged behind the mirefolk or rebels beat him until his pace increased.

Torchlight suddenly materialized through the vegetation. As we drew nearer the lights, habitation became visible. Thatch-roofed huts jutted out of the bog on stilts. Tethers kept long boats floating together by the docks. Animal skins stretched out to dry over wooden frames decorated narrow walkways connecting individual huts. We halted and three women carrying torches and carved staffs left the village to meet us. They wore little to cause discomfort in the humidity aside from strips of cured hide and intricate blue designs inked across their pale skin. They ignored the rebels entirely and spoke what I assumed to be swamp tongue to the mirefolk warriors who maintained their silence throughout the discussion, communicating solely through hand gestures.

Two of the three women broke away from the conversation and sauntered down the line of prisoners. They poked and prodded each of us in turn, trailing long sharpened nails down skin slick with sweat and riddled with bug bites. Before they reached me the third woman called them back to her side. They exchanged words, and the procession was moving again, though not for long this time. We passed under stilted huts while children called down to us from the aerial bridges in mocking tones. More and more mirefolk congregated around us on the march through to the village center.

We climbed out of the filth and up the shore of the island at the heart of the settlement, where a colossal bonfire raged. More blue-inked women cavorted around the crackling inferno, so close I marveled that their hair did not catch flame and their skin blister from the heat, while a pair of tall silhouettes wearing horned masks honed wickedly curved knives.

"Are the mirefolk cannibals?" whispered one captive over his shoulder to the man walking in front of me.

"Not according to the Royal Anthropological Society," the man whispered in reply.

"Oh feck, that seals it then. It's a bloody barbeque for sure," said the first man loud enough to earn a rifle stock to the side of the head.

A great saurian idol towered over the fire pit. Why the mirefolk had constructed a two-story alligator statue baffled me, but nothing confounded me worse than the question of where they found such large bones to lash together. But it was the pair of shadowed forms in the midst of the dancing that turned my blood to ice. Not human.

They were too tall, too lean. The slender fingers with which they wielded the knives had extra joints, and matted fur clung to their bodies. One of the spindly silhouettes directed its gaze our way and I saw the tapered beak and crown of antlers I presumed to be a mask was indeed a face. The sweat coating my skin felt like frost and I began to shiver uncontrollably. My breath caught in my throat, and hot piss ran down my leg. I clenched my teeth together to prevent them from chattering, as a murmur travelled down the line as my men beheld the creatures.

A kick from behind buckled my knees and sent me sprawling in the soil. I spit the mud from my mouth as a pair of hands hauled me to my knees. To my left and right white-painted warriors coerced the other prisoners into kneeling before the blaze. Father Fehervari was positioned adjacent to me and I took comfort in his presence.

"What are they?" I whispered to him.

"Demons," he said with casual certainty. "Though if I'm correct the mirefolk are referring to them as 'stewards'."

"You speak swamp tongue?"

"Not specifically but a related dialect," he replied.

A warrior strolled by, dragging the butt of his spear through the dirt, and I held my tongue until he passed. "Have you seen anything like them before?"

"Not in my wildest nightmares," Father Fehervari whispered.

One of the stewards directed a willowy, claw-tipped digit at one of the kneeling captives further down the line and two inked women went to fetch him. He began to struggle, the men nearest him doing likewise, unwilling to give up their comrade without a fight. The mirefolk warriors pummeled them all into submission and dragged the chosen one, now limp, up to the demons. One of the inhuman creatures plucked the prisoner off the ground and held him up by his ankles with unholy ease while the other hunched over to examine him. A mirewoman stepped forward and addressed the congregation. She spoke forcibly, punctuating her words with precise gesticulations.

"What is she saying?" I asked Father Fehervari. "Are they going to cook and eat us?"

He sighed. "No, I don't believe so. From what I can interpret, the stewards intend to reanimate their god 'Potabek' by offering living flesh to grant him new life."

"Oh, feck."

The stewards turned, eyes alight as they licked blackened lips with blackened tongues. Then one slid its blade through their captor's flesh. I squeezed my eyes shut as the demons butchered the soldier, my heart lurching with every fresh shriek. After a minute I found myself hoping his heart would fail or his lungs would collapse and end the interminable screeching, but it carried on and on and on. Worse than the anguished squeals, I think, was the wet sound of their blades parting flesh.

It wasn't until the stewards cackled that I opened my eyes to find the soldier's remarkably intact skin draped over the saurian idol. Flesh and innards dripped from the structure – none of the man's remains had gone to waste.

Another laugh, and I looked back to find a demon's extended finger hovering over me, and I prayed harder in that instant than ever in my life that they choose anyone else but me. My prayers were fulfilled. The demon's finger halted on Father Fehervari. Relief washed over me, followed by crippling shame. Father Fehervari nodded once, stood of his own volition, and strode forward with squared shoulders and raised chin.

"No," I howled, lurching forward only to be yanked back into line.

"Courage and faith men. Courage and faith," he called out as the stewards snatched him up, securing him to the altar. "The Lord prepares a place of honor for his martyrs this night."

"No," I yelled as they made long, calculated incisions at Father Fehervari's wrists and ankles, prayer spitting between the man's gritted teeth.

I lost my damn mind and lunged to my feet, bowling over an unsuspecting warrior. Behind me I heard other captives echoing my cry and engaging the guards as best they could with their hands bound behind their backs.

I locked eyes with Father Fehervari as a blade split him from neck to sternum, and as the warrior I had knocked over got back on his feet, I brought my forehead down on his nose like a war club. The cartilage crunched, exploding in a welter of blood, but he dragged me down into the mud with him.

He beat me until a mire witch interceded. Dragged to my knees, I spat blood, cursing at my captors as they held my head, forcing me to watch the desecration of my friend and mentor. They peeled back the flesh from his limbs in slow, deliberate motions. Each tear summoned a new shriek from Father Fehevari, who locked eyes with me once more. He gave me a smile that was more grimace as the demons began to shuck him from his skin.

I surged to my feet, my roar drowning out Father Fehevari's shriek as I drove my shoulder into the warrior, lifting him off his feet. The man lay into me with kicks and punches; the witch took her time before intervening. Tears mingled with blood, sweat, and snot upon my swelling cheeks. The inked woman spoke a string of syllables and the warrior hoisted me to my feet and shoved me into motion. Had I any fluid left in my bladder I am sure I would have pissed myself all over again, but instead of guiding me up to the demons and their gleaming blades, the warrior pushed me away from the fire, down the shore, past two dozen of kneeling comrades, through the press of villagers, before slogging out into the shallows.

Every time I cast a look over my shoulder, I received another shove, but I was not the only Sharpshooter being escorted back toward the huts. Mire witches selected a few men who seemed to be causing the most grief and rebel irregulars dragged them off to join us.

"We will save you for last," taunted the blue-inked woman in heavily-accented-but otherwise-perfect Imperial, "so that you may have our undivided attention."

Father Fehervari's cries followed me, each one a phantom knife paring away at my soul.

We arrived at a cluster of moored rafts bearing cannons and additional rebel equipment. Prodded with the butt of a spear, I managed to scale the dock without use of arms or hands. The mireman continued jabbing me until I shuffled up the walkway to a round hut.

The hovel was empty apart from some baskets and hides. I sat on the floor without further prompt and he took up post along the wall. I locked eyes with Corporal Fadley and Doc Dunbarr as they entered. Fury and hatred smoldered in the pits of their eyes.

Then Commissar Normann stepped through the door, the turncoat Antony Lovatt at his back. I stifled a laugh at the twist of irony. Lord knows there was little else to find amusing about our situation. Lovatt propelled the Commissar to the floor and made to leave as Father Fehervari's screams cut off abruptly.

My choler boiled over. "Was it worth it? Was it worth it, you scum-sucking bastard?" I spat at Lovatt.

His demeanor hardened but he remained immobile.

"What did they pay you to spread your legs like a common whore?" I snarled.

He stalked over and delivered a right hook to my head, knocking me sideways.

"Enough," barked a burly man I pegged for a rebel officer. "The priestess wants them unsullied for the offering."

"He had it coming, sir," Lovatt growled.

"I don't give an adder's arse. He'll be dead before sunrise anyway."

Lovatt lifted me by my bound hands, nearly dislocating my shoulders in the process. My mouth moved to form a few choice expletives, but the words died in my throat when I felt something hard and sharp pressed into my palm. A knapped stone belonging to a spear head or similar cutting tool. My fingers closed around it instinctively. Lovatt cuffed me once more for good measure and vacated the hut without another word. I expected the rebel officer to storm over and confiscate the spear head from me, but he proved oblivious, stroking his beard and then addressing the lone mireman standing by the wall.

"Come on, let's rejoin the festivities," he said. "No need for you to miss the rebirth of your god, on account of these

Imperial lapdogs. I'll leave behind some of my boys to guard the prisoners."

Whether or not the warrior understood the words he must have perceived their intent because he followed the officer out of the hovel. I began sawing at the rope lashed around my wrists. The angle was poor, and I had a limited range of motion, but I cut at the cord until my fingers cramped. Then I cut some more. Through the insubstantial walls I listened to the officer directing his men to keep an eye on us. I restrained the rate of cutting but did not cease entirely as a pair of rebels entered the hut, the screams of another sacrifice fouling the air.

With wary eyes scrutinizing us I made slow progress. Half an hour passed. One of the rebel's eyes grew heavy while the other fidgeted incessantly. The stewards made bloody offerings of five more of my men based on the screams before I finally felt the ties give way. The desire to stretch my arms nearly overwhelmed my sense of self-preservation as I waited for an opening.

It came as the sacrifice of another Sharpshooter commenced.

"What's wrong with you? Why won't you stop squirming?" asked the tired rebel of his companion.

"My guts are tearing me up," said the fidgeting rebel.

"That's what you get for eating their fucking stew. I told you that meat floating around in there could be anything," said the first.

"I need to relieve myself. Can you cope without me for a minute?"

They both turned and assessed us.

"Go ahead, better that than messing your trousers in here for me to smell," said the tired man.

"I owe you one. Andrei and Dav should be nearby. Just give them a holler if you need anything."

"Yeah, yeah, just be quick about it."

His companion bolted out the doorway. The lone guard made a show of shaking off the drowsiness, but he did not remain attentive for long. Each time he blinked his eyes stayed shut for longer and longer. It was only for fractions of a second, but I knew I would not get a better opportunity to act. I anticipated the next blink and when his eyelids began to descend, I launched from the floor and brought my hands around. I covered the distance between us in the time it took for his eyes to flutter back open. Sidestepping the wavering bayonet, I jammed my left hand between the hammer and the musket's frizzen, gouging the area between my index finger and thumb but preventing the rebel from firing it. As he opened his mouth to shout a warning, I rammed the spear head into his throat.

I eased him to the floor when his legs stopped twitching and rummaged through his kit, trading the blood-slick spear head for a proper knife. I sliced through Corporal Fadley's binding first.

"Grab the musket and watch the door."

"Wha' are we goin' to do?" asked Doc Dunbarr as I cut his binding next.

"Free the Commissar, Doc," I said, ignoring his question and handing him the knife. I shuffled along the wall over to Fadley.

"How long do we have?" I asked.

"He's still squatting with his pants around his ankles," Fadley responded.

"Any sign of the patrol?" I asked.

"Nothing."

I popped my head out the portal. The mirefolk had left few torches unattended back in the village but the bonfire flared bright in the distance, casting enough light to survey our surroundings, my gaze falling to the floating rafts tied to the dock and the contents they held. A smile split my face for the first time that night. A leathery hand clapped me on the shoulder and I turned to see Commissar Normann offering me the rebel's knife. I shook my head, displaying my tattered hands.

"He's finishing up," said Fadley. "We need to move."

I led the three of them out of the hovel and down the walkway. We moved as quietly as we could but every creak of the planks under our feet sounded like a musket going off to my ears. We reached the dock and found one of the missing patrolmen leaning against a post, puffing on a pipe and observing the ritual from afar. Normann acted with the startling speed that had served him so well hunting down deserters, driving the knife through the bottom of the smoking man's jaw and into his brain.

"I see the lantern, he's heading back," whispered Fadley.

"That one," I said, pointing to one of the wider, cannon-laden rafts secured to the jetty.

We climbed into the boat, cautious not to upset the balance, and once we were all aboard, I unmoored us. I picked up a long oar and directed us away from the dock. Commissar Normann and Doc Dunbarr settled in alongside the cannon at the bow while at the stern, Corporal Fadley continued to track the second guard down the barrel of his musket.

"Get that thing loaded," I hissed to Normann and Dunbar.

The raft skimmed across the black water toward the heathens and their idol. The mirefolk appeared no less demonic than the stewards by the hellish luminescence of the bonfire. We edged closer with each sweep of the oar and I worried the cannon would not be loaded in time. The doctor and the political officer fumbled around in the dark, hurrying to prepare the gun to fire.

"He's almost to the hut," warned Fadley, rifle at the shoulder.

"Is the cannon loaded?" I asked my improvised gunnery crew.

"Aye," said Doc.

"Aim for the idol," I told them.

"We'll never hit it from this distance," Commissar Normann sneered.

"I will get us as close as I can. Just be ready to fire," I spat back.

"He's found his dead mate," said Fadley. "And there's the other patrolman."

Outside the hut the second guard began shouting to raise the alarm. A head or two at the fringe of the crowd perked up at the bellowing but the wails of the stewards' latest victim provided several seconds more cover.

"Now," I said.

"We're still too far," Normann snapped.

"They've spotted us," said Fadley.

Two muskets cracked from back at the village. Both shots flew wide, splashing into the water meters away. Fadley's own musket replied and he immediately set to reloading. The shots alerted the congregation who stood confused Unlike the rebel irregulars who reacted with experience, racing to secure the perimeter but still unable to determine the source of the disruption. The stewards paused midway through shucking the skin from their offering and looked out into the swamp. Right at us. They opened their beaks and emitted a screech so dreadful it muted the din of the swamp. For the span of a single heartbeat all was still, all was silent.

The idol twitched. Twitched again. Then with a creak of bones old and new, its shoulders rose as it shrugged into its new skin. Gore ran in rivulets from the flesh of what had been my company and dripped from the bone framework. It lifted its malformed head, eyeing those near before snapping luminous eyes to the raft.

"Oh, feck…"

It opened its maw, and darkness deeper than anything I had ever seen swirled behind teeth of sharpened bone. It spewed a hiss that bent nearby trees, snapping one beneath fetid breath that washed like sewerage across the water.

Commissar Normann sprung from the raft, disappearing beneath the water as one of the stewards charged, splashing toward us, blade raised.

"Now! Fire now!" I roared, and the cannon added its voice to my own.

The might of the gun's discharge capsized the small raft and spilled us out. Foul water rushed up my nose and down my throat. I could not see in the inky blackness to judge up from down. I thrashed my arms about, colliding with sinking crates of supplies borne by the boat. I kicked out and my bare feet finally touched the muddy ground. I corrected my orientation and surfaced to find the world had descended into chaos.

The cannon ball had missed the idol entirely, the cast iron projectile tearing through a few rows of spectators before striking the bonfire and pitching blazing lumber across the island. A burning branch, thick as a man, jutted from idol's shoulder as it roared.

Captives splashed into the swamp, scattering in every direction. Mirefolk warriors chased after them while rebels fired their muskets into the swamp indiscriminately, hitting panicked villagers more often than not.

I turned to a shriek, and the steward closed in on me, but as it raised its blade, water erupted in front of the demon, and its shriek was met by the hate-fueled roar and glinting knife of Commissar Normann. The big man ducked the first swing, then drove his shoulder up into the steward, the knife punching fast – once, twice, three times into the thing before the two went under, thrashing.

Upon the island, the idol hissed again, snatching up a rebel and stuffing the still-screaming man into its jaws. I made for shore, keeping low in the water as it feasted upon a mire witch next – she offered no resistance, a beatific smile on her face as she was devoured.

As I pulled myself onto land, Fadley floated past, eyes unseeing, but it was Doc Dunbar I watched charge the idol, hair alight as he drove a burning piece of wood deep between the saurian's legs. The doc was still laughing as the idol tore him in two.

The saurian stomped its pain and rage, squashing mirefolk and rebel alike as it hissed, dropping to its knees.

I took one last look as I crept from the water, and we locked eyes, the false-god and me. In those depths raged eternity, of gods cloaked in the skin of men, children's hearts beating in their chests as humanity was sacrificed on their endless altars.

I blinked and it was gone – both the promise of mankind's annihilation and the false-god who wore the face of my priest.

FAILURE TO EXTRACT

Kevin Wetmore

Strayer had never seen anything blacker than the entrance to the tunnel. Even out in the bush with only starlight above, the tunnel's mouth looked like a deep and dark void. If he focused, however, and looked all the way into the blackness, he could see the slight flickering of what must be a small fire hidden around the corner, down a dozen yards.

Shit.

Strayer was in his third month of a Long Range Reconnaissance Patrol. He was weary and wary. In front of this bunker, they had achieved their goal and having found the enemy they had to engage. He said a quick prayer and held his M16 a little closer.

Strayer had been in country for almost a year. He had not been drafted though. His father fought at Guadalcanal, and his grandfather had been in the Connecticut Horse Guard between the wars. This sense of duty when there was conflict carried on down the line to a distant great-great-grandfather who fought the Pequots in King Philips' War. His was not a career military family, but a fight-when-called-to family. So, just after finishing his divinity degree, he found himself a chaplain in the infantry and staring into a bunker late at night on a mountain somewhere north of the A Shau Valley.

Sarge motioned for everyone except Jacobs to pull back. One hundred yards from the cave he whispered the plan.

"All right, here's how this is going down. Holquist, you go in. Anything or anyone even looks at you cross-eyed, you fill them with lots of holes."

Holquist moved his Stevens model 77E an inch or two in front of his chest. "Roger that. Locked and loaded."

"Lopez, you stay here with Mamacita. Anyone tries to come up the backdoor, you teach them the fear of God."

Lopez, who rarely spoke, just kissed The Gun and nodded. The M-60 looked like a toy in his giant hands, but when he opened up with it ten rounds found their target every second. Lopez loved The Gun as much as he loved his own mother, naming it 'Mamacita'. Right before going into a fire fight, he'd kiss it, put his Virgin of Guadalupe medallion in his mouth, and then unleash hell.

"Reverend, Quinn, you're with me. We give Holquist a twenty count and then follow."

Strayer and Quinn both nodded. Fresh magazines were quickly and quietly clicked home. They moved forward silently, safeties off. Strayer was ready for anything but knew nothing about what they might find in there. As they crept closer to the cave entrance, Strayer swore that it grew darker. No, not darker – it seemed to swallow the light. Though they were in the jungle, and even at night the humidity was off the charts, he shivered, a chill running down his spine. This wasn't pre-fight jitters or adrenaline. Something about this set up was just wrong.

Nine weeks earlier Strayer stood at attention in a wooden building outside Saigon. A full bird colonel stared at him, assessing him silently.

"You're not the average grunt, are you, son?"

"No sir."

The colonel looked him up and down.

"I've read your jacket, Strayer. Yale man, degrees in anthropology and divinity. What the hell you doing in the 'Nam, son?"

"My family has always served when the country has needed us, sir."

"That so?"

"Sir."

"I mean you're a chaplain, but you also have commendations for combat."

"Guess I know how to shoot, sir."

The colonel laughed and flipped open the file on his desk. He wiped his neck with a handkerchief, already sweat-soaked before the full heat of the day had even begun.

"Awards for marksmanship from the goddamn Boy Scouts, your high school rifle club, basic training – hell, you're the best shot in your platoon and you're the goddamn fucking chaplain! You have a deadeye, son. Never knew a preacher who could take out a man at a thousand yards with one bullet."

"Different skill sets, sir."

"That right, Padre?"

"Reverend."

The colonel looked up. "Excuse me?"

"Not Padre, sir. I'm not Catholic. I'm Presbyterian, so technically my title is Reverend.'"

The colonel grunted and puffed on his cigar, then waved the smoke around him and mumbled something about it being the only goddamn way to drive off the mosquitos. He then looked down at the file again before speaking. "Says here you speak the language."

"Picked up some of the local lingo while in country, sir. Not really fluent. Just have an ear for languages."

A grunt in response. "Your background – you know about religion? Not just yours – theirs?"

"I guess, sir."

"Do you believe in the devil?"

Strayer broke attention and looked right at the colonel. The question had come from so far left of field that he wondered if he had heard it correctly. "Excuse me, sir?"

"It's a simple question, son. Do you believe in the devil?"

"Well…" he paused. "The devil certainly appears in scripture and our Lord was tempted by him, but is there a personification of evil that is responsible for all evil in the world? Well, it's a little more—"

"That's what I'm talking about," the colonel snapped. He stood and came around the desk as if to examine Strayer. "Do you believe in evil?"

"Permission to speak freely, sir?"

"Granted."

"I've been in country for almost nine months. I've seen evil. Lots of it. I don't think we need a fallen angel to explain it, though."

"What about something else?"

"Sir?"

"What if it's not the devil? What about demons? Monsters?"

"Are you pulling my leg, sir?"

"No, Corporal, I'm not pulling your goddamn leg! Now answer the goddamn question! Do you believe in supernatural evil?"

"Sir! I do, but I'm skeptical that everything that goes bump in the night is a ghostie."

The colonel stared at him, then something shifted in his eyes, a decision made. "Good. I'm reassigning you to a new unit. You're going in the field, on a lurp.

Strayer started at that. Why would a long range reconnaissance patrol need a chaplain, even one good with a gun?

"After we took Signal Hill we thought things would get better. But there is some dinky dau shit going down in the A Shau valley and I am putting together a lurp to check it out and put a stop to it. Padre, you're my man."

Strayer didn't bother correcting him again. "May I ask the colonel what kind of dinky dau shit, sir?"

"Lurps vanishing without a trace, boys drowning in one inch of water, soldiers going insane overnight and talking shit about a fire speaking to them."

"Combat fatigue?"

"No. This is not the usual stuff, Corporal."

For no reason he could explain, Strayer suddenly felt like a spider was walking slowly up his spine. When he was younger his mother told him that meant someone had just walked on his grave. He pushed the thought away; this shit was already weird enough.

"Does... does the colonel think there are monsters in the A Shau valley, sir?"

"No, I sure as hell do not think there are monsters, soldier! But morale is low, GIs are scared, and I've heard enough scuttlebutt that I think sending a preacher out with a lurp will calm folks down. Then we can get back to the business of stomping Charlie a new mud hole. You get out there and say a prayer, bless the bush, do an exorcism on the goddamn NVA, I don't care what. Just do your thing. You are to report to your new unit at 0600 hours tomorrow. Be a good chaplain, and give me reason to tell the troops that *you* took care of the problem. Dismissed."

Without a word, the colonel returned to his seat, Strayer already forgotten as the next issue on the desk became the man's focus.

As always in his life, Strayer found himself once again the odd man out. The rest of the unit had gone through 5th Special Forces school in Nha Trang. Lopez, Quinn, Holquist, Jacobs and Sarge were all lurp veterans with multiple tours. He was a chaplain with a gift for hitting the center of the target almost every time. Now they were going out into A Shau, gathering information but also with the purpose of, apparently, finding talking fires.

That's how Corporal Strayer found himself late at night in the A Shau valley in front of the blackest cave mouth he had ever seen with less than a month left in country.

Sarge motioned them forward. Holquist took point, with Strayer, Quinn and Sarge following as quiet as possible. Within ten minutes they were back looking at the cave mouth. Jacob, who had been left guarding the entrance, merely nodded. He lay in the bush with the muzzle of his shotgun pointed in the direction of the cave.

With a few quick hand signals from Sarge, Holquist started forward, silent like a jungle snake. After a twenty count, the others followed. Holquist was already in the cave, invisible to his companions.

They had just arrived at the cave mouth when they heard the Stevens go off. They hurried ahead as fast as the low ceiling would allow and stopped just short of the turn. This far in the flickering firelight was clearly visible.

Sarge gestured, and he and Quinn crept forward as Strayer watched their six, keeping his focus on what was happening in front but making sure nobody was sneaking up from behind.

After a moment Sarge whispered, "Reverend, I think we require your services."

Quinn came back around the corner and swapped places with Strayer, who kept his M-16 up as he edged forward and confronted the scene.

The small tunnel opened into a larger room, one with boxes and bags and a small fire in the center.

Next to the fire were the remains of an NVA soldier and another Vietnamese man in black peasant garb. Both had been shredded by the shotgun blast. The boxes and wall behind them were spattered with blood and covered with bits of bone, hair, and brain. The air smelled of copper and gunpowder. A single plastic shell lay on the ground between Holquist and the fire. He still held his Stevens up, aiming at something beyond the flames. Strayer turned and squinted, finally seeing who Holquist had in his sight.

On the other side of the fire calmly sat an old man. He appeared unfazed by the shotgun blast in the tight quarters. As soon as Strayer focused on him the old man's eyes brightened. A look of expectation crossed his face.

"Services as a clergyman or as a translator?" Strayer asked Sarge without taking his eyes off the old man.

The old man spoke before Sarge could reply, "Tại sao bạn ở đây? Bởi vì những người bị đốt cháy hoặc những người bị chết đuối?"

"The fuck's he saying?" Sarge barked.

"He's asking why we're here. I only understand some of the words. Something like are we here because people burned, or because people drowned?"

"Ask him what the fuck he knows about it."

Strayer thought for a moment and spoke, "Bạn có biết về những người bị đốt cháy và những người bị chết đuối?"

The old man smiled. "Con Hoa và Bá Thủy đã ở cùng họ. Bây giờ họ sẽ ở bên bạn. Người của bạn đã thả napalm trên các làng của tôi. Tôi nghĩ rằng bây giờ bạn sẽ biết những gì nó là để có lửa đuổi theo bạn."

Strayer gestured at him to slow down for a moment. He rolled the words around in his head, searching for their meaning. "He says Ba Thuy and Con Hoa have been with them. That they will be with us now. He said something about how we used napalm on them, so now we will have fire chase us."

"Who the fuck are Ba Thuy and Con Hoa? These guys?" Sarge pointed to the bodies opposite the old man.

The old man just smiled. The only sound was the snap and crackling of fire. Somehow that was worse than the earlier firefight. Strayer felt the weight of something or someone else in the cave with them.

"No, Sarge," said Strayer, glancing around to confirm no one lurked in the shadows. "Ba Thuy is a water goddess who causes noi."

"Noise?" Sarge stared at the old man with the eyes of a rattlesnake.

"Not noise. Noi. It's a traditional curse. It makes people push their own heads down in water so they drown even in very shallow amounts."

"He expects us to believe a goddess has been killing American soldiers? Commies don't believe in gods, Strayer. What's the other thing?"

"Con Hoa? I think they're the ghosts of people who burned to death. They make other people set themselves on fire."

All three soldiers fell silent, staring at the old man, who in turn stared into the fire. The flames surged but could not chase the shadows from the cave. Rather, the flames and shadows danced together, never illuminating the dark spaces. Strayer suddenly felt very vulnerable. He noticed the others also seemed on edge. He wanted to attribute it to the claustrophobia, to the VC and NVA in the cave, but he knew this was something else.

"Chẳng bao lâu," the old man whispered.

163

The shadows crept closer. The flames let them.

"What does that mean?" asked Sarge.

Strayer stared at the man staring ever deeper into the flames. Strayers mouth was dry, almost too dry.

"Soon," he managed to croak out.

"Soon? What's fucking soon? He thinks he can scare us? Because I don't think fire ghosts or water goddesses are going to fuck with us." Sarge pointed at the two bodies. "Because that is an NVA soldier wearing a special operations patch, and that looks like a goddamn PLAF soldier missing a head, thank you for that, Corporal Holquist. Now why is our friend here sitting down with an NVA commando and a Viet Cong soldier in a room full of supplies? Please ask our friend here."

Strayer asked. The old man answered.

"He says they came to him. They wanted his help."

Sarge smiled grimly. "And why would the NVA and Charlie need ole grandpa here?"

"He says he is a 'Ong Thay Phap'?"

"And what the fuck is that?"

"I'm not sure. Hang on." Strayer asked the old man a series of quick questions, which the old man answered more slowly, never once taking his eyes off the fire. With each exchange, Strayer grew more hesitant. It wasn't the language, but what he was being told. "Near as I can guess, Sarge, it's a kind of sorcerer."

"Like a witch doctor?"

"Yeah."

"How do you say 'bullshit' in Vietnamese?"

"Nhảm nhí."

"Hey, grandpa! Nhảm nhí. I don't give a fuck if you're a witch doctor, a werewolf, or the fucking Wizard of Oz. What is all this, and who are they?" He pointed at the corpses again.

The old man looked at Sarge, then back into the flames.

"Chẳng bao lâu," he whispered again.

"Nhảm nhí, grandpa. What's this stuff?" He indicated the boxes behind the old man and the dead men.

Strayer asked. The old man answered.

"Supplies – food and medicine for the villages napalmed just south of here."

Holquist spoke up. "He talking about Khe Sanh?"

Strayer shook his head. "I don't know. He just said 'his' villages. The NVA guy and Charlie here brought this stuff to buy his services."

"And what services were those?" Sarge said, his voice quiet and dangerous now.

"Apparently he can summon Ba Thuy and Con Hoa."

"Gods and ghosts," said Sarge. A statement, not a question.

"Yes," said Strayer.

"Gentlemen, it seems this is the one we have been sent to find."

Knowing what was coming, Strayer paused. "Yes, sir. This would appear to be the one the colonel wanted us to find."

Sarge pulled the trigger on his M-16. The old man flew backwards as the bullet struck him in the chest, and he slumped against the boxes.

"No telling what's booby trapped around here and no time to figure it out. Let's drop some willie pete and start the skedaddle back to daddy to tell him we done good. Di di mau."

Strayer started to follow Sarge out of the cave as Holquist pulled two white phosphorus grenades from his bandolier. He looked back at the old man who, amazingly, was not dead yet. He smiled at Strayer through bloody, black teeth. "Chẳng bao lâu," and then in English, "Con Hoa, for you."

Strayer suppressed a shiver and turned, following Sarge and Quinn.

"Fire in the hole," Holquist yelled, barreling out of the cave just as fire and smoke started to pour from the opening. They kept moving, no longer bothering to stay quiet until they caught up to where Jacobs waited.

"Sarge?" Jacobs asked.

Sarge looked back at the cave as smoke continued to pour out, the glow slowly dying.

"Problem taken care of. Jacobs, call in some snake and nape to make sure this area is very fucking off limits to whatever dinky dau shit they thought they were doing."

Jacobs looked at the four men standing in front of him. "How dinky dau?"

"Sarge wasted a witch doctor," Quinn said, "and Holquist brought an NVA and a VC closer to Buddha."

"Okay," Jacobs said, not sure if he was being made fun of. He got on the radio and called in the strike request. "Snake and nape coming here at first light, Sarge."

"Good. Should make sure whatever Charlie had been planning here is no longer a concern—"

Mamacita open up on full. Ten rounds a second streaming off into the bush. They dropped low.

"Fuck, Lopez! Move!" Sarge led the way, the soldiers running back to the rear position where Lopez had been watching the back door.

The Gun cut out.

Silence screamed across the jungle.

They found Lopez lying against a tree, his uniform charred and smoking. The Gun lay a yard from his feet. As they neared, the skin on Lopez's face and hands had been burned, and some of his hair under his helmet was more than a little singed. As they stood watching, blisters began to form on the man's hands and face. The smell of burnt flesh bit strong. The terror in Lopez's eyes was obvious.

Quinn, Holquist and Jacobs immediately took up defensive positions while Sarge and Strayer tended to the giant man.

"What was it? Where are they?" whispered Sarge.

Lopez stared at him.

"Who were you firing at?"

Lopez looked off into the darkness of the jungle, and simply said, "Them. They came from out of the jungle."

"Them? How many? Did you get them all?"

Lopez looked at him, terror in his eyes. "I didn't hit one."

"Fuck, stay alert," Sarge hissed. "Light up anything that

moves out there, boys. We got us some hostiles." The men all drew in a little tighter.

Sarge turned back to Lopez and put his hands on either side of the man's head. "What happened here, soldier?"

Lopez was panting, terrified, but also like it hurt to breathe. The burns on Lopez's arms and face turned from red to white with black edges. Almost as if his skin was still being burned. The smell of the burnt flesh, hair and clothing filled Strayers nostrils. He tried to ignore it but heard Holquist quietly retching behind him.

"Lopez!" Sarge barked, "Focus up, soldier."

Lopez looked at Sarge. "Mamacita did nothing."

"What?"

It clearly hurt Lopez to speak, but in his terror there was also a kind of confusion.

"Mamacita didn't hurt it. Why?"

He looked off into the jungle. "The flame."

"What flame? Lopez! Stay with me!"

He forced Lopez to focus back on him.

"No." The skin around his mouth began to split, and pus oozed out as he spoke. "A five-foot-tall flame. It was fucking walking towards me!"

"Okay, Lopez. I don't know what happened, but you're shell-shocked."

Lopez gripped Sarge's arms. Some of the skin on his fingers began to slough off. "No! It was a flame. It was moving towards me. I shot at it and it kept coming. It spoke to me! 'Soon', it said. Then the flames went away, and it was an old man. 'Now', he said, and then there were all these children. They were naked and on fire. The old man smiled at them, and they all ran and grabbed me. Mamacita told them not to come, but they ignored her. Everywhere they touched caught on fire. So, I threw myself on the ground and rolled around to get rid of the flames.."

Strayer looked up from examining Lopez's body, disbelief in his eyes. "Some of these burns are pretty bad, Sarge. But look at this one."

There was a burn mark on Lopez's arm. The red and black outline of a child's hand was clear. The center of the burn was streaked with white and black as the flesh continued to crisp.

Sarge straightened up, his eyes moving back and forth across the jungle. "I don't know what the fuck is going on here, but we are making a beeline for the evac zone for an extraction. Jacobs, call it in."

"The fuck is going on, Sarge?" Panic obvious in Jacobs' voice.

"Keep your shit together, Jacobs. Keep it together all of you! Stay focused."

"Roger that," said Holquist, but he was scanning the jungle incessantly. Everyone gripped their weapons a little tighter.

"I want a bird there to get us the fuck out of here. Lopez, I don't care what the fuck happened to you. What I need to know is can you walk?"

Strayer helped Lopez up, and the man tested his feet. He looked badly hurt.

Lopez nodded and mumbled, "Someone will have to carry Mamacita."

"Roger that. Quinn, you get the honors. All right, gents, look alive. Change in plans. We are heading back the way we came in. We have an extraction point that is supposedly free of things that want to kill us about ten clicks from here. We know the jungle behind us 'cause we just came through it. I don't know what lies down the planned evac route, but whatever the fuck is going on here, I want us gone before it comes back. We need to be there at first light. We move as fast as Lopez will let us. Move out."

They started down the trail, Holquist on point, the rest back about a dozen feet, guarding Lopez like a treasure they were afraid Charlie might try to steal.

Lopez stumbled through the bush, but Strayer kept a hand on him to keep him steady. Lopez's eyes were unfocused, and he moved like a marionette. He was shivering and stumbling. Fear, maybe, but Strayer knew the burns had probably started Lopez down the path to hypovolemia and hypothermia. Strayer hoped they'd get him all the way to the evac point, but Lopez was fading.

They had been moving down the mountain for about fifteen minutes when Holquist stopped and raised a hand. He peered into the bush, then sank down. The others followed. Strayer helped Lopez get low. He tried to hand the soldier a .45.

"Just in case," Strayer murmured. Lopez couldn't close his fingers around the weapon, and Strayer put it back in his belt.

In silence they waited. Only the sounds of the jungle met them – animals, birds, a water flowing nearby. They waited. And waited. Nothing from Holquist. Sarge motioned for them to stay in place while he crawled ahead. He moved through the bush towards where Holquist was, and after a minute they heard a quiet "Shit." Sarge called them forward.

Holquist was face down in a stream coming down the mountain. They ran forward. Sarge had pulled him out of the water and started mouth to mouth and CPR. Strayer moved to support while the others stood guard over them. Quinn, Jacobs and Strayer all exchanged glances. Quinn was starting to panic, eyes darting. Jacobs kept turning in a circle after that, looking for who or what did this to Holquist. The only sound was Sarge trying to breath for Holquist and the stream flowing on. Moonlight reflected off the stream, creating a glow around them.

"What the fuck, man? What the fuck is going on?" Quinn yelped.

"He tripped. Must have hit his head," snapped Sarge as Strayer took over CPR.

"It's that old man," muttered Jacobs.

"Stow that, soldier! I don't want to hear that talk. The next man to go all heebie jeebie on me is going to regret it."

Strayer fell back from Holquist, exhausted – it was clear the man was gone.

"Fuck, man," said Quinn.

Strayer wiped his face with a bandana and looked up at Sarge. "He drowned in six inches of water, Sarge. He didn't hit his head. He put it down into six inches of water and held it there."

"Time to move, Reverend."

"Can't leave him here, Sarge," began Jacobs.

"You gonna carry him, Jacobs?"

The men stood staring at Holquist.

"Y'all knew the rules when we set out," said Sarge. "Get fucking moving. Jacobs, grab his effects for his family. Lopez, the Stevens is yours now."

Lopez looked down at his devastated hands and held out his blackened fingers.

Softening, Sarge looked at his men. "It was an accident. He was one of us. But he's gone and we are in hostile territory. Grab his stuff – don't leave anything for the gooks."

The men took the gear from their fallen comrade begrudgingly, as if they were robbing a grave.

When they were done, Sarge looked at Strayer. "Reverend, a few words."

Strayer bowed his head and closed his eyes, clutching the M16 tightly. "Lord, we commend our friend and fallen comrade James Holquist to your hands. He was a good friend and a good soldier, and he deserved a better end than this. May he find peace and rest in your bosom. Amen."

Sarge nodded. "Jacobs, take point."

The men started through the bush again, and Strayer quickened his pace and caught up to Sarge.

"Don't," said Sarge.

"Got to admit, it is a hell of a coincidence."

"Don't have to admit shit, Reverend. And lower your voice, Charlie will hear you. Stow your crap and keep moving."

"The men are starting to panic, Sarge."

"The men are professional soldiers and will do their job. Now fucking do yours, Reverend."

They hit the valley floor and could move a little faster now, although Lopez was starting to slow.

"Sarge, Lopez is badly burned. He needs water and rest. Let's a least catch ten."

Sarge looked at Lopez, nodded. "Ten."

The men dropped and opened their canteens. Strayer held

out his. "Lopez – have a drink, man. You need water. Let me take a look at those burns."

Lopez took the canteen with both hands, holding it like a child, but didn't drink. He stared off into the jungle as Strayer conducted his examination. Lopez was covered in second and third-degree burns. They looked far worse than when he had first examined him. Anyone else, thought Strayer, and they would have died of these wound a mile ago.

For the second time in an hour he said a prayer for a comrade, this one silent.

Jacob's voice rose in panic. "The fuck is that, Sarge?"

Jacobs was pointing his M-16 at an old man standing in the bush twenty yards off who was staring at them... and smiling. Quinn let out a shriek and began firing, the bullets going nowhere near the old man.

Sarge raised his M-16 and fired.

Jacobs also opened up, and when he saw the leaves to the left of the old man take hits, he adjusted his aim and pulled the trigger. It jammed.

Sarge kept firing wildly at the old man, who simply turned and disappeared into the bush.

"The *fuck*..." said Quinn. "We need to get the fuck out of here and now." He started to put on his pack in anticipation of fleeing.

"He's right, Sarge. This isn't what we signed up for. This shit is crazy."

"Stow that shit, both of you," growled Sarge.

"This has gotten too fucked up. Lopez is slowing us down. He's dead already. Let's just leave him and get to the LZ!" Quinn was practically screaming.

Sarge raised his M16 again, this time pointing it at Quinn. "I will shoot the first swinging dick that walks away from us."

Strayer looked down at Lopez, who was white-eyed with terror. "Lopez, you okay? You hit?"

"The flame! You all saw the flame, right? It came back. It came back for me. It was talking to me. Sarge's bullets just passed through the flame."

Sarge stormed over to Lopez. "Stow that shit. It was just some old VC. This shitty country has a million of them, and they all look alike."

He turned to Jacobs. "What happened to your fucking weapon?"

Jacobs was examining the M-16. "Failure to extract, Sarge."

"Clean out the goddamn thing, Jacobs. That kinda cherry mistake gets people killed." He turned to the others, seething. "Lopez, calm the fuck down. Strayer, calm Lopez the fuck down and stop eye-fucking me. Quinn, with me."

They quickly moved towards where the old man had stood.

Strayer watched them disappear into the scrub, then turned to help Lopez to his feet, who was holding his medallion and praying. Strayer turned to his back to get the first aid kit, and when he turned back, he was greeted by a pillar of fire standing next to a whimpering Lopez.

Strayer scrambled back like a crab. Heat radiated off the pillar in shimmering waves. Lopez started screaming. Small flames dropped off the pillar around him, and their form shifted and morphed into naked children. The large flame solidified and became the man from the cave.

"Ba Thuy gave your friend the gift of noi," he said.

Someone was screaming. Strayer realized it was him.

Lopez screamed too.

Jacobs had been cleaning his M-16, and the screaming snapped his focus to Lopez and Strayer, and he stumbled away from the fire.

The old man looked at the children who had surrounded Lopez then turned to Strayer and smiled. "They want your friend to know what napalm feels like."

The flame children struck like vipers, reaching out and grabbing Lopez. The smell of burning flesh hit the air as white-hot flames engulfed the man. Lopez writhed and shrieked as the flame consumed him, calling for help until his blackened body collapsed in a heap. Strayer dry retched, and crab walked farther back to get away from the heat and smell.

"Jacobs, Reverend, get the fuck down!" Sarge's yell rang out as he burst from the bush and began firing. Bullets passed through the flame children, who seemed to gutter out like candles, leaving only wisps of smoke in their wake. Quinn opened up with Mamacita, and the old man looked at them as if they were mosquitoes. He smiled, turned, and walked back into the bush.

"What in the name of fuck was that?" panted Quinn.

"Con Hoa," Stayer said, and promptly bent over, retching. He realized he had the stench of burned Lopez in his nostrils and retched again. His body felt like it was underwater, and he sat awkwardly on the ground. Nothing in his training prepared him for this.

"*Bullshit*," bellowed Sarge. "There were some drugs in that cave or something. The spooks use that sort of shit! No such thing as ghosts or goddesses. Somebody is *fucking* with us."

"Yeah. Ghosts and goddesses," said Strayer simply.

"You've gone dinky dau, Strayer. You're in shock. Stand up, Corporal."

"Could be," Strayer answered, pushing to his feet. "But Holquist died in six inches of water and Lopez was just set on fire by children who turned into flames. There are more things in heaven and earth, you know?"

"No, I don't know, Strayer! I'm not in heaven or earth. I'm in the 'Nam, same as you. And this situation has seriously gone south."

"He was speaking English," said Jacobs. "I could understand him."

"I think he was in our heads. I'm not sure he's fully real," said Strayer.

"Stow that shit. Jacobs, get me an ETA on the evac. We're close to the extraction point, I intend for all of us to reach it. Whether the VC have some new weapons, China is testing new mind control drugs or the goddamn ghost of Christmas past wants to make a bonfire of us all, we are getting the fuck out of here. Gather up your stuff. Sorry for Lopez, but we can move faster now."

"How do you fight that, Sarge? How do you fucking fight that?" Quinn was coming apart. Tears ran down Jacobs' face. Sawyer knew panic and shock were stripping their training and professionalism. He didn't care. They needed to get as far from this shit as they could.

Sarge grabbed them each in turn and pushed them away from Lopez's still smoking remains and down the all-but invisible trail.

"Enough of this bullshit, we're burning daylight." Then, as if recognizing the poor choice of words, he pushed ahead of the group and set out south again.

"I'm taking point. You don't want to be left behind, then don't get left behind," he called back.

Strayer thought Sarge night just be coming apart, too.

The four of them moved at a quick clip through the bush. Fear is a great motivator. It was still two hours until sun up, but the birds wouldn't wait if they missed their rendezvous. Strayer puffed heavily with the exertion. He saw the old man behind every tree, the children under every bush. He could hear the others' breathing hard as well. He said a quick prayer, thanking the Lord for being forgiving, because the jungle was not.

"Sarge, quick break?" asked Jacobs.

"Keep moving!"

"I need to piss!"

Sarge gave him the eye but relented. "Thirty seconds. Everybody relieve yourself. We've got to keep on." He looked back from where they came, searching for the old man who stalked them.

Strayer relived himself on a tree and turned to Quinn just as he was bending over and moving his face towards the small pool of urine on the ground.

"Quinn! What are you doing?" Strayer grabbed him and pulled him back. Quinn's eyes had gone white like a blind man's and he resisted Strayer with all his might, struggling towards the piss rapidly soaking into the loam.

"Sarge! Help!"

Sarge and Jacobs rushed over and grabbed a hold of Quinn too. He strained under their efforts. Finally, something in him seemed to break. He stopped struggling, and they all fell backwards away from the puddle. Quinn's eyes returned to normal but grew wide. Strayer tuned his head to see what Quinn was looking at.

The old man watched them, a menacing grin on his face. "If you do not want noi, the Con Noa can have you, too."

Sarge picked up his M16, but the man was gone. Instead, a low mist swirled out of the jungle and began to coalesce into a grayish black smoke. Its tendrils began to wrap around Quinn.

"What the fuck is happening?" he screamed and his skin began to smoke and bubble. The others backed away as his body burst into flames. Strayer could hear children laughing as Quinn screamed, his skin melting from his body.

The men didn't wait. All three began running south, all sense of coherence gone, branches whipping at them as they fled. It was every man for himself. Fifteen minutes later, Sarge collapsed by trailside to catch his breath.

Strayer made sure there was no water nearby then turned on Sawyer, grabbing him by the pack strap. "Sarge, you shot him in the cave! We've shot him several times since. Quinn emptied Mamacita into him an hour ago, and he's still showing up. Time to face facts. He's not human. He might not have been human in the cave."

All three were breathing heavy. Their hands and faces dripped blood from cuts and scratches. Strayer used a handkerchief to wipe the blood from a cut under his right eye.

"So what do you propose, *Reverend?*"

"Run. Fast. He doesn't want us here. We don't want to be here. Maybe if we can get to the evac point, we climb in the bird at first light, head south and then be done with this place."

"We've been moving!"

"We move faster. Leave anything we don't need. Drop these packs. Who cares if Charlie gets ahold of The Gun? We're being mauled out here. Three of us left. Worse comes to worst, I can think of one other thing."

"What?"

"I'm going to be saying a prayer for the dead the whole time we're running. Even if the old man isn't human, the kids are supposedly ghosts. So let's lay them to rest."

"We run, you pray. That's your fucking plan?"

"Got a better one?"

Sarge grimaced. "No. Jacobs. Drop your pack. Take only weapons, ammo and the necessaries. We're gonna double-time it to extraction point."

Jacobs looked ill. He took off his pack and stared at it as if he had never seen it before.

"Di di mau. Let's get moving."

They set off, running for their lives.

Strayer lost track as they ran, but he assumed Sarge knew the route. Didn't matter at this point. The important destination was far away. Maybe the farther they got from where the little ghosts had died the safer they would be. Nothing was certain, though. He kept smelling smoke and hearing voices, but nothing materialized. They seemed to be following a trail south. The path snaked up and down and the sky started changing from black to blue, signaling dawn.

They'd arrived at the top of a hill, and Strayer estimated they were less than half an hour from the LZ. They quickened their pace even more, loping downhill along the trail. As they reached the bottom Sarge halted suddenly.

The old man stood before them, blocking their path..

Jacobs fumbled with his weapon. He pointed it at the old man and fired.

The old man sighed in response, like a disappointed teacher dealing with an inept student. "You do not know this land. You do not know what spirits walk here. You have angered them, and you must pay a price."

The day was growing brighter. Strayer heard engines in the distance. The huey had to be on the way. They just needed to get past the old man. Before Strayer could move, however, the old man smiled and pointed to the sky.

Strayer suddenly realized the smoke they had been smelling for hours was from the cave. The cave they had fragged hours earlier. The one where the old man had been killed. Somehow they had run in one big circle right back to the cave. And now the old man started to giggle as Strayer fell to his knees in despair.

The engine he heard wasn't a helicopter.

It was a jet. An angel of death.

Jacobs turned to Sarge. "Snake and nape!" He turned to run back the way they had come, but the trail was blocked by dozens of burnt children and adults.

"The Con Hoa have come to see what napalm can do to Americans," said the old man.

Sarge pulled the trigger on his M16, only to find his had jammed as well.

"You have failed to extract," said the old man, his smile growing ever wider.

Sarge pulled out his K-Bar, snarling. "Come on, witch doctor! You don't scare me." He threw himself towards the old man, stabbing him over and over. The old man simply smiled and wrapped his arms around the soldier. Sarge began to smoke as the old man became a pillar of fire.

The jet grew closer, the roar of its engine singing across the valley.

Strayer climbed to his feet and began moving as fast as he could down the hill, shouting a Buddhist prayer for the dead as he ran. He asked that the burned dead of Khe Sanh and all of Vietnam be released from their suffering, and that they be reborn in Buddha's paradise. The Con Hoa stood and watched him run past, making no move to stop him. He threw himself hard down the side of the mountain, sliding through the bush until he heard the jet pass over him with a loud shriek. The world lit up brighter than the sun, and then everything went black.

When he finally woke he heard voices. Voices speaking English.

"This one's still alive."

"Jesus."

"Let's move out."

A bird, rising with him in it. A bed. Sheets. Doctors. Nurses. Pain. Sleep.

A week later the colonel came to the hospital in Saigon.

"They tell me you're going to make it. They also say you're looking at a long and painful recovery. Lot of burns. Sorry to be the one to tell you, but you're the only one that made it out. The rest of your lurp was KIA. Brave of you boys to call a strike on your own position during a firefight. I assume there was something on that hill that needed to be blown up good?"

Strayer could only nod. Once.

"So no more boogey men and monsters? I can tell the troops that the good Padre blew them up?"

Strayer looked around the room. He heard panicked breathing and realized it was him. Summoning all his strength he nodded a second time but could not make eye contact with the colonel.

"If you blew them up, then all I have to say is a-fucking-men. Hope you have a fast recovery, son."

The colonel walked away, but Strayer didn't know what, if anything, had been accomplished. He was heading home a broken man, and his friends were now all dead.

That night as he slept, an orderly came to remove his bedpan and replace it. Strayer stirred. It was the old man, smiling down at him.

"You prayed for them, yes?" he asked in Vietnamese. "Asked the Buddha to give the Con Hoa peace?"

Strayer nodded. It hurt to do so.

"You have the compassion of a Buddha. You pray for your enemies, for their souls."

Another nod.

The old man looked at the table next to Strayer's bed. "You are a man of faith?"

Strayer nodded.

"A shame the Americans insist on making more con hoa. You were almost one yourself."

The old man placed his hand on Strayer's bandaged hand. The burns on Strayer's arms and hands were so bad they had been wrapped up completely in gauze. He'd never use his hands again.

"The con hoa let you live. That is good." The old man stopped smiling.

"But you did not propitiate everyone. Ba Thuy is still angered at what you do. You did not pray to her. No matter how devout to your god, Ba Thuy cares little for your faith. She gives you the gift of noi."

With that, he smiled again and turned to smoke, which slowly dissipated until only the memory remained.

Despite his bandaged hands, despite the burns on his body, despite the tight bedding and heat of the day, Strayer worked patiently, diligently.

He placed the bedpan on the pillow next to him. In more agony than he had ever known, he turned his body over slowly. Even at the end he could not have said why, he only knew he would know no peace until he lowered his head into the liquid and give himself to Ba Thuy.

Strayer heard screaming. Could not tell if it was the nurses or his own, but knew he would not have to hear it for long.

HUNTER

Steve Lewis

Sector Eleven, Alpha Company barracks

The barracks was dark and still, with only the slow flicker of lights to show it wasn't as empty and deserted as the shattered buildings around it. It had been built to house 140 troops. Now it had just three.

Sergeant Jason Barnes lay in his cradle, power cables plugged into his cybernetic implants. He hated them, but he needed them to stay in the fight. With everything else gone, the fight was all he had left.

Across the barracks were the only two other men left from the original company – Gibbs and Williams – both heavily cyborged and jacked into their recharging cradles. They had both been good soldiers, but nothing special. They had survived where better men had died. That gave them the one quality that couldn't be trained – luck. Given the way the war was going, it was the only thing that was going to get any of them out of it alive.

The comms unit next to Barnes' cradle flickered to life, snapping him to full consciousness.

"Hunter One, this is Command. We have alien activity in your sector. Standby for data."

"This is Hunter One," Barnes replied. "What you got for me, Piper?"

Corporal Narelle Piper and Barnes were old friends and had dated when they were both corporals together. It had ended when he'd been promoted to Sergeant. When the aliens invaded, Barnes was one of the first to undergo cybernetic rebuilding, having lost almost everything in that first crazy day when the alien portals had opened. Hundreds of thousands of crazed

180

monsters had spilled out across the planet, ripping people apart. Barnes was one of the lucky ones to survive long enough to make it to the medical labs.

Their relationship now strictly professional over the radio network.

"Multiple portal signatures, at least three major clusters," Piper replied. "Data suggests two opening within minutes of each other, the third with a delay of fifteen minutes or so. Best bet, this is a synchronised attack. They're coming, and they mean business."

Barnes scanned the data on the screen beside him. Three clusters all right. At least five portals on each, with a few minor portals scattered around the three cluster points. He hit the alert button on his console, lighting up the barracks.

"We'll take the clusters," Barnes said, swinging his heavy metal body upright in the cradle. "You got someone to take care of the outliers?"

"Not yet," Piper said. "I'm working on it, but there's not much more than drones available in your area."

"Let me know how you go, we don't want any friendlies getting in our way."

Gibbs and Williams were up now, moving quickly. Barnes joined them, and they went to the armoury to draw weapons.

Gibbs – Hunter Two – grabbed a seven-barrelled brute of a weapon from the weapon rack, an electrically-driven Gatling gun that was usually aircraft mounted for area suppression work. The weight of the weapon and its ammunition hopper was something that only a cyborg could carry, and Gibbs was almost completely 'borged – only his face wasn't metal or Kevlar composite, that being the line that he wasn't going to cross.

Williams – Hunter Three – grabbed a two barrelled, over-and-under combination with a 40mm automatic grenade launcher on top and a 15mm machine gun below, meant for bunker defence work. Even for a cyborg the weapon was considered 'heavy' – Williams' body of titanium bones and polyfibre muscles could carry it, but the recoil was horrendous, and even a cyborg needed a tripod mount to fire effectively.

Barnes loaded up with a simple battle rifle, a 30mm weapon that looked like a much-upsized version of what he carried before he'd been rebuilt. Capable of firing in multiple modes, it was simple, accurate and lethal – the lighter weapon meant he could carry three thousand rounds into battle and still stay light on his feet.

Barnes inspected the two other men as they gave him the once over. He was the least 'borged of them all, with only his arms, legs and spine replaced by metal and polyfibre, all held together by the Kevlar nano-composite that made up his skin.

His vital organs were all his though, and he still had functioning genitalia, which marked him apart from the others. He figured that if he had his own junk he was still a man, even if that was *all* he had left.

Piper had prepared the deployment packets for their inboard tactical computers. "I've marked the three clusters on your maps, gentlemen," she said as they accessed the data. "I've designated them Clusters Alpha, Bravo and Charlie on your maps, and the outliers are numbered Oscar One through to Oscar Seven."

"Good work, Piper," Barnes replied. "I'll be taking Alpha, Gibbs will take Bravo, Williams on Charlie. We'll sort the outliers after we clean out the clusters, so we'll need you to keep an eye on them until we're clear."

"Roger that, Hunter One," Piper said. "I've got drones on their way. I'll keep you informed."

"Sounds like a plan," Barnes said, then looked at the other two men. In the dim, flickering light Barnes thought they looked like misshapen trolls ready to head out into battle, and he wasn't entirely sure that image was necessarily wrong. "We ready?"

"Born ready!" Gibbs said, raising the heavy Gatling gun. "Been sleeping here too long, time to pay the rent."

Williams grinned and slapped Gibbs on the shoulder, sending a metallic echo through the building. "Ain't nothing keeping us here, Sarge," he said. "Let's get out and show them how it's done."

"I couldn't agree more," Barnes said. "Piper, this is Hunter One, heavy metal moving out."

The three cyborgs left the barracks and moved quickly and carefully through what was left of the city. It was a mess. Streets were piled high with the rubble of collapsed buildings, torn down by rampaging aliens or blown to pieces by desperate defenders who had quickly lost all interest in preserving real estate in order to stay alive. In most cases it hadn't worked, and scraps of military uniforms, discarded weapons and human bones littered the ground.

Mercifully, most of the dead were out of sight, buried beneath the rubble, but the three cyborgs knew they were there, their enhanced senses picking up the smell of rotting corpses coming up from their graves of fallen concrete, glass and steel.

Barnes had plotted a course that kept the three men together for as long as possible before splitting up to make their way to their respective targets. Partly for security, but Gibbs and Williams were all that was left of the old days, and he knew that every battle could be their last. They didn't talk about it much, but he knew the other two felt the same.

They were silent with their thoughts as they advanced, finally reaching the point where their paths separated. Gibbs and Williams gave each other a quick fist-bump then went on their way, leaving Barnes to watch them go.

Only when they were out of sight did he continue on his own course.

Cluster Alpha, formerly the corner of Main Street and 4th Avenue
"Hunter One, this is Command."

"Go ahead, Piper."

"I have eyes in the sky above you."

"Thanks, Pipes." Barnes closed his eyes and activated the data feed. The three drones in his area each pushed information directly into the chip in his skull. He cycled through them quickly to give himself the best read on the ground he could.

Five portals four hundred metres ahead. By the time he

climbed atop a mound of rubble high enough to get a good line of sight, they were starting to sparkle. It should have been a beautiful sight, but the inner light of some alien dimension shining through was generally followed by clawing hordes of death. Barnes hated it. The sight triggered the fear and anger he'd felt the first time he'd seen it – he had his fear mostly under control now, but he'd stopped trying to hold the anger back, letting it consume him during battle.

"All units, Hunter One in position," he said over the comms channel, trying to keep the growing anger under control a little longer. "It's gonna get busy here, so if you have anything you need to say, now's the time."

"Hunter Three here," Williams said. "Still en route to Cluster Bravo. Terrain here is a mess, might not make it before those portals open."

"Understood, Hunter Three," Barnes replied. "Command, I won't need my drones much longer, you might want to send him some support."

"Roger," Piper responded. "Redirecting some eyes your way, Hunter Three."

"Much appreciated, Command,"

"How's things looking at your end of town, Hunter Two?" Barnes said, jumping to a higher position on what was left of an adjacent building, his cyborg legs clearing the fifteen-metre gap easily. "You going to make it in time?"

"We have a problem, Hunter One," Gibbs said. "I think we have mice in the area."

"Fucking civilians," Williams cut in. "You'd think they'd have the sense to leave by now."

"How many?" Barnes asked, mentally agreeing with Williams.

"Not sure," Gibbs replied. "I can see signs of them every-where. I'm picking up some fleeting heat signatures, but nothing concrete."

"Keep them alive if you can," Barnes said. "Don't get yourself dead doing it though."

"Wouldn't dream of it," Gibbs said. "Some support here to clear them out of the way wouldn't go astray."

Barnes frowned. "Command—"

He stopped talking as the portals at Cluster Alpha opened, and creatures came spewing out.

Whatever alien dimension had spawned them had little in common with Earth evolution. There were several different breeds amongst them. Most were four legged with long-snouted heads, like dogs; some were round-faced like great cats while others were sharp-beaked like birds. They all had thick hide, and some had slabs of chitin that provided some slight armour protection. Barnes had long given up wondering how and why they'd evolved the way they had.

Two things they all did have in common though were sharp claws and fangs, and a serious hatred of humans – they seemed to want nothing more than to kill every human they could.

Barnes raised his battle rifle, thumbed the selector to auto and squeezed the trigger, bracing himself against the recoil. He fired short, controlled bursts into the closest groups. The 30mm rounds were copper-topper hollow-points, with a tungsten penetrator core, and they punched through the creatures hide before blossoming to tear them apart from the inside.

The creatures turned towards him, snarling in fury, and charged at him at full speed, without any thought of seeking cover or trying to flank him. The scrape of their claws on concrete sounded like an avalanche, and they struck sparks with every step.

The natural lay of the rubble channelled them into four distinct lanes, and Barnes let his rifle play for a few seconds across each lane in aimed bursts before moving to the next. The carnage was horrendous, but they kept coming.

By the time they'd reached two hundred metres, their howls had built into a shriek, a primordial sound that cut Barnes to the core, and for a moment he felt the terror the sound had caused the first time he'd heard it. He pushed that aside, giving in to his anger, and let loose a howl of his own, all thoughts of aimed fire gone as he fired long bursts from the hip.

He focussed his fire onto the right-most approach, being the closest, pouring round after round into them until that entire group was gone, and then he switched to the far left.

At one hundred metres, that group was nothing more than alien flesh decorating the rubble, so he switched to the next group, spraying rounds into them, his fire just one long burst now. He knew he was burning through his ammunition too quickly but he didn't care – he wanted them dead, and ammunition was only going to be a problem if he survived this battle.

At fifty metres, their shrieks and the drumming of claws on concrete blended with the echoes of his rifle fire, filling the area with sound. It was maddening, so intense it threatened to overwhelm his other senses, making it almost impossible to think clearly.

He gave in to it, advancing towards the last group of approaching aliens, spraying quickly to thin them out as they charged towards him. They were fast, and he knew that a couple would get through – the press of a button on the trigger grip extended his rifle's bayonet, impaling the first as it leapt towards him, and the second was met with the metal-shod butt with a blow that caved in its skull, sending fluorescent alien brain-matter splashing to the ground.

The area was silent and Barnes raised his battle rifle and scanned his surrounds.

Nothing moved.

"Command, this is Hunter One," he said, slowly letting his rage subside. "Cluster Alpha neutralised. Send the next target coordinates."

🌍 🌍 🌍

Cluster Charlie, formerly the corner of Queen Street and 2nd Avenue.
"Command, this is Hunter Three," Williams said. "In position overlooking Cluster Charlie."

"Roger that, Hunter Three," Piper replied. "Look sharp, expect company."

The surviving satellite network could analyse the energy readings from the portals and accurately predict their opening to within a few seconds. Williams watched the small timer on his data feed tick down. Right on zero, the portals in the square some three hundred metres away and thirty metres below him spiralled open, their bright alien glow lighting up the shadows, and aliens spilled out. The drones around him counted the creatures as they emerged, the counter quickly tripping past three hundred.

He'd set his over-and-under weapon on its heavy tripod, its clawed feet dug into the rubble and stable. Williams fired both barrels at once, the lower barrel spitting 2400 tungsten-tipped rounds a minute towards the aliens as they emerged, while the upper barrel coughed a high explosive grenade every second or so.

The volume of fire from the machine gun was considerable, but the tungsten penetrators lacked real killing power unless they struck something vital. They punched straight through the alien bodies, ripping out flesh and spraying their fluorescent green and yellow blood everywhere, but only a kill shot stopped them from moving towards him. Even with limbs torn off and gaping holes in their bodies, the creatures came on, crawling on bloodied stumps, dragging themselves forward by their claws, their shrieks all the louder in their pain.

The grenades, on the other hand, exploded amongst them and scattered their remains all around. With a lethal radius of ten metres, every second created a hole in the enemy swarm, one that took time to fill.

Williams tripped the filters in his cybernetic ears, reducing their shrieks to almost nothing. For a long while the only sensation he had was his hands tight on the spade grips of his weapon and the shake of recoil through the tripod.

Their numbers began to thin and he stopped firing grenades, concentrating long bursts of machine-gun fire on the closest groups, letting the penetrators do their work, slowing them down if they didn't die outright.

Soon, there was nothing left on its feet moving towards him, only dozens of wounded aliens doing their best to get to him before they died of their wounds. Williams turned his cybernetic hearing back up, enjoying the sounds of the creatures in pain.

He moved to finish them off. Some things had to be done up-close and personal, and payback was one of them.

"Command, this is Hunter Three," he said, the armoured heel of his cyborg foot crushing the life out of the first alien he reached. "Cleaning up here, will be ready for new orders in a few."

◉ ◉ ◉

Cluster Bravo, formerly Central Station

Gibbs was having a rough time of it, his advance blocked by fallen buildings and walls of rubble. His internal timer told him he had plenty of time to get into position before the portals opened, but he'd rather be there early and take the best position than settle for whatever he had to.

"Command, this is Hunter Two," he said. "Roads are blocked, looking for another way in."

"Better get the lead out, Hunter Two," Piper replied. "We have your portals opening in twelve minutes twenty, and I think everyone would really like you to be there for that."

Gibbs' navigation AI pinged, showing a workable path. "On it, Command."

The new route took him back a half-block, and he cut down an alleyway, aiming to approach the cluster from a different direction. Despite his bulk, Gibbs' cyborg legs pushed him three times the speed of a normal man. He sprinted through the alleyway, turned right and leapt up a mound of rubble in his path. The top was surprisingly even, with most of the girders and concrete blocks tipped over to make it almost level in parts, which was going to save him a lot of time.

He was halfway across when he saw the portals on the other side. He had just enough time to see they lacked the tell-tale

sparkle that meant they were about to open, before the ground beneath his feet gave way and he fell into darkness.

Oscar Three, formerly St Michael's Cathedral, Main Street
Barnes was perched atop of the one remaining turret of the old cathedral, firing controlled four-round bursts from his battle rifle at the aliens milling around below. From his position he had could see all the outlying portals in his area, and he had fired a short burst at each of the alien mobs as they emerged, baiting them to him.

It was easier than tracking them all down and dealing with them in small groups.

"Hunter One, this is Command," Piper said suddenly into his earpiece. "Hunter Two is missing, never made his cluster."

"Shit," he said. "Are the drones tracking him?"

"Negative, Hunter One," Piper replied. "But there's a huge hole in the ground along the path his onboard AI had mapped out for him."

"Aliens?"

"Portals haven't opened."

"All right… keep an eye on them, I'll finish up here and head over."

"I'm done here," Williams cut in. "I'll see you there, Sarge."

"Will do," Barnes said. "Stay alert though, there might be something out here we're not aware of."

"Roger that."

Barnes switched to automatic and sprayed his fire all around the base of the cathedral. He was in a hurry, and conserving ammunition was even less of a priority now. Gibbs was one of the few men left from his original company, and he desperately needed to find him.

City North Subway Line, below Cluster Bravo
Gibbs fell heavily, but not enough to cause him any harm. The drop was a good thirty metres, which would have killed the pre-cyborg him. As it was, it just rattled him a little, and he stood and dusted himself off.

The darkness was lit only by the small hole above him. His artificial eyes enhanced the available light; bodies of aliens surrounded him, some just broken from the fall, others impaled on spikes and stakes set around the area. Looking up, it appeared the hole he'd fallen through had been covered with light wood and a thin layer of rubble. A trap. And he'd fallen into it like a dumb animal.

He brought up his map AI and plotted his position. Looked like he'd fallen into an old subway line, and the latest drone information suggested there was an open subway station about two hundred metres to the south. No way was he climbing out, so he turned south and moved as quickly as he could, hoping he'd get to the surface in time to be of use.

Oscar Seven, formerly the State Library, South Avenue
Barnes joined Williams along the way towards Cluster Bravo, and they moved fast yet wary. The portals weren't due to open for another five minutes, but neither of them wanted to be surprised by anything out there that might have done Gibbs some harm.

"Hunter One, this is Command," Piper's voice cut in. "I have bad news."

"Tell it, Command," Barnes said, and his heart sank, fearing the worst.

"Easier to show you," Piper said. "Sending you the video feed from the drones."

Both men closed their eyes and watched the feed played directly into their optical nerves. It showed the area above Cluster Bravo, with a dozen portals, large ones, as yet unopened.

"Seems quiet," Williams said softly. "No sign of Gibbs though."

There was movement, and the drones zoomed in, showing a dozen people moving amongst the rubble towards a large hole in the ground. They were armed with a mix of military weapons and civilian hunting rifles, and they looked gaunt and hungry.

"Looks like Gibbs found his mice," Barnes said.

"Or they found him," Williams replied. "That looks like a pretty neat trap, just right for alien swarms or walking machinery."

Barnes nodded, jaw tightening in anger. They all expected to be killed by aliens one day, it was just a matter of time before their luck ran out, but to be killed by a bunch of *civilians* by mistake, that was just too much to bear.

The civilians circled the hole, looking into the darkness, and some of them uncoiled ropes and started to climb down.

At that moment the portals opened and the aliens spilled out, heading straight to the nearest lifeforms.

A handful realised they weren't going to make it to cover and stood their ground, buying time for their comrades to finish their descent. They killed maybe a dozen before the swarm reached them, but it was never going to be enough.

Alien claws sliced through human flesh and bone, spraying blood everywhere to soak into the rubble. There was no precision to the attacks, just a frenzy of destruction that struck at whatever they could reach; arms were torn off as their terrified victims threw them up in a vain attempt to protect themselves, and then the long claws sliced deep into their bodies, organs spilling to the ground.

The scent of blood enraged the creatures more, and they jostled amongst themselves to reach something to kill, attacking with savage ferocity even after their victim was clearly dead. Their shrieks and howls drowned out human screams, until there were no human screams left to hear.

It was over in a heartbeat.

One of the civilians had the presence of mind to pull and

prime a grenade before the aliens struck them. It wasn't enough to save them. It fell from dead hands and exploded amongst the milling aliens, blasting a hole in the swarm the aliens barely noticed.

They had brought enough time, however, for their companions to finish their descent, and the aliens swarmed around the hole, looking down as their prey escaped.

They shrieked and clawed at the edges of the hole in fury; already weakened by the grenade blast, the edge gave way and sent another forty or so aliens to their deaths. The rubble around it collapsed in a landslide, turning one side of the hole into a gradual slope, and the aliens poured down into the depths, out of sight of the drones.

Barnes and Williams opened their eyes as the video feed ended.

"Command, where does that hole go?" Barnes asked.

"Subway line, heading north-south," Piper replied. "Looks fairly intact from the air, no gaping craters or massive falls along its path."

"Any exits?" Williams asked. "They could have cleared them by now."

"There's a possible exit to the south, about two hundred metres," Piper said. "The northern route has some known blockages, but otherwise runs all the way north into the next sector, some five kilometres until the next known exit."

"I want drones running along that subway route, looking for any signs they've exited," Barnes said. "And get in touch with their sector command. I want to know if they have troops ready to deal with something this big."

"Roger, Hunter One," Piper replied. "Already on it."

Sector Twelve, City North, 1ˢᵗ Platoon
Barnes and Williams made good time to the adjacent sector. There was an infantry platoon dug in not too far from the subway

exit, and Command had authorised the two cyborgs to cross the boundary to assist.

His drones counted fifty soldiers, none of them cyborgs, dug in in four main locations, giving them a frontage of three sections and a section in depth. Heavy weapons were well sited, the three forward sections had interlocking arcs of fire, and there had been some solid effort put into making the approaches as difficult as possible. All in all, it was better than Barnes had expected.

The platoon commander was waiting for him, a female Lieutenant that looked barely old enough to be in uniform. The look on her face told Barnes she hadn't had much exposure to cyborgs, which meant that she hadn't seen real action at all.

"Good afternoon, ma'am," Barnes said formally as he and Williams halted in front of her. "Sergeant Barnes, Sector Eleven, call sign Hunter, come to give you a hand."

"Lieutenant Miles, First Platoon, call sign Aries," the officer replied, coolly. "I'm not sure why you're here though, Sector Twelve has this under control."

Barnes and Williams stared at her. She was young all right, clearly sensitive about accepting advice, and they'd both known pig-headed junior officers who put their pride above their troops.

"You know the situation ma'am?" Barnes asked politely as Williams turned away in disgust. Miles nodded.

"Aliens headed our way," she said. "I'm sure there's lots of devils in the details, but that's the gist of it."

"There's about eleven hundred devils in the detail," Barnes said. "You can probably handle them the way you're set up, but this started as a Sector Eleven problem, we're just here to finish the job."

Miles shrugged and led the two cyborgs back through the platoon position, and the dug-in troops all stopped what they were doing to watch the two men as they passed. Barnes had seen that look before, that sense of awe that gave way to terror as the watchers realised that being modified like that was the *best* thing that could happen if you lost a battle, and trying to decide whether surviving was worth the loss of humanity.

Barnes couldn't blame them, he'd been a cyborg for over a year, and he still couldn't decide.

⊙ ⊙ ⊙

City North Subway Line
Gibbs had travelled south, picking his way through the scattered rubble that littered the subway line. It made for difficult going, and he was in a foul mood after falling victim to a simple trap.

He'd almost travelled the two hundred metres his AI had mapped out for him to the southern exit, when he heard a faint noise behind. He paused and listened, turning up the microphones built into his ears.

He recognised the chittering immediately – aliens on the move. It took him a moment to realise they were moving away from him. He cursed as he turned around and quickly made his way back the way he'd come.

⊙ ⊙ ⊙

Sector Twelve, City North, 1st Platoon HQ
Barnes had toured the defensive position quickly, trying to work out where he and Williams would fit in. Miles had no experience with cyborgs and didn't really want them there but let the two men position themselves where they'd do the most good – as long as they kept out of her way.

Williams set up to the rear of Three Section, on the platoon's right flank, setting up his tripod on an elevated position with good fields of fire and limited approaches. It was well suited for a static heavy weapon, and Barnes left him to get himself acquainted with his new comrades.

Barnes expected the aliens to come barrelling out of the subway exit and straight towards the platoon position, and One Section in the centre was right in their path. Corporal Miller, the section commander, seemed capable enough, but obviously had no idea how to integrate Barnes into his position. Barnes decided he was best employed to the rear, slightly elevated so he could apply the weight of fire from his battle rifle to wherever needed it most. Miller seemed relieved to have him off the position, probably as much to ease any command issues as well as not wanting a cyborg upsetting his men.

"Hunter One, this is Command."

"Go ahead, Command," Barnes replied.

"Got all sorts of news for you," Piper said. "Some good, some not so good."

Barnes sighed. "All right, give it… if it's general intel, patch Lieutenant Miles in first."

"Already here, Hunter One," Miles said. "I'm patched into your Command frequency, and vice versa."

"Good work, Piper," Barnes said. "Hit us with it."

"First, the good news: we got a hit on Gibbs. He emerged somewhere south of the hole he fell in, was in range of a drone for a few seconds, then disappeared again. Best guess is he went back underground and is somewhere in the subway system."

"That doesn't sound good," Miles said. "If the aliens catch scent of him, he could be in trouble."

"Gibbs can look after himself, ma'am," Barnes said. "Any more good news, Piper?"

"I have some resupply drones headed your way, should be there in a few minutes."

That *was* good news. Barnes and Williams had both fired about half their ammunition in dealing with their clusters and the outlying portals, and a stand-up fight like the one heading their way would use up the rest.

"Nice work, Piper," Barnes said, and touched a stud on the back of his hand. "I've got my resup beacon on… there's lots of troops around, so land it nice and gentle somewhere close by."

"Roger Hunter One, picking up your beacon now," Piper said. "And there's Hunter Three's beacon… drones should be coming in fast and low, landing, not dropping."

"I'd better tell my men not to shoot them down," Miles said. "It's been an out-of-the-ordinary kinda day, and they're mighty jumpy."

Barnes felt Miles disconnect from the network.

"Alrighty Piper," he said, "Miles has gone… what aren't you telling us?"

"It's not what I'm not telling you, it's what she's not telling you," Piper replied. "There's chatter all over the Sector Twelve network about portal signs. Lots of them, all over the place, but nothing from their command HQ."

"Not something to keep quiet," Williams said. "Anything confirmed?"

"Sector Twelve is a mess," Piper said. "Their drone grid is shot, holes everywhere, and I think whoever was coordinating it has gone missing. Everything is being done visually, and they don't have the resources to confirm any sightings at all."

"Can you swing some drones this way, on the quiet?" Barnes asked. "These troops might be able to hold off a straight-line charge from a few hundred aliens, but this position isn't built or equipped for a major assault."

"I'll see what I can do," Piper said. "But anything I send your way is going to weaken our own sector."

"Chance we're going to have to take," Barnes said. "If this sector falls, it's that much more for the rest of us later on."

There was a soft ping as Lieutenant Miles rejoined the command net. "I've let them know to expect drones," she said cheerfully. "Did I miss anything?"

"Just small talk while we waited, ma'am," Barnes said. "Anything from your Sector Command we need to know about?"

There was a noticeable pause, which told Barnes plenty.

"Nothing worth passing on," Miles replied. "I've arranged for a resupply of our own, after this battle is done, but that's about all."

"Good to know, ma'am," Barnes said. "I'd hate something to come out of left field in the middle of this."

Another pause.

"One hundred percent agreeance, Sergeant," Miles said. "If I hear anything worth passing on, you'll be amongst the first."

Sector Eleven, Command Headquarters

Piper had only a limited number of drones at her disposal and lots of ground to cover, but she had friends in neighbouring sectors, and managed to scrape up four drones to send to Sector Twelve to help Barnes.

Other sectors had drones flying on tight sweeps, constantly looking for portal signs, and you couldn't stick another drone over a sector boundary without setting off all sorts of collision alarms. Not in this case though. Her drones crossed the boundaries without causing a ripple, and she sent them, in pairs, on a programmed sweep on the area around Lieutenant Miles' position, five hundred feet in the air and cameras recording everything. Visually, she couldn't see much from that height, but the electronic sensors could pick up anomalies that might require a closer look.

And there *were* anomalies.

Plenty of them.

Sector Twelve, City North, 1st Platoon

Six men from Four Section were out in front of the platoon position laying mines, their rifles slung as they focused on the delicate task of setting their charges; the corporal in charge of the detail wanted it done quickly and figured that having half of his men as sentries would take twice as long, which increased the risk of being outside the position.

It was a poor decision.

One minute the area to the front of the platoon position was clear of aliens, the next it was filled with them. Hundreds and hundreds of them, pouring out of the subway exit fifty metres away from the mining detail. It took them fifteen seconds to cover that gap, and the detail lost much of that time taking in what was happening.

The corporal managed to unsling his rifle and start firing, and two of his men joined him a few seconds later, while the other three turned and ran.

10mm hollow-points blossomed on impact and shredded alien flesh as it tore through them. The three men fired rapidly, not really bothering to aim. For a moment the alien charge faltered, but the weapons only had thirty rounds in the magazine, and they emptied quickly. Before any of them could reload, the aliens closed the distance and tore into them.

Claws sliced through their bodies, spilling blood and organs onto the ground and shredding the bodies until there was nothing left but a bloodied pulp, the creatures behind them pushing around to close-in on the fleeing humans

The three men who ran died under a flurry of alien claws and teeth, their cowardice granting them an extra ten seconds of life.

The sounds of firing and their screams, however, brought the rest of the platoon to full alert. Machine guns opened fire, long bursts punching into the swarm – the nearest creatures were targeted by several fire teams and riddled by a dozen or more rounds before they fell, the combined weight of high-calibre fire tearing their bodies apart.

The carcasses formed a barrier, and the aliens pouring from the subway began to spread out to get around them. Some of them struck the leading edge of the thin minefield that had already been laid and paid the price, the small hollow-charge mines firing directly up into the bodies, turning them into a pale yellow-green mist that drifted on the strong breeze and wafted across the platoon position.

The minefield was only so dense however, and soon they were through it, not caring about their losses in order to get close and kill. They seemed to be endless, and each one that fell seemed to be a little closer than the last.

"All units, this is Aries One," Barnes heard Miles say over the general platoon net. "Be advised: we've received authorisation for a reserved demolition, expect fireworks to your front."

A reserved demolition was a previously set up series of charges, often used in very specific circumstances. Barnes hadn't been briefed that one had been set up, and there weren't many places where a controlled demolition would be useful about now.

"Aries One, this is Hunter One," he said over the command net. "We weren't advised of a demolition plan."

"Hunter One, we have charges on the subway exit," Miles replied. "We're going to blow it, seal the aliens inside."

"Ma'am, I have a man down there," Barnes said. "You blow that and they'll head right back to Sector Eleven and down his throat."

"Not my circus, not my monkeys," Miles said. "I have my orders."

Barnes felt Miles disconnect, and cursed.

"Williams... did you hear all that?"

"Sure did," Williams replied. "Not particularly friendly of her."

"Once she blows that exit, we're heading back to Sector Eleven," Barnes said.

"Roger that," Williams said. "I can be ready to move in a few minutes—"

A massive explosion rent the air ahead, and Barnes looked up in time to see the subway exit collapse. The charges seemed well placed, with just enough force to close the exit without blowing everything to bits, and part of Barnes admired the demolition team's precision.

It hardly had any impact on those aliens already out, however, and they kept coming, charging towards the dug-in platoon and into the furious weight of small arms fire that filled the approaches.

In the centre of One Section, Corporal Miller was doing his best to give fire control orders to his men and to stay alive. He was finding it difficult to do both. Aliens just kept coming, even after the subway had been sealed.

Three had avoided the bursts of machine gun fire and were bearing down on his position. Miller took careful aim, doing his best to ignore the shrieking howls that sent waves of terror over him. His first round went wide, but his second struck the alien centre-mass. The hollow-point exploded, tearing out chunks of alien flesh, but the wound did little more than stagger it. He fired again, blowing one of its front legs off and dropping it to the ground.

The other two kept coming, and Miller turned to the man next to him who was cowering in the bottom of the pit, his hands over his ears to block out the alien sound. Miller kicked him, hoping to nudge him into action, then gave up and turned back to the aliens.

They were too close now, and he switched to automatic fire, spraying quick bursts, doing his best to control the recoil and his nerves, and failing badly at both. One of them went down, a three-round burst hitting it in the head and torso, exploding it, and then nothing as the bolt of his weapon locked back, out of ammunition.

He pressed the stud and dropped the empty magazine to the bottom of the pit, reaching for a fresh one. The shrieks were getting closer and he looked up, freezing as he stared into the multi-faceted eyes of the alien only metres away. He screamed, his magazine falling from his shaking hands, and then the alien was in the pit, its claws and teeth tearing him to pieces before turning on the other man, who died crying with his hands still covering his ears.

Barnes saw the breach but could do nothing to prevent it. He charged down the slope to the pit, putting a burst into the creature as it tore into the remains of the two men, then jumped in after it and began firing at the aliens in front of him. The stink of human and alien blood and flesh mingling at his feet stoked his anger again, and it took everything he had not to give in to it.

In the background, heavy weapons fire resounded as Williams opened up with his over-and-under. Somewhere, there was the soft cough of mortars that had finally been given clearance to fire, and the shouts of terrified men and the screams of the dying ... but none of it mattered. It was just the aliens in front of him and the rise and fall of his trigger pressure.

The aliens died by the hundreds; their battle howl slowly subsided as their numbers dwindled, replaced by shrieks of anger and pain as they lay dying in the killing ground to the front of the platoon.

Barnes became aware that someone was calling his name, and realised Williams was on the comms channel.

"Barnes!" he said, urgently. "Priority message from Piper, tune yourself back in!"

"Tango! Tango! Tango!" Piper's voice cut through the noise into his command net. "Portals opening all over Sector Twelve! I can make out a dozen clusters and their outliers, but with my limited drone cover there's likely others that I can't see."

Barnes cursed. A dozen clusters was a major assault, and there wasn't much in Sector Twelve that could cope with that.

"Piper, keep an eye on things, let me know where they're headed," Barnes said, climbing out of the pit. He had planned to head back to Sector Eleven but couldn't leave a rookie platoon to face things alone.

"Roger that, Hunter One," Piper said. "You and Williams stay safe, it's going to get ugly in there." Barnes felt Piper drop off the Sector Eleven net.

"Aries One, this is Hunter One," he said on the local command net. "We have portals opening all over your sector. Are you aware?"

There was a long pause, and Barnes was about to ask again when Miles replied.

"Hunter One, this is Aries One. We have no reports of any portals in our sector. Where are you getting your information?"

"Sector Eleven Command has sent some drones on a fly-over," Barnes said. "Twelve clusters, maybe more."

"You've got a nerve flying drones over our turf, *Sergeant*," Miles said. "But I'll check with Sector Twelve Command, see if they can confirm." She cut the connection, and Barnes went back to check on Williams and draw fresh ammunition from the resupply drones.

City North Subway Line

Gibbs could hear the aliens ahead. By their sounds he figured there were hundreds of them, and he wasn't in too much of a hurry to catch them in the confines of a tunnel system. On the surface he could make better use of terrain to maximise the range of his weapons.

Underground, they'd come at him in a wall of teeth and claws and sooner or later something was going to get through.

In the distance he could make out the sounds of firing. It was faint, and his map AI placed the noise around the next known clear exit in Sector Twelve. He had no idea what troops were there, but whoever they were they seemed to be dealing with the aliens quite nicely.

Then, the noises changed. There was a sharp explosion, and then chaos as dirt and concrete tumbled about. The alien noises scrambled about furiously, and then suddenly turned back his way.

Something had happened, and that wall of teeth and claws was now heading right back for him.

Sector Twelve, City North, 1ˢᵗ Platoon

"Hunter One, this is Aries One," Miles said over the local command net. Barnes thought she sounded pissed off, which matched exactly how he was feeling. "There's no confirmation of *anything* happening in Sector Twelve, you might want to tell that Piper of yours to mind her own business and get her facts right."

"Command, this is Hunter One," Barnes said over his command net. "You there Piper?"

"Always here, Barnes," Piper said.

"Lieutenant Miles doesn't seem to believe your reports of major alien activity, thinks you might have it wrong," Barnes said.

"Well, that's interesting," Piper said, "and by 'that's interesting' I mean she can go fuck herself."

"I'll have you charged when this is all over," Miles said, clearly angry. "I'm not sure how Sector Eleven does business, Sergeant Barnes, but this is unacceptable."

"I'll take it up with Command HQ when this is all done, ma'am," Barnes said. "Until then, you might want to take Corporal Piper and her drones seriously."

"There's nothing out there!" Miles said. "Sector Twelve HQ can't see anything, portals or aliens!"

"No disrespect, ma'am," Piper said, "but Sector Twelve drone coverage is worth jack. You want the direct feeds from my drones in your area?"

"I'd advise you take the offer, ma'am," Barnes said. "If your drones are down, and it's as bad as Piper makes out, we're going to need everything we can get our hands on."

There was a long silence, and Barnes could feel Miles struggling with a decision.

"Fine," she said at last. "Put it through to my command terminal."

"Yes ma'am," Piper said cheerily, and Barnes felt Miles drop from the net.

City North Subway Line

Gibbs ran as the aliens swarmed towards him. Knowing he couldn't outrun them, he looked for a choke point he could use to hold them off.

After backtracking a few hundred metres he found an area that was mostly caved in, with only one track accessible. That still gave him a frontage of six metres to defend, and a lot of aliens could pour through a hole that big.

He could hear them easily now without his enhancements and raised his Gatling gun, bracing himself for the onslaught.

🌐 🌐 🌐

Sector Twelve, City North, 1st Platoon HQ
Miles watched the video feeds coming through from Piper's drones. The early footage showed a dozen clusters of portals, all opened, and she recognised the areas, so it clearly wasn't dummied-up data to put the wind up a newbie officer.

She also knew the sector well enough to know there were areas the drones clearly hadn't covered, and there might easily be another few clusters out there Piper hadn't found.

"Command, this is Aries One," she said as she sent the video footage directly on to her own Sector Command. "We have a potential situation here."

"Aries One, this is Command... where are you getting this data?" Miles didn't even know the name of the person at the other end – they seemed to change daily – and she felt a moment of envy at the relationship and trust between Barnes and Piper.

"Sector Eleven has lent us some drone support," she replied. "Looks legit, I might need support out here."

"Aries One, we have no way of confirming that data at this time," the voice said. "Resources are currently allocated to higher priorities."

"When *will* you have confirmation?" Miles asked. "If it's real, I need to know, and soon."

"We'll have satellite coverage over your position in two hours, Aries One," the voice said. "Until then, hold tight." The connection went dead.

Miles looked at the data feed. The images looked real enough, and Miles had seen the resupply drones come in for Barnes and Williams... Piper was good enough to get drones through that far, so could easily have sent recon drones in as well.

Outside, the sounds of firing had stopped, replaced by the sounds of cheering. For many of the men, this was their first battle, and she'd lost only a handful, and that would lift morale a little.

"All hands, this is Aries One," she said, making up her mind. "Tango! Tango! Tango!"

City North Subway Line

Gibbs fired burst after burst at the horde surging towards him. His Gatling burned hot as he pumped out hundreds of hollow-points and tungsten rounds, but still they kept coming. He'd never worried about running out of ammunition before, but now he knew he wasn't going to have enough.

Alien bodies continued to explode and paint the subway tunnel as Gibbs slowly backed up. Then his Gatling ran dry, now nothing more than a whirring machine. He threw it to the ground in disgust and drew two long trench knives.

Rather than wait for them, he charged, roaring and slashing wildly with both weapons. Their soft flesh gave no resistance at all to his razor-sharp blades and supernatural strength, painting the walls with blood and gore as a pile of victims grew around him. But still they kept on, showing no sign of relenting.

Sector Twelve, City North, 1ˢᵗ Platoon

The live feeds were being streamed directly to Barnes and Miles now. It looked bad because it was. A swarm of thousands upon thousands all heading towards 1ˢᵗ Platoon's position.

Miles joined Barnes at the rear of One Section's position. She was out of her depth, and she knew it. This was her first command, likely to be her last, and she owed her men the best chance they had of getting through it. She knew she wasn't it, and found Barnes in the position he'd made for himself at the rear of One Section.

"Sergeant Barnes," she said quietly. "I think I need your help,"

"Sure, ma'am," Barnes replied. "What do you need?"

"My platoon sergeant is dead," she said. "I need a replacement and can't afford to take one of my corporals away from his section."

Barnes looked surprised. "I didn't realise they'd got through to your command post."

"They didn't," Miles said, putting her finger under her chin and cocking her thumb back. "He took the easy way out but left me in the lurch."

Barnes nodded, he'd known many men who'd gone the same way rather than been torn to pieces by aliens. "Are you sure, ma'am?" Barnes asked. "Williams and I haven't been exactly met with open arms since we arrived."

"We're in this together," Miles said, and then shrugged apologetically. "Besides, you've done all right by us, and if we'd listened to you in the first place, we might be in a better situation about now."

"Any word from your Sector Command, ma'am?" Barnes asked, knowing the response wasn't likely something he wanted to hear.

"Nothing helpful," Miles replied. "And if I get through this alive, I'm going to make whoever's responsible pay."

"Looks like we're on our own then," Barnes said. "I know Piper is working on support, but it'll take a while for her to get anything here."

"If it comes," Miles said bitterly.

"Oh, it'll come," Barnes said. "Just a matter of whether it'll be of any use to us."

"Fair enough," Miles said. "So... what's your best plan to buy time here?"

Barnes surveyed the area. "We need to get your troops set up for all-round defence. The aliens are going to try and over-whelm us from all directions – we can't leave any gaps."

"Makes sense," Miles said. "I was thinking of moving further up this hill and digging in up there."

"That'd work if we had time," Barnes muttered, "but I don't think we have more than ten minutes or so before they get here."

Miles frowned, thinking furiously. "How about we pivot the two flanking sections outwards, pull Four Section in to cover the rear, and bring the Heavy Weapons section into the centre."

"Sounds good, probably the best option we have. I can give you Williams to coordinate the Heavies, he can add to their firepower, and I'll stay with you as a counter-penetration reserve."

Miles nodded and moved away to give her section commanders their orders.

Despite his calm tone, Barnes wasn't feeling particularly confident about their chances. He'd been in an attack like this in the early days, when everything was a surprise and no-one knew what to expect. Their defences had been breached within minutes, and the aliens had swarmed through and killed almost everyone. His company commander had called in an airstrike on their position, killing hundreds of aliens and dispersing them to be mopped up by the rest of the battalion, and it was only luck that Barnes and others had survived.

Survived to become a cyborg, and that was a dubious privilege at times.

"Hunter One, this is Command."

"Go ahead, Piper."

"Thought you might want to know Sector Twelve Command HQ has gone silent," Piper said. "No signs of alien activity, just looks like everyone has left the building."

"Well fuck."

City North Subway Line

Gibbs was in trouble. Claws and teeth slashed at him from all sides, and he was finding it hard to move. Unlike Barnes, Gibbs had no problem at all in giving in to his anger, and his own roar of rage matched the alien shrieks as he struck with short thrusts into the creatures that pressed around him.

Then something came writhing through the alien mass towards him, moving incredibly fast. It was long and serpentine, and it launched itself at his face, mouth wide with row after row of sharp teeth. He barely managed to get an arm up and block it, the jaws closing on his forearm and gouging deep lines in his armour. He tried to shake his other arm free of the mass of bodies to bring his other knife up, but the creature was too fast. Its tail whipped forward, driving a long needle-sharp spike of chitin into his right eye that punched deep into his brain, killing him instantly.

His cyborg body thrashed on the ground as random electrical impulses swept through it. The aliens, seeing him moving, kept attacking, not stopping until they had finally torn his cyborg body to pieces and his random twitches stopped.

The swarm moved on, leaving his mangled body in the darkness.

Sector Twelve, City North, 1ˢᵗ Platoon
The largest swarm Barnes had even seen was just over five thousand, and this swarm was vastly bigger, more than enough to completely surround the human position. Instead of attacking immediately, they milled about as their numbers grew.

Their howling was different from anything Barnes had heard before, an almost triumphant keening, as if to signify to their waiting victims that death was gathering for them.

The idea that the aliens could be taunting them was worse than the noise itself, and sent a shiver through Barnes he had to fight to control.

Sector Twelve, City North, 1ˢᵗ Platoon, One Section
One Section hadn't had to re-adjust and was notionally the platoon's strongest defensive position. It had lost a few men, including the section commander, but had good fields of fire and priority of effort from the guns of the Heavy Weapons section behind them.

Lance Corporal Dillon, now in command, stood in the pit his former section commander had occupied. The bodies had been removed and his men had thrown in about a foot of dirt to cover what they couldn't scrape out, but the place still reeked of death.

The smell made him physically sick, more than the howling spewing from the swarm about four hundred metres in front of his position. He'd been told to hold until they were two hundred and fifty metres away before he opened fire, but the noise, the smell, the waiting and knowing he was standing in the very pit his predecessor had been torn apart finally got to him.

Dillon scrambled to the edge of his pit and opened fire, a long burst that emptied his magazine in seconds. The men around him joined him, their fear and anger bubbling out into long screams. Even at that range it was hard to miss, and aliens started to fall, but the hollow-points needed kinetic energy to be truly effective, and very few of the creatures died. The wounded howled, turning their attention on the humans firing in the distance, then the rest of the swarm charged towards the centre of One Section's position.

Dillon fell back into his pit, scrambling to replace his magazine. He wasn't sure how effective his fire had been, but it had drawn their attention, and that couldn't be a good thing.

Sector Twelve, City North, 1ˢᵗ Platoon, Heavy Weapons Section
Williams cursed as Dillon open fire, too far away to be effective at anything other than pissing the aliens off, which he seemed to have done admirably.

With command of the heavy weapons section – a combined group of light mortars and heavy machine guns – there was plenty of ammunition for the guns, but only thirty rounds for each of the mortars. The standard rate of fire for mortars in these circumstances was twenty rounds per minute, but Williams halved their rate, giving them three minutes of fire, which wasn't going to cut it against a swarm this big.

He had the mortar crews concentrate their fire on the ones streaming towards One Section. They fired by rote, the six seconds between shots enough to adjust the tube slightly and allow the natural variation of the charge bags to move the fall-of-shot a few yards from the previous round.

The mortar rounds pulverised anything close to their point of impact, tearing bodies apart and scattering what was left. The aliens didn't comprehend where the fire was coming from, but really didn't care either – they didn't bother taking cover, they just charged, their shrieks getting louder as they came.

After three minutes the mortars were out, and Williams had the crew take up their rifles and form a screen in front of the machine gun positions.

Sector Twelve, City North, 1st Platoon HQ
Piper's drone feed had an enormous field of view, but the aliens filled it, and more continued to pour in from its edges. They seemed endless, and Miles wondered where the hell they were all coming from.

Dillon's opening shots had triggered a response from the entire swarm, which charged, those too far away to reach the humans circling the position to find a way to get closer. With the support of the heavy guns, One Section seemed to be holding, the area in front of their position filling with alien bodies. The heavy guns could only support one front at a time however, and elsewhere things weren't looking so good.

Sector Twelve, City North, 1st Platoon, Four Section
Corporal Harris had been in command of his section for only a few weeks, and like his men had little real combat experience. He had re-positioned his section quickly when the order came through, which meant makeshift defences at best, and his troops weren't sited as well as he would have liked.

"Aries One Four, this is Aries One," he heard Lieutenant Miles through his radio earpiece. "How are you holding up back there, Harris?"

"Aries One, this is Aries One Four," he said. "Not good, ma'am, not good at all. I have dead ground all over the place, if you have anything spare, I could use it."

A scream brought Harris's attention back to the battle… a small group of aliens, thirty or so, had made their way through a pile of fallen concrete everyone had assumed was solid and impassable. The aliens had found a way, however, and burst clear of the pile only twenty metres from the section's left flank.

The men on that flank turned quickly to deal with them, concentrating their fire on the small group as they left their positions and backed away. The last of the aliens fell only a few metres from the withdrawing troops, but the men were now out of position and left a huge hole in the defensive line. Aliens poured through that gap, unchecked and spreading out as they charged across the rubble at full speed.

Sector Twelve, City North, 1ˢᵗ Platoon HQ
Barnes was tapped into the drone feeds, his eyes closed briefly as he watched the battle unfold. He cursed as the men in Four Section abandoned their position, knowing a breakthrough was imminent.

"Williams, this is Barnes," he said sharply. "Four Section is about to go under... anything you can do to help?"

"By the time I turn the guns around, it'll be too late," Williams replied. "And the mortars are out."

"Shit!" Barnes said, getting the same sinking feeling he had over a year ago when he'd lost almost everything. "I'm going myself, I'll see if I can buy some time."

Barnes raced back to the rear of the platoon position, passing terrified men who looked ready to break. They saw him running and started to climb out of their pits to join him, thinking he was withdrawing, and he had to shout them back into their positions.

He crested the slight rise at the top of the position and looked down at the swarm pouring towards the gaps in Four Section. There were more aliens than his rifle had rounds, but he opened fire in long bursts, hoping to cut down enough to give Four Section the few minutes they'd need to regroup.

Sector Twelve, City North, 1st Platoon, Four Section
Harris watched the men on his left go under, finally standing their ground and firing at the swarming aliens until slashing claws and ripping teeth tore them open. Body parts and entrails flew in every direction, covering the remaining troopers in blood and carnage. Most of them didn't even notice, but he saw one man drop his rifle in horror to look at the blood on his hands, only to be torn to pieces by the same creature that had killed the man next to him.

The aliens didn't stop. There were two other soldiers with Harris in their makeshift trench, and they turned their fire on those that had broken through. They were close enough for grenades now, and the two men poured on fire while Harris threw grenade after grenade, blasting alien bodies to pieces and sending concrete shrapnel everywhere. The alien advance finally slowed, but it didn't stop completely.

Screams were coming from everywhere. Harris' two forward positions had fallen. All that remained were pulpy messes.

"Aries One, this is Aries One Four," he said into his microphone as he reloaded. "The aliens have broken through Four Section… I say again, aliens have broken through."

He raised his rifle to fire and looked right into the eyes of an alien barrelling towards him. Another dozen were right behind it, and he froze, too terrified to even pull the trigger.

Sector Twelve, City North, 1st Platoon HQ,
Miles was patched into Piper's drone feed, watching the aliens close in. She heard Harris's cry but could do nothing about it, and cringed as aliens tore their way through Harris and the two men in his pit, wishing that Piper hadn't chosen that moment to zoom the high-definition camera in.

"Aries One, Hunter One, this is Command," Piper said urgently over their combined command net. "Hold tight, the cavalry's on its way!"

"Command, this is Hunter One," Barnes replied. "You dug up support?"

"Roger, Hunter One," Piper said. "No troops available, but we're diverting tactical assets your way."

'Tactical assets' generally meant artillery, missiles or rockets, which were great against large swarms of aliens but sometimes lacked the accuracy needed for close in support work. Worse, their exploding warheads generated secondary shrapnel from the fallen concrete, which tended to multiply the danger zone of any blast.

"How much do we have?" Barnes asked.

"And how long until it gets here?" Miles added.

"I'd say a few minutes, no more," Piper replied, "and you have pretty much everything spare from any sector in range."

Barnes whistled aloud… that was a *lot* of firepower. Whoever was calling the shots on this one wasn't taking any chances against an attack this big.

"All right, Piper," Barnes said. "We might be able to hold out. Give us a thirty-second warning before impact, if you can."

"Will do," Piper said. "You and Williams stay safe." There was the briefest of pauses. "You too, ma'am."

Barnes felt Piper drop off the net.

"You going to let your people know, ma'am?" he asked. "It might give them some hope if they know they only have to do this for a few minutes more."

"Good idea, Sergeant," she said, and turned away to pass on the news.

Through the video feed, she could see Barnes standing atop a mound of rubble and single-handedly trying to stem the breakthrough at Four Section. It was a heroic effort, firing his battle rifle in short controlled bursts that splashed aliens apart every time he pulled the trigger. It wasn't going to be enough though, and she could see the other sections were about to be overrun as well.

She switched off the video feed and picked up her rifle. She was going to die, so might as well take as many of the bastards with her as she could.

⊙ ⊙ ⊙

Sector Twelve, City North, 1ˢᵗ Platoon, Heavy Weapons Section
Off to his right, Williams saw the breakthrough in Three Section developing seconds before anyone else, so he pulled his over-and-under from its tripod mount and raced in that direction.

He braced himself and started firing as he moved, grenades spitting out to blow holes in the enemy advance. It wasn't enough. Three Section disappeared under a massive wave of aliens that only slowed because the lead creatures stopped to rip the humans into chunks of flesh and bone.

Those behind swarmed past them and up the slope towards the Heavy Weapons Section. His grenades gone, he opened fire with the lower machine gun barrel…without the heavy tripod to support it, the brutal recoil pounded into him, and he screamed in pain and anger as he fired. He cut down the ones at the front of the swarm, but others came, a wide line that he was never going to stop.

He charged into them, still firing, drawing the creatures towards him. Aliens died all around him, then the machine guns from the Heavy Weapons section opened up, adding to his fire. For a moment he was clear of aliens, but then they swarmed up the hill towards the men on the guns and they turned their fire to protect themselves. The swarm surged forward again, and Williams disappeared under it, still firing and kicking as alien claws and fangs tore his cybernetic body apart.

⊙ ⊙ ⊙

Sector Twelve, City North, 1st Platoon, Four Section
"Hunter One, Aries One, this is Command," Piper said urgently. "Thirty second warning – incoming fire, get under cover!"

"Roger that, Piper," Barnes said. "Might be a little late, but better than nothing."

"All units, this is Aries One," Miles said over the global net. "Incoming fire support in thirty seconds… hold out!"

Three Section and Four Section were both gone, with aliens swarming up the hill. Barnes was isolated where he was, so withdrew slowly towards the Platoon HQ position. He expected to find Lieutenant Miles inside, taking cover from the incoming artillery, but she was out with her HQ team, firing at the aliens as they scurried up the hill towards them.

Barnes could see the incoming fire streaming towards them from all directions, an impressive sight under other circumstances.

"INCOMING!" he shouted. Miles looked at him and then at the sky, then ordered her men back into the bunker.

Barnes scooped her up as he raced past and bundled her into the bunker, ignoring her protests. It didn't have a door so he blocked the entrance with his armoured body and braced for impact.

Thirty-two warheads detonated on and around the platoon position, ripping the landscape to pieces, along with anything not under cover. The shockwave threw Barnes into the bunker, nearly crushing the troops he was trying to protect, and then everything was silent.

Sector Twelve, City North, 1ˢᵗ Platoon
Barnes and Miles stood atop the position, watching the relief force sift through the rubble looking for survivors. There weren't many, and those were horribly injured and would require serious medical attention.

Miraculously, Corporal Harris had survived, the only man from Four Section to make it – he had lost both arms and had punctures to a few major organs. Other men had similar injuries, some from the aliens, some from the artillery fire, and stretcher parties were carrying them to waiting ambulances for evac and treatment.

Barnes watched them go. Sector Twelve was about to get their first batch of cyborgs, and he hoped they'd do as well as his own men had.

"I'm sorry about your friends," Miles said, thinking much the same thoughts. "We wouldn't have made it without them."

Barnes nodded. "Most likely not, no," he said quietly. "They died well. That's what they would have wanted."

Piper had located Gibbs's body in the subway. A small swarm had emerged from the southern exit and had been dealt with by an infantry force in Sector Eleven, and Piper had sent in some drones to check for more. His body was surrounded by dead aliens, which was fitting.

Miles looked at Barnes, then reached out to tap his chest with her knuckles. She seemed surprised when it made nothing but a soft thud.

"Expecting a metallic sound?" Barnes asked. Miles nodded, suddenly looking sheepish. "Don't worry, everyone does."

"Do you miss it?" Miles asked. "Being fully human I mean."

"Some days I do," Barnes said. "But I'd be lying if I said I'd give it all up."

"Really?"

"By rights I should be dead, and if I wasn't dead, I'd be an invalid somewhere unable to fight, just waiting for the aliens to finally catch up and finish what they started. These implants, this armour," Barnes said, "gives me a second chance, like I've come back from the dead."

"Must be hard."

"A small sacrifice for the greater good," Barnes said, nodding towards the survivors of 1st Platoon. "Knowing I helped here today makes up for a lot of it."

"I'm heading to Sector Command," Miles said. "I don't suppose I can convince you and Piper to transfer over to this sector. You know I could use you both."

Barnes laughed and shook his head. "We're Sector Eleven people, we've spilt too much blood to be moving."

"Thought you'd say that," Miles said, "but thought I'd ask all the same."

Barnes drew himself up to his full height and threw a salute to the young Lieutenant, taking her by surprise. She returned it with a puzzled look.

"You did well, ma'am," Barnes said, "if you don't mind me saying so. You might have a bit to learn about trusting your superiors as much as you do, but you did well."

Miles smiled. "Thank you, Sergeant, you did pretty well yourself," she said. "Once we get the sector set up again, you and Piper should come over, maybe we can work on some better coordination protocols."

"Piper can't leave sector command, ma'am."

"No-one's indispensable, Sergeant," Miles said with a grin.

"I mean literally," Barnes said, a touch of sadness in his voice. "She was caught up in the same attack I was and got mauled worse." He hesitated, the words tasting bitter as he explained. "She's just a brain in a box now, tied directly into the command and control grid."

Miles looked at him, horrified, then reached out and put a hand on his chest. After a moment she turned away and Barnes watched as she went to look after her people, then he turned away himself and made his way slowly back to Sector Eleven and his barracks.

Sector Eleven, Alpha Company barracks
The barracks was dark and still, with only the slow flicker of lights to show the building wasn't as empty and deserted as the shattered buildings around it. Until recently it had housed three soldiers, now it just had the one.

THE CRUST

Justin Bell

"It's the end of the world, Sergeant Graves. Does it really matter how your hair looks?"

Peter Graves looked over towards Doctor McCally, his hand halfway paused through his shock of brown hair. The beating blades of the Blackhawk slammed air down upon his head, battling his fingers for supremacy over the fall and design of his carefully manicured locks.

"I thought you military boys had strict guidelines on that sort of thing?" The scientist's thick, Australian accent put a twist on the last word of the sentence.

"We're not traditional military, Doc," the sergeant replied.

"No, apparently we're a glorified taxi cab for a snotty scientist," Greer barked from the pilot's seat.

The doctor chuckled. "Fair play, Ms Greer. Fair play!"

The broad belly of the Blackhawk AH-1 drifted as it cut through the evening sky, moving like a black shadow among indigo curtains.

"So, you really think this is the end of the world?" Graves asked, turning towards the scientist. His hand navigated from his hair to the week-long growth of stubble along the firm contours of his broad chin.

"Tough to say," she replied, "though typically when my American counterparts call me over from halfway across the world, I tend to think the worst."

"You a geologist, then?" Graves asked.

"Biologist," McCally replied.

"Did you say biologist?" Yarvis moved the M-249 Squad Automatic Weapon from his lap so he could lean in further. "The hell do they need a biologist for? Last I heard it was tectonic plates throwing that geyser outta whack."

McCally forced a broad smile across her smooth features. "I guess we'll all find out together, won't we, darling?"

Graves looked out the open door of the Blackhawk at the mountains retreating in the distance. When he'd woken this morning, he'd been preparing his team for a training operation in the Rocky Mountains, not expecting a call from his least favorite contact in the CIA. One benefit of running his own off-the-books outfit was that those clueless spooks couldn't boss them around, yet here they were, being bossed around by a clueless spook. At least the money was good.

The team was small tonight, with only him, Greer, and four others. They hadn't expected to get diverted to prevent the supposed end of the world. One of the largest geysers west of the Mississippi was throwing off all sorts of weird shit, and the federal pukes needed a quick escort for the good doctor. As Greer had said, being a glorified taxi driver wasn't in their job description, but when the CIA threw a couple zeroes on the end of the contract, they felt a little more obligated.

"So what happens if this thing blows?" Graves asked.

McCally shrugged. "I haven't seen the analysis yet, but if it's anything like the Yellowstone protocols we could be talking about enough debris to block out the sun for a few decades. Plunge the planet into its next ice age. All sorts of fun stuff."

"And what the hell are a bunch of soldiers for hire with automatic weapons supposed to do to stop that?"

"Maybe you should give your CIA friend a call and ask him."

"Tried. He's not answering."

"Surprise, surprise."

"Sarge, I've got visual!" shouted Greer from the pilot's seat. "Night vision's shot! Infrared is going off the charts. Whatever is up with that geyser down there, it's smoking all instruments."

"Can you put us down N-O-E?"

"Bringing us in, nap-of-the-Earth, on your order, Sarge."

"Warrant Officer, you outrank me!"

"Not in this outfit I don't."

The Blackhawk's propellers slowed to a successive *thump thump thump* as the dark aircraft eased its way down from the sky towards the uneven ground below.

Sergeant Graves turned towards the cargo hold and the four other men seated inside. "Yarvis, get that SAW ready! Quezar and Brady, M4 Carbines with suppressors and scopes! Grab those NVR's!"

"I thought night vision was toasted?" asked Luis Quezar, even as he swept the automatic rifle up in two hands.

"Grab 'em anyway, kid!"

"Brayshaw, make sure you've got the tactical shotgun. I want something with a punch, just in case."

"In case of what?" Brayshaw asked. "The geyser gets pissed and throws rocks at us?"

"We don't know what we're dealing with," Graves barked. "Treat this like a hostile engagement, do you understand me?"

"Aye, aye, Sarge! On it."

The Blackhawk slowed and eased its way down towards the ground, its running lights washing over the scene below. Equipment lay in broken splashes, spread in scattered arcs across a wide expanse of the rocky terrain.

Graves turned towards McCally. "When was the last time you talked to the team here?" he shouted over the whirling thump of the rotors.

"Six hours ago!" she replied. "We figured the residual energy was interfering with communications, but I think that's another reason they asked you for escort services!"

The sergeant gestured out of his open compartment and Dr McCally leaned over to glance outside. He saw her eyes widen in surprise.

"Where are they?" she asked, though she knew nobody there would have the answer.

"Touchdown in one!" Greer shouted from the pilot's seat. The second she finished speaking the rotors clunked and the Blackhawk lurched left. Graves shot upright, reaching out and gripping the seat.

"Fucking hell!" Yarvis shouted, the M-249 back on his lap and fully loaded.

"Engine sputter!" Greer shouted back. "Instruments are going haywire!"

The helicopter dipped forward and charged as if trying to headbutt the ground, and Greer yanked back on the stick with both hands, struggling to get the aircraft level.

"Going in hard!" she yelled. "Everyone buckle up, this bitch is fighting me!"

The AH-1 banked left, coming around in a rumbling semi-circle. Dust kicked up around them as they neared the ground, the whirring blades picking up small stones and dirt, pelting the aircraft and everyone inside.

"Hold on to something!" Graves shouted right before the Blackhawk pounded into the ground belly-first.

"Well, that could have been a hell of a lot worse," Greer said, looking at the Blackhawk. The front landing gear had snapped off in the harder than expected landing, so the nose now tilted forward, the blunt and rounded front of the aircraft worn and twisted by the impact. Light smoke spilled from the rotor joint and the propellers spun in lazy haphazard circles over their heads as the momentum wound down. Around the broken bird, Graves' team had filtered out in a defensive perimeter.

Several portable light posts bracketed the site, forming an eight hundred-meter perimeter around the research area, four hundred meters from the geyser itself. Pale, artificial light baked down upon the ground, illuminating the rock-covered area and showcasing the damage that had been done.

Every workstation and their metal crates stood pulverized into twisted clutches of iron and polymer. Shattered monitors sprayed all over the rocky surface of the surrounding ground. Eight-inch-thick beams holding geological sensors and long-range scopes were twisted and pulled apart like Twizzlers, laying in shredded halves among the rocks and sand.

The scientists were nowhere to be found. The geologists had detected the shift in tectonic plates ten days ago, identifying it as a massive earthquake deep underground. The land had split underneath the geyser and released a cacophony of molten water and lava that sprayed into the air for forty-eight hours straight. Then, it had stopped. All that remained was a huge vacant hole in the ground. A doorway into the Earth's tough hide.

Kari Greer made her way over towards the fissure, her pilot's helmet cast aside, and an M4 Carbine clutched in her gloved hands. Everyone in Graves' crew was expected to multi-task, and Greer was no exception. A former Warrant Officer in the Army, she knew how to handle combat just as well as the flight stick of a Blackhawk.

"Don't get too close!" shouted Graves. "We don't know what we're getting into yet."

Not too far away, Mitch Brayshaw crouched in the dirt, his hands making strange patterns among the rocks. "Sarge, you might want to come check this out."

Graves approached Brayshaw and crouched as he drew near, narrowing his eyes towards the rough pattern of sand and dirt near Brayshaw's hand. Thin divots were dug out of the hard material in even, three-pronged patterns – trenches dug among the material. A faint copper-hued patch of dirt dragged along the same path, making an almost attractive artistic statement in the sediment.

"These marks," Brayshaw whispered, pointing to the trenches. "They almost look like claw marks."

Graves glanced up at him from under the carefully maintained comb over of thick hair. "You been watching X-Files again, Mitch?"

"Seriously, man," he said. "And check this out." He gestured towards the copper-colored dirt and moved it around with his hand. "See how this is clumped together where it's discolored? I think it's old blood."

"How old?"

"Few hours maybe?"

222

"Maybe six hours?"

Brayshaw locked eyes with Graves, both thinking the same, uncomfortable thing.

"Guys, what are you looking at?" Quezar asked, coming up on their flank. His pace slowed as he neared the swath of rust-painted ground. "Oh damn," he whispered. "That what I think it is?"

"This makes no bloody sense," Dr McCally complained as she stormed past them. Her eyes affixed on Greer who bent low near the mouth of the geyser, closer than Graves was comfortable with.

"Hold up, Doc," he said. "And Greer, back away from there a little, wouldya?"

"Something got you spooked?" Greer asked, standing and turning towards them. "Just a big hole in the ground, right—"

Her chest exploded without warning, a vicious and angry outward burst of thick red, clumped with torn muscle and shredded fabric from her tactical vest. A twisted and gnarled barb ejected through her flesh, coated in gore, then clacked apart into splayed, bony fingers. Her eyes glared down at it as the appendages spread, latching into her skin like a grapple. It tugged, and she whirled backwards, toppling into the silent darkness without even a scream.

"What the hell!" screamed Yarvis, as he took two cautious strides forward, his Squad Automatic lifted into the crook of his arm.

"God dammit!" screamed McCally, taking an unsteady step backwards. There were a few beats of silence after Greer's disappearance, and the low clatter-click of insect legs on rock echoed from the darkness of the geyser. Dozens of narrow green eyes blinked into illumination just beyond the crest of the geyser, all of them glaring up at the small team of operatives who converged behind the scientist, weapons ready.

"Fuck me sideways," hissed Brady, coming up on Graves' left.

"What did they dump us into?" Brayshaw asked.

The clacking footsteps halted, but the eyes remained, peering out at them, curious and hungry and attempting to test their purpose here. Suddenly, four pairs of them charged, hurtling forward, their claws smacking on stone and dirt.

Graves glimpsed one before they reached the team. Its pale skin was thick and leathery like the hide of an albino crocodile. Two long, narrow legs were bent backward at the knees, ending in three protruding talons. Its four spindly arms wrapped around Dr McCally like a sick embrace, coiling her up into the creature. Its head was flat and wide, the skin just as empty of color as the rest of its body, creatures that appeared to have not seen the sun in a very, very long time. The monster dragged McCally backwards, her arms wheeling as three of the other creatures charged Graves and his team.

"McCally!" Graves screamed, but she disappeared from view as the remaining creatures stormed towards them; twisted, bone crusted fangs extended, their green slits for eyes narrowed and glaring. "Open season on these mother fuckers!"

Brady swiveled left and opened-up in full auto with his M4, the silenced weapon snapping in his hands. Bullets stitched a lazy diagonal line down the skinny torso of the first approaching creature and split its hard flesh into ribbons, spraying a dark ichor in thick rivulets down onto the sand. It slumped forward and tumbled, limbs flailing.

"They're fast, but not bullet-proof!" Brady shouted, altering his aim and seeing two other creatures had already collected behind the first three, covering some serious ground in less than a handful of seconds.

Yarvis moved to intercept, his M-249 exploding with a shattering noise. The drum-fed machine gun sprayed 5.56-millimeter rounds into the tight clutch of approaching pale creatures, shattering through them and splintering limbs and shredding flesh. Graves moved forward, stepping through a pair of exploding beasts, ducking away from their spraying blood and taking aim at two more that approached quickly. Keeping it on semi-automatic, he squeezed off three shots with the M4 into the forehead of an approaching geyser monster, swiveled and pumped two more rounds into the second.

He rounded on the opening to the fissure, his weapon at the ready but the eyes had vanished, and the crest of the crevasse was clear. No monsters. And no McCally.

"They got her," he hissed. "Fuck!"

"We got a few of them, too," said Yarvis, glancing around at the half dozen torn, pale corpses surrounding them.

"Jesus did you see how many eyes there were?" Quezar said. "Big deal we killed six of them. It looked like there were six fucking hundred."

"What the hell are these things?" asked Brayshaw, dropping into a crouch, touching the rigid flesh of one of the creatures.

"Spent too much time underground," muttered Graves. "Buncha fucking morlocks or something."

"So what do we do now?" asked Brady. "Time to call in reinforcements?"

"Like who?" asked Graves. "Freaking Ghostbusters?"

"I say we call a damned bomb strike in here," Quezar mumbled. "Shove a tactical nuke up their asses."

"Yeah, I'm sure that would do wonders for the unstable tectonic whatever the fucks down there," Brady said. "Blow this geyser and blow the entire world to shit."

"McCally was here because they called her. They wanted her here, and they wanted her here quickly. That means some shit is about to go down," Graves said. "We just gotta figure out what that shit is."

"And how do you suppose we do that?" Brayshaw asked. "Go down after her?"

Graves looked at him.

"God dammit, Sarge. You've got to be fucking kidding? And end up like Greer?" He halted for a moment, as if Kari Greer's fate had just occurred to him.

Graves was thinking the same, staring up into the dark sky and picturing his pilot's face, her vacant, staring, unknowing eyes as the thing's barbed fingers dragged her down into the darkness.

"We owe Greer better than this," Graves said. "We owe her more than cutting and running. Her and McCally. Comms are down, and the bird is broken. We can either sit on our asses and wait for help to come, or we can toughen up and see what's going on down there. I know which choice I'm making." As if emphasizing that fact he yanked the magazine from his M4 and checked the load, then slammed it back home.

"You with me, or what?"

Graves crested the lip of the geyser, looking down into the looming darkness. His M4 Carbine now had a tactical flashlight bolted underneath the suppressor to go along with the top-mounted sight, and it cut a pale path through the inky darkness. Halting for a moment, Graves passed his weapon left then right, illuminating the section of entrance where they stood.

"It goes down deep," he said, turning to speak over his shoulder. As he'd known they would, Quezar, Yarvis, Brady and Bradshaw had all volunteered to hit the geyser with him, if not for McCally or for the future of the world, then for the Warrant Officer they'd spent the last three years of their lives with. The woman who had flown them into and out of some of the hairiest shit imaginable. Although none of them agreed on what the rest of the world deserved, they knew Greer, and knew she deserved better.

"Looks like some kind of tunnel system," Brady said, moving up next to Graves, his own light shining down through a narrow passage. "Some kind of anthill bullshit going on down there."

"Fuck. This is sounding better and better all the time," Quezar muttered.

"We need you, man," Graves said. "You and your C4. You're

our explosives guy, the combat engineer. If we're bringing this thing down, that shit in your backpack is what's going to do it."

Quezar nodded and sighed deeply. "Whatever you say, Sarge."

Graves stepped onto the rock and followed the passage down, drawing in a deep breath and holding it as the walls closed in to a narrow, circular passage surrounding them. They could only walk two at a time, shoulder-to-shoulder, and even that was a little too close for comfort. They walked for a long time, going down into the blackness of the Earth, moving farther and deeper than any of them felt comfortable with. A dull, wet heat soaked the air around them as they walked, like thick, hot hands gripping and pressing on them, slowing their pace.

Bringing up the rear, Quezar turned and looked up from where they'd come. "I can't even see the stars or sky anymore," he said. "How deep are we?"

"Not deep enough," Graves replied.

"Hold up," Brayshaw whispered. The former recon specialist had what seemed like a sixth sense for tracking, and he pushed up past Graves and Brady, holding his hand up and moving his fingers as if feeling the air. "I'm feeling a cross breeze," he murmured. "More passages are likely linking up to this one ahead."

Noise exploded from deeper within the earth. Claws scraped and clacked on the rock, and the air grew thick with menace.

"Oh, shit," hissed Brayshaw, lifting his weapon and back-pedaling. "Shit, shit, shit!"

"Where are they?" barked Yarvis. "Where the fuck are they? I can't see shit with this light!"

"Whose dumb ass idea was this?" barked Quezar.

"Calm down, all of you," Graves hissed. "Take it easy! Sound carries in enclosed spaces, if we're hearing them, then they're hearing us. Shut your damn traps and let's move, quick and quiet."

They froze, silencing their movements as much as possible, slowing their breathing and taking quiet steps. Graves inched forward, one step, then another. Yarvis placed a hand on his shoulder and pulled so that Graves would move aside and let him come up on his left, placing the heavy weapon at the front. The clicking sounds were still coming from up ahead, a near avalanche of clawed footfalls. A low, red light throbbed in the distance, barely illuminating the far end of the access tunnel. It revealed a few branching tunnels along each wall.

"This isn't going to end well," Quezar whispered.

The group continued in silence, step by step, muscles tensed as they heard the skittering of clawed feet all around them. Graves could now hear them above him and to either side and knew there must be countless passages throughout this buried ecosystem. Dozens of those creatures, if not hundreds.

Perhaps even thousands.

He kept watching the low, red illumination from up ahead, focusing on that, the mythical light at the end of the tunnel. As he took one more step clacking footsteps rattled from just ahead and to the right. He shifted, moving the pale cone of tactical flashlight just far enough to see an opening where another passage connected. A shift of motion in the gap of the wall caught his eye.

"We've got movement! Two o'clock! Brady, Quezar get up here with those 203s. I think we're getting company!"

The two specialists pushed forward with their M4 Carbines that were underslung with 203 grenade launchers. Yarvis clung to the left wall, his automatic drifting towards the opening on the opposite side. The claw clicking stopped, a sudden and swift cut of noise, draping the tunnel in a disorienting silence.

"Slow," Graves whispered. "Take it slow."

They burst from the opening like water from a broken fire hydrant, exploding outward in a flood of pale-skinned skitter, clamoring over and around each other and swarming the tunnel with flailing limbs and smacking claws.

"Hoooly shit!" Yarvis yelled as they poured out, several of them peeling away and scrambling up the sides of the tunnel and over the ceiling. Within a second the 249 was up in his arms, stock rammed shoulder-tight, his other hand supporting the barrel as it roared loud and long in the dark confines of the tunnel. Rounds shredded the first group of approaching creatures, blasting them apart in strips of pale flesh and bone.

Graves moved forward, shifting and firing his M4. Two others dropped as a dull whump and streak of smoke sailed over his head, the grenade clunking along the curved wall for a moment before exploding amid a group of them, throwing shrieking, broken forms in all directions.

"Press forward!" Graves shouted. "Head for that red light!" He broke into a run, charging through and around disoriented creatures, shifting and firing a swift burst every few paces. Yarvis discarded his spent ammo drum and retrieved another, punching it tight into the weapon and turning and firing again, battering another group of creatures with lead.

Brayshaw moved on Graves' flank, firing his M4 in bursts, sending two more creatures scrambling for the ground. Another 203 launched from Quezar's rifle, striking the wall and exploding, showering rocks and wet clumps of flesh over the group as they raced forward.

Graves glanced to his right as he ran past an opening in the passage; another horde of creatures charging up that tunnel to attack them.

"Quezar!" Graves shouted. "You're last in line, seal that passage!"

Brayshaw and Brady hurried past the opening, the floor of the tunnel now piled and slick with the broken, bloodied bodies of the beasts they'd already slain. Quezar halted by the passage just as a creature lunged from it, screaming. It lashed out with its narrow, boney right arm, fingers pressed together into a jagged barb. The soldier shifted to the right, the barb skidding over his left shoulder and carving a hunk of thick flesh from it. Wincing, Quezar lifted his foot and kicked, smashing the creature high in the chest and throwing it backwards. As it toppled back down the hole, he slammed a 203 round into the ceiling. It detonated with an ear-shattering blast, blocking it from within.

"Passage sealed!" Quezar shouted, picking up the pace, his left arm hanging limp at his side.

"He get ya?" Graves called back. Quezar nodded but didn't slow his run. They all looked ahead as the passage dipped deeper, sloping downhill on a steeper trajectory as they neared the red light. Their clothes were wet and heavy, the temperature at near unbearable.

"What are we getting into down here, Sarge?" Yarvis asked as he removed another empty ammo drum and replaced it.

"Savin' the world, Ronnie. Savin' the fucking world."

"I didn't join this outfit to save the world," Quezar said. "Just wanted to make some money and maybe live a few years longer."

"Can't have both in this line of work, kid," Brady said, shaking his head. Sporadic clicking echoed inside the walls around them.

"Keep moving," Graves hissed as they angled further downward and picked up the pace. More clicks echoed off the curved walls, these coming from behind them.

"How the fuck did they get behind us?" Quezar asked, turning around. He could see the faint glistening of eyes in the darkness, converging and approaching.

"They're moving fast!" shouted Graves. "Seal the tunnel!"

Quezar whirled on him. "What? That's our way out!"

"Doesn't matter if it's filled with fucking Morlocks! Seal the God damned tunnel!"

The skittering grew louder and longer as the eyes charged towards them. Quezar lifted his weapon and Brady lifted his. They back-pedaled with the 203s raised, hoping that maybe the eyes would take one last-ditch swerve in either direction, stopping what they had to do.

"Now!" Graves roared, and the two men launched their grenades.

The slamming blast of twin explosions howled in the confined area. Smoke filled the central tunnel, dropping large chunks of ceiling and wall. When the dust finally cleared their only exit was closed in a pile of broken rock.

They stood there in silence, looking down at the faint red light a hundred yards away, then back at the sealed tunnel on the other side. The entire passage pulsed, a deep and aggressive heat radiating from the walls.

"Well, that settles that," Quezar mumbled. He rubbed at the seeping wound on his shoulder.

"If this is a maze down here," Graves said, "there's probably another way out. We just need to find it."

Quezar glared at him through narrowed eyes and pushed past towards the faint red light.

The five of them moved in silence the rest of the way, continuing down the tunnel amid the scattered scratches of claw on rock from surrounding passages. Graves kept quiet. He had a lot he wanted to say to the men and women who had put their trust in him. He'd led them down here, sealed them in, and likely sealed all their fates.

What difference would any of this make in the grand scheme of things? How would five independent contractors stop this fissure from detonating? How could they stand against a horde of pale-skinned, four-armed creatures born in the bowels of the Earth's crust?

Nearing the edge of the main passage, Graves held up a hand to halt the approach of his team. They slowed to a stop near where the throbbing red light shone on the passage walls and floor.

There was a gradual curve towards the left. Graves approached it, leaning forward to look around. The passage opened into a wide, sprawling cavern, an opened maw of pointed rock and stone that glowed red as a thick stream of lava coursed around it. In the center of the chamber two figures huddled on the ground, coiled in fetal positions.

Graves dropped into a crouch, gesturing to his team to fall in behind. Looking back, he motioned to Yarvis. "Let me hold your binos for a sec, Yarv," he whispered.

Reaching into a pouch on his vest, the machine gunner

pulled out the set and handed them over. Pressing them to his eyes, he leaned around the corner and adjusted the range.

"McCally looks to be alive," he whispered. "She's there with another unidentified person." Without looking at Yarvis, he passed the binoculars back. "The immediate area is clear," Graves reported. "Wide room, about a hundred yards circular. Two females in the center." He looked at the group. "Straight across the room looks to be another wide passage, I'm betting that one also leads somewhere towards the surface. If we move in, you guys grab the scientists and exfiltrate through the other passage. I'll stay behind and cover your six."

"The fuck you talking about, Sarge?" asked Brayshaw. "We're not leaving you down here to get chewed up by these bastards."

"It's my fault you're all in this mess," Graves said. "I'll be damned if I don't get you out of it."

Quezar looked around at the other members of the team, thinking his words through carefully. "You know, Sarge, I'm damn tempted to take you up on that. But we started it, I suppose we might as well finish this shit."

Graves swung around the corner of the tunnel and crouch-ran across the chamber towards McCally. The heat was near unbearable. Everywhere Graves looked he was glaring through waves of rippling heat, his clothes and flesh soaked as he came up on the two women laying on the ground motionless.

"McCally!" he hissed as he neared. "You alive?"

She spun on the ground, eyes widening. "Graves? What the hell are you doing here, you idiot?"

"Saving your thankless ass," he replied.

"You shouldn't have come," she whispered. "They're all over the place. Everywhere."

"What are they?"

Behind and around him, the other four fanned out in a loose

perimeter, weapons raised. The cavern was high and wide, a rough circular shape with low stalagmites dangling from the roof like liquid stone poured then frozen in place. Steam from the lava rose and formed a persistent humidity. Several small openings were scattered along the walls, though the skittering noises were disturbingly silent this deep within the ground.

"I'm not sure what they are," McCally replied. "But they've been here long before us. They were probably trapped down here, but then the tectonic shift opened a pathway to the surface, releasing this strange energy… and them."

"It's poised to release much worse," another voice hissed, and Graves turned towards the second woman on the ground.

"This is Genevieve Poirot. She was with the geology team," whispered McCally, coming up into a seated position.

"Those lava streams," Poirot said, pointing at the boiling red fluid rolling along the edge of the room. "They are interlaced throughout the entire substructure down here. Like veins and arteries all throughout this compound. They've formed this symbiotic relationship with the organisms. A delicate balance, holding this whole structure together."

Graves looked up and around, lifting his weapon. For a moment, he thought he heard that telltale skittering noise, but it seemed to fall silent the moment he had.

"How do we get out?" Graves asked. "The tunnel we came down… well, it's impassable now."

Poirot pointed to the wide passage on the opposite side of the room. "I think… I think that may lead to the surface. I've seen steam venting through it and felt the cool gust of air."

"Then get up, ladies," Graves barked. "We're getting out of here."

He hooked a hand around McCally's elbow, helping her to stand while Brady moved in on his right and did the same for Poirot, moving them slowly but steadily to their feet.

"We can't just leave," Poirot breathed. "The geyser could detonate at any time."

"What can we do to stop it?" Graves asked.

Poirot smiled a knowing smile and opened her mouth to speak.

They never heard the trademark claw-skittering of the approaching Morlock. It leapt down from the roof, one of its narrow, twisted limbs shooting out. The barb struck Poirot straight in the face, splitting her skull in a wet snap that sprayed blood and brain in a wide upward arc. As the creature landed, it withdrew its arm, leaving Poirot's body standing there, confused, a ragged mess piled on top of her shoulders. Poirot took one curious step backwards, then toppled to the ground.

McCally stared, her eyes wide and unblinking.

"We've got one!" shouted Graves, but Brady was a step ahead, moving towards it and popping three swift shots through the hardened crust of its forehead. Bone splintered and sprayed, and the underground dweller flopped backwards, limbs twitching.

The skittering returned. Graves turned, not wanting to see what he knew he would. Every single hole along the curved, arched wall of the cavern was full of monsters.

"Go go go! Fucking go!" Graves roared, lifting his weapon and unloading the M4 in a rapid chattering of automatic gunfire. The creatures scattered from their perches in the holes, scrambling down the rock walls on all their six limbs like nightmare man-sized insects, claws snatching chunks of stone and rock as they went along.

McCally stumbled backwards, turning and running towards the other passage as Yarvis came up next to Graves, firing his own automatic. As the rapid chatter of claws on rock echoed around them, Graves heard a louder, harder sound. Deep, powerful, and thudding footfalls sounded over the skittering. Something bigger than what they'd seen so far.

"These holes," Graves hissed. "We've been calling it an anthill… these must be the drones."

"If there are drones," continued Yarvis.

"Then there's a fucking queen," finished Brayshaw, coming up on their left. Just ahead of them, along the south wall of the curved cavern, a large opening filled, half a dozen blinking eyes emerging in the darkness.

"Three of 'em straight ahead!" Quezar said, moving to intercept.

"That's not three of them!" Graves shouted. "That's one. One big one!"

The queen charged from the darkened cavern, a large, lumbering beast loping on all six limbs. She was the same as the drones, but far thicker, like old and off-white twisted tree trunks. Her head had an ornate rounded crown of thick cartilage perched above six narrow, gleaming eyes. With a snap and stomach-churning flutter, fibrous wings cracked from her contorted spine and extended into a quartet, frantically buzzing and carrying her airborne. She was the size of a large horse, and much more powerful.

"Quezar!" Graves shouted, his voice rising to a pitch.

"One step ahead of you, boss man!" the specialist called out, moving up on his flank and lifting his M4. He moved his hand towards the front-facing trigger under the 203 grenade launcher and let a thick slug fly with a thump. The grenade struck the queen on its left, just under the twin fiber wings on that side. Dark ichor fell in streams as it shrieked, lurching to the right and threatening to topple over sideways.

"Nice shot, Luis! Nice fucking shot!" Graves shouted even as a few dozen smaller Morlocks made their way down the curved surface of the cavern and charged across the rocky terrain towards them.

With a loud, angry scream, the queen corrected its sideways pitch, wings beating hard as it turned and headed straight for the soldiers.

Brady charged past Graves on the left, firing his M4 and knocking down half a dozen creatures as he did. Yarvis unloaded again with the 249, carving a swath through the horde around them.

"There's way too many of them!" Graves shouted.

"We were tryin' to tell you that an hour ago, Sarge!" Quezar barked back.

Brayshaw swiveled right. "They're coming from everywhere!" His weapon chattered, holding back an approaching group. Two of the beasts veered apart, letting his weapon fire pass harmlessly between them as they lunged forward.

"Brayshaw, watch it!" Yarvis screamed, but the Morlocks met in the middle with the soldier caught between them, sharpened bone claws slashing at his vest and the muscled flesh beneath. He screamed once, and then went down within the rushing swarm.

"Keep going!" Graves shouted, hot on McCally's heels. "Head for that shaft!"

Brady, Yarvis, and Quezar angled after them, turning and firing as they ran, trying to take down as many of their pursuers as possible. Quezar launched another grenade, dropping it in the center of a group of six Morlocks.

Yarvis shifted left as Quezar fired right, sweeping his weapon back and forth in an arc.

No matter how many they took down more just kept coming, the horde growing into a pale tsunami of shuffling bodies. The queen continued to surge forward, guiding her winged body towards them as they approached the wide shaft and escape. Graves glanced to his left as he backpedaled, seeing the trench of thick, rolling lava right next to him.

"What did the scientist say about the lava?" Graves barked to McCally as they continued their frantic motion towards the exit passage.

"I don't know what you mean!" she screamed back over the buzz and chatter of wings and bony claws.

"Delicate balance? Isn't that what she said?"

"Something like that!"

"What if we upset that balance?"

"I'm a biologist, Sergeant Graves. Your guess is as good as mine!"

Brady pulled up near him, turning right and slamming a fresh magazine into his M4.

"Boss, we getting the hell out of here or what?"

"Absolutely! Fall back on me, now!"

Brady half-turned and prepared to move.

"Look out!" Graves screamed his warning, but the queen dove and snapped out one jagged front leg, burying it into Brady's back and impaling him on a narrow, barbed limb. The soldier glanced at Graves for one split second, his eyes wide with disbelief.

The queen snapped her leg back and released the barbs, throwing Brady two dozen meters backwards, his body rag-dolling through the air. A swarm of pale creatures was on him as he landed, devouring him in seconds.

Graves' stomach lurched. This was all his fault.

The distinctive chatter of 249 fire grew louder as Yarvis approached, Quezar right next to him.

"We gotta break for it, Sarge!" Quezar yelled. Graves nodded and looked back, seeing that McCally was crossing a stone platform over the lava trench. The passage was close now.

"I'll hold here," Graves said. "You two break for it. I'll take as many down as I can."

Yarvis and Quezar glared at him then each other, not sure what to do for a moment.

"Just fucking go!" Graves screamed and charged forward, away from the passage, his weapon exploding in fire.

Yarvis shook his head. "I'm staying with you!" He shifted, his weapon lifting just as three of the Morlocks struck from his blind side, slamming into him and knocking him backwards. As Graves turned, he saw two Morlocks tear Yarvis apart, their limbs striking like pistons, blasting blood and gore upwards in spurts.

"Ronnie!" screamed Quezar, headed his way.

"Luis, fucking watch your back!"

Another stray Morlock leapt, jumping from the approaching horde and arching through the air. Quezar turned too late as the creature smashed into him, front legs slamming down through his shoulders, pinning him to the stone ground. The creature reared up and whipped his legs apart, tearing off Quezar's arms and sending his weapon skidding across the ground towards Graves. The sergeant fired the last of his rounds, then tossed the M4 aside and scooped up Quezar's.

Graves firmed his lips, drew a breath, and turned and ran, his team no more.

"Go go go go!" he screamed to McCally as he charged, hoping they could make it.

McCally stared at the carnage in horror as Quezar was torn limb from limb. She turned as Graves shouted, seeing him running over the stone floor, waving for her to run. The nearby lava was cooking her skin, crisping the flesh as she stood in the mouth of the passage.

Graves halted for a moment, turning and firing his M4, taking down a trio of creatures that led the pack chasing him. He spun back around and ran, nearly catching up with the scientist as she entered the passage. She turned and faced him

"Keep running!" he yelled.

"Graves, behind you!"

The queen's barbed arm moved quickly, ramming down through Graves' shoulder as he turned. It thrust with such force it punctured his torso where the arm met the body, burying itself in the stone floor and pinning Graves to the ground like an insect in a museum.

To his credit, Graves didn't scream. He clamped his jaws and lips together in a firm, narrow grimace, his hand still wrapped tight around the trigger of Quezar's M4.

"Sergeant!" McCally shouted rushing towards him.

Graves reached into his holster and pulled out his Glock 19 pistol, throwing it to her. "Take this. Take this and run."

"I... I can't—"

"Just go!" he screamed, the tendons in his neck pulling taut, his face flushed and red.

"What are you going to do?" she yelled back, backtracking up the passage. She could already feel the soothing cool air of night blowing down on the back of her neck. It was like a cool glass of water on a hot, summer day.

Graves turned his head back towards the queen. She was lowering herself towards him, snarling. "I'm going to see about upsetting this balance."

He swung the M4 around and pulled the trigger on the 203 launcher, driving a grenade into the face of the queen. The detonation shook the passage, knocking chunks of rock and stone down around McCally, who ducked and retreated as it showered over her. The queen's arm separated at the torso with the explosion and she reared up, screaming, her horde of drones swarming to her aid.

"Come with me!" McCally shouted at the sergeant as he wrapped his hand tight around the severed barb of the queen's arm. He poised there, ready to yank, but must have realized the jagged barbs of the severed leg could tear something vital open and he'd bleed out.

"No," Graves said. "I need to see this through." Before she could reply, he had thrown himself to his feet and was fishing a large shell out of a pouch on his vest, pumping it into the round tube mounted below his gun barrel. McCally tensed her fingers around the handle of the Glock, turned and threw herself up the passage at a dead run.

Graves bit down hard, fighting back the pain as he dashed back out into the cavern. There was a chance he could see this through and live to fight another day. A small chance. His eyes narrowed at the rolling river of lava as he worked out his plan of attack.

As he scanned the ground ahead, his eyes locked on the mangled form of Luis Quezar. The drones had pulled back to attend to the Queen, leaving the soldier's half-eaten body unattended. Graves broke into a run, charging forward and hoping they wouldn't spot him, but knowing they probably would. Quezar's twisted and torn form was thirty yards from the trench of lava, the heat an oppressive wetness this close.

Graves slid next to Quezar's body, not wanting to look at him. Because his arms had been torn off at the shoulders, his backpack slid off quickly and smoothly. A hissing screech snapped his head around, and his eyes widened as the queen lowered her bone-crusted head towards him and charged.

Graves tore open the satchel and removed the device, spinning from the corpse and running as a bony limb punched a jagged crater in the rock just behind him. A flurry of buzzing and screeches assaulted his hearing as the queen howled in anger. Graves flipped open the lid of the control panel, then triggered an activation mechanism.

A small digital clock on the front side of the bundled device blinked into life, showing a five-minute timer. Graves knew that was five minutes he didn't have. The queen wrenched her limb free of the rock and screeched again, racing towards him. Her mouth opened wide, wider than Graves thought possible. His fingers frantically dug at the metal device, peeling away another panel as he searched for the manual override he knew was there.

Another bone twisted limb shot out and dug deep into the meaty muscle of Graves' thigh, and this time he couldn't hold back his scream as agony ratcheted through his entire body. Dropping to his backside, he could hear the soft gurgle of lava carving hot divots through solid stone and kept thinking of the scientist's words.

A delicate balance.

The queen moved in for the kill, placing her remaining legs either side of Sergeant Graves body as she lowered her massive head to tear his flesh apart.

"I've got you right where I want you," Graves sneered as he triggered the manual override.

Susan McCally's lungs burned, the heat still tugging and pulling on her as she climbed. Far below she could hear the mangled, twisting scream of the queen, then Sergeant Graves called out, a single barking shout of pain.

She didn't turn back. She kept running, her legs aching and arms pumping, sweat streaming over her face and forehead. She longed to look back, to glance over her shoulder and make sure she wasn't being followed, but she wouldn't allow herself to. She didn't want to risk slowing down, especially when she felt cool air slamming her in the face as she climbed. The night sky would be just ahead, she was sure of it, the stars almost within reach.

The shattering blast shook the entire tunnel system, and she stumbled forward, feeling the shock-wave of heat at her back as the ground shifted beneath her feet. Chunks of curved rock broke away and scattered at her feet, and the entire passage felt as if it dipped down to the right. McCally scrambled to her feet, smoke flowing past her as the tunnel rumbled and bucked.

"Run, you stupid woman, run!" she shouted to herself. She could feel the ground giving way, the entire passage beginning its slow, inward crumble. McCally pushed forward as debris rained down around her. She was so focused on running she didn't notice the squirming, pale-flesh figures scrambling along the curved roof above her head. She only realized they were there when they dropped to the ground ahead of her. She could see the sky just behind them, the indigo blackness of a wondrous South Dakota night.

One of the drones hissed and lunged, its barbed upper left hand lashing out towards her. She scrambled backwards, moving her hand to catch her fall against the wall. Her fingers brushed against something metal, and she closed her hand around it in desperation. The Glock. The second drone launched into the air as she swung her arm around and fired a bullet directly into its face.

The creature's head exploded in a hot shower of bone and gore, and before she even felt the splatter of Morlock blood spray her face she'd shifted left and fired again through the disjointed, twisted neck of the next pale creature, tearing its spine to shreds and sending it toppling sideways onto the stone.

With a sudden downward jerk, the floor beneath her began tearing away. Dr McCally drew in a breath and leapt forward, making several long strides before she finally burst out onto firm ground. As she sucked in fresh, cold air she glanced up at the geyser and saw one last gasp of steam burst up and fade into nothing, then the entire mound of stone, rock, and dirt crumbled in upon itself with a deafening crash.

Her ears ringing, Doctor Susan McCally crawled over the ground, eyes still stinging with spent steam and blasted earth. Shrouding the world in darkness, she covered her face and buried her head, trying to force the images from her mind – they'd never be gone, she knew that, but it didn't stop her from trying.

As her ears began clearing, the soft scuff of shoe on stone brought her head up, her eyes blinking away the dust and dirt.

A man in a dark suit stood before her, his arms crossed over his narrow chest, his suit, shirt, and tie a little too immaculate given the surroundings. She could tell who he was the moment she saw him, and even more frightening, she could tell what agency he represented.

"Dr McCally," the man said softly, looking down on her. "I'm glad you made it out of there alive." He bent slightly, offering one hand while the other wrapped around the Glock Graves had given her. "Now I think it's best you come with me."

CALL UP THE DEAD

A Griffin and Price Novella

James A Moore and Charles R Rutledge

*"There Shall not be found among you, anyone who casts a spell, or a
medium, or a spiritualist, or one who calls up the dead."*
-Deuteronomy 18:10

Wade Griffin parked his truck in front of a pawnshop, which
sat in one corner of a past-its-prime strip mall. The mall also
contained a dry cleaner, a store that sold used cell phones, and
a Thai take-out restaurant. Griffin had tried the food there once.
Once.

Griffin stepped out of the truck. It was springtime in northern
Georgia and all the cars in the parking lot were covered with a
film of yellow pine pollen. Pure hell if you had allergies. The
only thing Griffin was allergic to was fish, and you didn't get a
lot of airborne fish in the small town of Wellman. He entered the
pawnshop and stopped just inside the front door. There were
two men inside, a skinny gray-haired man behind the counter,
and a fat guy with a buzz cut seated on a stool in a corner.

"Help you?" Skinny said.

Buzz cut just practiced his thousand-yard stare.

Griffin stepped up to the counter and placed a small
diamond bracelet on the glass surface. He said, "This was pur-
chased here."

"Don't recognize it," Skinny said.

"I wasn't asking. This is one item from a jewelry box that
was taken in a burglary two weeks back. I want to know who
sold it to you."

"You a cop?"

"Private investigator."

"Then get the fuck out of my shop."

"I'm thinking not," Griffin said. "But speaking of cops, the guy you sold this to would be willing to tell them where he got it if I asked him. Probably lead to all kinds of embarrassing questions."

"Eddie, throw this guy out on his ass," Skinny said.

Buzz Cut, aka Eddie, slid off the stool. "Time to go, Ace."

Eddie was big and he was fat, but it wasn't all fat. He had scar tissue around his eyes, and his nose had been broken more than once. A bruiser, and probably a game one. He extended one hand, as if to take Griffin by the arm.

Griffin slapped the hand aside and brought his knee up towards Eddie's groin. Eddie twisted his leg inward to block and brought his hands down as any street fighter would. That was what Griffin wanted, of course. He grabbed the back of Eddie's head with his left hand and slammed his right elbow into Eddie's nose. The restraining hand kept Eddie from pulling away and he took the full force of the blow. Eddie fell.

Out of the corner of his eye, Griffin saw Skinny reaching under the counter. Griffin shuffled sideways and kicked the counter, causing it to topple over backwards. Skinny went down in a crash of broken glass and a shower of shiny objects. Griffin moved quickly around the wrecked counter and saw that Skinny had been reaching for a chrome .45 automatic.

"I'm betting you don't have a license for that gun," Griffin said, as he kicked the weapon away. "That's going to go badly when the cops get here."

Skinny said, "Look. We can make a deal. I got money."

"I don't want money."

"Okay, sure. I'll tell you where I got the bracelet."

"That may not be enough now, seeing as how you were going to shoot me and all."

"No, no. I was just going to scare you. Look, I got something better. This is something big."

"I've seen your shop. I don't think you've got anything big

enough to keep me from calling the cops. Step it up. The smell from the Thai place is making me sick."

"Listen, a guy came in two days ago and sold me a ring. It's on that list."

Griffin felt his gut go cold. "What list?"

"The list the cops sent out after that last home invasion."

Griffin said, "You have an item from one of the invasions and you didn't tell anyone? Those fuckers killed both those families."

Skinny must have seen what Griffin was thinking because he began to scuttle backwards, oblivious to the shards of glass on the floor. "I was going to tell somebody. I swear I was."

Griffin took a long, slow breath and blew it out. He suddenly realized his fists were clenched. No wonder the guy was freaking. Griffin knew what he looked like. Six-feet four inches, and 235 pounds. He could imagine his expression just now.

Griffin said, "Who sold it to you?"

"I don't know his name. He was never in before."

"You got a camera in here?"

Skinny shook his head. "Too expensive. But if you help me make a deal with the cops, I can describe the guy."

Griffin took out his phone. "The only deal I'll make with you is I'll try and keep the sheriff from killing you when he gets here."

Carl contemplated the third chilidog sitting innocently in the bag of food he'd just picked up at The Dawg Shop. The place had been open for all of two weeks, and as a good citizen and the sheriff in the area, he'd made a point of going by and giving them business the day they opened.

Since then he'd been by at least once a day, except for Sundays, when the bastards had the gall to be closed.

He needed a third chilidog like he needed a massive coronary. Yet, here he was, looking at that bag and seriously thinking he could just go back and pick up a few more for Angie back at the station. She'd never know. No one had to know.

He found himself wondering, and not for the first time, if the bastards running the place were lacing their chili with cocaine. It would explain the addictive quality and his lack of willpower.

The parking lot was full, and a goodly number of people were sitting in their cars and getting curbside service. Carl had actually gone inside, but now he was thinking he could just honk the horn and get those extra dogs on the go.

"No. Dammit. You're gonna get up and walk off a few calories if you're going back for more."

It was justifiable, really. He hadn't even tried one of their jalapeño slaw dogs yet. The very thought made him salivate.

As he was opening the door of the truck he used instead of a county issued squad car, he saw two young men squaring off and getting ready to throw down on each other.

They were young bucks, maybe out of high school and all the way into their first year of college. To look at them he figured their hormones far outweighed their common sense and as if to make his point for him, the object of their pending fisticuffs stood with her arms crossed and an amused smile on her face.

Carl made sure he had on his big voice when he spoke. The sound carried past all the people starting to look at the two would-be brawlers, and as quickly as they had gathered for the potential fight, the crowd dispersed. "Boys. I'm gonna make this short and sweet. Either one of you takes a swing and you're both going to the county lock up. I promise you, I will find reasons for you to spend the night." He smiled as he talked and moved closer to the two kids.

Jolene Blackbourne looked his way and her smile changed, growing more predatory.

Damn. She was feeling playful.

The two boys looked at Carl and then looked toward Jolene.

The thing about Jolene was that she was very nearly supernaturally pretty. Men looked at her and they wanted her. Hell, a lot of women looked at her and they wanted her. Carl looked at her and he wanted her, but he was smart enough to know that a lot of poisons came in shiny packages.

"Hey, Sheriff Carl…." She threw a smile his way and waved her fingers.

"Jolene, honey, are you trying to get these boys to bust each other into pieces?"

Her blue eyes went all kinds of wide and innocent. Her dark mane of hair bobbed gently as she shook her head. "No sir. We were just having a talk and then Remy over here got a little edgy."

"Yeah? Why is that?"

"He wants me to be his girl."

Carl smiled thinly. "Why is that a problem?"

"Bobby was thinking I should date him. Exclusively."

Carl nodded. "You planning on dating either of these boys exclusively, Jolene?" His smile grew a smidge wider and he ground his teeth together. The paperwork he filed as a result of exactly this sort of incident took more time than he cared to think about.

"Well, I mean you never—"

"Jolene, honey, just this once, be truthful. For me?"

Jolene's smile would have lit up the Vegas strip. "Naw. You know I like older men."

"See, boys?" Carl put a heavy hand on each shoulder and gave a friendly squeeze that didn't quite make their bones creak. "Nothing to get riled up about. Neither one of you has a chance in hell." He leaned in closer to Bobby, who looked like the one most likely to take a swing. "Let's just call this a draw and you both get to go home instead of coming with me."

Jolene batted her baby blues at Carl and he made it a point not to look too closely.

"But—"

"No, Remy. No buts. Get yourself on your way before I forget to be friendly." He stared daggers until the boy got the clue and sulked all the way to his new Ford Mustang. College. Probably a bribe to make sure junior went to class. If everything went well, Carl wouldn't be the one to scrape the boy and his bribe off the interstate in a few months. Parents just loved giving their kids muscle cars, as if the things were designed to survive a DUI and the impulse most kids had to impress their friends by doing a hundred around tight corners.

Maybe he was being cynical. Maybe not. It was hard to say.

He gave the other kid the stink eye until he clued in and moved toward his beat-up Town Car. Jolene always did love a class war.

"Jolene, what are you doing here, anyway? This isn't your normal stomping ground."

The smile was pure honey and the promise of a thousand sinful delights. "I decided I need some spending cash, so I got a job here."

"Really?"

"Well, I just had the interview, but Derek? The owner? He's pretty sure he can use me."

"Oh, I'm sure he can." Carl tried to smile, but it wasn't easy. He'd have to get a few extra dogs, and then figure out how to get here when Jolene wasn't working. Otherwise this would be his last visit for a while. "Say, Jolene?"

"Yeah, Sheriff Carl?" She put her hand on his forearm as she sashayed next to him. He managed not to walk into the door.

"You know if Derek has a delivery service?"

Her smile was as bright as ever. "I'll go find out for ya."

"Thank you, sunshine."

He stood in line and contemplated what he was going to order. When his cell rang, he reached for it and smiled when he saw the name.

"Wade Griffin! What can I do for you, brother?"

Interview room two at the Brennert County Sheriff's Headquarters always made Griffin think of hospitals, with its antiseptic smell and its institutional green walls. Griffin was leaning against one of those walls while Carl Price questioned Skinny, whose name turned out to be Barry Long.

"I've told you everything I can," Long said. He was seated at a small table in the middle of the room. The table held a bottle of water and the cuffs Carl had taken off Long once they got him to headquarters.

"Tell me again," Carl said. Carl was playing bad cop. So was Griffin. There were no good cops in the room.

Long sighed. "The guy came into the shop right after I opened on Monday. He showed me the ring. I could tell it was a nice piece. We argued a bit about the price and then I paid him and he left. Like I told your pal here, I never saw him before."

"And it occurred to you to check the ring for identifying marks, and to compare it to the list we sent out, but not to call us."

Long said, "I've been in trouble before, Sheriff. I didn't know what to do, you know?"

"You knew what to do," Carl said. "You just didn't do it."

Long said, "I'm cooperating now, aren't I? I helped your guys get a sketch. I looked at the mug shots."

"And I've got some more for you to look at."

"How long are you going to keep me here?"

Carl said, "Depends on how happy you make me and whether or not Mister Griffin there decides to press charges. You think about that."

Carl turned and went to the door. Griffin followed. They stepped out into the hall.

Carl said, "What do you think?"

Griffin said, "I think that's all he knows."

"Not much to go on."

"More than we had," said Griffin. "What I'm wondering is why just the one ring? The bad guys took a whole lot of stuff from those houses. Why fence just one piece?"

Griffin shrugged. "Testing the waters? See if the stuff was too hot to move?"

"Doesn't feel right, Wade. Both invasions were carefully planned and executed. This feels more like a mistake."

"Maybe one of the crew suddenly needed some fast cash?"

"Maybe. And he slipped something out of the loot. Which suggests a sudden need, drugs being the most likely."

"Might be worth talking to some of the local dealers."

"Might at that," said Carl.

The door opened at the far end of the hall and one of Carl's deputies, a guy named Perez, stuck his head in. "Someone to see you, Sheriff."

"Who is it?"

Perez shook his head. "Says she's with the army."

Carl shrugged, and he and Griffin went out to the lobby. A tall, blonde woman was at the front desk. She wore a black skirt suit, medium heels, and a slender string of pearls at her throat. Classy.

The woman said, "Sheriff Price. I'm Major Sandra Thorne. Military Police." She flashed an ID badge. "We need to talk."

Carl said, "Kinda busy just now, Major. Care to tell me what this is about?"

"Private would be better," Thorne said.

"Okay, we can use my office."

Griffin said, "I'll go check on that lead, Carl. I'll call you later."

Thorne said, "This concerns you as well, Mr Griffin."

Griffin raised an eyebrow. He'd never been in the military. Why should Thorne want to talk to him or even know about him?

Carl led the way to his office. He seated himself behind his desk and Thorne took the room's only other chair. Griffin leaned on the wall. He did that a lot.

Thorne said, "We've reason to believe that a man named Avery Mason is in your area."

She was looking at Griffin when she said it. *So that was why she wanted me in the meeting.* Griffin said, "Yeah, I know him. We aren't friends."

"We didn't think so," Thorne said. "You turn up in one of the files about Mason. You and he were both working as mercenaries in Iraq at the same time. Don't worry, Mr Griffin. We aren't keeping tabs on you."

"I wasn't worried," said Griffin.

"Pretend I've never heard of the guy," Carl said. "What's he doing in my county?"

Thorne said, "Mason was an Army Ranger. Top of the line special ops. Simply put, he went bad. He started using his position in the army for profit. Drug smuggling, extortion, all kinds of things. He was dishonorably discharged but managed to stay out of jail. Witnesses tended to not want to testify against him."

"Convenient," said Griffin.

"Very. Mason became a mercenary. We've kept track of him as best we could. At one point he was privy to a lot of military secrets. He's still operating in various trouble spots around the world. We also believe he's been behind a string of high-dollar home invasions throughout the Southeast."

"Hot damn," said Carl.

"Thought you might see it that way, Sheriff," said Thorne. "Mason usually employs other ex-military personnel. Runs a tight ship. Leaves no witnesses."

Carl nodded. "That's the pattern. Speaking of which, I don't suppose you know anyone who looks like this?" He handed her a copy of the sketch of the suspect.

Thorne looked at the drawing. It showed a man with a narrow face, a thin nose, and close-cropped hair. She said, "He doesn't look familiar."

"Too bad," Carl said. "Would have been nice to have a name. He sold a ring that was taken in one of the invasions."

Thorne said, "Tell me about that, please. I just have vague outlines of the two home invasions in Brennert."

Carl said, "Two houses in two different neighborhoods were hit. Both places belonged to wealthy people. As you said, the crew leaves no witnesses. The first invasion was three weeks back, a lawyer named Cameron Weston. He had a wife and two kids. All four of them were lined up and shot."

Thorne grimaced. "Sounds like Mason."

"The other target was a doctor, Terry Roth. One bullet each for him and his wife. Luckily their only daughter was away at a sleepover. In both cases, the perps had to be in and out quick. These were gated neighborhoods with security patrols. The invaders got in, took what they wanted, and got out. Well planned operations. The term 'military precision' was bandied about, come to think of it."

"Do you have any idea how the invaders chose their targets?" Thorne said.

"Not really. Both men were known to be wealthy, but so are a lot of other people. I know where you're heading, Major. The sad truth is most high-end home invasions happen to drug dealers or other types who can't use banks, so they have a lot of cash lying around. Background checks on Roth and Weston didn't turn up anything shifty."

"Random isn't Avery Mason's style, Sheriff. There will be a reason he chose those men."

"I'd be awful obliged if you could provide it," Carl said.

"I'm afraid I don't know either, but I know how Mason operates."

"Maybe you could let me in on that. A picture of the guy would be nice, too."

"I'll email you a copy of the report, minus classified material, of course."

"Of course," said Carl.

"But even if you know what he looks like, you can't just pick him up. That's been tried. You don't have probable cause and I guarantee you won't find anything on him or wherever he's living."

"Which raises a point," Griffin said. "Given what Major Thorne has just told us, everything changes. If the ring guy is still alive it's only because Mason doesn't know about the ring yet. Mason would never fence anything locally. Guy must have skimmed it like we figured. He can ID Mason and we have a witness who can put him with the ring from the Weston invasion. Mason *has* to kill him."

Carl said, "Meaning we got a ticking clock on finding the guy."

"Yeah, which means maybe you'd better check the drug angle while I try some of my business contacts."

"By that you mean mercenaries?" Thorne said.

Griffin smiled. "I'm a private investigator, Major. Got a license and everything."

Carl said, "Yeah, I'll ask around. The pawnshop guy paid Ringo pretty good. If he was looking for quality drugs, he'd have had to deal with some of Junior Hulsey's people or one of the Blackbournes."

"Neither of who are likely to be overly cooperative," Griffin said. "Watch yourself, brother."

"Yes, Mom. Get out of here and let me get to work."

As Griffin was leaving, Thorne said, "You're going, yourself, Sheriff? Most commanding officers I know are big on delegating."

Carl grinned. "Oh, I'm a delegating fool, Major. But not on this one. I want to find these bastards myself."

"Thank you so much, Mr Thayer," Sue Townsend said. "It was a beautiful service. And you did such wonderful work. He looked as if he was only sleeping."

Henry Thayer took her withered, arthritic hands carefully into his warm paws and stared gently into Mrs Townsend's eyes, his face kindly, his mane of salt and pepper hair just so, and said, "And so he was, Mrs Townsend. Your husband will awake in a better place."

They were standing in the hallway of Thayer's funeral home. They were the only people left after George Townsend's funeral. Thayer looked down at the tiny old woman and smiled his compassionate, sincere smile, the one he practiced in the mirror. He was perhaps three times her size. His clients seemed to find his bulk comforting, somehow. He supposed it gave the feeling of solidity and permanence.

Sue said, "Well, my son is waiting out front. Thank you again."

"I'm only glad that I could offer some comfort in this time of sadness," Thayer said. *Now please hurry up and get out of here so I can be about something that actually matters, you simpering old fool.*

Thayer escorted the old woman to the door and closed it gently behind her, watching as her son, William, led her away from the building toward the waiting car. Then he turned and hurried toward the rear of the building. His employees could finish cleaning up and getting the room ready for the next viewing. He went out the back door and followed the path that led to his house.

Thayer's home was hidden behind a wall of tall pines. He had chosen the slightly out of the way location for house and business because it offered the privacy he wanted and needed. People had said he was foolish to build so far from downtown Wellman. That out of sight meant out of mind. But Thayer knew things those people didn't. Oh, so many things.

Thayer entered his house and went directly to his study in the far west corner. He loosened his tie as he opened the door at the back of the room and then descended a short flight of steps to a second door, this one sealed and guarded by a security panel. Nimble fingers punched in the numbers that opened the door. There was a whoosh of air and then a slight smell of corruption wafted from within. It didn't bother Thayer. The smell of death was as familiar to him as a lifelong friend.

The chamber beyond the security door was vast, far larger than the house above. It was another reason he'd chosen this secluded location. He'd had the natural cave expanded by contractors who were paid very handsomely for their discretion before they died in an unfortunate construction accident not long after the work was finished.

Thayer went to one of the many metal tables that filled the room. The body of the late George Townsend lay upon the cold surface. It had been so easy to have the body removed from the casket before the coffin was taken to the burial ground. Thayer's servants in the hidden room in the mortuary had performed that function many times.

They had also taken the time to remove the suit from Townsend's corpse. There had been a time when the rituals had taken hours on end for him to finish, but these days the movements were virtually as common for him as walking. Two fingers moved into the thick, black lotion he'd prepared during the last full moon, and he made the seven marks required by his master on the cadaver laid out before him.

Thayer mumbled a few words and waved his hand over the corpse's face. Townsend's eyes snapped open, but they didn't focus as those of a living man would. His pupils did not dilate, nor did his eyes wander about the room, much as Thayer expected they might want to. The corners of Townsend's mouth twitched.

"You'd like to scream, wouldn't you, George?" Townsend said. "I can imagine finding your soul back in your moldering body would be quite the horrifying experience. Don't worry though. You won't be trapped there forever. My lord Nsnigoth has use for you."

Thayer turned and walked across the twilight of the room to the farthest wall of the cavern, his steps echoing hollowly in the vast chamber. That wall was lined with rectangular niches. A corpse lay in each niche of Thayer's personal catacomb. He needed one in particular. He did not bother looking at the corpses. He knew exactly where each rested.

"Awake, Joshua Collett," Thayer said.

The body of a man in his early twenties jerked twice, spasmed and shivered and then slid from one of the apertures as a serpent might. The dead don't move like men. Collett rose to a standing position in front of Thayer.

Thayer said, "Your father has become a problem, Joshua. He suspects there might be something wrong about your burial. I'm not sure what set him off, but this morning he threatened to call the police and have you disinterred. I can't have that. I want you to go to him tonight."

He stared at Collett's face. The changes to the jaw line, the slight bulge where lips hid teeth, were all Thayer needed to see to know his pet was ready to handle the work he demanded of it.

The corpse gave a slow nod, the eyes shifted to looked at him and then quickly looked away as if the very sight of him was enough to inspire terror in the dead man. Henry Thayer smiled.

"Joshua, when you are done, I want you to bring me his heart. Do you understand me?"

There was no hesitation in Joshua's nod, no sign of any hint of remorse at the command. "You'll need to move quietly. Prepare yourself. And if any living thing should see you, make certain that thing dies. Do you understand me?" Collett nodded again, and then squatted, knees popping noisily. While the corpse of Joshua Collett waited for the sun to set, it moved through a series of slow, meticulous motions that made tendons stretch and joints pop until the body no longer made a sound. When Thayer was younger those sounds had made him cringe. Now they were music, a song that promised his words were law, and would be obeyed.

A quick look at his watch told him the Berringer funeral was coming up soon. It was time to get back to the funeral home and prepare. Linda Berringer was killed when a tractor-trailer jackknifed on the interstate, and her car ran under the thing. Her body had been torn and shredded until it was barely intact. The service would be closed casket out of necessity.

Pity. She had been a lovely young lady.

Oh, the fun they could have had together if she'd been less of a mess.

The sun was shining through the windshield and played across the Major's hair. She was a good-looking woman, in a severe, military sort of way. At least she managed a smile when Carl cracked a few of his jokes. At first, she just sort of blinked, like maybe he'd lost his mind but eventually she relaxed.

She made sure not to smile when he was talking to Denny Willis and Billy Harper, both of whom were standing next to Carl's truck and trying not to look too put out by the zip-tie cuffs he'd used on them. They were big fellas, in the case of Billy a lot of that size came in the form of fat, but Denny was all steroidal body builder muscle and fresh tattoos.

Neither of them was smiling. Hell, they looked positively put out by the Ziploc bag full of plastic wrap twists he'd confiscated. Street value was probably around seven grand. They wouldn't be getting that back, which meant their boss, Junior Hulsey, was going to be extremely annoyed with them.

Currently they were all standing in the parking lot of the Dawg Shop. The boys had planned a lunch break, which was a mighty fine idea, but they'd made the mistake of trying to sell a few hits while waiting on their order.

Carl took offense at that. So did Derek, who wanted his place to be family friendly and called on Carl the second they showed their wares.

Billy was being a good boy and behaving himself, but Denny was doing a lot of flexing and trying to break his restraints. All he'd done so far was make his wrists all kinds of red and angry with him.

"Denny, if you don't stop working those bonds I'm gonna go ahead and strap your ankles together. Then we're gonna have to call for back up and a wagon to get you where you're going."

"Why don't you go fuck yourself?"

"Denny, son, I have a lady present. She doesn't want to hear that kind of language and I don't either. So you're going to behave yourself before things get much worse."

"How they gonna get worse?"

Billy answered for him, because Billy was wise in the ways of the Brennert County Sheriff's Department and the methods the Sheriff would employ if he were made unhappy. "Delousing at the jail. Full cavity search. Might could lose your clothes and give you something from the lost and found when you manage to make bail. If you manage to make bail." Billy closed his eyes and shivered. As Carl was the one who'd chosen his clothes from the lost and found the last time, he could respect and appreciate that reaction.

"We also reserve the right to confiscate any property used in the commission of a felony crime here in Brennert County. Now I don't do that too often, I kind of think it's a shitty way to act." Carl smiled. "Say, Denny, what are the chances that if I check your house I'm gonna find even a single twist of crack cocaine?"

Carl knew for a fact that Denny had just bought himself a nice little ranch over on Gibson Street. He made it a point to know who was doing what in the Hulsey extended family of douche bags and dealers.

Denny puffed up his chest and looked like he wanted to argue. Billy looked at him, frowned heavily and shook his head so fast his features nearly blurred.

Denny was a fairly fresh import to Brennert County. His ignorance could be overlooked once or twice. Billy, on the other hand, was a native son.

Denny deflated.

"Now, boys, I have a few questions to ask you."

Denny glared.

Billy nodded and offered a weak smile. "Nothing too personal, Sheriff Carl?"

"Just a few questions about someone who might be looking for the high-end stuff."

Denny was doing his best to look crafty It wasn't an impressive expression. "How high-end are we talking?"

"Sort of stuff a low-rent type like you could never afford. Probably someone new to town."

"New?" Denny was giving him the squint eye.

"Last three weeks or so probably." Carl smiled. "Now do you have anything for me, or should I look some more, and maybe start taking your truck apart."

Denny had a wonderful singing voice. He gave up three names, and where they were most likely to be found.

"Boys, I'm confiscating your supplies. Oh, and the brass knuckles, the two hunting knives and all three firearms."

Denny started to protest, and Carl smiled. "But I'm gonna leave you your truck this one time."

Denny smiled with relief.

"There's a catch. I ever see you over here again, anywhere near this place, and I'll bust your asses so hard you can't sit for a week."

"What?" Billy sounded desperate. "Man, I fucking love the slaw dogs here."

Carl smiled. "That's okay, Billy. Don't you fret. I found out just today that Derek delivers in a three-mile radius. Any further and he charges extra."

⑥ ⑥ ⑥

Griffin left the Sheriff's HQ and climbed into his truck. He pulled out his phone and selected a number he seldom called. The owner of that particular number usually called him. Mel Broderick picked up on the third ring.

"Griffin," Broderick said. "You need work? I got plenty."

Broderick was a broker for mercenaries. If you needed a bodyguard or someone to help you storm a fortress in Afghanistan, he could hook you up. Griffin specialized in bodyguard work these days. It kept him close to home for Charon's sake, and it rarely required him to do anything illegal.

"Not today, man. I'm looking for information on Avery Mason."

Broderick gave a low whistle. "Even I won't work with that nutjob these days, Griffin, and you know how low my standards are."

"I do. Thing is, I think he and some of his rent-a-mercs may have pulled a couple of home invasions in this area."

"I've heard rumors about Mason being involved in that sort of thing."

"But no hard facts?"

"Nothing I'd swear to."

Griffin rolled his window down. The day was turning warm after a cold start. Spring was definitely out of whack. "Do you know anyone who might have a line on Mason, then? I want to find him before he kills any more civilians."

"What will you do if you find him?"

"Better you don't know."

"Let me make some calls," Broderick said. "I'll get back to you. And watch your back, Griffin. Mason is a seriously bad guy."

"Me too," said Griffin.

"Yeah, but you're still mostly human."

Broderick rang off.

Brian Coleman knew he had screwed up. And he knew he needed to get out of town before Avery Mason learned about it. Taking the ring had been stupid. Selling it had been worse. He still remembered what Dwayne Haskell had told him.

"I'm sticking my neck way out vouching for you," Haskell had said. "You stay clean until this job is over and we'll both be rich men. But so help me, Brian. You fuck up and Mason will kill you without a second thought."

Brian had thought he could do it. But once he saw all that money in the lawyer's house and got some idea of what his cut would be, man he just had to have the coke. He had told himself he wouldn't go crazy. Just a couple of snorts. Didn't have to turn into a binge.

But it had. And now the money for the ring was gone and he wasn't going to get anything else. He just needed to pick up a few of his things and go. The small rental house he and Haskell were sharing sat on a back road north of Wellman. Brian had sworn it was the last dump he'd ever live in. They hadn't known where Mason was staying with the other two members of the team, and they hadn't told him where their place was either. Safer that way.

Brian parked in the trees some distance from the house and made a wide circle through the woods so he could come at the house the back way. It also allowed him to see all around the place and make sure no vehicles were parked anywhere near.

He didn't think Haskell would sell him out, but then Haskell was afraid of Mason, so who knew?

He came up to the backdoor and saw that the trip wire was still in place, attached to the edge of the door and hidden in the doorjamb. Gingerly he unhooked it. It was rigged to the pin of a flash-bang grenade. Wouldn't kill an intruder but it would mess up their day real good. The front door was similarly rigged.

He slipped in through the kitchen and went into the living room. Avery Mason was seated on the beat-up sofa that had come with the place. Dark hair, a body sculpted by years of combat missions. He was smiling, which was a bad thing.

"You know, Brian," Mason said in his gravelly voice, "You have to be some special kind of fucking stupid."

Brian said, "Look, I'm sorry, man. I know I screwed up."

Avery shook his head. "I don't think you know just how badly. The police are circulating an indenti-kit sketch of you. It's not a bad likeness, really."

"Had to be the pawn shop guy. I—"

"Brian," Mason said, cutting him off. "Do you know the term pump and dump? No? You probably think it's something one of the hookers you hired with my money does for you. But no, it's a stock term."

"Stocks?"

"Yes, Brian. Stocks. Didn't you wonder why the doctor and the lawyer had so much cash hidden in their homes when neither of them was involved in the drug trade? I'm sure if they'd had any drugs, that runny nose of yours would have sniffed them out."

Brian could feel sweat running down his back. Mason never talked this much. Brian's 9mm was in a flat holster at the small of his back. Mason wasn't holding a gun. But he'd seen Mason pull a piece before. The guy was scary fast.

"See what happens is," Mason went on, "a broker buys blocks of stock from basically worthless companies, usually with the help of a partner or two. They inflate, or 'pump up' the share price by bogus trades and such. They persuade a bunch of uninformed people to invest, because it looks like the stocks are continuing to rise in value. Then the lawyer and his pals dump the investment at a profit. The stock prices collapse, and everyone else loses whatever they put in."

Brian said, "That's what Wesson and Roth were doing?"

"Yeah, and a friend of mine with his ear to the financial ground noticed that the two of them were suddenly liquidating some investments, which meant they were cashing out and covering their tracks before anyone found out just what was going on. And so, you and me and our friends came to Georgia to get that cash while it was available. Some of the money was in offshore accounts, but Wesson and Roth had over a million each hidden away, plus all that jewelry and stuff we got."

"Christ. I didn't realize it was that much. I'm really sorry, Mason."

"Yeah, well, I just wanted you to know just how much you'd lost, and what you almost cost me before I killed you."

Masons last words registered, and Brian jerked his jacket aside and reached for his 9mm. Without seeming haste, Avery pulled a Glock .40 from inside his coat and fired twice. Brian felt the impact but was dead before any real pain reached his brain.

🌀 🌀 🌀

Avery Mason stood and walked over to Brian Coleman's body. He was sure Coleman was dead, but he kicked his gun aside anyway. A careless mercenary was soon a dead mercenary. He considered putting an extra round through Coleman's head, but since the police had worked so hard on their sketch, he thought he might as well let them see how close they'd gotten.

Mason sighed. He had hoped to make a couple more scores before blowing town, but things were too hot now. They needed to go. Haskell's buddy had screwed everything up. Mason figured he'd kill Haskell too, but he was now one man short and he did have an idea for one last hit on the way out of Brennert County, something totally unrelated to the stock swindle. After that, Haskell was toast.

Mason pulled out his phone and made a call. "Come pick me up. Yeah, it's done."

Turned out Hulsey's men were easier to deal with than the Blackbournes. With the possible exception of Jolene, that whole clan could hold a grudge. As he pulled away from the third location where the Blackbournes should have been openly selling, Major Sandra Thorne was looking at him with a slightly amused expression on her face.

"Everything okay, Sheriff?"

He smiled. "Oh, not even close, Major. First, please call me Carl. Second, the Blackbournes recently lost a major lawsuit against me, and the leader of the clan, a lady with the cheery name of Lament, has made it a personal task to make my life as miserable as possible."

"Okay, Carl, then I'm Sandy. And why are you trying so hard if they're just going to run whenever you come around?"

"Well, Sandy, no one ever said being the sheriff was supposed to be easy. Besides which, if I let them win on these little grudges, they get to win on other stuff, too. On important stuff. I can't allow that to happen."

"So, politics?"

"Sort of. Only the politicians here are some particularly stubborn types."

"So what next?"

Carl looked at the sky, which was darkening a bit, then at his watch, which confirmed sunset was right around the corner. His stomach growled. "Well, I figure if we play this just right, I can meet with a less hostile Blackbourne and you and me can have about the best chilidogs ever placed on this planet."

"What if I'm a vegetarian?"

Carl frowned. "Are you?"

Sandy shook her head. "Not even a little."

"Oh, good. We can still be friends." He paused. "I'm just

kidding. Some of my best friends are vegetarians." He paused again. "Okay, no, that's a lie. But I've met people who claimed they don't eat meat." One more pause as he moved the truck in a tight one-hundred-and-eighty-degree turn. "Something wrong with those people."

Ten minutes later they pulled up at the Dawg Shop, where parking was at a premium. He found a spot near the building and then flashed his blue lights for exactly one second, long enough to get noticed and nothing more.

Jolene Blackbourne showed up a moment late, her brilliant smile in place. "Hey, Sheriff Carl." She looked toward Sandy and managed to keep her smile in place, but her voice chilled by a few degrees. "Who's your new friend?"

"Hey, Jolene. This here is Major Thorne, a friend of mine who needs a little help with a case I'm working on."

Jolene kept her smile in place as she examined the other woman from head to toe. He would have admitted that Sandy Thorne was a fine-looking woman had Jolene asked, but the girl would never ask in a million years. "Anything you want me to help with?" She already sounded bored.

"Well, honey, I need to know if your people have found any new buyers. Strictly high end, and only come to town in the last few weeks."

Oh, the smile she shot him was pure saccharine. "Oh, you know I don't pay any attention to that stuff, Sheriff Carl."

"Of course I do, Jolene. You'd be doing me a personal favor."

That changed her entire expression. "Oh, really? The sort you'd owe me for?"

It was his turn with the purely artificial smile. "Well, I think we could probably work something out later."

When she leaned into his window, he smelled the light musk of her body and some sort of flower he couldn't have hoped to name in a million years. The scent was pleasantly distracting even though he didn't want it to be.

"You got a pen, Sheriff Carl?"

He held up his pen and pad. She rattled off a list of names. Four in all.

Two of them matched the list that Hulsey's boys had offered up. Jolene was not as accommodating when it came to addresses.

"You know, Junior's boys actually gave me addresses." He smiled to take the possible sting from his words.

She smiled at him her eyes practically glowing in the dimming light of the growing darkness. Actually, they were glowing but the lights from the restaurant suppressed that inner glow. "Now, Sheriff Carl, you know I'm working right now, but if you came by later, after my shift, maybe I could show you those places personally." Her fingers rested on his forearm. They were tiny, delicate looking appendages, but they burned with their own warmth.

"For now, darlin'? I'd just like to order a few dogs from you."

Her pout was exactly as fetching as her smile, and just as theatrical in nature. "What'll it be?"

He gave his order and then ordered for Sandra when she was done reading the large menu. They sat in the parking lot and ate, and he loved watching the Major's face as she came to understand the glory of the Dawg Shop properly.

Nathaniel Collett was not a happy man. He had been once, but that was before his wife took ill from a brain tumor and never recovered. Even then he'd managed a bit of joy in his life. Josh had brought him joy. The boy was smart, he was good looking enough to have a few constant companions of the female variety, and he was popular enough to have good friends. All of those factors made Nate a happier man.

And then Josh died.

It was a dumb death, too. He drank too much one night when Nathaniel was out on a run – long distance trucker was not an easy life, but it paid well enough – and he went and got sick while he was sleeping on his back. He drowned in his own vomit.

A damned foolish way to die.

Finding his son dead that way? It had taken the last of the joy from Nathaniel. Crushed it out of him. Now there was nothing. Not a damned thing in his life that made him happy.

To make matters worse, Nate was pretty sure someone at the Thayer Funeral Home had done something to his son. He had no proof of that, just a gut feeling, but as he was taking time from his route to mourn, he also took the same time to make a few complaints and to look into what he'd need to have his boy disinterred. It wasn't something he wanted to do. He did not have any desire to see his dead son's corpse, but he was also pretty sure that if they tore open the ground and pulled out Joshua's coffin, he would not find his son's body in that casket.

It was a horrible feeling, but one that would not leave him alone. His grandmother, Eloise, was supposed to have been gifted with special senses. Most times he just wanted to shrug that sort of thing off, maybe even laugh about it like his mother always did, much to his daddy's chagrin. Sometimes he couldn't just chuckle it away. He thought maybe he had some of her gifts, because now and then he got a feeling and when he got them, they were inevitably true.

That was the problem here. It was one of his *feelings*. The ones that were never wrong.

He wanted it to be wrong. He did. He prayed for it, but still the feeling would not leave him alone.

Joshua would not be in his grave.

That thought would not leave him be. It haunted him. It made him do things like call the Brennert County Sheriff's Department three times a day and ask about the possibility of disinterment.

It made him walk back over to the small bar he had in the living room, the one his son had used to drink himself to death, and grab the bottle of Johnny Walker Red he kept there. The seal was still intact. He'd picked this one up after he found Josh. Every bottle that had been opened had been watered down. Oldest trick in the book but he never considered checking it out, because, you know, Josh was a good boy.

His vision blurred for a moment as he considered his son.

Nathaniel was lost now. He knew that. With his wife gone and their only son dead, he was lost.

He looked at his long list of phone numbers. Most of the important ones stayed on a clean sheet of notebook paper that he rewrote once a month. This month's version was sitting on the counter next to the previous version. He gave thought to calling on Jolene Blackbourne, just to have someone to talk to, but decided against it. She was mercurial. Sometimes she could talk and sometimes she couldn't, and he didn't think he could risk a rejection right now, besides, really she was almost as young as Josh had been.

The sliding glass door at the back of the house opened, letting in a cool breeze.

Nate looked away from the phone numbers and stared at the door. For one second he thought maybe Jolene would be there. She'd come by once before when he was at his lowest. The very night he'd thought about taking his own life, actually. She'd talked him down and reminded him that Josh still needed him.

She was a fine girl.

It wasn't Jolene.

It was Josh.

There was something wrong with his face. The jaw was too broad. His mouth looked like he was hiding and orange slice under his lips, and if he smiled there would be a wide orange grin instead of his perfect, white teeth. Like he used to do when he was ten or so. That always made Nate smile.

Nate stared at his boy and his eyes watered right on up.

"Josh? Son? Is that really you?"

Josh didn't smile. He said nothing. He just stared at his father with a blank expression.

"Josh?" Nate's voice broke and he felt the jagged air he sucked in as it caught and struggled with his throat and lungs. God, how could grief hurt so much?

Josh nodded. The way he moved? It was wrong, as wrong as whatever the hell was going on with his jaws.

Nate didn't care. His little boy was alive! Whatever was wrong, it would be better simply because his little boy was alive!

He stumbled, dropped his glass onto the carpet as he walked, and reached for Joshua.

Joshua stayed exactly where he was for a moment and then took a step forward that made absolutely no sense. It was different enough from Josh's gait that Nathaniel was completely taken aback.

"Josh, what the hell?"

It made no sense. His boy was walking. His face was off, okay, but he'd been away and maybe whatever medical miracle had brought him back required some sort of implant or something. In the dimming twilight Nate realized that Josh's skin was the wrong color, too. He almost overlooked it when they were further apart. It was just the light in the house, he hadn't turned on the overheads, so a little discoloration, that was just a trick of the light. But no, he looked closer now and frowned. This wasn't a trick of the light. This was something very wrong. Josh was too pale, and his eyes looked... wrong.

"Josh? Son? What's wrong?"

When his boy spoke, the voice was completely out of tune. His tone was inflectionless, and his facial expression barely changed. His eyes never even really looked toward Nate.

"I'm hungry, Dad."

"Well, why didn't you say so? I'll get you a sandwich. Just picked up some bologna today. I haven't had much appetite since you, well, since you went away." He couldn't bring himself to tell his son he'd died. Maybe after they ate.

"No. Not that sort of hunger. I need meat." Josh's voice still sounded off. Breathy. Like he couldn't figure out how to talk. He'd drilled his son on speaking loud and proud, because, really if you gave off a bad first impression it was all downhill from there. You only got the one first impression. He wanted better for his boy than what he'd been given. Don't all parents?

"Well, sure, son. We can go get a steak if you want." He frowned. Not a lot in his wallet, but he could always break out the emergency credit card, just this one exception for the emergencies only rule. It wasn't every day his boy came back from the—

Dead! Josh is dead! D-E-A-D! DEAD!

Josh took three steps toward him. Each one was off. He moved like he never even put his feet on the ground, he didn't just walk. He sort of *slithered* on his feet. It made no sense but the image was unsettling and *wrong*.

"Josh, what's wrong with your feet?"

"Hungry. So hungry."

Josh's hand pushed against his chest. Nate looked own at those fingers he'd known ever since the boy was born and saw the thick dark claws where his nails should have been.

"Josh. What?" That was as far as he got before the pain bloomed in his chest. Nate was still watching as Josh pushed his fingers forward and drove them deep into his flesh. Sliding past bone. The pain was bigger than the entire room. It grew even bigger until it stole Nate's breath from him.

No. That was the holes in his lungs. He was still looking down when the air gasped out of those holes, spraying pink foam past the three fingers that had pierced the delicate organs.

The fingers squeezed, breaking bone and tearing internal things that should not be torn. The grip around his heart was a crushing weight.

"He wants your heart, Dad. And I am so hungry." The words were whispered in his ear, right before Josh opened his mouth and showed the changes that had taken place there.

The pain in his heart was horrible on so many levels. It was the breaking of physical and emotional doppelgangers.

But the agony of the teeth that slid through his stubble and then met in the side of Nate's neck?

That was so much worse.

Joshua took his time feeding on his old man.

Nate stayed awake far longer than he would ever have thought possible.

Griffin came fully awake when Charon groaned in her sleep. Her eyes snapped open and she sat up with a sharp intake of breath.

He said, "You okay?"

Charon looked over at him, her dark eyes troubled. "Yes. No. Jeez."

"What is it?"

She shook her head. "I felt something. Like when those two demon things attacked Carter and me in that parking lot."

Griffin didn't like to think of the events of the previous fall. "Do you think it's connected?"

"No, this is different. But it's what Carter would call an incursion. Something moving around on this plane of reality that shouldn't."

Griffin got out of bed and stretched. He was wide awake now. It didn't take a lot to wake him and he always had trouble getting back to sleep. "I don't guess there's any way of knowing what or where?"

"Not for me, wild man. I'm not psychic like Cindy Kane. It didn't feel like it had anything to do with us. Just something weird out there in the dark."

"Is Decamp still out of town?"

"Yeah, he's in Scotland with that creepy friend of his, Jonathan Crowley."

Griffin had first encountered Carter Decamp a couple of years earlier. The man was a retired professor of English literature. He was also an expert on the occult and some sort of monster hunter. Somehow Charon had drifted into being his apprentice. As impossible as it seemed, Decamp had some form of actual supernatural power and he was teaching Charon the same thing.

"I guess we can't call and ask him, then."

"He said he might be difficult to reach for a while. Besides, this might be nothing. It's not like we don't have enough weird stuff around here with the Blackbournes and all. If anything else happens I can try and call him."

"Guess that's all we can do for now then," Griffin said.

"You could get back in bed and hold me until I go back to sleep," said Charon.

"I could do that."

Unlike Griffin, Charon had little trouble falling back asleep and she was soon snoring softly. Griffin drifted off close to sunrise, which was also the time his cell phone chirped. He rolled over, grabbed the phone, and slipped out of bed. He checked the screen as he walked into the hallway. Carl, of course.

"Hate to wake you this early, Wade," Carl said, "But I'm at a crime scene and I may need Decamp. I called him, but just got his voicemail."

"Decamp's out of the country. What's going on?"

"Hell if I know. I got a body with a missing heart and some weird wounds. Looks like someone's been chewing on the victim."

Griffin was quiet for a moment. Then he said, "Charon had some sort of warning last night. A feeling that something was wrong. Could be connected."

"Be a hell of a coincidence if it wasn't."

"Do you want me to ask her to come to the scene?"

"Not sure she should see this, Wade."

"You know she's seen plenty of bad things, already. Her call, but I'll ask her. Tell me where you are, and I'll be there as soon as I can in any case."

Carl gave him a name and an address. Griffin went to wake Charon.

Close to an hour later they pulled up in front of Nathanial Collett's house. It was an older house, probably built in the sixties, but clean, and well maintained. Two Brennert County Sheriff's Department cruisers and Carl's truck were in the driveway.

"Sure you want to do this?" Griffin said.

Charon said, "No, but given what happened last night, I think I have to."

They got out of Griffin's truck. Carl was sitting on the front steps and he stood as they approached. He said, "Thanks for coming, Charon."

"Don't thank me until we see if I can be of any help."

"Hey, I appreciate the effort. I've got protective gear for you both."

Griffin and Charon stopped to put on paper booties over their shoes. Then they followed Carl into the house. The front door led directly to a well-kept living room. What was left of Collett was sprawled on the floor. A lot of blood had seeped into an old rug that covered the hardwood floor, and Griffin's footsteps made an unpleasant squelching noise.

Griffin crouched and looked at the bite wounds. He said, "Basic size and shape of the bites looks almost human, but..."

Carl said, "But the bites are too deep and too savage. Yeah, coroner said the teeth would have to be sharp, like an animal's."

Carl had sent the two uniformed deputies who had been guarding the room outside. Griffin said, "Some of the less human moon-eyes eat human flesh like this."

"Thought of that," Carl said. "Might have to talk to Lament, whether I like it or not."

"I'd hold off on that as long as you can."

"Plan to."

Griffin said, "The chest wound looks really weird."

"It's a puncture wound made with a multi-pointed weapon. Like someone with claws stuck his hand into the old man's chest."

Charon said, "Griffin said the heart is missing. How about any other internal organs?"

"It doesn't look like it," Carl said, "But we won't know for sure until the autopsy has been performed."

"That suggest something to you, Charon?" Griffin said.

"A human heart is a prized ingredient in any number of occult rituals. If whatever did this carried it away, it could mean something."

"Or maybe they just ate it," said Carl.

Charon said, "Possible, but since they didn't take any other organs, it's not as likely. If they enjoyed viscera, there was plenty available."

"Good point," said Griffin. "How are you holding up?"

"I'm not going to hurl yet."

"Good to know."

"Here's another weird thing," Carl said. "I didn't make the connection until I got over here, but Nathaniel Collett has been calling my office every day for the last couple of weeks, saying he thought something had been done to his son's body at Thayer Funeral Parlor. He wanted us to dissenter the kid."

Griffin said, "He give any reason?"

Carl shook his head. "No, just said he had a feeling. Figured him for a loon. I've been letting one of the deputies talk to him. Maybe I should go and talk to the owner of the funeral parlor."

Griffin said, "Thayer. That's that huge place outside of town, right?"

"That's the one."

Charon said, "Starting to feel a little queasy here, guys. Maybe I should go and do some research on entities that eat flesh and steal hearts."

"Yeah, let's get you outside," Griffin said.

"Let me know if you turn anything up," Carl said. "And thanks again for coming out. I know this isn't pleasant. I've been looking at corpses for way too long and it doesn't get any easier."

Someone was aware of him. Henry Thayer had felt it just at the moment Joshua Collett was taking his father's heart. That shouldn't have been possible. The only magus of any power in the area was Carter Decamp, and Thayer had gone to great lengths, using the necromantic powers granted by Nsnigoth, to shield himself from Decamp. Thayer had come to Wellman because the walls between worlds were thin there.

This could be a problem. He had perhaps gotten a little carried away in allowing one of his servants to roam free. The local police might find the elder Collett's body and wonder what had happened, but they wouldn't jump to a supernatural conclusion. It wasn't part of their mundane thinking.

If the details of the condition of the body got out and someone with the right sort of eldritch knowledge made a connection, it could interfere with his plans. His time in Wellman was growing short. Soon would come the reaping of souls. But he wasn't ready to leave just yet. He would need to find out more about this person, whoever it might be.

Thayer went all the way to the far end of his private catacomb. There, on a stone slab, lay the body of one of his first converts since arriving in Wellman. The man had been trapped in his own dead body for six months. Only Thayer's dark arts had kept the shell in one piece. Even so, the dead man, a fellow named Darren West, was little more than a pile of bones and blackened flesh. He was also hopelessly mad.

Thayer leaned down over Darren and spoke an incantation. Darren's eyes snapped open. They were completely black and without irises. Just two, gleaming ebon orbs.

Thayer looked deep into those eyes, still mumbling the words of power, summoning the guidance of the ones who walk behind the angles. And in Darren's eyes, Thayer saw the one who had felt his presence. A small woman with dark hair and eyes...

The Thayer Funeral Home was a big, sprawling place.

Carl looked at it for several seconds and scratched at his chin. Seemed damn near every funeral home he saw was big – most of them were houses he wouldn't have minded owning, too, if not for the whole dead people in there thing – and kept up better than any of the houses around them when they were near residential areas.

He'd met Thayer a few times. The man had about the same sort of sincerity as a snake oil salesman, but that sort of came with the territory, he supposed. You spend your days working on corpses and then smiling into the faces of the grief stricken and you sort of had to put up layers of emotional padding to avoid killing yourself. Happened in all sorts of businesses, his included.

Still, he delayed a few more minutes before going in.

The place was laid out tastefully, with earth tones and the sort of furniture designed to offer comfort to folks who'd just had their loved ones die. A lady in a dark dress with thick red hair of the sort that came out of a box of hair dye rose from her seat behind the desk and smiled at him. He knew her. The hair was real. It was one of those mysteries he would never understand, how some people got those colors naturally, but he'd known Missy Kincaid since she'd been in middle school with him.

Her smile brightened the room. "Carl. How are you? It's been forever."

"Missy. How come you never get any older?"

She waved the compliment away with a chuckle. "You and me both know that's a lie, but you're sweet for saying it." She moved in closer for a hug and he let her. Missy was about as sweet as honey, and happily married to the best of his knowledge – her high school sweetheart, a man named Burt Kincaid, who was a pharmacist these days.

"How are those kids of yours?"

"Pure trouble." She giggled like she was still in high school, a fact that he found endearing. "But I love them just the same."

"Long as you talk them down from the hard stuff I'll let 'em pass on being guests at my jail."

"Oh, they're only five and seven. I think we've got a while before I have to rein them in." He'd met them both. They were cute as buttons.

Missy got a serious look on her face. "Is everything all right? Are you here professionally or personally?"

"Professionally, I'm happy to say."

She smiled and nodded. "Well, you tell me what you need and I'll see what I can do about getting it handled."

"Well, if he can spare just a few minutes, I needed to talk to your boss about a case."

Missy frowned. "I'm sure he'll make the time." Her smile crept back in place slowly.

"Well, thank you, kindly." He put on his best smile. "It's nothing too bad, just a few questions about a man who made some calls."

Her face grew stormy and then switched to a politely sad expression he knew was another case of snake oil sales. "I expect I know who you mean, but there's no reason for wagging tongues, hon. I'll got get Mister Thayer."

Carl nodded and looked around the room, contemplating sitting down while he waited. A quick scan of the chairs showed exactly two types: the sort you don't sit in and the sort that just pull you in and never want to let you go. He chose to stand instead. The former would break under his weight and the later would entice him to take a nap.

When Thayer came out of his office, the man had a smile plastered on his face. His eyes were just a bit wider than usual, and his dimples were deep creases. If Carl were the sort that bet on poker, he'd say the man was hiding something. What that something was he could not say, but his guts said Thayer was guilty as hell of something.

"Sheriff Price! How good to see you. How can I help you today?" He offered his hand and Carl took it. Thayer was a big man, lots of muscle and a bit of padding. His grip was soft and the other hand moved to enfold Carl's in a double grasp that he was certain came automatically to the man these days. He was used to offering comfort.

Carl resisted the urge to wipe his hand clean. He offered up his best hundred-watt smile. "Well, I was wondering if we could have a talk somewhere a little more private?" Aside from Missy there was no one around. "I don't want anything said that might start ugly rumors, and if someone were to come through the door...."

"Understood." Thayer let go of his hand and smoothly made his way back to the solid oak door to his office. The carpet they walked across would have muffled the sound of stampeding buffalo. Carl figured it was the sort of carpet a man could sleep on and never for a second miss the comfort of his bed.

Thayer turned and smiled at him even as he settled into his office seat. Like everything else, it was a damned fine piece of furniture.

"What seems to be worrying you, Sheriff?"

"Well, not worrying me so much as it's a little on the worrisome side." Carl thought about going the country bumpkin route and making himself sound ignorant but didn't feel that was the right way to go with Thayer. The man was not a local, but he was also the sort that seemed capable of understanding when a man was playing him.

"How so?"

"Well. We're keeping the details closed right now, as we're dealing with an open investigation, but last night we had a murder here in Brennert. A man named Nathaniel Collett got himself killed in a rather grisly fashion."

There it was. Not exactly a tell, but a shift of the eyes. Was it the sort of thing that was admissible in court? Or that he'd ever mention? No, but it was enough for his guts to tell him Thayer was likely dirty on one level or another. It could also just be that he knew about the police reports.

Thayer made a sympathetic face and *tsk*ed. "That's horrible. Why, it was only a few weeks ago that I buried the poor man's son."

"That's one of the reasons I'm here, actually. While investigating the situation it turns out that Mister Collett made several calls to my offices."

"Oh, he did?" His look of surprise was almost perfect.

"I'm afraid so. He had a few complaints about your funeral home, actually. He believed someone on these premises was doing something… unnatural… with his son's body. He made multiple requests to have the body exhumed in order to examine it."

Carl made sure to keep his expression neutral, but it wasn't easy. The man wasn't actually squirming in his seat, but he wanted to. Might be he'd done absolutely nothing wrong, but he surely was doing everything in his power to make sure he didn't fidget more than the bare minimum.

Just to make his point, Carl said, "Under the circumstances. I might well have to look into his request to have the body exhumed."

Thayer kept the same expression, but his color changed a bit. First, he got paler and then he got a bit of a blush going. Not the sort that said he was embarrassed, but the sort that said maybe he was a touch on the annoyed side.

"Really, Sheriff Price, I can't begin to imagine—"

"Thing is, Mister Thayer, while I can't get into details, there were certain aspects of this particular crime scene that indicated possible occult beliefs and practices."

Couldn't have made the man flinch that hard without actually slapping him in most cases. He tried to control it, but some actions are purely involuntary.

"'Occult activities?'"

"You'd think that wouldn't be a thing, right? But we've had a few occasions over the last few years that have meant studying up on that sort of thing. I have a couple of local experts looking into the situation right now, seeing if they can find any correlations between the sort of activities that were performed on the deceased and different occult organizations."

Thayer put on a perfect poker face. He'd been caught off guard, but he recovered very well.

"Not to worry. I doubt it'll come to exhuming anyone, but if you can think of anything or anyone who you might suspect of dealing with occult beliefs, no matter how obscure, I'd be obliged if you let me know." He pulled a card from his shirt pocket. "That's got my cell number on it. Please don't hesitate."

Thayer stood and took the card in one smooth movement. "You may rest assured, Sheriff, that if I learn of anything at all, you'll be the very first person I contact."

"I appreciate that. I hope you can understand why I asked to speak to you alone. That sort of talk could cost a business a good deal of, well, business."

The smile that crossed Thayer's face was cool and professional. He kept his teeth hidden, which was good, because Carl could see the muscles in his jaws clenching tight. "I appreciate your discretion, Sheriff."

"Last thing I ever want to see is an innocent man's business hurt by nasty rumors. Well, last thing after a murder, of course."

"Of course." Thayer herded him toward the door, and Carl let himself be herded.

"If there's any other news, I'll be sure to keep you in the loop, Mister Thayer."

"I appreciate that, Sheriff."

"We're here to serve and protect." He smiled as he nodded to Missy and moved toward the main entrance. "Have a nice day now, ya hear?"

The spring air smelled sweet after the perfectly conditioned air inside the funeral home.

Carl did his best to suppress a chill as he climbed into his truck. A moment after he left the site, he was calling Wade Griffin.

He sat at his office seat for a long while with his hands clenched together in front of his face, his lips pursed tightly and pressed against the double fist of his interlocked fingers.

His stomach wanted to churn. His breath wanted to come in a dozen rushed gasps but he would not allow it. He couldn't let this stop his plans. Not now. He was too close.

He'd been foolish. He's made a dreadful mistake. He'd thought the local yokels incapable of dealing with the sort of efforts he'd put forth. He'd assumed they would be foolishly ignorant to all matters occult.

It was the heart, of course. He'd taken it, and he hadn't really needed to, but he wanted to make a proper offering to Nsnigoth, and really, why not kill two birds with one stone? But the Sheriff was smarter than he looked, or he knew someone with knowledge of the occult. Perhaps the woman from the vision Darren had shown him. That seemed the most likely.

"Nothing to worry about." Thayer's voice was a hoarse whisper that he'd not have recognized had he been paying attention. "I can fix this. I shouldn't have left Collett's body to be found. I should have just made him disappear. And when I find this adept, whoever she is, that's exactly what will happen to her."

He moved his hands away from his face and placed them on his desk, wide fingers splayed, and snorted like a bull. He was so close to the reaping of souls. He had spent almost a year collecting them, keeping a low profile and catering to the oafish residents of Brennert County. He needed only a few more souls to have the exact number for the ritual. And then...

If Nsnigoth smiled upon his offering, Thayer would ascend to the level of an Outer Lord. It had happened only a few times in centuries, but the Outer Ones had raised humans to the level of minor gods before. He knew about the Soul Eaters and The Queen of Flies. Shadowed legends spoke of others, as recently as the Victorian era. Nsnigoth would recognize him. He felt it. He knew it. And nothing must jeopardize that.

He would tell the Kincaid woman that he was unavailable for the rest of the afternoon. His deacons could handle the two viewings currently in the parlor. Thayer had things to attend to.

Wade Griffin sat in a recliner in his living room with a legal pad and some notes he'd made earlier. He was lining up possible avenues of investigation into Mason and his crew. So far he'd hit one dead end after another. He still hadn't heard anything from Broderick, and none of Griffin's local sources had turned up anything.

It didn't help that his mind kept drifting back to the other matter at hand. The partially eaten body with the missing heart. He and Carl had run into too many weird things since Griffin had moved back to Wellman. The town had always had a strange reputation, even when he was a kid. But the last couple of years, the place had become weird central.

He glanced over at Charon, who was seated on the couch surrounded by books. Her brow was furrowed in concentration. Griffin smiled, despite the seriousness of both their researches. Charon always threw herself into everything with laser-like focus. It was one of the things he loved about her.

Charon put a hand to the side of her head. "Griffin, something just passed one of my wards."

Griffin sat up. "Any idea what?"

"No, but it isn't human."

One of the first things Carter Decamp had taught Charon was how to set up protective wards, a sort of supernatural early warning. If anything crossed one of the wards, she would know it. She had placed them around Griffin's house, and unknown to Carl Price, around his place as well.

Griffin stood. He lifted his Beretta from the coffee table and slid it from its holster. "Do you know where they are?"

"Around the side of the house, near the garage."

"Okay, you know the drill. Stay by the basement door. If they get past me, head for the safe room."

"Jesus, Griffin. How can you be so calm?"

"I'm not. But panicking won't help."

Charon caught his arm for a moment. "Don't get killed."

"I'll do my best."

Griffin went out the front door. He wished he'd had time to grab some of Decamp's 'special' ammunition. He'd just have to hope plain old bullets did the trick. He went around the corner of the house, gun pointed at the ground, but ready to bring up for target acquisition. Just like they teach you in cop school.

Griffin's night vision was good. It only took him a few moments to adjust to the dark. As he came around the back of the house, he saw two figures fumbling at a window.

"Hey," Griffin said.

Both figures spun toward him with speed that reminded him of a striking snake. Two men of average size. At a glance they looked human enough, though both had very pale skin. Then he got a good look at their hands. The fingers were long and gnarled and tipped with sharp claws. Charon was right. Not human.

One of the men, who had a wild bird's nest of salt and pepper hair, started toward Griffin in a crouch. He came forward in an odd gait, not moving at all like a human being, almost as if his body was boneless. Again, Griffin thought of snakes.

Griffin said, "One warning. Don't come any closer."

The man grinned, showing sharp, ragged teeth. Griffin thought of the bite marks on Nathaniel Collett. The man crouched lower and then lunged forward with amazing speed.

Griffin fired two rounds, but the man twisted and one of the shots went wide. The other caught him in the shoulder, but he ignored it. A moment later he slammed into Griffin, grabbing his wrist with one clawed hand and seeking Griffin's throat with the other.

Another man might have worried about trying to free the hand that held the gun. Griffin reacted to the moment. It was one of the things that had kept him alive. Instead of worrying about his weapon, Griffin smashed his forehead into the creature's nose, shattering it. Whatever the thing was, it felt pain, because it jerked its head back, blackish blood leaking across its face.

With his free hand, Griffin grabbed the wrist of the arm holding his, stepped past the creature and then pivoted and swept the thing's arm downward. It was a picture-perfect Aikido wheel throw and it sent the creature sprawling on its face. Griffin stepped up, put the 9mm to the back of the thing's head, and pulled the trigger twice. *That* did the trick.

Griffin heard the other creature running up behind him. It was almost on top of him as he turned, and he drove a side kick into its ribs, knocking it backwards. The thing landed in a crouch, then leaped at Griffin like some pouncing animal, claws spread wide.

One of the lessons Griffin's karate sensei had taught him was to stay away from jumping kicks. Yeah, they look great in the movies, but once you're in the air you can't change direction. As the creature left the ground, Griffin took a step backwards, leveled the Beretta, and fired three shots into the thing's face. It fell to the ground and didn't move. The headshot was the way to go, apparently.

Griffin's nose was assaulted by a terrible stench. He walked over to the first creature. The thing was… *liquefying* inside its clothes. He'd worry about that later. Griffin went back around the house, still scanning for more enemies.

He let himself back in. Charon was near the door leading to the basement. Her hands were empty but Griffin knew her pockets contained some of Decamp's conflagration dust and other items she could use if she had to.

"Are you okay?" Charon said.

"Yeah, for once they weren't bullet proof. But they were fast and mean. Pretty obvious they were the same sorts of things that killed Nathanial Collett. They had claws that looked like they could have torn his heart out."

"I should have a look at them," said Charon.

"They're melting or something," Griffin said.

"Even more of a reason to hurry."

"Not sure we should be outside."

"You mean you're not sure I should be outside," Charon said. "Nothing else has passed my wards and you'll be there to protect me. It might help if I can identify the things."

Griffin said, "All right. But we'd better hurry. One of them was almost gone when I came in."

Charon grabbed a flashlight and they went outside. Griffin was alert to any sound or movement. The night had turned cool. He hadn't noticed on his first trip out. Too pumped with adrenaline.

When they reached the fallen creatures, one was indeed completely gone. The other, apparently 'fresher' was still there, though fast falling apart.

"Wow, the stench is awful," Charon said, breathing through the sleeve of her shirt.

Putrefaction is never pleasant," Griffin said. "I was at a mass grave once where—"

"No stories, just now, dear," Charon said. She played the flashlight beam around on the creature. "Jesus. Some sort of walking dead, but not a zombie exactly."

"They didn't move like zombies for sure. They were fast, and their movements reminded me of the way snakes move. And they seemed smart. Something was behind their eyes."

Charon crouched by the remaining figure. "These claws are interesting. Whatever possessed these men changed them."

"Their teeth were changed too. Big and sharp, like a shark. Have you seen enough? I don't like staying in the open like this."

"Yes, we can go in. I have some more research to do."

"Any guesses as to what these things are?"

"Not yet. But I'm really glad they didn't kill you."

Griffin said, "Me too. But whoever sent those things won't be nearly as happy when I find him."

Charon said, "Or her. Don't go getting sexist on me." She was joking, of course.

@ @ @

Early the next morning, Griffin met Carl at their favorite Waffle House out on Hwy 41. A slow drizzling rain was falling, making the day cold and gloomy. Spring was determined not to spring, it seemed. That was fine. It fit Griffin's mood.

"You dig up anything on Thayer yet?" Griffin said.

"Not much. He moved to Wellman not quite two years back. Before that he lived in Virginia. He doesn't have a criminal record. Pays his taxes. Smarmy as hell, but he seems to be a solid citizen. Little old ladies love him."

"And you don't like him."

Carl smiled. "Not one damn bit."

Griffin said, "Looks likely that he sent those things to my place last night."

Carl waved at the waitress to bring him more coffee. He said, "I'd say yes. Nathaniel Collett complains about Thayer and something nasty kills him. Charon has a vision, or whatever the hell you call it, and something similar comes after her."

"Which makes him what, you think? Some kind of sorcerer?"

Carl said, "Something like that, I guess. Charon got any insights?"

"Not yet, but she's still looking."

"And I guess no word from Decamp still?"

"Nothing. So it's just Thayer and us," Griffin said. "If he did it, things aren't going to go well for him."

Carl gave a quick nod. "Yeah, he came to your home and threatened the woman you love. Can't let that pass."

"I'm going to swing by his place later. Have a little chat."

"I'll go too. Unofficially this time."

Carl's phone buzzed. He looked at the screen, then took the call. He listened for a minute, then said, "Yeah. Okay. Tell him to stay put. I'm on my way." He rang off, then said to Griffin, "Looks like we found the guy who bought the ring."

"He's dead, I'm betting."

"Very. Want to take a ride to a crime scene?"

Griffin stood. He spotted their favorite waitress and said, "Susan? Two large coffees to go."

"We can take my truck," Carl said. "I'll bring you back here later."

Moments later they were on the road and headed north. Griffin said, "Where are we going?" "The body was found in a rental house a little ways north of town. I don't recognize the address, but I know that area is pretty sparsely populated."

"Who found the body?"

"The landlord. Apparently he was out doing some work on his property early this morning and he spotted his tenant's car parked out in the trees like someone had hidden it. He went to check on the guy and got the hell scared out of him when he tried to open the front door. Deputy said someone had rigged a flash-bang on the door frame."

Griffin nodded. "Simple but effective. Serves as an alarm and blinds the intruder so you can kill him at your leisure."

"Something a mercenary would do," said Carl.

Griffin said, "Indeed. Fucking mercenaries."

They found the place after making a bewildering series of turns on some back roads. The small house sat off in the trees at the end of one of the roads. A county cruiser and the medical examiner's van were parked side by side in front of the place. A deputy was leaning on the van, talking to a guy in dirty work clothes. The landlord, Griffin presumed.

Carl parked beside the cruiser and he and Griffin stepped

out of the truck. The rain was intermittent now, though the sky was still dark.

The deputy pushed off the van and walked toward Carl. He said, "Morning, Sheriff. Dr Morales is inside. This is Mr Brice, who owns the place. I've already taken his statement."

"Good work, Lew. Go and see if the doctor needs anything while I talk to Mr Brice."

Lew did as he was told. Brice, who was tall and lanky and older than Griffin had initially thought, said, "I've never had anything like this happen in all my years of renting properties."

Carl said, "I understand you found your renter's car hidden not far from here?"

"Yeah, he'd pulled it back into the trees like he was hiding it from someone."

"What was the man's name, sir?"

"Ted Keever. He had all the proper identification and stuff, Sheriff. No funny business."

"I'm sure," said Carl. "How long did he want the place?"

"Just for a month. He said he and his friend Mr Erwin were in town on a construction job but he wasn't sure how long they'd be here, so he didn't want to get into a lease on an apartment or anything. Asked if I'd let them rent month to month. I said I'd help them out."

"For the right fee of course."

Brice grinned. "Keever paid cash up front, which helped his negotiating quite a bit, I can tell you."

"That didn't strike you as a little suspicious?"

Brice shrugged. "Sure, but like I said, he had the ID and such. Nothing illegal about a man paying cash."

Griffin said, "Did you meet Mr Erwin too?"

"No, never met him. Keever made the deal."

Which is probably why you're still alive.

Carl said, "Did you rent any other houses to any out of towners?"

"No," Brice said. "This is it."

"Okay, Mr Brice. You can go. We may have some more questions for you later."

"Um, am I going to have to clean the mess up in there or does the county handle that?"

"We have a service, sir. Thank you for your help."

Brice didn't look thrilled, but he didn't ask any more questions. After he left, Carl said, "We're figuring Mason's crew was bigger than three men, so that means some of them are living somewhere else. I can run some checks on real estate companies locally."

"Worth a shot, "Griffin said, "but I'm guessing wherever the others were staying, they're not there anymore. Mason would know we'd follow that kind of lead once we found his dead former employee."

"Speaking of the dead guy, we should have a look."

They went into the house. Lew the deputy was leaning against the doorframe of a small den. He stepped aside to let Carl and Griffin pass. The deceased lay on his back. The front of his shirt was stained brown and a pool of dark blood had spread from under the body.

Lisa Morales, the new head Medical Examiner, was crouched by the body. She looked up and said, "Morning, Sheriff. Griffin."

Carl said, "Morning. What have we got?"

Morales stood. She was petite, with large, expressive eyes. She said, "Two to the heart. Nice shooting."

"Glad you approve," said Carl. "I'll let the shooter know when I find him."

"I bet you will."

"Any observations?"

Morales said, "The place has been cleaned out. No clothing or personal items in the bedrooms or bathroom."

"Covering their tracks," Griffin said. "Including this guy."

Carl said, "You get his prints before you bagged his hands, Lisa?"

She gave him a look that managed to say 'I know my job' and 'jeez you can be a putz', at the same time.

Carl said, "He may not be in the system, but if he's ex-army, maybe Sandy can get his prints identified."

"Sandy?" Griffin said.

"Major Thorne."

"Sandy."

"Shut up, Wade."

Henry Thayer sat in his office staring into space. He should have been out in the viewing area, pressing the flesh and making sad noises to the bereaved. He just couldn't work up the enthusiasm.

Somehow the woman had managed to destroy two of his servants. Thayer didn't know what upset him more, the fact that she was still alive, or that he had lost two of his carefully collected souls. He wondered how she had finished the ghouls. They weren't invulnerable, but they were hard to kill.

For a moment he considered sending more of his creatures after the woman and perhaps the sheriff. But no, that could just draw more attention to him and possibly lose more souls. He needed to renew his supply of the tormented, not risk depleting it further. He was glad he had only one service today. Once that was over, he could send his employees home. There were four new bodies in his mortuary. He would have them moved to the cavern and then spend the evening calling up the dead and consigning them to their own private hells.

When they were finished at the crime scene, Carl dropped Griffin back at his truck. Griffin headed for Gatesville, where he kept an office and where Charon had her occult bookstore, Baba Yaga's. Griffin had checked the Thayer Funeral Home website earlier and found there was only one memorial service that afternoon. Afterwards he ought to be available for a little heart to heart.

Griffin parked in front of Baba Yaga's and went inside. Charon was standing behind the counter sorting a pile of newly arrived books. She sold everything from crystals to dream catchers, but her specialty was books, and she actually made most of her money tracking down hard to find grimoires and occult texts for collectors. That was how she'd first met Carter Decamp.

Charon looked up as Griffin entered and said, "Ghouls."

Griffin said, "What?"

"Carter finally got back to me. He's in London. He told me that we're probably dealing with a form of ghoul. A type of creature that devours the flesh of other humans. There are several different kinds, but Carter thinks that's the most likely explanation."

"He have any advice on how to kill them?"

"Ha. I told him that was the first thing you'd ask. He said doing enough damage to the head would usually do it. Though their second life is artificial in nature, they do have to have some semblance of their former body to keep the spirit connected. He advised you wait for him to get back before trying to deal with them. He's flying home tonight."

Griffin said, "Might not be that easy since whoever is controlling them is trying to kill you. Those things were fast and determined. I don't want to give him a chance to send more."

"You sound like you know who it is."

"I think I do."

Griffin told her about Thayer. Charon said, "He's been in here a time or two. He's definitely creepy. And a funeral home would be the perfect cover for a necromancer."

"Is that what he is?"

"A sorcerer who works magic through dead people is called that, yeah. Carter says a necromancer can have a lot of different abilities. That's probably how he found me once I became aware of him. A circuit opened and he followed it back by scrying."

"Even more reason to talk to him sooner rather than later."

"Griffin, this guy could be seriously dangerous. I really think you should wait for Carter to get back."

"I'll give it some thought."

"Why am I not convinced?"

"You have a suspicious mind, kiddo."

"I thought you said this guy lived alone," Rick Haskell said as he pulled on his flak jacket. "Why are we going in full gear?"

Mason felt a flash of irritation. He didn't like having his orders questioned. But he reminded himself he'd probably be killing Haskell soon anyway. He said, "Guy's shifty. Not sure how, but the same source that told me he might have a lot of cash in the house, said the cops have been looking at him lately. Which means he may have some security we don't know about. Best to go in heeled and ready."

Haskell nodded. "Makes sense."

"Glad you approve. Now make sure you've got all your stuff. We're heading straight out of town when we leave the guy's house."

Mason looked around. The house was completely empty. No furniture. Nothing. And why not? The place was for sale and nobody knew he and his three men had been camping there for the past two nights. They'd abandoned the house they were renting when things had gone south with Coleman. Mason still wondered if he should have killed the guy they were renting from, but Muller had made the deal. No one had seen Mason.

Haskell said, "How long we got?"

"Not long. Give the guy time to close his business down and go to that nice, isolated house of his."

"And you really think he's got something stashed away? A funeral director?"

Mason said, "My guy says this Thayer invested in a top end security door and panel. He's hiding something in that house. Muller and Hicks should be back soon. Be ready to roll."

Griffin and Carl pulled up outside of Thayer's place a little after eight. They had taken Griffin's truck this time. This wasn't an official visit, so no county vehicles anyone might recognize.

Lights were on in the big house and Thayer's Mercedes was parked in front of his four-car garage. Looked like he was home. They got out of the truck and walked up to the front door. Carl rang the bell and pounded on the door with his fist.

When they didn't hear anything for several minutes, Carl hammered on the door with more force and rang the bell repeatedly. Finally, they heard heavy footsteps and then the door swung inward.

Thayer looked out, his heavy features distorted by rage. Griffin could almost see him master himself as he realized who was knocking on his door. His expression shifted to something more amiable. But his eyes didn't change.

"Sheriff Price," Thayer said. "You caught me at a bad time."

Carl said, "Sorry about that, Mr Thayer, but I need to talk to you."

"Can't it wait until morning?"

"No, it really can't." Carl stepped inside without waiting to be asked.

Griffin followed Carl through the door. The foyer of Thayer's house was impressive, with high ceilings and a lot of expensive furniture. Thayer still had his work clothes on, though he had divested himself of coat and tie.

"What's this about, Sheriff?" Thayer said.

"My associate Mr Griffin would like to ask you a couple of questions."

"Is he with your department?"

"He's a consultant on those home invasions we were talking about the other day."

Thayer said, "Very well. I can give you a little time, but this is really very inconvenient."

"You mentioned that."

Thayer said, "Let's go to my study."

Thayer led the way to the back portion of his house. Griffin noted more luxurious furnishings as they moved through the place. Apparently, death was a good business.

Thayer took a seat behind his desk and offered chairs to his visitors. Both men declined. Griffin was keeping a close eye on

Thayer's hands. Didn't want him going for a gun or anything in his desk. There was no reason to think the guy was a shooter, but then again you never knew.

"What was it you wanted to ask me?" Thayer almost managed to look amiable.

Griffin said, "I wanted to talk to you about necromancy."

Thayer tried to hold his expression steady but failed. He said, "I'm afraid I don't know the term."

"I'm thinking you do," Griffin said. "Here's the thing, Henry. A couple of men came to my house the other night and tried to kill me and someone I care about. The really odd thing is both men were dead, but still moving around."

Thayer looked at Griffin and then at Carl. Slowly the guarded expression left his face, to be replaced by something unreadable. Thayer said, "That explains what happened to my servants. You destroyed them."

Carl said, "This may be the point where I need to read you your rights."

Thayer smiled. "What are you going to charge me with, Sheriff? Sending dead men to kill your friend here?"

"I'm sure I can find all kinds of things, Mr Thayer." Carl's face at that moment was nearly unreadable, too. Wade understood the look well enough. Carl had selected a new target for his rage.

Griffin became aware of an unpleasant odor. He spun, just in time to see the door to the study fill with shambling figures. Griffin pulled the Beretta, yelling a warning to Carl as he did so.

Half a dozen of the ghouls flowed through the door in a wave. Griffin shot one in the head but a moment later three more slammed into him, pushing him against a wall.

Carl shoved a chair into the path of two of the creatures as they came toward him. They avoided it cat quick, but it gave Carl a moment to line up on the closest one and put a round through his skull. The second one managed to reach Carl and tried to grab his gun hand. Carl pulled his hand away and jammed the barrel of the gun under the ghoul's jaw and pulled the trigger twice.

Griffin used the butt of the Beretta as a bludgeon and crushed the nose and teeth of the ghoul in front of him. He knew the thing could feel it. Griffin pulled his knee up close and kicked out, sending the ghoul staggering backwards. Carl Price shot the thing in the head before it could recover.

Griffin was still struggling with the remaining pair. He elbowed the one to his right, then used the gap to shoot that one in the face. He felt a searing pain in his shoulder as the thing to his left dug its claws into his shoulder. Griffin whipped his arm around that of the ghoul, trapping its elbow. He leaned backwards, exerting pressure until the arm broke, then pivoted and threw the creature over his hip. He shot it as it was trying to roll to its feet.

Griffin looked over at Thayer's desk. The big man was gone of course. A door in the back of the study stood open. Griffin and Carl moved to the threshold, guns at the ready. A short flight of stairs led down to another door, this one a heavy security model. It hung open as well. A reek of decomposition wafted up from below.

Carl watched the undertaker heading away and shook his head. "Guess we have to go after him." He was speaking to Wade, of course.

"Can't see any way around it."

"I seriously wish, just once, one of these assholes would surrender and make life easy."

"Got to worry about these things realistically, Carl. Kill the ghouls and then see if Thayer wants to surrender."

"I don't like the odds."

"Me neither."

They started down the stairs and found Thayer had apparently fled into a sub-level of the place that was carved from stone. The house was fairly new, and this construction was new as well. Carl made a note to look into the construction company to see if they were working for anyone else who needed new bat-caves carved under their homes. It was Wellman. He needed to check those things.

Down into the subterranean pit they moved, weapons at ready. The place stank of death and Carl would have bet a month's salary on there being more of the things down there. He didn't want to, but he would have, and at a guess he'd have won.

The talk with Thayer was supposed to be a quick conversation. His radio was in the damn truck. His shotgun was in the damn truck. Carl was not at all amused. "I find that bastard he's not gonna be happy."

"I got dibs. He made a run at Charon."

Carl said nothing. But he understood all too well.

The room they entered was vast, a substantial ceiling and distant walls that faded into the murk. That was the best word for it. There was light, but not enough to leave him comfortable with the notion that he was seeing everything.

None of the bad guys ever wanted to have good lighting, either.

"Whatever he's up to, he spent a fortune on this place."

Thayer answered from a good distance away. "I don't have time for this. I have plans, Sheriff. They do not involve you or Wade Griffin. Leave now and I can forgive this transgression. You can live to see another day. Otherwise, you will be joining the dead in my personal catacombs."

Wade said, "Well, that's it. I guess we should go."

"Thayer, you have ten seconds to get your ass over here and surrender. Otherwise it ain't the two of us joining the dead."

The man laughed at him. *Laughed.*

"Sheriff, you have no idea who you are dealing with, I am days away from becoming a god. Do you understand me? The reaping of souls shall come and my lord Nsnigoth will make me a god!"

Wade looked his way and Carl looked right back, the both of them not sure if they should laugh at the very notion or be genuinely worried. It was hard to tell sometimes in Brennert County if people were properly crazy or of the world was.

Carl said, "Nsnigoth?"

Wade said, "Never heard of him. I really wish Decamp would hang closer to town."

"I really wish the crazies around here had less ambition."

Thayer laughed. "'Crazies?' I'm not crazy, you fool. I simply understand the world better than you do. Others have been anointed before me. Others have ascended to the ranks of the gods. Not many. It's not an easy task and you've already inconvenienced me."

The man was out of sight, but he was close. He also sounded odd. His voice modulated in the same way some of the kids back in their football days had when they were changing clothes, looking up and down while talking, putting on their pads, or tying their shoes.

"He's up to something."

Wade nodded. The big man's eyes were narrowed, and he pointed with his chin. There was a wall to the right. It was a support structure but anything at all could be behind it.

A moment later Thayer came stepping from behind that support wall and, sure enough, he'd put on a flak vest and a few pieces of ballistic armor that covered his vitals. The arms, the legs, the head were all bared, but a body shot probably wouldn't do too much good.

That was okay. Both of them qualified as marksmen.

"Gentlemen, I offered you a chance."

Thayer raised his right hand. There was a damned big .45 semi-auto in it.

What the hell? When did the evil overlord types start using guns?

He didn't hesitate. Thayer took aim and fired.

Things didn't go the way Thayer had planned. The two men were big but they were also quick. They ducked low and each went in a different direction. Their movements upset Thayer's aim and his shots went wild.

So much for the element of surprise.

Both men returned fire. One of them managed to hit him in the shoulder, the bullet creasing flesh and cutting a trench of fire across his left arm.

He screamed an obscenity and backed around the corner. They could not reach him without him seeing their progress. They could not merely fire and hope to hit him. For the moment it was a draw.

"We could work together, gentlemen. I will be a god and I could be benevolent."

A complete lie. He hadn't gone through the years of preparation to share his glory with anyone. These two were interlopers, and they'd be dealt with.

The wards he'd placed around his home gave off warnings. There were more people on his property. The parlor was closed for the night. No one was expected, and he knew for certain the Sheriff had not called for backup. Just the same, the man could have had people waiting. Enough. He'd closed his eyes and called on the ghouls to do his bidding. He would handle these two. Seven of his departed moved from their resting places and slipped toward the house above. They moved through the darkness and quickly changed course toward the funeral home.

"Well, shit, Wade, that's about the best offer I've had all day. We could serve some asshole that thinks he's a god. You with me on this? We could polish his shoes, maybe bring him breakfast in bed and we'd be like personal servants to a new god, a better god."

"I'm not really much for gods. The one's I've met haven't impressed me much."

Thayer had to control his outrage. They were unbelievers. They did not understand the power that would soon be his.

"You are fools! I'll enjoy tearing your souls from your bodies."

"I'm going to enjoy blowing out your kneecaps, asshole." The sheriff had a gutter mouth.

He risked a quick peek around the corner of his wall and saw only the sheriff. Somehow, the bigger man had vanished when he wasn't looking. Fear bloomed in his chest. No! He was too close to fail. He had to take control of the situation again and soon.

Upstairs the dead were moving, and he was aware of what they did, what they saw, as if their actions were distant memories.

The night was profoundly dark, and the funeral home was no exception. Mason took his time scouting out the area. Muller took a long walk around the perimeter and saw nothing.

Hicks waited for the signal and when he got it, his gloved hands attacked the security control box. In a surprisingly short amount of time he signaled the all clear and the four of them moved.

"That was easy." Mason didn't like surprises. His compliment was just as much a query.

"Never even turned on his security."

Mason nodded and felt a flash of irritation. On the one hand, laziness made their job easier. On the other, that sort of security system was a very expensive addition. Not using it was foolish and meant there might be something unexpected ahead. Like the truck. They had no idea who the 4x4 belonged to; only that Thayer likely had nothing to do with it.

"Be cautious. I don't like surprises."

All of them nodded their affirmative. He needn't have worried and he knew it. Most of the guys had been with him since the beginning, unlike the one he'd already removed from the equation. Well, Haskell was a pro, but he'd be erased soon enough. He couldn't forgive getting screwed over by Coleman. It wasn't in his nature to forgive.

The house was empty, quiet as a tomb. The notion brought a quick flash of a smile to Mason's face. Silent was the best sort of structure to enter.

A few quick hand gestures was all it took to send everyone on their way, sorting through the rooms as quickly and efficiently as they could. Mason headed for the den and was happy to see that the door to the room was not only unlocked, but open. Still, part of him felt uneasy, first the security system was off and now the man's personal home office door was unsecured. Was it sloppiness? Or was there more to it?

He hadn't survived for years by ignoring his instincts and at the moment they were saying there just might be some serious shit rolling his way. He checked Thayer's office before closing the door. He wouldn't be caught off guard.

Three seconds after he'd walked away from the room, the door opened behind him.

It wasn't one shape that came through, but several. The house was dark, but his eyes had long since adjusted. The shapes were human, but they were wrong on a level that sent every bell and whistle in his mind screaming.

"We've got company!" He let out the call even as be back-pedalled and drew his 9mm. The first burst of three shots caught the closest of the shapes in the chest and sent it staggering back into the rest of the group. The body jerked once for every perfectly delivered shot, and Mason knew the bastard was going down, and probably taking a couple more down with him that would buy him more time to shoot.

That was the way it was supposed to work in the real world. Instead, the first one came back up with a bellowing hiss, and charged, dropping lower to the ground and moving on all fours. The ones behind his human target were already up and coming for him.

There was no panic. Mason was a trained killer and he'd learned long ago to suppress the sort of fear that would cripple him. Instead he focused the heightened senses offered by adrenaline, used the bump in his reflexes to his advantage and prepared to eliminate his enemies.

That all sounded perfect in his head, right up until the time he saw the dead man's face. The jaw bulged and the mouth opened –a mouth full of razor-edged teeth. He could see well enough to know the thing in front of him was not a man at all, but something far, far worse.

Panic saved his life in that moment. He jumped back with a shriek and the thing coming for him missed as it tried to bite through his face.

The next few rounds from his pistol were entirely handled on autopilot. Muscle memory took over and let him blow new holes in the creature. Open wounds bloomed across the chest, the neck the face and the head above the left eye. The nightmare fell down and did not get back up.

There was no time to celebrate as another of the things lunged toward him, mouth open in a screech that bared impossible teeth. Do enough damage and they fell. That was what he'd taken away from the fight. He opened fire, blowing half of the chest of the thing away. He pulled the trigger twice more before he realized his gun was empty. He dropped the clip and slammed another magazine home.

Haskell stepped into the room and did exactly what he should have done. He took aim and fired at the next in line. The thing spun as the bullet tore through its left arm. Then it slither-ran toward Haskell at high speed. He tried to compensate, tried to recover from the unexpected shock, but he was not fast enough. Haskell let out a short scream as the thing landed on top of him and drove him to the ground.

There was no time to worry about Haskell after that, because another of the things was moving toward him. It moved in impossible ways. The very notion hurt Mason's head. The human body has physical limits, but the thing bobbed and weaved even as it walked, and no human torso could move that way, not even the most adept contortionist could manage it.

A perverse sort of anger bloomed in Mason's chest. The fear was still there, but his mind was outraged by the notion of the laws of physics being so casually shoved aside.

"You need to back off!" He roared the words and fired at the next of the things, refusing to accept they were human any longer, and refusing to accept the possibility they were anything else at the same time. Mason's heart was hammering as hard as it ever had, but his hands were still steady.

From behind him he heard the sounds of Muller and Hicks coming his way. They were wise enough to announce themselves.

Haskell let out a loud, wet scream and fired his weapon wildly. Mason had no choice but to step back and look.

Sometimes looking only makes it worse. The man-shaped thing tore away Haskell's scalp and a large portion of his skull in the same move. Blood and other fluids spewed across the area and Mason shivered even as he took aim and fired round after round into the thing on top of Haskell.

A moment is all it takes, really. That, and a simple mistake in perception and Mason's life changed forever. The mistake was merely that he thought he'd killed the first of the nightmares to come his way when he'd blown out most of its chest.

While he was putting holes in the thing that killed Haskell, the first creature he'd blown to pieces took a massive chunk out of his left thigh.

He screamed.

He was still screaming when one of the other shapes jumped past him and by the sounds of things, attacked Muller.

Then Muller was screaming, too.

The thing on his thigh clawed its way up his chest, biting and tearing as it pulled itself higher.

He had time to wonder why Hicks wasn't screaming before the darkness tore away pieces of his consciousness.

While Carl kept Thayer busy talking, Griffin turned and moved away from the support wall and into the gloom. Time to take advantage of the shadows that dominated the chamber. Truthfully, Griffin didn't much like the idea of going too far into the huge space, knowing what could be waiting there.

Griffin's night vision was better than most. Once he reached a point where he could no longer see Carl, he moved forward, keeping parallel with the support wall, hoping he could spot Thayer before the fat man could see him.

Griffin paused as he heard sounds of distant gunfire. Someone else was in the house above. No way of knowing if they were friend or foe, and he couldn't worry about it now.

Thayer must have heard it too, because Griffin saw some motion off to his right. Griffin had fed a fresh magazine into the Beretta before leaving cover and now he brought the weapon up and started toward where he judged Thayer too be. He spotted the man at the same moment that Thayer saw him coming. Thayer tried to swing the .45 up, but Griffin had the advantage of already being ready. He put two rounds into Thayer's leg.

The fat man screamed and fell as his leg gave away. He lost his grip on the .45 as he clutched at his injured limb. Griffin sighted on Thayer's head. If he tried to regain the semi-auto, Griffin would finish him.

But Thayer wasn't going for the gun. His attention seemed focused elsewhere. Griffin could hear him mumbling to himself. Then, his hands moved away from his leg and he got up. *Shit. Had he healed himself?*

"You've ruined it," Thayer said. "You're making me use too much of my power." He looked up and Griffin saw that his eyes had begun to glow with a pale green luminescence.

The hell with that. Griffin fired and saw a jagged hole appear in Thayer's forehead. The man staggered, but he was still coming.

Griffin said, "Carl, we got a situation here!"

Carl leaned out from behind the support wall and saw the shambling form of Henry Thayer. He said, "Jesus, this just gets better and better."

Both men began firing. Thayer's massive bulk jerked and twitched with each bullet strike, but he stubbornly refused to fall.

Griffin sensed motion to his left and spared a glance to see that several of Thayer's minions were slithering from the recesses in the walls. He ignored them. Thayer was puppeteer. Drop him and the puppets would fall too. At least he hoped so.

"I warned you, goddamn it," Carl said. He took careful aim and Griffin saw one of Thayer's knees explode.

That made the fat man go to one knee. It also made him tilt forward so that Griffin could see the top of his skull. He put two rounds into it. Thayer fell face down, his body still twitching.

Griffin turned immediately, prepared to line up on the closest ghoul. But the closest and the farthest and all the little ghouls in between were on the ground as well. Finally, something had worked out.

@ @ @

Thayer was dead, or at least he should have been with the damage he and Wade had delivered to him. By all rights he was a goner. The man certainly wasn't in a fighting mood anymore and Carl was glad of that.

Still, Thayer moved. He sat up, blood running from the wounds in his head and from every other spot where they'd managed to put a bullet into his heavyset body.

Thayer's face was a distorted mask, warped by pain and something worse.

He was afraid, genuinely terrified, but Carl didn't think he was scared of dying.

No. This was something worse.

From the farthest reaches of Thayer's personal chamber of terrors, a shape lumbered toward them. It was a corpse, but so far gone that little remained aside from blackened flesh stuck to bones. The eyes of the thing were as dark as midnight, far darker than the mummified remains.

Thayer looked at the shape and his eyes bulged with terror.

Carl understood why.

It wasn't the corpse. That was bad, but, frankly, he and Wade had seen far worse in recent months. The dead walking happened enough that the apparition should have seemed almost commonplace. That was the sort of thought that made Carl twitchy enough, but there was a presence hidden within the dead thing, something that loomed ponderously, until its energies filled the entire room with an oppressive pressure, like he was swimming underwater, though the air was still perfectly breathable, if a bit rancid.

Had he ever felt anything like this before? Of course he had, once upon a time when the head of the Blackbourne Clan had torn a hole in reality and tried to unleash a god upon the world.

He did not have to guess. This was Nsnigoth, the thing Thayer worshipped, the very thing supposed to make him a god. He cast his eyes toward Wade for only a moment, to make certain he was not alone in what he felt. Wade's face spoke all that he needed to hear. His best friend's expression was an open book, a study in fear. He knew without benefit of a mirror that his own expression was close to identical. He could feel the hairs on his arms and neck standing on end.

The dead thing spoke with a dark god's voice and it was not a thing meant to be heard by sane people. The words were uttered in a language long dead on the planet. But Carl heard them translated in his mind and cringed at each and every syllable. Someone whimpered. It might have been him or Wade or possibly the both of them, he could not say.

You have called my name countless times and summoned me to see your sacrifices. You have failed me this night. There will be no reaping of souls, though I shall take what you have. You have done battle in my name and fallen before your enemies. Let them see your fate. Let them know your misery and remember the cost of disappointing Nsnigoth.

Even as the rotted remains moved forward, a greenish light burned within the bones, a pallid, sickly color that spread like flames across flash paper until the whole body of the thing was ablaze. The light grew in intensity and Carl wondered if the fiery essence might somehow be contagious, diseased or radioactive. He backed away from it, turning his eyes from the thing as it reached for Thayer.

Around the room, in niches carved for the sole purpose of holding cadavers tortured into a mockery of life, the bodies of Thayer's victims took on the same glow and began to burn. A thick, acrid smoke burst from each of the bodies and Carl turned, dragging himself away from the light that called to him, that wanted him to see Thayer's final fate.

Wade still stared, eyes wide, and Carl grabbed his arm and shook him.

In an instant Wade recovered and shook himself. "Carl? What the hell...?" His voice sounded strained, hoarse as if he had been yelling when he had not. It wasn't Wade's vocal chords, it was the air, the insane, growing pressure in the underground fortress.

"Don't know! Don't care! Run!" His own voice carried the same unnatural tone of strain.

Wade didn't have to be told twice. He moved for the door, eyes alert and his movements as precise and ready as ever. Carl envied him his calm – he was pretty sure he was going to piss himself.

Behind them the room bloomed with a green fire that burned as cold as an arctic blast.

Thayer screamed, a long, lingering wail of fear, sorrow and pain. He was still screaming when Carl pounded up the stairs, following his best friend.

If he thought escaping the catacomb would make the world better, he was wrong. The house was on fire as well, burning with the same hellish illumination.

Several bodies raged with the unnatural flames and a few more were pinned by them. Carl shoved for the back door and pushed past a separate duo. One man locked in position, a silent scream marring his burning face, while another of the dead things burned across him. Fingers locked on the man's flak vest and melted though the material. The head of the thing on top of him had been blown away, and whoever the poor bastard had been, he'd died trying to escape the thing he'd already killed.

Carl moved toward Wade's truck, coughing as the fumes from the fire tried to find their way into his lungs. The thought of those burning corpses tainting the inside of his body was enough to make him hold his breath, lest whatever had been done to them might somehow be contagious.

Neither of the considered waiting around. Even the most civic minded parts of Carl's mind refused that notion. They had to get away. They had to escape the thing that had spoken to Thayer.

Wade Griffin was the bravest man he knew, but he was just as determined to get away as Carl himself.

"They'll call me back here, Wade." His voice sounded normal again, his mind was starting to feel normal again, too. "Once someone spots the fire."

Wade nodded, his face set like stone. "I know. Should take some time though, the place being so far out of town."

"I'll have to come back. It's my job." Sometimes that fact weighed on him like a boulder across his chest.

Wade nodded and drove on. Like as not he wanted to lead foot it out of there, God knew Carl wanted him to, but Wade was wiser than that. No point in drawing attention to themselves in case anyone *was* around.

Slow and steady got the job done, even when you wanted to run like all of the demons in Hell were on your ass. Sadly, they both knew more about that than they wanted.

"When they call you, I'll come along for the ride."

Carl nodded and stared out the windshield, while behind them the Thayer house and all of its secrets burned, the flames moving slowly to the natural colors one expected to see.

"I wonder who those guys in the house were."

Wade looked his way. "One of them was Avery Mason."

"No shit?"

"None. The others were probably his crew. Looks like two of our problems got solved tonight. We can let Major Thorne know she won't have to worry about Mason anymore. I guess Thayer's big house did make him look like a good target."

Carl nodded again, just for the moment content to let the silence hide the sound of Thayer's screams in his mind. Thayer's screams, and the laughter of a mad thing with the powers of a god.

To the Reader,

Thanks for reading SNAFU: Resurrection.

We hope you've enjoyed it as much as we did putting it together.

Please consider leaving us a review if (and anywhere) you see fit. Any and all reviews are gratefully accepted.

If you have any questions, or want to quote from the book, please contact us at any time.

I would ask please, if you DO review online, send a link to Geoff via editor@cohesionpress.com or via our Facebook page messaging system. If you review for a magazine or paper, let us know and we'll buy it.

Thank you.

Geoff Brown - Director, Cohesion Press.
Mayday Hills Lunatic Asylum
Beechworth, Australia

Amanda J Spedding - Editor-in-chief, Cohesion Press
Sydney, Australia

Matthew Summers - Editor, Cohesion Press
Sydney, Australia

9 781925 623253